MW00928425

SINABAR

Deborah May Marshall

Bloomington, IN Milton Keynes, UK

AuthorHouse™
1663 Liberty Drive, Suite 200
Bloomington, IN 47403
www.authorhouse.com
Phone: 1-800-839-8640

AuthorHouse™ UK Ltd.
500 Avebury Boulevard
Central Milton Keynes, MK9 2BE
www.authorhouse.co.uk
Phone: 08001974150

© 2006 Deborah May Marshall. All rights reserved.

No part of this book may be reproduced, stored in a retrieval system, or transmitted by any means without the written permission of the author.

First published by AuthorHouse 9/12/2006

ISBN: 1-4259-3433-1 (sc)

Printed in the United States of America
Bloomington, Indiana

This book is printed on acid-free paper.

Acknowledgements

Thank you God for your unending love and inspiration.

I would like to thank
my husband Bill and
my mother Doreen Potter
for their unfailing encouragement and support.

I offer my loving gratitude to
my father, the late Ron Potter,
who instilled in me the knowledge that
we are all capable of achieving whatever
we firmly desire,
and for his indescribable expression
when he witnessed these achievements.

I would also like to thank my dear friend Norma Rowe
and my dear sister-in-law Linda Potter
for their great encouragement.

Many, many thanks to my great friends and helpers
Bonnie Howard and Janet Montgomery
for their editing of the finished story
and Jacquie Craig who helped with
the early editing.

If it hadn't been for each of these wonderful people
this story would have never gone to print.

And last but not least,
Thank you everyone for purchasing this book
and taking the time to read it.

Enjoy!

Blessed Be,
From Deb Marshall

Chapter 1

DIVORCE!

D is for – Dissolved. Poof; gone. Sometimes, I feel that I'd like to do the same.

I is for - In shock, future shock.

V is for - Voracious for life, I've been held back & stunted by marriage to that man.

O is for - Out in the world at last, freedom.

R is for - Reality, I've craved freedom for some time but I also fear the unknown.

C is for - Cavity, there's a big cavity in my life now. Do I ever want to have it filled again?

E is for - Everyday in every way, I will overcome, and make my life better and better.

Maria wrote this verse out, after great introspection. She was numbly trying to analyze how she really felt at this momentous juncture in her life. She had done it. She had struggled through the big D. Now it was time to close that door and get on with Her New Life.

Her husband's indiscretions and infidelity had just been the excuse that she needed to make the big change. She knew that there was a better life out there, if she just had the guts to go after it. Their married life had been unsatisfying for some time, so in her dissatisfaction with everything else, she had focused on the one wonderful thing in her life, her daughter Sylvia.

Sylvia was growing up now and very soon she would be going off to college. Is this what they mean by the empty nest syndrome, she had thought to herself as she looked for an apartment? It doesn't matter; I have to plan a life for myself, starting right now.

Two days after she had packed Sylvia off to college and helped her get settled in, she was reading the classified advertisements in the Globe & Mail when she found a very interesting one. It read:

Seeking successful, responsible
female Equestrian Coach
and Recreational Supervisor
for young lady. Must
have a suitable list of references
and be willing to relocate.
Contact Mr. Green
416 345-9267

I wonder what they mean by successful female equestrian. This sounds very interesting.

She immediately called Mr. Green and made an appointment for the next day.

On arriving at his address, she found that the sign on the door read Mr. Albert Green - Barrister. "How very British," Maria quipped, trying to affect an English accent. A tall, older lady ushered her in to see Mr. Green right away. He was a very surly, abrupt, little man who proceeded to asked her many questions about her past; her horse business, her sports and recreational background, as well as her success level in teaching children.

"Would you have any difficulty in moving out of Toronto, Ms. Stark? The estate is a forty five minute drive to the east."

"No, I'd actually much prefer living in the country."

"The position will entail being a companion to a young lady of seven years as well as instructing her in horsemanship and other recreational pursuits. She is the daughter of Sir Edward Warner. You would be living on the estate with Sir Edward, his two brothers and their families. So if that suits you Ms. Stark, the information you've given me leaves me with much to look into. After that if you appear to be suitable for this position, I'll then set up an appointment for you with Sir Edward. That will be all for now, Ms. Stark. Good Day."

He ended the appointment so abruptly that it left her head spinning with questions. She knew though, that she wouldn't be getting any more information out of him.

Mr. Green called her four days later to ask if she could travel to SINABAR – the Warner family estate, to meet Sir Edward.

"Be on time Ms. Stark, 7 p.m., sharp. You'll have an interview and then stay to dinner. Oh, Ms. Stark, they do 'dress' for dinner."

Now that sounded scary. Well, I guess I'll find out how scary when I get there, she thought to herself. Between meeting Mr. Warner and 'dressing' for dinner, she didn't know which made her more apprehensive. In the morning she realized that she had a friend from her horsy life, who had emigrated from England some ten years ago, so she could call her for some information regarding British customs. On the one point about proper dinner attire, her friend was successful in clearing that matter up. For this occasion and the season she suggested a long skirt, a demure blouse and a soft feminine sweater.

Well luckily I've a few days left to find these items. I wonder what she would consider as a demure blouse, she asked herself.

Maria went shopping that afternoon and although she was looking at clothing, three facts kept rotating in her mind: Sinabar Estate, three brothers with Edward being the employer, and a little girl to instruct. Needless to say, with all of this in her head and an almost numbing excitement, it took her till the next evening to decide on her dinner attire.

She had a petite figure except for her height of 5"5', which would have made her seem almost boyish if it hadn't been for her gently, well-formed breasts and her below shoulder length, dark hair. Actually, the opposite sex admiringly referred to Maria as being vitally beautiful. However, Maria, having married early and having never straying out of that relationship naturally hadn't had the opportunity to hear the opinion of other admiring males.

The next day she nervously prepared for her venture into a new life. She took a long, hot shower. She had awakened that morning with a very positive feeling but because she didn't, as of yet, know how to accept these intuitive expressions, she let a small doubt creep in, to devour her calm. It had been a while since she had instructed children and her riding classes had been a far cry from working on a 'one to one' basis. Had she been a successful role model to her own daughter or had her marital problems affected the choices that her daughter was now making?

Now, she would be meeting a man whom she would have to impress suitably, in order for him to be interested in hiring her to instruct his daughter. Meeting men was still an uncomfortable task, for her. She hadn't been comfortable thinking about men and or dating, yet. Even though her divorce was soon to be final, her emotional state was still quite shaky.

Something from her subconscious kept trying to calm her relentless, nervous energy, trying to reassure her that this was right, definitely the right direction to take. She didn't totally comprehend this influence but it did steady her a bit.

Maria was always worrying about being late and as a result she often was. It was imperative that she be on time, this time. Not knowing the area east of Toronto, she decided to leave early to find the estate and then make her entrance at precisely the right time.

As she drove the forty-five minute drive from her modest apartment on the outskirts of Toronto, east along the north coast of Lake Ontario, she deliberated on her life's situation. The dissolving of their marital estate; the selling of their stable, equipment and all of the stock; except for her own faithful horse, the paying of the debts and the half and half split with her ex-husband didn't leave her with anything near complete financial security. Her ex didn't care to and wasn't able to give her much in the way of monetary support and they had agreed to go half-and-half on their daughter's education and board. She had to go to work in order to support herself, help her daughter and board her horse.

Besides, even if she could afford to stay at home, what would she do at home?

She was used to an active, work filled life and there were few or no opportunities in the equine world, that didn't involve having a facility to work out of and a big bankroll. She had made the mistake of never developing a credit rating of her own. She knew now that if a woman ever expects to do any business without her husband, it makes things a lot easier if she has a credit rating in her own name. Having any involvement with the banking institution unnerved her.

For her it was going to be; waiting on tables, working as a sales clerk, or taking advantage of this opportunity. Please Lord let it be this. At least this recreational instructor job would be within her field of interest and could possibly even be fulfilling if she liked the people.

Chapter 2

*A*s she drove along she was thankful for this beautiful day. It was one of those glorious fall days filled with amber sunlight and mellow warmth - chased by crisp cool breezes now and again, just enough to remind you of the cold days to come. At six thirty she found herself driving through an area that was vividly picturesque; her vehicle's tires rolled over an older highway winding and bowling over the repetitive, round topped hills of the orchard country, past rows of well-groomed, fruit trees which stood like centuries lining the road. Here in the hills sheltered from the lake, the warm air had a golden, fall mustiness, heavy with the wine scent of overly ripe fruit. Maria considered what wonderful riding country this would be. As she drove closer to the shore area, and the land began to flatten out as it reached out to one of the truly Great Lakes, Lake Ontario, she noticed that a strong breeze had whipped up. In contrast to the bucolic fall scene of just a few miles back, here she was surprised at the dark grayness of the waves relentlessly lashing the shore.

As per Mr. Green's directions, she rounded the next corner and the distinctive stone arch that she had been looking for, came into view. She drove up to the arch and sure enough there was the bronze plaque simply stating "SINABAR".

Inside the arch, all that could be immediately seen where rolling pastures on each side of a paved lane. Along the narrow private drive, and down over a hill she came in sight of a gray stone stable building, complete with stone arches, individual turn out pens and Dutch style stall doors. The stable was sheltered from the lake by another hill and a mixture of fruit and evergreen trees. Consequently, she found the air here intoxicating; the musky, sweet smell of over ripened fruit contrasting with the clear astringent pine scent. Amid this rich sensual stimuli, Maria was also visually entranced by this picture postcard scene. However, there was still no sign of the Manor House that Mr. Green had spoken of.

Maria had her 35M camera beside her on the car seat, as usual, photography being a favorite interest of hers. This vision was just too good to let escape. She had to capture it on film. So she got out of her car and without being too intrusive, she took two good shots from the side of the lane. But where was the house? The only thing left for her to do was to get back into the car and keep following the lane. She was anxious to arrive at the house. Simultaneously she felt electric currents of excitement and nervous anticipation.

"Follow the paved black lane. Follow the paved black lane," she sang out loud, as if this was a yellow brick road. She did exactly that.

Several seconds later her mouth dropped open at the wondrous sight that appeared in front of her as she topped the next hill. The sky had opened up and there it was, SINABAR, Manor House. The black ribbon of pavement stretched down a long hill and out along a rocky causeway to a large island. White capped, gray blue waves on both sides of the causeway stretched up to the horizon, which was crowned by a fantastic, purple pink, sunset vista. There, at the end of the causeway silhouetted by the vivid sunset, was the huge, gray stone manor house with the waning sunlight reflecting on its many windows of its west side.

Maria scrunched her eyes shut and opened them wide again. No, it wasn't a mirage. There it was. In this hazy violet light, the

Manor made an unbelievable vision of angles, shadows and brilliant reflections. I have to try to get this on film, she thought; being so moved by this beauty that she had forgotten her hurry to get to her appointment. Maria was out of her car before she could think about Mr. Warner, and was hurrying to a high abutment that overlooked this wondrous sight.

This cliff top was high above the swirling torrent of waves crashing against the shore, where the causeway met the main land. Maria struggled with her long skirt as she tried to run to a prime vantage point. As she came to just the right spot, she dropped the skirt, which she had hiked up with one hand. She fumbled with the settings on her camera. She wanted this shot to be perfect. While still peering through the lens, she took several steps sideways to change the angle of the view through the camera's aperture. The long skirt annoyingly restricted her steps. Her calf muscles stretched the skirt's seams to the extreme. In her heightened paradoxical state of elation and annoyance, to her great misfortune she made that unforgiving mistake of not paying attention to her footing. Panic was knocking at her door but she wasn't aware enough to answer it.

The sandy, mossy top of the precipice shifted under her stance. She took a restricted step back, seeking security, but it wasn't enough. She had no way of knowing that the upper cliff face was giving away under her weight, but as she felt the movement, she began to sense what was about to happen.

For a split second, she looked down at her feet and began to recognize her ultimate fate. Time seemed to slip into slow gear. She fought to regain her balance, but it was too late. As her feet both started to go out from under her, she arched backward throwing the camera over her head to its safety. Her body had begun to slide away with the earthy material around her. Still facing her supposed destination - the island, all she saw was a blur of sky and water.

Realizing that she was starting to fall she attempted to reach back to catch the edge, but there was nothing there for her straining fingers to grab hold of. In her last try for abstract security, she arched herself backwards once more, only to succeed in bashing the back of her head against the underlying rocky face of the cliff, mercifully knocking herself unconscious.   Her body dropped through the air, hitting savagely against the stone face several times before plummeting into the crashing waves.

She came to, seconds after hitting the cold water. It seemed as if she was waking from a long tormenting bad dream, only to begin another. Her first thought of course was - where am I? After the swift, chilling realization that she was under water, her second thought was - which way is up? As if from a lightening bolt, her body experienced the first powerful shot of adrenalin. Her arms and legs jolted into action, in unison with her brain. Eyes: try to stay open, try to focus. Where is the light? That'll be the surface.

In the waning, evening light the surface was just barely discernible, the lighter gray above her. She had gone into the water feet first, but her unconscious state had robbed her of any opportunity for a last gulp of precious air before descending into the depths, and leaving her head already full of water. She tried frantically to blow the water out, causing yet another significant loss of vital air. It's lighter there. Muscles rallied to fight towards the light, the surface. Blue-gray cold was everywhere, dark gray and light gray. Arms reaching, legs thrusting now with all of her might, she fought her way towards the light, but the surface still evaded her. One more valiant stoke, you can make it. It seemed like a very long way.

Maria gasped, just as her mouth cleared the surface. Air, all of her body had been crying for air. Now as she gasped for her second gulp of life giving, precious oxygen, a wave crashed down on her, pushing her under again. Her body received another shot of adrenalin as it reacted for survival. She was going to have to struggle madly for every gulp of air.

Maria was a very strong swimmer. If the water had been calmer she could have floated or treaded water long enough for her head to clear, to replenish much needed oxygen, and get her eyes to focus, to find the shore. But the water was rarely calm here and she was going to have to fight the waves if she was going to live.

Thrusting, kicking, struggling upward, muscles screaming, head pounding, she bobbed up, struggling for that gulp of air, swallowing water, white frothy water prevailing everywhere. Choking, not being able to take in hardly any of that precious commodity, her chest felt as if her lungs were exploding. She was hit by the next wave; those cold, dark velvety, gray waves. Her mind was starting to get lazy now. Hypothermia was taking control. Strive to get to the light! She was coming up for the third time and her body was telling her that she wouldn't be able to do this again. She was bracing for another wave to hit. She was almost unconscious again. She was starting to slip away. Where did the light go..?

In the cold, gray darkness, in the white froth and cramping pain, something or someone grabbed hold of her body from behind. Half conscious she didn't know if she should struggle or just give in. A strong arm had come under her arm and across her chest and was lifting her backwards against a warm body and propelling her through the water. Maria didn't have time to struggle or open her eyes again. As soon as she felt that strong arm and warm body against her back, the black, velvety hood of unconsciousness engulfed her mind once more.

The strong body who was struggling to reach the shore with her almost lifeless body in tow was none other then that of Sir Edward Warner.

Chapter 3

*E*arlier that day...

Edward was having another bad day. He'd been having more frequent migraine attacks lately and suffering their ravishing symptoms. Through his agony, he had called Dr. Adams earlier in the day to ask him to come to see him as a patient and also to invite him to stay for dinner.

After accepting the invitation, Dr. Bill Adams asked his secretary to juggle his afternoon appointments, so that he'd be able to go out to Sinabar. Two delights in one day, it'd be well worth the trouble. Getting to visit with the renowned scientist Sir Edward Warner was always an intellectual treat, which brightened his otherwise mundane existence. Then, to also experience dinner at Sinabar, what a rare treat! Edward had one of the best European chefs to ever set foot in Canada.

"If I can get away from here before three o'clock, I might even get there early enough for the added pleasure of having tea with the Warner's," he chortled gleefully to himself. I don't know why a man like Edward would drop his British title while here in this country,

Dr. Adams reflected to himself. I certainly wouldn't feel awkward about using it here. It's too bad that he suffers from those dreadful migraines.

Dr. Adams was a middle-aged man who lived for fine food and craved intellectual stimulation almost as much. He'd been the Warner family physician, ever since he could remember. Edward had known that the promise of dinner would bring Bill Adams out on a house call without any trace of an argument.

Edward's headaches had been getting much worse lately. The amount of the prescription medication that he needed to take to get any relief was becoming very dangerous as well as having an affect on his memory. Lately, he had spent little time with his daughter, Anna Belle. He'd also forgotten that Albert Green, his barrister, was sending a prospective recreational instructor for an appointment with him. Thankfully, Albert called him at three o'clock to remind him that Ms. Stark would be arriving at Sinabar at seven o'clock. Edward had been anxious to find someone to spend time with Anna Belle, someone to teach her proper horsemanship, swimming and other healthy forms of recreation, but above all to get her out doing something active. Since her mother had left when she was an infant, Anna Belle had only had Emma, who was now showing her advanced age. Emma had also been nanny to Edward and his brothers, Brian and Gregory, back in England and then here in Canada. Brian, who was still single, was quite attached to Anna Belle and was of immeasurable help. He spent as much time with her as he could, in his busy life. Thankfully, due to Brian's strong affection for animals, Anna Belle had likewise developed a love for animals as well as the commitment to care for them. Hence, the pet population at Sinabar was extensive.

Today, Edward had started the day with a particularly bad headache and his medication left him slightly dizzy and unsettled. It wasn't the best day to be interviewing new employees, but it couldn't be helped. After he had tea with Dr. Adams and they had discussed possible new migraine medications, Edward decided that a walk along the causeway in the cool fall air might help clear his senses before he was to meet with Ms. Stark. It would undoubtedly improve Dr. Adam's appetite, he thought with a smile. Edward left instructions with Emma, that if Ms. Stark was to arrive before he returned, she was to introduce her to Anna Belle.

Albert Green hadn't told him very much about this Ms. Stark, only that she was well qualified in horsemanship, swimming and other ladies sports. That name, Ms. Stark, conjures up visions of a mannish prig of a woman. Edward shrugged at the thought.

Dr. Adams arrived just in time to devour more than his share of the teatime fancy sandwiches, petit four cakes and crisp, green and red grapes. Brian and Gregory were absent as they'd gone to a community meeting in the village. However, they were joined by the two ladies of the house, Gregory's pouting, pretty, blonde wife – Mallory, and of course the pale, timid Anna Belle. Edward tried discussing new treatments for migraine, with Dr. Adams, but Mallory kept interrupting.

"Dr. Adams," she simpered, "Have you chosen your costume for our annual All Hallows Eve masquerade ball?"

"Oh Mrs. Warner, it had totally escaped my memory. Thank you once again for the invitation." It hadn't really escaped him at all but he didn't want to get into a lengthy discussion with her about costumes, let alone the fact that as of yet he didn't have a date for the ball. I may just have to come stag as usual. Now there's an idea for a costume, I wonder if I could find a Stag costume, he questioned himself? That would be unique, but I'd probably have to have it custom made.

Mallory had asked the doctor something about ideas for costumes, but he'd been lost in thought, so she went on talking to Anna Belle about her costume. Edward rose to his feet sensing that this was an opportunity for the two of them to make a break for it, to get out of this conversation.

"Mallory, I hope that you'll excuse us, Dr. Adams and I would like to take a walk before my appointment with a prospective employee," Edward stated, as he started to walk out of the room with the doctor hot on his heels. Then he remembered something and turned back to Mallory, "Oh, the lady's name is Ms. Stark. She, as well as Dr.

Adams, will be joining us for dinner. Anna Belle, if I don't get a chance to come to your room before your bedtime, I'll see you in the morning." And with this the two men made their escape from Mallory and her preoccupation with the masquerade ball.

Dr. Adams wasn't really looking forward to the over exertion of going for a walk with Edward. He always had a dreadfully hard time keeping up with Edward's long striding walk, but on the other hand he felt that Edward was annoyed with Mallory's prattle and needed to get out in the air.

The walk through the garden, into the woods and to the start of the causeway, was enough for Bill Adams and he was looking forward to turning back but Edward continued on, out the causeway toward the mainland. Bill had thought that Edward might want to discuss his illness, now in private, but Edward had fallen broodingly quiet. So he decided that he had better respect Edward's mood and devote all of his attention to trying to stay on the path and keeping up. Edward had chosen to walk along a narrow path close to the water's edge. The late evening light was strangely violet. On glancing over his shoulder, Edward realized that the color was being reflected from the vivid purple to pink sunset. Under different circumstances a person might have derived great joy from witnessing such a vista.

Bill was starting to puff as he struggled along, squinting to find good footing on the treacherous path, while Edward walked along easily.

"Edward, can you slow down?" he croaked. "Are we turning back soon and can we walk on the pavement, for Heaven's Sake? I don't want to end up in the water!" Bill exclaimed as he glanced at the approaching high embankment of the mainland. Just as the last syllable escaped from the doctor's mouth, Edward stiffened and abruptly halted.

Some seconds earlier Edward had noticed the figure of a woman, standing high above on the edge of the embankment, her body bathed by the violet light of the sunset. After stopping so fast that Bill ran into him, Edward stood transfixed by this fanciful sight.

He also, immediately remembered that the sand footing along the edge up there might be faulty because of constant wind erosion. As Bill was exclaiming how sorry he was for running into him, Edward gasped "SHE'S FALLING!" and he lurched forward down the path, running with tremendous speed.

Bill was astonished. He hadn't seen the distant figure, at the top of the headlands. He hadn't seen Maria lose her balance and fall from the cliff, her body bouncing violently against the cliff face and plunging into the waves below.

Edward had some distance to cover to reach the location on the causeway, far below the headland where the woman's body crashed down into the roiling water. He didn't know if he could get there in time. The wave action would be pulling her out away from the stone wall. He was running recklessly, and certainly much faster then he could ever remember running before. He ran on, heart pounding wildly, trying to measure his breath, pushing harder and harder, eyes straining all the while to catch a glimpse of the woman's head bobbing in the waves.

Where is she? As he ran, nearer the water's edge, he struggled out of his jacket and dropped it in his wake. The water is so rough; all I can see are waves, he thought. Then a slit second later, "There," one word rasped from his throat as he spotted something bobbing between the waves. It was she, some distance out from the causeway. He dove, without even kicking his shoes off. The cold water hit him full blast like a frosty blizzard in winter. Luckily there was no trace of the powerful migraine drug in his brain now. Urgency had taken over, the very second that he'd seen her body falling. The waves were extremely strong as he fought to plunge through them. I must try to keep her in sight. She disappeared under the waves. Will she be able to fight her way up again? He was almost to the point where he had seen her go down last. He dove to find her. His eyes struggled to adjust to seeing under the water. It was all a blur. He was going to have to surface for air, but before he could, just ahead of him some feet away, he could just make out the outline of a darker blur. GOD, LET THAT BE HER!

He fought his need for oxygen and dove further and deeper, struggling to get to her. IT IS! He locked one arm under hers and across her chest. Instantly, he started fighting to reach the surface and much needed air. They were both in great need! He had no way of knowing if she was still alive. Her thin body felt very limp. As he broke the surface of the water he felt as if being reborn, being reborn into that quenching atmosphere of oxygen. I've got to get her head above water and keep it there. How far is it to shore? He craned his neck and struggled to focus his eyes to scan for land. Got to get her to shore as quickly as possible! The cold water had numbed his body, but his soul felt great relief because he had a firm hold on this person that he must save. He reached the shore and was having difficulty lifting himself and this limp body out of the water, which definitely was trying to pull them back into its depths. Dr. Bill Adams was there, lifting her weight from him so that he could climb up over the slippery rocks. The doctor immediately started to performed mouth to mouth resuscitation on the woman and after a few minutes she coughed up gulp after gulp of water and started to breathe raggedly.

As luck would have it, they were near the old boathouse. It was imperative to get her out of this cold wind and to start to warm her. After taking a few labored breaths she'd lapsed back into unconsciousness. The two men carried her into the living quarters of the boathouse. It hadn't been used for many years but it was still furnished. They lay her on a dusty couch and Dr. Adams began to check her vital signs. Edward found several blankets. Dr. Adams peeled off her sweater and blouse, and removed her skirt. After he'd quickly checked her extremities, they wrapped her in two of the blankets. Dr. Adams was relieved by the fact that she was breathing, even if her breathing was still a bit ragged. An insignificant amount of blood was trickling sluggishly from a wound on the back of her head. As they had undressed her he noticed that one hip and her other entire side were also very badly scraped.

"What was that?" Edward said as he swung around to face the door. Before either one could recognize the sounds, Brian flung the door open and rushed in, with Gregory not far behind him. Gregory turned and closed the door, while struggling to catch his breath. Brian leaned on a chair, also puffing. Before anything could be said, all eyes went to Maria's body lying on the couch. Brian moved to the couch and leaned down over her, looking for any sign of life. He tilted his head and looked up at Edward, who was standing near by, wrapped in a heavy blanket, "We saw you in the water. Is she going to live?"

Edward deferred to Dr. Adams, "What's your opinion doctor?"

Dr. Adams shrugged and replied, "I think she'll recover. She may have a serious concussion. I can stop the bleeding from the laceration on the back of her head. She has bad abrasions and contusions down one side. However, I don't think she has any broken bones, which is a great wonder after the fall that she had. I think the most important thing is to get her up to the house and get her warmed up."

"What about getting her to the hospital?" Edward asked, in great concern.

"There's no point in trying to move her further tonight, I'll stay with her. It's more important to get her settled quietly and get her temperature up. We'll need to get her to the hospital tomorrow, for a full battery of tests."

"Who could she be?" Edward asked, peering down at this petite pale figure, looking very worried and just a bit confused.

"Edward Warner, meet Maria Stark." Gregory stated, as if making a formal introduction. Gregory had recovered now after making a mad dash down to the boathouse from the lane on the causeway. Brian and he had been returning home after the meeting, in the nearby village. They saw a car stopped along the lane near the headland where Maria had fallen. The car had been left running so they assumed that the driver must be near by. They thought that it might be someone sightseeing, so they walked to the cliff to see if they could find anyone. At the cliff they found a camera on the ground and noticed that a prominent section of the edge of the crag had sheared away. As they scanned the waves below, they caught sight of someone, in the water about one hundred and seventy five feet from the headland. Edward had just reached the woman and started pulling her back to the shore of the causeway. They ran back to the cars and drove them both down the causeway and stopped near the boathouse. Gregory drove the woman's car and he'd grabbed her purse from the car seat and ran to find Edward.

"This is Ms. Stark?" Edward exclaimed in shock, his nerves still gangling from the excitement of the rescue and the extreme exertion. "Albert Green must've lost some of his marbles. This girl is too young for the job that he was asked to fill."

"Well her license says that she is thirty nine," Gregory informed them, having searched through her wallet for identification.

"Gregory, put that back into her purse, we don't want to invade her privacy any further. It's enough to know who she is," Edward barked at him. Gregory grumbled as he stuffed the wallet back into the purse and put it on the table.

"She sure doesn't look thirty nine," Brian acknowledged, as he slumped into a chair.

"Precisely," agreed Edward, "Shouldn't we move her to the house now doctor?"

"Let me try to bring her to," said the doctor, as he gently lifted the locks of lush dark brown hair away from her delicate face. He lifted her hand, felt her pulse and loudly repeated her name, "Ms. Stark, Ms. Stark." Maria rolled her head to one side and slowly opened her eyes. Her arms shot up immediately as if she was still fighting to swim.

"It's all right Ms. Stark. You're going to be all right." the doctor said, assuredly. She laid her head back and stared at the distinguished doctor.

"The cliff... I fell... the cold water," she sputtered, wincing as she clutched the blanket around her. "Where... who... who?"

"You're safe Ms. Stark. Relax my dear, I'm a doctor," crooned Dr. Adams.

"Who?" She whispered, once more. As she grudgingly managed to tear her eyes away from that pleasant doctor's face, she saw the other three men who were looking on anxiously. As she looked from face to face, for some reason her gaze rested uneasily on Edward's countenance.

"Yes." The doctor had been aware of her uneasiness and her need to know. "Yes, this is Edward; he's the one who saved you."

"Edward?" she hesitated, "Edward Warner?"

"Yes," Edward said, as he approached the couch, "You are quite safe now. Dr. Adams has examined your injuries. He's sure that you are going to be all right, but we need to get you to the house and into a warm bed."

"Mr. Warner, thank you. Are you all right? You're very wet," Maria said weakly, ending with a cough.

Edward's face broadened into a wide boyish grin, "I'm alright. I just decided to go for an evening swim."

"We had an appointment," she said, with a small smile. "Am I early or late?"

Edward laughed, "That's enough from you young lady. We need to get you tucked into a nice warm bed."

Brian and Gregory glanced at one another in wonderment; they hadn't seen Edward grinning playfully since before his ill-fated marriage.

"Brian, give me a hand and we'll get her out to the car. Oh Ms. Stark, these are my brothers, Brian and that is Gregory, and your new doctor is Dr. Bill Adams," Edward said, gesturing toward each of the men. Gregory nodded and Brian smiled shyly as he approached to help Edward.

"Hello gentlemen, I guess I'm at your mercy," Maria said, as Brian helped lift her up into Edward's arms. As she rested her head against Edward's chest, she had a fleeting flashback, of thrashing in the icy, gray water then feeling that arm around her chest, pulling her through the water. She shivered violently, at first remembrance. Then she pressed her head against his reassuring strength and drifted off. Edward held her in his arms as Brian drove to the house. He was relieved now that she was sleeping, quietly. She must be totally exhausted.

Chapter 4

$\mathcal{M}$aria awakened in a beautiful canopy bed, surrounded by an exquisite white and gold decorated bedroom. A tiny, white, fluffy dog startled her awake by jumping on her chest and licking her face. A little, dark haired girl giggled from where she was peeking around the partially open door. She giggled again and ran away. The little dog jumped from the bed and ran after her. Dr. Adams was dozing in a plush chair beside the bed.

Maria remembered the kindly face of the doctor. As she began to recall the near fatal event of the day before, that icy feeling started to creep over her body once again. She cut that thought pattern off in mid shiver, by thinking of his face. She didn't want to remember anything more about it right now, except, except that face of the man who had saved her, that face and that warm feeling. She moved to reach toward Dr. Adams and caught herself as a dull pain raked her side.

"I guess I'd better take stock of myself," she muttered to herself. As Maria moved about in the bed, to find out what hurt, Dr. Adams woke up.

"Take it easy there Ms. Stark," he said, while stifling a yawn as he stretched, "we'll be going to the hospital today to have you completely checked over. I thought that you were stable last night and that it was much more important to warm you and make you as comfortable as possible. Edward wouldn't let me go home; no, we both thought it would be better if I stayed with you, just in case."

"My name is Maria. I think that you're probably familiar enough with my person, to call me by my first name. It was you, who partially undressed me at the boathouse, please say that it was. And then here..."

"Whoa, right there Maria, let's not jump to conclusions! Yes, I helped Edward undress you and quickly wrap you in the blankets. Please don't be embarrassed, I was strictly acting as a physician and Edward was so besought with worry and exhaustion, I - I don't think that he would have noticed anything other then your very pretty face. And as for here in this bedroom, Emma the housekeeper has been instructed to care for you."

Maria was momentarily embarrassed, but that feeling was quickly overwhelmed by one of gratitude. To help hold the tears back, she tried to concentrate on surveying the golden beauty of the room's décor. She scanned its two, large, rounded-topped windows with their creamy, sheer curtains, softly blowing over golden brocade, window seat cushions. The morning sunlight was pleasantly warm on this side of the manor and the windows emitted the gentlest of fall breezes. This was too fantastic. She had never lived in such splendor. After everything that had happened, she would be very lucky if Edward Warner would even consider her for the job of supervising his daughter. As Maria was looking around, her eyes fell on a beautiful, golden statue of a stallion, standing on an antique table in the middle of the room. It was as if the room had been decorated just for her. Don't dwell on fairy tales, my dear girl, she thought to herself.

Chapter 5

$\mathcal{E}$dward had started his morning off early with a brisk walk around the rose garden. As he walked his mind slipped discriminatively back to the events of the previous evening. His memory didn't dwell on the high adrenalin moments of the actual rescue, but instead he zeroed in on the memory of that first glimpse of Maria's face, as she lay on the old, dusty, floral couch in the boathouse. He fondly remembered that delicate, pale face, with the wet, dark hair clinging to her skin. A bevy of emotions began to swirl; I'm a mature man of forty five years who has survived one hideous marriage, I've an exemplary career as a scientist, and I'm trying to raise a young daughter. I can't afford to be thinking about a woman, even if she could possibly be interested in a man like me. OUT OF BOUNDS, he thought to himself as he walked back towards the manor.

All of that firm resolve, but he couldn't help glancing at the windows of her bedroom, once more before he entered the manor and went to his office.

"Dr. Adams, there was a little girl peeking around the door, a short time before you woke and she had a little, white dog that jumped up and gave me a good morning kiss," Maria said, to the sleepy man.

"Oh that would have been Anna Belle, the little darling. I'm surprised that she had only one dog with her. You see, it's quite isolated out here and Edward likes to keep it that way, so he makes up for the lack of child companions for Anna Belle with animal friends for her. There's a smaller stable here on the island. I guess you could call it a petting zoo and there are more than a few dogs running around here. Before you move around the house by yourself, you'll have to be introduced to them. A few of them have strong guarding instincts."

"Well Doc, I don't know that I'll be here very long. What's the plan for the hospital visit that you mentioned?"

Dr. Adams got up from the chair slowly, holding his back and stretching, long, "Edward has asked me to take you to the hospital as soon as you can comfortably get ready and to have you checked over thoroughly, of course."

"All that, won't be necessary. I think I'll be all right." Maria said, pushing herself up into a sitting position, with some difficulty. Dr. Adams moved quickly to support her as she attempted to slide her legs over the side of the bed. The pain of doing so, showed vividly on her face. The doctor sympathized, "Edward wants you to have the best treatment available, and for you to be brought back here to recuperate. I believe he said something about you still having an appointment for a job interview."

"He still wants to talk to me about the job?" Maria asked, through a pained expression.

"Apparently that's his wish," Dr. Adams answered. "Are there any family or friends that we should contact to let them know that you are all right, but that you'll be staying here for a while?"

"No, and I can't stay, I haven't anything with me other than my purse," Maria stated, firmly. "No there is no one to contact, my daughter is away at school." Maria looked forlorn. Her head was starting to ache.

"I'm sure that Mallory Warner will have things that she can lend you, for now," he assured her.

Maria for some unknown reason, felt even more dejected now, "You mean there's a Mrs. Warner?"

"Oh yes," Dr. Adams said with a tiny hint of a smile, "Yes Mrs. Gregory Warner, Edward's sister-in-law."

Maria automatically turned her head in an attempt to hide her reaction of relief, even before she knew that she felt it. Dr. Adams missing nothing, smiled to himself. As if on cue, there was a faint rapping at the door. The door opened widely and a blonde woman carrying an armload of clothing, hurried into the room.

"Well now, Maria Stark I'm Mallory Warner. Edward has asked me to bring some comfortable fitting, day wear outfits for you to use until you have your own clothes here. I can see that I could've brought some of my more fitted things and they would've been fine for you. That's a man for you - no judge of size. Oh, I hope that you are feeling better this morning. You must've had quite an ordeal. The men didn't tell me very much about it. When you are feeling better you'll have plenty of time to fill me in. I hope that you like some of these outfits. If you have any problems just send Emma to my rooms. It's going to be so nice to have another female to talk to." Mallory whirled around after throwing the clothes on the bed and walked back out of the room.

Maria looked at the doctor with large eyes full of astonishment and asked, "Does she ever take time to draw a breath? I won't have to worry about what to say to her, she'll never give me a chance to say anything."

Dr. Adams laughed uncontrollably, "You've got her pegged." He walked to the door, while asking, "Do you think that you can get dressed alone or should we send for Emma?"

"I think I can manage," Maria said quietly, while thinking to herself, I will one way or another.

"I'll wait in the hallway," the doctor assured her. "That's your bathroom over there," he said pointing to another doorway. "Just call if you need anything."

Maria met him in the hall about fifteen minutes later. She was finding it quite difficult to walk. From the clothes that Mallory had thrown on the bed, Maria had picked a loose fitting, blue pantsuit, definitely wishing to dress for comfort. Dr. Adams had a wheel chair for her to use, making no mention of where it had come from. She was grateful, as it seemed that the hallway went on forever before they came to an elevator that took them down one floor to the main entrance hall. The huge, main hall was crafted of stone, with a circular staircase, chandeliers and a glass wall looking into a flower garden.

Dr. Adams wheeled her into a small, sunny breakfast room or sunroom, just off the large formal dinning room. This room was bright, warm and very inviting. A long wall of glass looked out to the north into an English style rose garden, the rest of the room was a warm green with yellow accents. The large table was glass and wrought iron. This room would gleam as if by sunlight even if the weather didn't co-operate, actually the lighting was coordinated to do just that. The doctor simply tapped on a white door at the end of the room, undoubtedly the kitchen door. A sturdy, older woman dressed in a classic, gray uniform entered the room, briefly introduced herself as Emma the housekeeper and asked Maria what her breakfast preferences were. She and the doctor agreed upon fresh fruit and croissants. After a quiet breakfast, the doctor wheeled her out to a sparkling gray, chauffeur driven limousine that was waiting to take them to the hospital.

"Maria, I can see that you're very weary so please save your energy and rest," he suggested, indicating that she might lie down across the wide seat, so she did. He went on to ask, "There is one request that I would like to make of you though. Would you please call me by my given name? It's Bill."

"Certainly Bill, if that's what you'd like," Maria answered softly, from behind already closed eyes. She slept until they reached the hospital. Once there, Dr. Bill took charge and it seemed to Maria that the ordeal of test after test went on all day; and indeed it did. At six o'clock she was lifted back into the limousine and she was looking forward to going to sleep again, but Dr. Bill was trying to give her a report on her condition.

"Maria, you've suffered a serious concussion. The contusions on the back of your head indicate that you must have hit your head quite hard when you fell and of course that has caused the concussion. Your left side and hip are badly bruised. This will cause some stiffness and lameness but there are no apparent internal problems. However, I'll be monitoring you in regard to a slight possibility of deep vein thrombosis. And just to be cautious I'll be prescribing some bed rest and the use of a wheel chair for as long as needed. As a result of the shock to your system and the after effects of the concussion you can expect to feel shaky and not at all well for at least a couple of weeks. You're going to require complete rest and continuous monitoring for possible side effects for the next two weeks."

"Is that so? I'm very tired," Maria muttered, as she sprawled out on the seat once again and went to sleep.

Bill Adams sat watching her as she slept, concerned for her comfort, yet confident that she'd be all right.

Chapter 6

*M*aria's next few days passed in irregular intervals; composed of a myriad of London fog like times, interspersed with fleeting, pleasant, sunny intervals and cushioned with thick, gratifying sleep. She didn't remember arriving back at Sinabar, from the hospital nor being dressed for bed and being tucked in.

Edward couldn't concentrate on his work. He felt befuddled. He didn't know what was happening to him. He'd never had this problem before; this lack of focus. He paced up and down in his laboratory, just above that golden bedroom, and later he paced back and forth on the white pebble paths of the rose garden. He paced up and down, back and forth.

Edward was an extremely successful scientist. He had recently completed a monumental project that would be a corner stone in the progression toward the nutritional well being of all humanity; a solution to the problem of how to supply superior nutritional sustenance to all people, everywhere. His completed documentation hadn't even been published yet, but already, among his colleagues it was being rumored that he would surely be nominated for the highest world recognition awarded by the joint members of NATO.

He wasn't self-impressed by these early accolades. He continued to be motivated by an instinctual need to help mankind, and was merely thankful that he'd accomplished what he knew would be of paramount aid to all of the populous of the world.

Now here he was, his strong constitution reduced to sweaty palms, quickened step, indecisiveness, lack of appetite and depleted attention span. "Is this a nervous system let down resulting from prolonged stress, now that the project of a lifetime is almost complete, or have I been bitten by a bug? Yes, maybe it's some flu bug. That's what it must be," Edward reassured himself as he walked down the second floor hall to the stairway. As he started to descend the stairs, shaking his head he murmured, "And now I'm talking out loud to myself."

A prim and smiling Emma met him in the grand hall, "Good morning Sir, how are you this bright morning?" she chirped, pleasantly.

"I'm fine Emma. How's our Ms. Stark?" Edward asked, while teetering back and forth on his heals with his hands tucked into his trouser pockets.

"She has slept on and off for the last two days, Sir. She slips in and out of a heavy, sometimes fretful sleep, being awake only for short times. I've had May sitting with her most of the daytime and the few times that she has been awake, we've assisted her with some soup and tea."

Edward's brow furrowed, "Keep some fresh fruit by her always, also some delicate cookies and a thermos carafe of tea. Let me know as soon as you feel that she might like some solid food or she might feel well enough to join us for meals."

"Yes Sir."

"You've taken care of obtaining the ladies clothing and accessories that I asked for?" Edward inquired.

"Yes Sir."

"Emma, you mentioned that Ms. Stark's sleep is sometimes fretful."

"Yes Mr. Warner, sometimes she thrashes around in the bed as if she's still in the water."

"Well, maybe that's to be expected. The poor lady has had quite a traumatic experience. Is Dr. Adams stopping in today to check on her?"

"I believe so Mr. Warner, I must say that the doctor has been quite attentive of Ms. Stark," Emma reported, with a smile.

"He has. Has he? Please tell him that I'd like to see him after he's seen the lady today."

"Yes Sir," Emma assured him as he strolled off down the hall. Emma had noticed that Edward was looking more attractive then usual this morning, and that this was the first time she'd ever seen him wearing those soft slippers that Anna Belle gave him last Christmas. Anna Belle will be so pleased, she thought to herself as she hurried off to amend the staff duty list for the day.

Emma would have been surprised if she'd found out why Edward had started wearing the slippers. As a result of his restlessness and insomnia he had taken to walking the halls whether by day or night and to his great disdain he found himself standing outside Maria's door more often than not. He worried about her hearing his steps in the hall and he didn't want to unsettle her, or startle her, so he had searched out the slippers and started wearing them.

The very night before, Edward had stood outside Maria's door, which he had opened ever so slightly. He marveled at the sight of the moonlight draping across the bed, softly highlighting the silhouette of her body. She lay slumbering quietly, her dark hair trailing across her forehead and down over her delicate shoulder. He reached out, only with his mind to see if he could sense her state of being. With the aid of the silvery moonlight, he perceived the gentle rising and falling of the light covering over her sweetly, sloping breasts.

"What am I doing here?" Edward moaned softly, as if in great pain. He hadn't experienced these thoughts, these stirrings, for a very long time; indeed not since well before his divorce from Reanna. The dreadful experience with his ex-wife had left him torn and bruised, feeling numb toward women kind, rendered incapable of anything beyond simple pleasantries with the fairer sex.

"I must remove myself," he ordered, regretfully forcing himself to turn from this ethereal moonlit vision. As he walked slowly away a tingling seemed to be playing over his aura, like the teasing soft touch of small finger tips. He shivered and mentally tried to push this feeling away, contributing it to the air in the hallway being cold; even though it wasn't. The house was completely dark except for the shafts of haunting moonlight, beaming through the large windows. He adeptly made his way back to the lab where he sat aimlessly starring at the computer screen. "I know very little about this creature. I know nothing about her personality, her interests. But that face! That image of beauty, I just can't get it out of my mind," he confided to himself.

Edward was so affected by that visage, that he had all but forgotten the woman's name and why she had originally come to Sinabar.

Chapter 7

$\mathcal{M}$aria's eyes popped open alertly for the first time in days. The room was still as magnificent as she had originally envisioned it to be, and had continued to marvel at through the haze of pain and fatigue of the past four days of her convalescence.

"I think I feel positively human today," she said aloud to herself, as if to confirm the fact. She thought pensively back to the extreme lethargy that she had experienced since the accident. How many days have I slipped in and out of the haze of sleep, nightmares and body aches and pains? I'll have to ask Emma. Emma, she vaguely remembered was an efficient, gray haired woman, who helped her in and out of clothes and tried to feed her. There also had been another young woman who had helped her. What was her name?

Maria stretched and gazed around the room. There were no clothes in sight, other than a dressing gown. There was no clock anywhere, nor any sign of anything that needed to be done. "I guess this would indicate that rest is what's expected. I can't rest forever. I came here as a possible employee. What must Mr. Warner think? I have to get out of this bed and make myself presentable and accountable." Maria pushed herself up to a sitting position and swung her legs over the side of the bed. As she did so she was uncomfortably surprised to find that her hip and side were quite painful, and that dizziness still welled up over her senses as she got used to sitting up.

"I guess the only thing I can do right now is pull the cord to summon help." She did so and then gratefully lay back against the pillows. On an elaborate marble table between the bed and the window seat, she now noticed an ample basket of fruit, a plate of cookies and a thermos carafe. So luxurious, she thought.

There was a soft knock at the door and Emma entered followed by the young serving girl, whom Maria had wondered about. She was pushing a breakfast cart.

"Good morning Ms. Stark, you look quite rested this fine morning," chimed Emma. "This is May. We thought we might bring you an assortment of breakfast dishes this morning and let you choose your start for the day."

"Oh, thank you ladies," Maria said, being overwhelmed in more ways than one. The effort of this offering impressed her, while the smell of bacon upset her delicate balance. The ever-observant Emma noticed the slight spasm of queasiness that passed over her charge's pale face, so she asked, "Maybe, I could suggest some lightly scrambled eggs, some stewed fruit and toast." Emma quickly had May take the cart back out into the hall where she prepared a dish of these selections for Maria and placed it on the marble table. Emma got the dressing gown, helped her into it, and then assisted her into a chair at the table. Maria bolstered herself and tried to nibble at the food.

"Emma, I must get back on my feet today and find out if Mr. Warner has time to see me. I can't go on like this, receiving his gracious hospitality," Maria stated.

"Oh, Ms. Stark..." Emma started.

"Call me Maria, please." Maria interrupted, in a soft voice.

"Very well Ms. Maria, but please don't worry about Mr. Warner's hospitality. He is a well-meaning gentleman and he simply wishes you to rest and recuperate. Dr. Adams will be coming to attend you this afternoon and Mr. Warner has asked that he report back to him afterwards."

"Thank you Emma, that suits me fine. I'd like a chance to dress and prepare myself to receive Dr. Adams. And if Mr. Warner wouldn't mind, I'd like to finally have that appointment with him." If I can last that long, she thought to herself. I will; I have to.

"Ms. Maria, there are clothes in the closet for you to choose from. Would you like to see some of them before I leave you?" Emma asked.

"Oh yes, Mrs. Warner was very kind to lend them to me." Maria shifted in her chair so that she could see the closet.

"No, Ms. Maria, these clothes aren't the ones from Mallory Warner. Mr. Warner asked me to purchase these especially for you."

"He did what?" Maria blurted out in amazement.

Emma nodded in the affirmative as she pulled many laden hangers from the closet and laid them on the bed for viewing. There were lilacs, pale yellows, several different beautiful shades of green, pale pinks, and crisp whites; blouses, sweaters and dresses, as well as basic black skirts and pants, a voluptuous, pearl gray sweater and a gray, suede, walking coat.

Maria sat with her mouth agape, her eyes growing larger as Emma displayed each item and replaced it in the closet. "There are also dainties and undergarments as well as sports sweaters and riding breaches in the drawers, Ms." Emma reported, smiling.

Maria was so overwhelmed that she could find no words at first. Then she said, "Emma, the colors, the styles, they're beautiful! How did you know what to pick?"

"Oh, my job wasn't that hard, Ms. I just had to locate the items. Mr. Warner was quite explicit about most of the items. He has an amazing eye for color, doesn't he? He did leave the underwear to my judgment, but he was quite definite that everything be of the finest quality of course."

"Why?" Maria exclaimed in wonderment.

Emma knew well enough not to try and answer a question that could only be properly answered by Edward himself, Master of the manor. She simply went on, "May will take care of any alterations that you might need. You should go back to bed now, for a while Ms. Maria. Dr. Adams will be coming at two o'clock. I'll send May to you later, with a warm lunch, and then she can stay and attend to your needs, well before the doctor comes."

Emma could see that the young lady certainly did need to rest. Poor dear! This really has been a lot for her to take in, all at once, she thought.

"If Mr. Warner is here I'll ask him if he'd like to meet with you this evening, and if all goes well with your appointment with Dr. Adams, would you like me to set a place at dinner for you?" Emma asked, as she helped Maria back into bed.

"Yes Emma, thank you for being so helpful," Maria said, as she rested back against the pillows that Emma had fluffed for her. After collecting up the breakfast dishes, Emma left Maria to her thoughts.

This indeed, was too much for her to comprehend and it had tired her greatly. She just wanted to pull the covers over her head, so she did. Why was Edward Warner, doing all of this for her? When she thought of this man that she really didn't know, it made her uneasy, because she didn't know how to accept any of this. However, upon searching deeper within herself, she found warm feelings there, accompanied surprisingly by a strange tingle of excitement. At this point she didn't even want to dwell on why she might have these feelings. They were very new feelings. WARMTH! She let this luxurious concept and the present reality engulf her as she slipped off into peaceful sleep, where she dreamt of her Prince in Shining Armor.

Chapter 8

*E*mma smiled to herself as she pushed the breakfast cart back to the kitchen. It'd be grand to have the mild, sweet Ms. Maria as "The Lady of the house", instead of the self-absorbed, pompous Mallory Warner; even as Mallory had been a great relief as "The Lady..." in comparison with Edward's ex-wife Reanna, who had left to pursue her strange life somewhere else. THANK THE LORD!

Emma had no way of knowing if this was what was on Edward's mind, but he sure was going above and beyond when it came to Dear Ms. Maria. Even his usually guarded daily routine had changed. He was looking more attractive and youthful then he had in a long time. Maybe, he had developed something in his lab, a youth potion that he was trying on himself. She doubted that. It was more likely the influence of Ms. Maria. Well, whatever the case, anything was better then the Jekyll and Hyde that Edward had become under the twisted, malevolent influence of Reanna, his first wife.

She hummed to herself as she walked back to the household office, where she sang out "Better Days Are Coming". Emma buzzed Edward's lab on the intercom, and finding him there, she informed him of Maria's request to meet with him.

"Yes indeed, please call me to the library to meet with Dr. Adams after he's seen Ms. Stark. I'll be asking him to join us for dinner. I hope Ms. Stark will feel up to it. If such is the case I'll interview her after dinner. Thank you Emma, you'll find me here this afternoon."

Emma wondered as usual, if he was working or if he was using his newly fortified laboratory as a place to hide out, away from the rest of the world. She didn't know what he had been working on for the last three years, but she did know about the unusual security refurbishments that had been made up there. The laboratory had much more security than the rest of the house. She couldn't understand this premise.

— ◆ —

Maria was awakened at noon by a gentle tap at the door. May entered pushing the serving cart, with Maria's lunch; steaming soup, warm biscuits, a raw vegetable platter and a selection of fruit tarts. Maria was grateful for the hot soup and light lunch. It suited the day, which was a typically dull, wet fall day. She hadn't seen May very often. Emma had just introduced them at breakfast, that morning. May was a pleasant, short, blonde girl of about twenty-two years. She had worked at Sinabar for six years.

"Ms. Maria, could I lay out some clothes for you to choose from while you enjoy your lunch?"

"Yes May, that would be nice. After I see Dr. Adams, I'd like to go down for tea and maybe take a walk in the garden before dinner, so I'll need comfortable slacks, a blouse and a sweater."

May pulled some items from the closet as she asked, "How about these dark green slacks, this light yellow blouse and the matching green sweater coat?

"That's fine, I'll try them... Shoes, what am I going to wear for shoes?"

"Oh, there are several pairs of shoes and boots here Ms. Maria. I'd take it that you would like the brown casual, walking shoes."

"There's a selection of footwear there as well?" Maria was once again awed by Edward Warner's complete anticipation of her needs.

After lunch, May assisted her with her toiletries and also helped her with her attire. They found that everything fit Maria very well. "Ms. Maria if you'll come and sit by the window I'll brush your beautiful hair for you."

"That sounds very nice, May. I'm not used to all of this pampering. I've never had anyone brush my hair, except maybe my mother when I was very young. May, did you ever meet Anna Belle's mother, Mr. Warner's wife?" Maria asked sheepishly, as May brushed.

"No, Ms. Emma hired me after Reanna Warner was gone. The staff was in a big upheaval right after she was sent away and those that hadn't been fired told me that I was very lucky to not have been here, when she was Lady of the house."

"Why is that, May?"

"Well they say that she is a tall, darkly beautiful woman, but very strange and cold. She was away a lot of the time, but they say that when she was here, the house always had an uneasy atmosphere."

"Did they really refer to Mrs. Warner as the Lady of the house?" Maria inquired.

"Oh yes Ms., that's the British way. The wife of the Master or landholder is always the Lady of the house," May explained feeling very self-important that she could teach this lady something. So much so that she added, without being prompted further, "Mr. Edward is the eldest of the three Warner brothers and therefore he inherited this estate as well as holdings in England. Mr. Brian, is an equestrian and outdoors type so he stays on here to manage the grounds and the stables. Oh, and he's a bachelor. Mr. Gregory is a businessman and he helps Mr. Edward with their many business interests. Now, they refer to Mr. Gregory's wife, Mallory as the Lady of the house," May finished with a chuckle.

"Why is that humorous, May?"

May smirked and explained, "Well, the Lady of the house is supposed to be interested in the goings on of the household. The Lady in a British household is the organizer. She would: oversee the food selections, order the flowers, hire the housekeeping staff, instruct the gardeners and so on... Mallory Warner is not interested in ever trying any of these tasks. Emma does all of that and more. She runs this household, and has had to ever since Edward's mother left to go back to England, after he married."

"I'm sure that Emma does a wonderful job." Maria made this simple assumption based on the short encounters that she'd had with the very efficient housekeeper. May surely is a well of information that doesn't require a lot of priming, Maria thought to herself. If I should be hired to work here and I need any information, I need only spend time with May.

"Don't you look wonderful Ms. Stark? You look a bit pale, no doubt from your dreadful accident, but with this glorious, dark brown, curly hair... the paleness is not unbecoming."

"I think I'll just lie back on the bed for a while, until Dr. Adams gets here. Thank you May, for all of your help," Maria said, being indeed very thankful for all of the information as well.

"Don't bother to thank me Ms. Stark, it was too enjoyable to be considered work," May stated, with a sincere smile before she left the room.

Maria liked May very much, but she was thankful for this quiet time before the doctor's arrival. She was very stiff and sore, as well as having to deal with dizziness if she moved too quickly.

I need this job, she was stressing to herself. I mustn't appear weak and fragile, or sickly and complaining. Of course she needn't have worried about that because it wasn't in her nature to be so. I'll meet Edward Warner today, properly, and I must make a good impression, if I hope to be allowed the responsibility of taking care of his only child.

Chapter 9

There was a brisk rap on the door, and after being bid enter, Dr. Adams appeared.

"Ms. Stark, you look quite divine today. I must admit, I wasn't prepared for such a pleasant surprise, so soon. Today is only the fifth day since your horrendous fall, not to mention your near drowning. Apparently, you are a very, lucky lady!" he exclaimed as he took a seat on the bed beside her.

"I agree with you totally, Dr. Adams. I haven't as yet, let myself dwell on the actual happenings of the accident, but I do know that I wouldn't be alive if it wasn't for Mr. Warner and you. Thank you, Sir," she said, leaning forward as much as she could from her propped up reclining position on the bed and gave him a brief hug.

"And what does our scientist friend think about your rapid rate of recovery?"

"Pardon me?" she asked.

"Edward... Mr. Warner."

"I wouldn't know doctor. I haven't even properly met Mr. Warner."

"Oh, that's strange, I thought that Edward would've been in to see you by now," the doctor said, shrugging his shoulders.

"Dr. Adams, other than a vague memory of being in someone's arms that night and dimly seeing a montage of male faces, I presently recall nothing else. I only remember you telling me, the next day on the way to the hospital, that it had been Mr. Edward Warner who saved me from the depths. Since then I've only seen Emma, May and yourself, and oh yes, that first day I seem to remember a little girl's face peering at me from around the door; a sweet, little face with warm brown hair, and a blonde woman by the name of Mallory bringing me some clothes. So you see, I haven't left these rooms since you brought me here from the hospital." Maria realized that her voice was beginning to get a bit shrill, which she by no means had intended, so she stopped for a minute and took a deep breath before continuing, "There now Dr. Adams, you're up to date."

She paused again, shaking her head ever so slowly before saying, "I'm sorry doctor, I hadn't intended on venting any irritation, indeed, I hadn't realize that I felt irritated," she lowered her head apologetically, "this is a very odd situation - to say the least."

"No doubt, my dear, I had overlooked the uniqueness of the situation that we have here. Anyway, the restfulness of your isolation has probably done you immeasurable good. That undoubtedly, has been Edward's consideration," he said, not totally sure of himself.

Maria glanced toward her closet, "Mr. Warner has apparently been extremely considerate."

"How are you feeling Maria, what symptoms do you have now?"

"I have painful areas on my hip, my back and the back of my head. My neck is very stiff and I have a problem with dizziness, if I move too quickly," Maria reported.

"You'll have to continue taking life very easy for a while yet, Maria. I've been a bit concerned about your concussion and also the possibility of deep vein thrombosis. Do you know what the latter entails?"

"No, I don't." Maria looked a bit shaken, so he hastened to explain.

"I'm speaking of any deep vein clotting that can occur in any of the extremities, and if it moves it can possibly cause a problem. Don't worry though, this condition was by no means definitely indicated by any of your tests, but it is always considered as a remote possibility following such a physical trauma. I'm speaking of this only as a precaution. That's why we wanted to be careful about your moving around, but now it'll be a good idea for you to get some mild exercise, under supervision of course. Have you had any problem with an upset stomach?"

"Yes, this morning at breakfast I was hungry but the smell of the bacon put me off a bit."

"As I said before, this is all going to take some time to resolve itself. I'll give Emma some instructions about your diet. As far as the dizziness goes, let me know immediately if it gets any worse and be careful to get up slowly and move carefully. I've brought some mild analgesic pills that I'll leave with you for any severe aches or pains, but please remember that if you have any changes at all, please call me, day or night. Do you understand?" he asked, with his warmest smile as he reached out to pat her hand.

"Yes doctor, thank you very much," she answered, while thinking to herself, that he was a very attractive man when he smiled. She went on, "In the past I've managed to keep myself quite physically fit. That is a main priority with me but right now I'm very stiff and sore."

"I credit you Maria, on your state of fitness," he assured her, worrying now that he might be blushing, a wee bit. "Your fitness was definitely an important factor in your lack of severity of injuries, your being able to survive until Edward was able to get to you, and of course your accelerated recovery time. It is truly a wonder that you are alive, I know - I was there! That, in itself, might lend one to ponder a bit about fate, in this situation - that Edward and I just happened to be walking out there and that he saw you falling. The whole thing is enough to make a person shiver."

She knew that he hadn't meant to be so suggestive, but she did shiver. Trying to hide it she said, "Well doctor, I know that with all of this great care I'll be just fine, very soon."

The medical part of his visit with Maria seemed to be over but he didn't want to leave her company. "Edward has graciously invited me to stay for tea and dinner. Will you be joining us for dinner?" he inquired, hopefully.

"I let Emma know this morning that if all went well I'd like to go out into the garden and then possibly join everyone for tea and dinner."

"Well, if you're intending to move around that much I must insist that you have someone with you and that you use the wheelchair."

"Doctor, I want to walk for some exercise!" Maria demanded.

"Then we'll just make sure that the wheelchair is there with you for when you are ready to sit. Please don't overestimate your physical capability and end up causing yourself further harm," he chided.

"I'll be careful, doctor." she conceded.

Dr. Adams got up and walked to the door, turning with a concerned smile and said, "Just don't bite off more then you can chew. Please!"

Maria smiled back, saying, "I'll remember to chew well."

"I'm going down now to give Edward a full report about your condition. He's a very thorough man."

"I'm beginning to understand that, about him."

"We'll send someone up to you, with the wheelchair," his voice stressing the wheelchair part, as he left the room.

Maria smiled to herself after he was gone. To think, that right now her very friendly and considerate doctor would be discussing her condition with her, as of yet, most unfamiliar hero. An icy shiver ran up her spine. What did he think of her? What would he think after they met formally, later this evening? All she could remember of him was a dim image of his face, his strength, and the feeling of being held next to his warm body, ever so tightly. And sandy, brown hair... yes she had noticed it when he had picked her up, and the scent of very discrete, yet manly cologne. "Get a hold of yourself, girl!" she said out loud. I've got to stop thinking along these lines. I'm here, trying to get a job! She slowly made her way to the bathroom to freshen up and make sure that she looked the best that she could.

Chapter 10

*B*ill Adams was still smiling as Edward entered the library. Edward, noting the doctor's smile, from under speculatively raised eyebrows, cut right to the heart of the matter, "From your expression, doctor, I would surmise that our guest, Ms. Stark is doing well."

"Extremely well, I'd say," Bill said with a 'cat just swallowed the canary' attitude, "although, she may have some hard times coming yet, possibly to be caused by her overly strong spirit. Yet it's that same, strong willpower that has succeeded in making her so well. Maria possesses such spirit, yet she also has humility as well. And she definitely has a sense of humor. What a package!" Bill gushed, oozing admiration for the lady in question.

Edward had lowered himself into one of the large leather upholstered chairs, facing the doctor. He languidly crossed his long legs and struggled to keep the surprise from his countenance. He was delighted to hear that the lady was doing so well, but he also was surprised at the ardor that Bill Adams showed for the lady's...'spirit'.

"Why doctor, you sound positively smitten," Edward said, in an accusatory fashion accompanied by a sly smile. "I ask for a medical report and you also give me a most insightful personality analysis. You impress me Sir."

Bill laughed uneasily as he lifted his brandy snifter and stared through the amber liquor, hiding his expression from Edward. "I guess I should never play poker," he said, quietly.

"How is the lady, medically, I mean?" Edward asked, with a hint of sternness.

"Medically, Maria is suffering from muscular stiffness and bruise soreness. She's also still having occasional dizzy spills, which are no doubt caused by her concussion. I feel that we should make sure to have someone with her if she moves around outside her room and that a wheelchair be available just in case she tires or has trouble with dizziness. She's quite anxious to get moving around. She's preoccupied with fitness and she isn't going to lie around in that bed. The problem may lie in protecting her from her own physical ambitions, long enough for her body to heal."

"Dr., please excuse me for a minute while I take care of this matter, right away," Edward said as he walked over to the large, ornately carved, cherry wood desk, where he pushed a button and spoke into the intercom, "Emma, please send May to the library before she goes back up to Ms. Stark's room. I have some further instructions for her." He came back across the room and sat back down in the chair across from the doctor.

"Edward, we can always trust in you to be straight to the point and to take the appropriate measures, immediately," Bill mused, once again staring into his brandy.

"Yes. Can you see any advantage to acting in any other manner?"

May knocked on the door and entered, "Yes Sir?"

"May, get the wheelchair out of the hall closet and take it with you up to Ms. Stark's room. Make sure that you or Emma are with her whenever she leaves her rooms, and for now, have the wheelchair with you also. I don't want the lady to feel that she's a prisoner in her room or that she's being shadowed, we're just concerned that she might suffer some further weakness or dizzy spells. So keep an eye on her and anticipate her needs. Thank you; you may attend the lady now." May nodded in answer and left to take Maria the wheelchair.

"Edward, you are quite considerate of this woman. She was coming here for a job interview, was she not?" Bill asked, with more than a hint of curiosity.

"Yes, my estate barrister had sent her here for an interview for the position as a recreational instructor and hopefully a companion for Anna Belle."

"And you haven't gone up to introduce yourself yet?" Bill asked, incredulously.

"No. Why do you ask?"

"Well, she mentioned to me that she hadn't properly met you yet and she seems to be having a hard time justifying your exceptional treatment of her."

Edward moved uncomfortably in his chair, "I hadn't realized that she might be uncomfortable with the situation." It was his turn now, to try and hide a look of dismay, "I've stayed away to further facilitate her recovery."

"Yes, well, I gave her that line in your defense, but I don't know if she fell for it." Bill finished with a wide grin.

"Thanks Doc for the try, I guess we men are going to have to stick together when it comes to dealing with the fairer sex," Edward said, allowing himself to laugh, "I take it that we'll be seeing Ms. Stark for tea. I'll have that interview with her this afternoon. Now if you'll excuse me I've a few things to do. Tea today will be served in the solarium. So please make yourself comfortable, and I'll meet you there at four o'clock."

After Edward excused himself, the doctor strolled around the library, looking at books and the magazines that were on the huge, cherry wood desk, but he couldn't get interested in anything that he saw. His mind kept coming back to the Maria / Edward situation. He smiled broadly as his mind rested on the brief experiences he'd shared, so far, with the lovely Maria. He realized that he didn't know much about her, aside from her medical history and her physical statistics, but he did know that he found her very attractive and stimulating. Maybe she was why he'd remained a bachelor all of this time, just waiting for the right woman.

And what do I know about Edward? Plenty, he'd known Sir Edward Warner since eight months before the birth of Edward's daughter Anna Belle. Edward had been married to Reanna, the strikingly gorgeous, tall, black haired, British socialite. When Reanna had become pregnant, which had been totally unexpected by her, Edward had been ecstatic, but Reanna said no, there was no way that she was going to have a baby. It had also soon become blatantly apparent that Reanna was an unfaithful, lurid, sexual deviant who posed a great risk to the baby that she carried as well as to herself. Edward had been desperate. Reanna was threatening to have an abortion as soon as she could. Edward had taken drastic action. He had locked her up and kept his wife under what he called, 'house arrest'. She was locked in the luxurious upper floor of the east wing. She was afforded every comfort, except the freedom to come and go and have visitors, other then immediate family members and Bill himself, her new physician   Edward had called him in on this unlawful case, with the understanding that Reanna would be very well paid off after the baby was born, and with of course, the conditions that she would leave the country and forfeit her right to use legal recourse against the family or him, and that she would keep her mouth shut about the whole thing. In return for his services the Warner family made a large endowment to provide him with a new, state of the art medical clinic. He had been hard to convince initially, because of possible legal repercussions, but once he'd been shown that this problem could be overcome by pandering to Reanna's greed, his feelings for the innocent child that this wanton woman was carrying, tipped the scales in Edward's favor. He had then willingly become part of Edward's solution to saving the life of his child.

This was history now and he had no cause to regret any part of it. As a matter of fact he was very glad of it every time he had the occasion to see the sweet and well-adjusted Anna Belle. As soon as Reanna had been delivered of the child, she took the fortune that Edward had given her for her ordeal as well as the quiet divorce he offered, and departed for destinations unknown.

The Edward of today had been knighted by the Queen, three years ago for his life saving, nutritional research and field work in third world countries. And it was now rumored that he was to be nominated for the Nobel Prize for Scientific Research; for his most recent body of work which was soon to be published. Yes, I guess anyone would consider him to be successful. Just look at him. He's forty something, six foot two, has a lean solid build, sandy brown hair, neatly kept mustache, an impeccably dresser (very British style). Yes, I imagine that most women would consider Edward to be very eligible. I should be so lucky!

In the case of Maria / Edward, I can only hope and pray that one plus one doesn't make a couple.

Chapter 11

$\mathcal{M}$ay knocked on Maria's door and made her presence known, "I'm back again Ms. Stark. Mr. Warner has asked me to accompany you this afternoon and also to bring the wheelchair just in case you might get tired. He doesn't want you to over do it, on your first walk. He also suggested that you might like to see the main part of the manor."

"What is it like outside, May?   I should like to go out into the garden," Maria asked as she came out of the bathroom feeling a bit more confident now.

"It's not raining now Ms. but it's quite cool," May explained.

"I'll take the suede walking coat," Maria said, starting toward the closet.

May moved ahead of her towards the closet, "Please let me do these things for you Ms."

"May, I'm just not used to being waited on," Maria stated with an uncomfortable little smile, "and please call me Maria."

"Yes of course Ms. Maria."

Maria just smiled and shook her head. She turned and started to the door as May got the coat from the closet. Maria tried in vane, not to let the other younger woman see how nervous she was. She was going to meet the other members of the Sinabar household either on her walk, at tea or later on at dinner. "May, lets start by going to the garden." She didn't understand it but some power was drawing her to the garden.

"Yes, very well Ms. Maria." They slowly strolled down the long corridor with doors on the same side as Maria's golden suite and huge windows along the south side of the manor. These windows looked out toward the water as if looking out to sea. It was Lake Ontario but she couldn't see the other side, so it looked as if it went on forever. Maria shivered uncontrollably at the sight of the water, so she looked down at the south grounds of the island. Apparently there was a circular driveway around the island, for as she looked down she could see the main entrance of the manor, with a terrace reaching out to the driveway which was covered by a roof running out from the main building. This way, people arriving could get out of their vehicle while under the arched roof. A valet might then come out of the small building at the other side of the archway, in order to park the vehicles. To the east, there was a wing of the main building, with the bottom looking like a large garage. To the west was another two-story wing. Earlier Maria had asked May if she lived here and she indicated that this southwest wing was the servant's quarters. All of the structure was built out of light gray stone and was adorned with carved, very decorative, stone work. Maria was trying to put the shape of this amazing structure into perspective. From her room, her window overlooked the center of the ornate garden that faced north, with a large wing on each side. So the manor was shaped like an H, with the main part being the joining crossbar.

The manor was completely surrounded by wooded area, with a paved lane also extending south into the trees and a garden pathway, leading north away from the house through the garden.

"How beautiful and sheltered," Maria uttered to herself, as she leaned on the window casement peering down into the yards.

"It's very grand isn't it Ms. Maria?" May exclaimed.

Maria jumped slightly, she'd been deep in thought, getting her bearings and she had forgotten that May stood behind her.

"If I get tired while trying to find my room, I can just sit down in one of these window casements," Maria said, with a chuckle.

"I think that's part of the idea Ms., this way you can sit in any of the windows and admire the scenery." They walked further down the hall till they came to a grand staircase and also an elevator in the center of the manor crossbar. Maria peered on passed the central staircase, wondering who else inhabited this floor.

May anticipated this question and said, "There are other suites on this floor but Miss Anna Belle occupies the only other one that is being used right now."

"Where does Mr. Warner live?" Maria asked feeling a bit nosey.

"There's one more floor above this one. Mr. Edward has a huge laboratory up there as well as his living suite. That's why he had the elevator put in a few years ago, to move things up and down from the lab. No one else is allowed in the lab, I hear that it has extraordinary security."

"I'd heard Dr. Adams refer to Mr. Warner as a scientist, but I'd no idea about his work," Maria said. May must also have no idea about his work or she'd have taken that bait and run with it, she thought silently.

They walked onto the elevator, Maria being glad that they could use it even though they were only on the second floor. "Where do the others live?" she asked.

"Mr. Gregory and Mallory have their suite in the north-west wing, and Mr. Brian has his in the north east wing. Mr. Brian has adapted the last several rooms on the ground level of the east wing into an area for horses; a kind of an animal hospital."

"Really!" Maria gasped.

"Well the rooms weren't being used... the rich can afford to be extravagantly eccentric," May almost whispered this last statement. She instantly wished that she could cram those last words back into her mouth. Maybe she had overstepped her bounds this time, she worried. Well if Maria is to stay here, she'll surely learn of the oddities here.

Maria sensed May's new found uneasiness, and not wanting her information well to dry up, she tactfully dropped the topic as they entered the grand hall from the elevator. The opulent staircase came down from the second floor, forming a spiral. And the huge crystal chandelier hung down through the center from the second floor ceiling. Smaller chandeliers encircled the expanse. It truly was an awe inspiring sight. Across the hall there stood a glass wall, facing north into the garden. The light gray stone of the walls, the glass wall and the chandeliers... everything was aglitter. Since the day outside was dull, and in answer to the lack of light being emitted through the glass wall, the chandeliers had been lit.

"What a beautiful entrance way," Maria said, coming to the center of the floor and looking up.

"It's called the grand hall," May explained.

"I can certainly see why," Maria said, while walking toward the garden entrance, "Do we have time for a walk in the garden, May, before teatime?"

Looking down at her watch May assured her that they did. May went to the closet and got her uniform coat and came back to assist Maria into her coat. They opened one of the large glass doors and went out onto the garden terrace.

The terrace was very large, with wrought iron tables and chairs as well as several swinging love seats with overhead coverings. The whole terrace was edged by stone, flower boxes, which were brimming over with riotously colored, late blooming annuals. The colors had been carefully arranged in ascending order from vivid violet through hardy bright pink, light violet pink and white; over and over again all the way around the raised stone sitting area.

In the center of the terrace a stone fairy danced merrily to a silent melody, while carrying a basket of real flowers with her arms softly extended, flowing with the dance. This beautiful fairy had been just about to step from one lily pad to another, lilting to the music, when she had been frozen in time. A large, stone hewn, water fountain yielded to her the pond which also sheltered four, stone frogs that seemed to gaze at her admiringly, while spouting their sparkling, water offerings of joy.

Maria was enchanted by this imagery. She walked closer and bent forward over the edge of the raised pond, reaching to touch one of those dainty expressive hands. The multicolored pansies in the fairy's flower basket, whispered of someone's great care as they bobbed delicately in the soft breeze, their little faces telling a story of love and patient tending.

Looking back down at the largest frog, Maria noticed that there was a brass plaque on the first lily pad facing the manor. Softly, she read it out loud:

Praise God for My Beloved Anna!
Humbly, God's Servant and
Your Adoring Husband,
Sinclair.

In smaller script, at the bottom there was a date and under the plaque in the concrete was the scrawled signature of the sculptor.

"There was truly great love here," Maria murmured, wiping tears from her chilled cheeks.

"It was meant to be joyful, Ms. Maria. The fairy was a tenth anniversary gift from Edward's father, Sinclair Warner to his wife Anna," May said, speaking softly, "It's filled with magic."

Maria pulled herself away from Anna's dancing fairy and the two women walked to the edge of the terrace and stepped down into the formal English rose garden. Here, precisely routed white stone walkways; lined with trimmed, rose hedges, as well as individual tea roses hovering over mounds of rich mulch, stretched out dividing the finely manicured lawns. While strategically placed, pedestal bird baths encircled by miniature rose bushes; as well as the occasional, decoratively carved, stone bench, made up the full composition of the garden courtyard.

Surprisingly, though it was late in the flowering season, some of the fragrant roses were still in bloom, undoubtedly because the garden was sheltered on three sides by the height of the manor and by the mature forest on the north side. A hint of rose scent wafted on the gentle breeze.

May had left the wheelchair on the terrace because of the stone walks. She would have to watch Maria carefully as they walked along enjoying the flowers and the season. Maria was enthralled by the scene and the scent of her colorful hosts. This must be a dream. She had longed to visit the beautiful garden that she had admired from her window, but she hadn't anticipated the full effect the garden would have on her as it engulfed her senses.

I know this place. I remember its sensual awakening in me. These thoughts echoed loudly in her brain and then deeper, deeper into her soul. Her mind and time itself seemed to slip a few gears. The garden seemed to grow darker. Warm light was now emanating from the many windows, especially from the grand hall. Soft melodic music reached for her ears, to remind her and tantalize her. She could see couples in formal dress, embracing knowingly, as they waltzed under the glowing chandelier.

Strong, new emotions began to flood over Maria's drifting existence; longing, emotional hunger, raw passion and sadness. Tears started to well up in her eyes. As her eyes misted over and her throat began to tighten, she fought to gain control once more. She succeeded. An ancient power from the past eased its grip on her and she began to stagger backwards holding her head, "What... where am I? Where did all of that come from?" Maria sputtered. She was once again back in the here and now.

Luckily, May was able to step behind her and steady her, but May had witnessed the sad expressions playing across Maria's face, and then the reflections of much more intense emotions. She feared that

Maria would pass out so she stepped closer to support her, which turned out to be just the appropriate move.

"Ms. Maria, there's a bench here beside us, please come and sit for a while." May put her arm around Maria's waist and helped her to the bench. Maria was still stunned by what had come over her so she let May sit her down.

May was already trying to comfort her, "You must've been thinking about what happened to you last week, your horrifying ordeal, my poor dear. All of this is too much, you need to rest."

Maria was relieved that May had jumped to this conclusion about what had just happened. She had no idea at this point as to what it was, other than the knowledge that what had just stormed through her mind had nothing to do with falling from a cliff and nearly succumbing to an icy, watery death.

'It', was very old and yet tragically familiar. The intensity of what she had just experienced, shocked her to the core of her being, and she knew that it was going to stay with her, haunting her until... Until what? Maria sat with her head in her hands and her elbows on her knees, eyes closed, searching the darkness of her consciousness for a clue as to what 'it' was that had come and gone again, so rapidly.

May stood and took her by the arm, "Let's get you back to the terrace and into the wheelchair, before you get a chill." She wasn't going to take any chance on Maria having another spell while out here in the garden, with no one else to help. Maria seemed not to have heard her so she made the suggestion again adding, "The Warner's will be gathering for teatime, soon." This time Maria nodded her head, as if in acknowledgment.

Maria murmured, just barely audibly, "It's gone."

As May had a hold of her arm and was offering to assist her to a standing position, Maria complied, absentmindedly. May succeeded in getting her into the wheelchair, but before she could take her inside, Maria spoke, clearly and strongly this time, "I'd like to sit here for a few minutes longer, overlooking the garden, alone please. You could come back for me in about five minutes."

May peered down at her charge with great concern.

"It's all right, May, I just want to enjoy the outdoors for a few minutes longer." May left her side and went into the grand hall, where she stood watching her new friend. She wasn't going to let Maria out of her sight.

The wheelchair was sitting near the fairy in her pond, so Maria maneuvered it until she sat facing Anna's fairy. In the waning, late afternoon light, Maria stared into the fairy's face, "Do you have any clues for me?" Maria whispered. She didn't know if she was asking this of God or Anna's spirit. It didn't much matter, she felt a magic that could've been from either. It was a positive, loving feeling this time which comforted her and eased her mental turmoil. Maria felt refreshed and strong, once again. She turned the chair and wheeled it back towards the door.

"Time to make my entrance and meet my destiny," she said aloud, in order to bolster her new found courage.

Chapter 12

$\mathcal{A}$t four o'clock the Warner family had started to assemble in the solarium for teatime. Dr. Adams was already comfortably seated there. Emma was busily setting out the tea service, as another helper brought trays from the kitchen. A beautiful, large bouquet of yellow roses crowned the center of the large round table. Emma's helper placed a large round platter of fresh fruit on the table just under this floral crown. The fruit had been cut in bite size pieces and arranged attractively. There were dishes of assorted cheeses and the accompanying crackers, as well as dainty cucumber, salmon and liverwurst sandwiches, a plate of petit fours and another of fancy sugar cookies.

Gregory and Mallory came across the grand hall, deeply enthralled in argumentative conversation. As they came into the room and noticed Dr. Adams they acknowledged him and made an attempt to engage him in polite banter. Anna Belle skipped into the room with two merry little dogs jumping and playing around her feet. She loved teatime.

Anna Belle's usual habit, after her driver returned her from school, was to run upstairs to check on her four legged friends, and then just having enough time to wash her hands and face she would run back downstairs for teatime. Emma quite often had her dinner plate ready for her at this time and she would have her evening meal early. This way, if she still had room in her stomach, she got to sample the teatime treats. Today her dinner plate was waiting for her at her usual place at the table.

Mallory sat down across from the doctor. "Dr. Adams, how is that poor lady that had the dreadful fall? I assume that's why you're here. Was anything broken?"

"Well, Mrs. Warner, Ms. Stark is doing just fine. Miraculously, she suffered no broken bones. As a matter of fact, I hear that she may be joining us for dinner this evening."

Gregory piped up, "My, so soon. She must be a very strong woman." He extended an empty cup to Mallory, for her to pour the tea. Mallory walked around the table to pour for Dr. Adams and Anna Belle. Gregory then went on to talk to the doctor about something that was totally inconsequential to Mallory. She was deep in thought about Maria, as she sat and sipped her tea. They were about the same age. Mallory had taken only a few glances at Maria, the day after the accident, when she had taken some clothes to Maria's room. Even in the woman's half conscious state, with disheveled hair laying about her oval face on the pillow, Maria had looked quite striking.

Mallory was of a split mind about this 'other woman'. What if she did end up staying here, for whatever reason? On one hand it would be divine to have another woman to talk to. It was so isolated here, even though she did go out quite often. On the other hand, Mallory enjoyed being the only resident beauty and she absolutely lived to impress the three men of the household. Having Maria around might shake up her indulgent little nest. Besides why would a woman like her be looking for a job here? Mallory deeply resented not being kept suitably informed about things like this. After all how could she be expected to plan things when she wasn't kept well informed? A look of total annoyance played across her pretty, but petulant face as she nibbled daintily on a sugar cookie. Mallory tended to be a bit plump and she became more than a little ill tempered if anything reminded her of the fact. She resented her own body type and lusted for that slim, trim look; if she had only known that men often thought of her body as being voluptuous.

Brian and Edward had come in while Mallory was musing over the possible new wrinkle in her smooth, pampered life. Brian was already deep in conversation with the doctor about some new drug that he was worried about the usage of, in his realm of the equestrian world. Edward was seated beside Anna Belle having a quiet discussion. Mallory strained to hear their conversation, but they were too far away. She did however hear the mention of Ms. Stark's name. Oh my, why would Edward be discussing Ms. Stark with Anna Belle? The first possible reason that Mallory could think of, stopped her thinking process, cold, "Oh, my God!"

Everyone stopped and turned to stare at Mallory. She hadn't realized that she had exclaimed her reaction out loud.

"I... I'm sorry everyone, I've just remembered something very important that I've forgotten to do," she explained. I hope that they've bought that feeble cover-up, she thought.

If anyone had realized that Maria might be out in the garden, and they had changed their line of vision just slightly, they might have seen her. Now she was on her way back into the manor, with May helping her through the door. She got out of the chair, once she had come in and was making sure that her legs were steady before making her entrance into the solarium.

"They're already in there Ms. Let me take your coat for you. I'll put it in the hall closet, over here," May said as she removed Maria's coat and took it and her own to put them away. Maria took this opportunity to run her fingers through her hair. She felt that her cheeks were cold, so she knew that they'd be rosy. She hoped that this didn't make her look flushed.

"I'll park the wheelchair just outside the solarium door Ms. and when you need me please just ring Emma's office."

"Thanks for your help May," Maria said and walked to the solarium doorway.

Edward just happened to be looking towards the door as Maria stepped into the entrance, "Ms. Stark!" he exclaimed, as he walked toward her with his hands extended, his eyes wide, taking in every aspect of her. Maria had made eye contact with Dr. Adams first, as he was the only one in the room that she knew. She now shifted her attention to the tall, extremely handsome man that was approaching her.

"Mr. Edward Warner, I presume," her eyes riveted to his.

"Precisely Madame, and at your service, I might add." Taking her hand in both of his, he led her into the room. "Ms. Stark this young lady is my Anna Belle. Anna Belle this is Ms. Stark."

"I'm proud to make your acquaintance, dear Anna Belle," Maria pronounced with genuine adoration. For this dainty, little girl, with soft, light-brown hair and large, brown eyes captivated Maria, immediately. She was so touched by this little dear, that in stead of taking her hand, she bent down and gave Anna Belle an affectionate hug.

Mallory, who had been shocked by Maria's well timed entrance, coupled with her snap assessment of this woman's vivid, classic beauty; watched these introductions in silence and following the same conclusion that she'd jumped to earlier, she thought, - my God, this can't be happening!

Edward broke the silence, "Ms. Stark, the rest of these faces you've seen briefly after your accident, so now please let me formally introduce you to them." He motioned to each of them as he spoke, "This lady is Mrs. Gregory Warner or Mallory. This is my brother Gregory beside her and this tall gent over here is my brother Brian. Everyone, this is Ms. Maria Stark, whom I've invited here for an interview for the position as Anna Belle's Recreational Instructor. As you all know, Ms. Stark had a horrendous accident last week as she was arriving to have that interview with me." Edward's eyes had locked with Maria's once again, before he moved beside her to put his arm around her shoulders and guide her to a chair.

A shiver ran down Maria's spine as she thought back to the last time that this man had put his arm around her. Edward sensed this and instantly understood why, however, the warmth in his eyes reassured her as she sat down.

Thankfully, it isn't what I had feared! Mallory was thinking, showing visible relief. He isn't introducing her to Anna Belle as her new mother to be. They had me going there, for a while. That's what I get for having such an over active imagination. Just the same, Mallory watched the eye contact between the two. I'm not imagining that connection. You can almost see the electricity between them.

Edward, taking control of the situation, served Maria the tea. Bill Adams was quite entertained, watching Mallory as she trying to assess the tone of this relationship. The other two men, Gregory and Brian were quite enchanted by Maria, and therefore seemed to be totally clueless as to the scene unfolding before them. Anna Belle was extremely excited and couldn't contain her questions. She had gotten up from her chair and had run to Maria's side, blurting out one question after another. Edward felt that he had to intercede, "Please Anna Belle, give Ms. Stark time and room to breathe. The lady and I'll spend some time discussing things after tea and maybe tomorrow we'll be able to answer some of your questions."

Wanting to reassure Anna Belle, Maria said, "Maybe we can have a visit of our own, tomorrow, Anna Belle." She winked at the little girl and that was enough to satisfy her.

"Ms. Stark," Mallory started, "in two weeks we'll be having our annual Halloween masquerade ball. I hope you'll have time to arrange for a costume. It's the party of the year and we're expecting around one hundred and fifty guests. It gives us all a chance to unleash our alter egos. Please plan to attend."

"If I'm here at that time Mrs. Warner, I'd be pleased to accept your invitation," Maria answered, as she contemplated the bottom of her teacup.

Edward couldn't stand this time being wasted in simple banter, pussy footing, skirting the issue of this Lady being part of their lives. "Ms. Stark," he got to his feet and came to the back of her chair, "would you mind if we adjourn to the library now?" No one could have taken this as a mere request.

"Certainly, Mr. Warner," Maria answered, as she got up. She took one turning step toward the door and her hip gave out. Luckily she was still close enough to a chair, to grab hold of it and keep from falling to the floor. Edward, standing close-by, was able to reach out and unceremoniously, picked her up. Dr. Adams came around the table and was at their side.

"I'm sorry gentlemen," Maria apologized genuinely, being very embarrassed. "I think that maybe I did over do my first bout of exercise. The tour of the garden must've been too much."

"I had no idea that you were out there," Edward stated, with great regret, "I'd have joined you if I'd known."

"Where is the wheelchair?" Dr. Adams asked.

"Just outside the door in the hall," Maria replied.

Brian retrieved the chair and Edward sat Maria into it. The doctor was quietly asking her about her symptoms. Maria assured him that it was simply weakness in her hip from the days exercise. She desperately didn't want this to keep her from having the interview with Edward.

"Are you sure that you feel up to this?" Edward inquired.

"Yes. I'm sure that you must have a comfortable chair in your library, however I'll rely on the wheelchair to get me there."

"Yes by all means, I shall make sure that you are comfortably taken care of," he answered as he turned to look at Bill Adams who was looking a bit left out.

"Bill, Emma will show you to a guest suite so you can rest and freshen up before dinner," Edward said, as he starting to push the wheelchair out of the room, and then he hesitated as he remembered his daughter, "Anna Belle, make sure that you've had enough to eat, and I'll be up around eight o'clock to tuck you in."

Edward was silent as he pushed the wheelchair through the hall and into the library. He knew that Maria couldn't possibly see his face so he used this opportunity to try and balance his concern for her well being with his need for this interview to go well. Like wise Maria used this time to her benefit. She had to marshal her complicated feelings and center her consciousness.

He wheeled her chair up to one of the plush leather arm chairs, "Ms. Stark, I'd suggest this chair for your comfort. There's a fur throw here if you're cool." He took Maria by her hands and lifted her gently forward and eased her down into the chair.

She admitted, "I feel very foolish Sir, at needing all of this assistance."

"Please don't feel that way dear lady. I'd do anything to assure your comfort. May I indulge myself and ask you for a great favor?"

"Yes, if you'll please call me Maria."

"Yes, you've read my thoughts. Of course that's the essence of my request, to have done with the encumbrance of formality, to have you call me Edward, please."

"For someone who has recently saved my life, I suppose that I could call you by your given name." Her eyes addressed his. "Thank you Edward - for everything."

Edward had seated himself in the other large, leather chair after moving it closer to hers and at a ninety degree angle so that they were almost touching knees at one side. He could reach out and touch the arm of her chair, if he wished. "No thanks are necessary, Maria. It has been my very great pleasure to be of assistance to you. If you don't mind though, I've several important questions to ask you. Please humor me by answering them, only if you feel that they're not too intrusive. Then I'll explain myself."

"Yes, for you, I'll try," Maria answered, turned toward him more and pulled the fur across her lap.

"Since the accident, have you changed your mind about working here?"

That was painless, she thought, "No, I haven't changed my mind."

"Are you married or is there a special man in you life?"

Ouch that was closer, but tolerable, "No, I've been divorced for eight months now and I have no other attachments other than my daughter who is away at college. Oh, I do have a horse that is at a friend's boarding stable and I'm very close to him... the horse that is," she answered, smiling shyly.

"Maria, I'm very sorry, I had to ask these questions just to know where we stand." Edward seemed to have relaxed significantly.

"That's being very practical, I appreciate that."

"I must explain something about myself, so that you understand where I'm coming from," he said, and continued, "I'm a very up-front person, I don't believe in subterfuge or artifice of speech. Some people find me too blunt and straight to the point. If there's one thing that I can't stand, it's unnecessary communication gaps. I feel that proper communication skills could solve many of the world's greatest problems."

"Ah ha," Maria murmured, nodded appreciatively.

"I must also tell you that I've been married once, to Anna Belle's mother, and it ended very badly, even before Anna Belle was born. The relationship was doomed right from the start because she liked to play sly and manipulative games; mental and emotional games, along with the fact that she had some other twists to her character." Now to quickly get off of that topic he swiftly changed gears. "What are your feelings about good communication practices?" Edward asked, getting up from his chair and walked towards the bar.

This gave Maria time to weigh her response, "I don't believe in blurting everything out right away, for in some circumstances I feel that we may need to protect ourselves a bit more than that, but I do believe in being truthful and straight forward."

"Would you like a drink Maria, perhaps a brandy?

"No thank you, I don't drink or smoke. My personal motto is that I don't put anything into my body that doesn't do the body some good," she elaborated.

"Admirable," Edward said as he poured himself a glass, "Some people would say that a moderate drink now and again might do some good when dealing with pain."

"More often then not, those people would be referring to emotional or psychological pain and for those cases, stalling off or numbing that pain usually only makes the pain worse to bear later on," Maria reflected, with a new softness of understanding in her eyes.

"Touché Madame! I find your wit, your depth and your candor greatly refreshing." Edward smiled as he sat down beside her once more.

"I find this to be a very positive and progressive discussion for an employer and possible employee to be engaged in," Maria said, managing to stiffen her expression a bit.

Edward's brows shot upwards, "Well, I guess that takes us off one track and back to a practical and safe one. Thank you, Ms. Stark." He had over accentuated the word "safe" and her surname. "Let's get back to our employment interview then." Edward got to his feet once again and began strolling around the room.

Maria watched his every move, admiring his long legs and slender, masculine torso.

"As I see it Maria, this job description can remain quite loosely defined. Anna Belle goes out to school now, but that's only because there has been no structured activities for her here at home. I suppose she may be benefiting from the social interactions of the public school system, however, I'd much sooner have a tutor come in for her schooling and a female companion working with her recreationally. Anna Belle has done extremely well at her studies, but she has had no physical development time and little active encouragement from any of us to develop her own interests and talents. Maria, can you see what we need? What could you do for Anna Belle?"

"Yes I can," she replied, her mind was going into overdrive now. She took a deep breath to compose her thoughts, and then began, "This is a wonderful opportunity for a woman of my background and what an exciting situation for Anna Belle." She could tell that this little girl was a very dear soul. "First, for exercise I would suggest dancercise. This will develop her natural grace and fitness as well as possibly spiking an interest in music. Also, I believe swimming would develop her muscle structure without too much stress. Then riding lessons of course, stressing horsemanship to develop the discipline of care for the animal as well as the responsibility for the animal. Then, if she is competitive at all, showing her horse would afford her the sportsmanship interaction with fellow competitors, but only if she wished to be competitive. For eye / hand co-ordination we could pursue archery, darts, and maybe eventually golf." She glanced up and noticed that Edward was leaning against his desk, eye brows raised high over a wide grin, so slowing down a bit she finished, "I could go on and on." She blushed slightly and lowered her gaze, realizing that she had gotten carried away. She swallowed, resumed eye contact, and took a stab at summing up her answer, "Mr. Warner, excuse me - Edward, I have a sound background in individual sports, exercise, dance, and of course horsemanship. I've had extensive courses in sports safety and first aid. Also, most importantly, I have raised a daughter. I feel that I'm well equipped for your needs and it would be a wonderfully fulfilling challenge for me."

"Yes Maria, I fully agree with you," Edward said, still grinning.

In her fervor over this subject, Maria just then realized how what she had said in her summation could have been taken. She blushed deeply and averted her eyes.

"Pardon me Maria, I'm just totally enthralled with your insight, your span of knowledge, experience and abilities, but above all, your enthusiasm. I believe that you'll be an invaluable roll model for my daughter." Edward left his half-finished drink on the desk and came back to sit beside her. He wished that he could reach out and take her hand, but he fought to restrain himself.

"What would our time schedule be like?" she asked, as she watched his long elegant fingers rhythmically stroking the leather of his chair arm.

"I'd think that Anna Belle should be able to take her classes in the morning and be with you from one o'clock to four or six depending on your day. This also depends on how well she does with her tutor, and, of course, wouldn't start until you are suitably recuperated."

"For the short time that I'll need to recuperate, we...uhh, Anna Belle and I, can spend some time getting to know one another. I'm quite excited about this. Thank you Edward for giving me this opportunity."

"Would you have any objection to my getting to know you better, as well?" He rushed on as if he was worried about her answer, "I'll try not to bore you or monopolize your time too much," while making this last plea, he looked down to watch her hands as they rested on the fur in front of her.

"I see no problem with that, Edward," she replied, giving him a discreet smile.

She has said it, the all-important answer that I've been waiting for. There is a God! These thoughts echoed in his mind. He loved to hear her say his name. He looked forward to each time that she might have occasion to do so. He felt like a teenager.

"As a matter of fact, you could help me solve a problem that I'm having with Mallory right now," he said, with a glance toward the door.

"Yes of course Edward, what could that be?" she responded, looking very concerned.

"Mallory is fixated on our Halloween ball. I guess I shouldn't be so flip with her about it. She does do all of the planning and helps Emma with the arrangements. The problem is that she's hounding me as usual about my not having a date for the ball. Would you do me the honor of accompanying me to the ball?" he asked, with a very serious look.

Maria was shocked at first, and considered this for a few seconds. "Do you think that wise, seeing that I'll be your employee?"

"The employer / employee situation will not be a concern between us, and as far as anyone else's thoughts on the matter, that'll definitely not be our concern."

This frankness of his is going to take some getting used to, but I do really like it, she thought before she stated, "I have no ideas for a costume."

"Please, let me take care of that, if you'll only consent to accompany me. I have a particular character idea in mind for you. I'd like to keep this to myself, if you'll just trust me until it's time for a fitting." He had a distinctively mischievous twinkle in his eyes.

Maria sat forward in her chair, "You have everything in hand, don't you?" she queried, feigning a stern look which softened slowly to a warm smile as she continued, "I guess the only thing left for me to do is accept. Thank you once again Edward."

He smiled broadly, "Well, now that we've covered all of the important questions that I can possibly expect you to answer, during our first conversation, would you like to retire to your room to rest and prepare for dinner? We can chat on the way as I accompany you to your door."

"That would be nice. This has been a very big day for me," she replied as she eased herself up, relying heavily on her arms. Edward wanted to help her but he refrained and simply moved the wheelchair closer for her.

"I'd like to try walking for a while," she said hesitantly, so Edward offered her his arm and they walked together behind the wheelchair.

"Speaking of your room," he started, "there's another room adjoining the one that you're using. I knew that until now you wouldn't have any use for it, so we hesitated in opening it up for you.

We'll be doing that soon, so after you've had the use of the full suite, you can tell me if it will be satisfactory."

"Oh Edward, you have no idea. I'm not used to being spoiled so. The room I'm using now is absolutely perfect. I love the view. I think of it as the Gold Room."

"Regarding your wardrobe, please make a list of your needs, for sports or dress or anything else that you can think of, and give it to Emma. She'll take care of everything for you."

Now this was too much. "I do have clothes!" she blurted out, surprising him with her quick retort and its hint of sharpness.

"Yes I'm sure that you do, my dear. I didn't mean to imply that you didn't. I simply would like to give you everything that you could possibly need, and in a week or so when you are feeling better, we'll arrange to have your belongings picked up. Your horse however is another matter. At dinner we'll speak to Brian about picking him up right away."

He had won her over once more. "That would be very nice, and then I'll be able to use him for Anna Belle's riding lessons," she said, smiling up at him. They had been walking arm in arm and she had needed to use his arm for support, the last few steps. They were near her door now, so he didn't insist that she sit down.

"I'm sure that you'll be happier to have your horse here where you can see him at anytime.

"Yes, that'll be perfect," she said, very happily.

He peered down into her face and he could see that she looked very tired.

"Here's your room, and just in time for you to have a rest. We hope to see you for dinner in the main dining room at seven o'clock. May will accompany you to the dining room, but if you don't feel up to it, just tell her and she'll let me know."

Chapter 13

On entering her room, Maria was surprised to find May already waiting there.

"How long do I have before dinner, May?" she asked, as she just barely made her way to the bed and collapsed on it.

"Two hours Ms.," May answered, having risen from the comfortable, easy chair by the bed. She had felt guilty, just sitting around, but the room was entirely clean and tidy and Emma had told her to wait there for Ms. Maria in case she should need any assistance. May was finding that she liked just having one person to attend to, instead of the many household duties that she'd been used to, especially when that person was as kind and easygoing as Ms. Maria.

"I think I'd better stay here, on the bed, for at least an hour," Maria murmured.

"I hate to intrude on you further Ms., but I need you to try on whatever clothes you'd like to wear this evening, in case I need to alter anything," May stated sheepishly.

"Yes, I think that I can manage that. Please bring out the lacy, lilac blouse and the long, black velvet skirt."

May pulled the clothes out of the closet, "Ms., there's a crocheted darker lilac shoulder rap here, would you like it also?"

"Yes, let's try it and what is there in the way of black, dress shoes?" With Edward's mind for details she was sure that he wouldn't have forgotten black dress shoes. Maria was sitting on the side of the bed preparing to try the clothes on. May laid the clothes by her on the bed and went back to look for the shoes. Maria put the blouse on and was buttoning it up. May brought the shoes out and set them on the floor in front of her charge.

Maria looked down to see that the shoes were shinning, black, patent leather with rhinestone hearts adorning their uppers. Her attention was drawn to the shine of the patent leather and the twinkle of the rhinestones. She felt dizziness slowly enveloping her and her vision began to blur. She was slipping again into another time. She was in a trance. These shoes were on someone's feet as they where dancing. The music was a lively, very old tune and she could also hear laughter through labored breath. She couldn't see who was wearing the shoes. The dance had begun slowly at first, but then, the shoes started to spin faster and faster. Maria tried to look away but she couldn't at first, then with great determination she managed to pull her eyes away from the shoes, breaking the spell. Dizziness overwhelmed her and she fell sideways on the bed. May having gone back to the closet to get the rap, had turned just in time to see Maria fall onto the bed. She rushed to Maria's side. "Ms. Maria, are you alright?" she asked.

With Mays help, Maria pushed herself further onto the bed to lie more comfortably. She definitely didn't want to stand up or even sit up again until she had rested. Seeing the look of extreme concern on May's face, she answered, "It's alright May, it was just another dizzy spell. Dr. Adams said that I still may be bothered by them." She had no intention of letting May know just how shaken she really was. "Don't worry about the clothes. I'm sure that they'll be fine. Just leave them over the chair. I need to sleep now."

"Yes Ms.," May said, as she helped Maria to undress and covered her up, "I'll be back to wake you in enough time to get ready for dinner." May immediately left to find Mr. Edward and the doctor.

She was very worried and quite sure that they both needed to know about the two strange spells that Maria had suffered today.

Maria felt numb. She had put all thoughts about the strange revelations that had taken place in the garden this afternoon and just now, out of her mind until she could be alone.

She had learned years ago that mental compartmentalizing is often the only way to stay sane and hope to solve your problems, when things start to build up. This meant taking each problem and mentally closing it into its own little box and temporarily storing it in the back of your mind, so that you can take it out later when you have the time and the strength to deal with it. She didn't know if she had enough strength right now, to deal with this big box full. Never in her life had she had such spells. Twice today something had taken her over. Each time it seemed to be brought on by different senses. In the garden it had somehow been the familiar scent of the roses and possibly a familiarity of the garden itself, while here in this room, it had been the sight of the shoes. Each time, she had seemed to be transported to another time where she was bombarded by bits of intense memories and emotions. It was like living some tragedy over and over again. Thank the Lord; she had been able to fight and eventually regain control, once again bringing herself back to this lifetime. The array of emotions had been staggering and had left her feeling drained. She knew that there was no way that this was due to her concussion. She just knew it, but why should the rose garden be so familiar? She certainly had never had the pleasure of frequenting the like.

Thankfully, meeting Edward had brightened her outlook greatly. This was going to be a great job and living here was only icing on the cake. Edward... Edward..... She was asleep.

Maria awakened much later to a scraping noise beyond the wall of her room. She lifted her head and listened apprehensively, but heard nothing more. Maybe I imagined it, she thought. Stranger things had happened today. She lay there visually surveying the room. I'm going to stay here. This is going to be my home. She pondered dreamily as tears welled up in her eyes. She hadn't realized how much of a worry, her future had been to her. Everything here was new and a bit intimidating, but at least here, she was needed.

There was a soft tap on the door and May entered, "Ms. Maria it's a bit later then you wanted to be awakened. Please don't be angry? Mr. Edward wants you to see the room next door before dinner," she said moving to Maria's bedside.

"Oh! Well, I guess I'd better get some clothes on then. Can you help me, please? I don't want to move too quickly. I really needed that rest," she said, sitting up slowly and swinging her legs over the side of her bed.

"Yes Ms., I'll be glad to help you." May went quickly to work and in fifteen minutes Maria was ready to face the world again. She couldn't believe her reflection in the large mirror. The effect of her paleness, as well as the color and the style of the clothing made an incredible difference from the image that she was used to. She'd never have thought of using these romantic and beautiful colors and of course she wouldn't have been able to afford such fine clothes.

"What a changed person. I'd never have thought of dressing in such colors. It took a man to show me the error of my ways." She had forgotten as she stared into the mirror that May was there and that she could hear her.

"It took Edward and his kindness," she said, to make her previous statement sound better. May snapped her out of this train of thought by bringing her the hairbrush and her lipstick. When she was ready to leave, May walked to the long side wall of the room and folded up the gold embellished dressing screen. Maria had thought that the elaborate screen had been placed there merely as a decorative accent to visually break up the expanse of the long wall. To her great surprise there was a door behind it. That's where the sound that had awakened her had come from. This door must be to the other part of the suite.

May opened the door and rays of candlelight shone from within. Maria moved to look into the room and stood in the doorway in total amazement, her mouth ever so slightly agape. It was a huge, huge room, meant to be a sitting room, guest parlor and private dining room all in one. The central area of the room was large enough to be a small dance floor. The side of the room overlooking the garden was almost all glass, although it was quite dark outside now so heavy, golden velvet curtains offered protection from the great outdoors. The walls were creamy white with tiny, golden lines that made the walls look like they were cushioned. The various pieces of upholstered furniture were done in ambers, rich browns and shades of cream. The elaborate dining suite was made of a light amber wood, polished highly. There was a fire burning merrily in the fireplace on the far wall. The warm luminous flutter of candlelight bathed the room.

Dr. Adams and Edward were sitting in luxurious leather armchairs, near the fire. They had obviously been waiting for her entrance, and as she stepped into the room, both gentlemen rose to their feet and bowed. "Good evening, Madame," Dr. Adams chimed.

"We thought it might be a good idea to bring dinner to you, dear lady," Edward announced.

Maria gave May a quick scolding look, meant to convey 'You told them!' and just as quickly forgiving her, she gave May a little smile. Maria pulled herself up into her best posture and with her most graceful movement, walked across the room to where the men stood.

The table was set for three. Edward stepped forward and taking her hand guided her to the table and sat her down. May went to the hall door and opened it. Two other servants pushed and pulled three serving carts into the room. These were placed strategically around the table, from where they went about serving the meal.

"The doctor and I thought this might be more relaxing for you then dining with all of the family," Edward explained further.

"You look divine, Maria," Bill Adams added.

"Thank you, Sirs. I'm quite taken by your consideration and I do appreciate it."

The meal was quite elaborate; freshly baked bread, tomato aspic, several varieties of salads, roasted potatoes, Brussels sprouts and carrots, thinly sliced roast beef with gravy and Yorkshire pudding, as well as guinea hens in a light, orange sauce. The repast was hot and delicious. Maria tried a tiny serving from each dish, savoring each individual flavor. She especially enjoyed the guinea fowl. The men obviously were both good eaters, they heartily enjoyed themselves.

"Isn't this a glorious room, Maria?" Bill asked, as he peered around the room. "We worked hard rushing around to get it ready for your dinner."

"I must thank you both then and your helpers as well. It's quite amazing. I'm truly overwhelmed by its grandeur and I can't yet imagine that I'm going to be living here."

The doctor shot Edward a look of surprise, "Then it's settled, Maria is going to be working with Anna Belle and living here."

"Yes Bill, we discussed the situation this afternoon and Maria is in favor," Edward assured him.

"Well congratulations Maria, but most of all I'm so very happy for dear little Anna Belle," Bill replied.

They left the shambles of the dinner that they had so heartily devoured and they adjourned to the comfortable sofas near the windows. The staff immediately cleared the remnants away. Following them to their sitting area, May set the long, low, coffee table with the tea service and a dessert tray of puff pastries, lemon, poppy seed cake and a dish of fruit. She then stood back and looked to Maria. The men were talking about the building of the fire when Maria noticed May waiting. "That's fine May, thank you. I'll serve the tea." May bobbed a quick curtsey and left.

Maria was pouring the tea as Bill said to Edward, "Anna Belle will be counting on us, Edward to make sure that Maria has a full, speedy recovery." He then turned to Maria, "That's not to say that you should be rushed my dear. Please let me know of any changes in the way you feel or just anything at all."

"Yes, doctor, at this point I feel that I just need some rest. I assume that May has told you both about the dizzy spells that I've had today. Well, that's all that they were and after I'm fully rested I'm sure that I'll be fine."

"Maria will be well attended to. There's a servants quarters next to this suite. May has been assigned to Maria and she'll move into the adjacent room, tomorrow," Edward assured them both.

"That isn't necessary Edward," Maria asserted.

"I thought you might say that Maria, however the arrangements have already been made. The main pull cord in your room and the one in here will still sound in Emma's office and a small buzzer will be installed by your bed that will summon May from her new room which will be next to yours."

"You're being very thoughtful as usual Edward," Bill complimented, "and it's an excellent idea."

Maria asked if anyone would like more tea as she poured some for herself. The men both had some and helped themselves to the desserts. Maria enjoyed the steaming cup. She sat back with the cup between both hands and thought of how nice it would be to melt right into it, as she gazed absentmindedly into the hot amber liquid.

"We'd better not keep Maria up to long Edward," Bill chided.

"Oh it's so early gentlemen. Please relax and visit with me for a while," she begged.

Edward smiled, thinking, she's starting to think of this as her home. The very idea warms me.

"We'll talk to Brian tomorrow about picking up your horse for you," Edward said to Maria.

"Oh you have a horse? Please tell us about your horse related interests?" Bill asked.

"I'm quite attached to the one horse that I have left." Maria's face lit up now that she had an opportunity to talk about horses, "His name is Shavano. He's a very well mannered, leopard, Appaloosa gelding. I've trained him English as well as Western."

"I had no idea that you were a horse trainer," Bill replied, with great surprise.

"Yes, I've had quite a successful career as a trainer, as well as an exhibitor and instructor," Maria explained.

"Brian will be ecstatic when he hears this, won't he Edward?" Bill went on and on....

Edward didn't need any of this new information about Maria to make him just mad about her. He already was, totally. He let the dear doctor go on conversing with Maria, making all of the polite inquires. He wanted to just sit back watching her, and learning more and more about her. Her skin seemed to glow softly in the candlelight. He wouldn't worry about Brian being a rival for her affections. He had enough trouble worrying about the dear doctor. She is enchanting; he could sit here mesmerized by her, forever.

After about an hour of chatting Maria yawned and stretched. Even though Bill was having a marvelous time, he took the hint and thinking of her health, he turned the conversation to the regrettable subject of leaving. He gave Edward a suggestive look, but Edward didn't choose to take his meaning.

"Maria, I'll plan on coming back in three days to check on you, but please call me if you notice any changes at all." At this point the doctor stood up and walked to the door. He had hoped that Edward would do the same, but it appeared that leaving right away was not his plan. Maria thanked the doctor for his concern and said goodbye. He called back to Edward, "I'm looking forward to the Halloween Masquerade, it should be a ball," he chuckled, "and make sure she gets her rest Edward. Goodbye." Then he left.

Damn that Edward, Bill was thinking as he walked down the hall. Well it is his home. He can leave and go up his elevator whenever he feels like it. He doesn't have to drive home. He sure was quiet this evening. I noticed him just sitting there watching her. I could never be that cool.

I'll bet he was just quietly waiting and wishing for me to leave. Then, to his mild disgust Bill realized that he had served as the chaperone this evening. Imagine! Me - their chaperone! Well, at least Edward has tact, but he has her all to himself now.

Chapter 14

Maria stood up and stretched again. She walked to the window and drew back one of the heavy curtains. She imagined what the garden would look like in the daylight. In the dark, aided by the moonlight she could just make out the outline of the east and west wings, which were still mostly in darkness. Edward had gotten up shortly after the doctor had left and went around the room blowing out the candles that had burned down low. The fire had died down to glowing coals. Two table lamps had been turned down low for the evening and four larger candles remained. Now the glorious room was bathed only by soft dreamy light.

Edward came and stood behind her without saying a thing. He was also staring off into the darkness. She hesitated for several long moments. "It's such a wonderful place," she whispered, subconsciously willing him closer, "It's so spacious and grand."

"I've lived here for most of my life. I guess that I probably take it for granted," he confessed.

"I have a keen interest in architecture and its history. You'll have to tell me all about Sinabar, sometime."

"Tomorrow, if the weather is nice I'll take you on a tour of the estate and start to give you the history of it," he said happily.

"A start to the history...?" she questioned.

"Yes, it'll be only a start," he said, speaking softly.

She could feel her energy field reaching back for his, trying to pull him closer. He was resisting.

Now that her eyes had grown accustomed to the filtered moonlight which was the only illumination of the garden below, she could make out the white, stone pathways and the bench where she'd been forced to rest this afternoon. She hadn't wished to tell Dr. Adams or Edward about the two spells that had taken her so very far away in time, while she had been in the garden and then later again in her room. She didn't want the doctor to know how she felt about it. She didn't really understand how she felt. As she suspected May had told them something about it, or at least Edward. That was probably why he had gone so far out of his way to present her with this dinner surprise. As she came out of her thoughts and gazed back into the moonlit garden again, those feelings that she had experienced - the sadness, the longing, the passion, started to invade her emotions again. This was a happy time, an exciting time, so why should she feel this way?

"Edward, my emotions have been running amuck today. I've been fighting a loosing battle with an overwhelming sadness, for which I have no earthly reason to feel. You've saved me once before, could you please help me again?"

"Yes!" he answered as he stepped up closer behind her.

She stood perfectly still gazing into the garden as if locked there. "Could you put your arms around me once again and hold me through this battle?" she whispered, not turning to look up into his face.

His arms came around her and encircled her gently, and supportively. He didn't want to hold her too closely, lest he give away the extent of his physical ardor. They stood this way for some seconds allowing their bodies time to relax together, letting their energies mingle, feeling the tingle of it. Maria sighed deeply, succumbing to this new feeling, as well as the memory of the deep longing that she had felt this afternoon in the garden.

Edward lowered his head and brushed the hair on the top of her head with his lips. "I'll be here always... always for you!" he said, softly but with great emphasis.

They both heard these words echo. It seemed like these words echoed out of the past and at the same time, into the future. Now Maria felt assured that she could confide in him. She didn't know why, but she knew that she could. Later she would talk to him about her spells, but for now she wanted to just bask in his warmth and lean on his strength. He held her close until he felt her legs start to weaken, then he reached down and picking her up. While holding her close to his chest, he buried his face in her hair and kissed her head softly. "You need to rest. Don't worry I'll sit with you and I'll not leave you for long," he said as he carried her into her bedroom, laid her on the bed, took her shoes off and pulled a cover over her.

"Shall I call May for you," he whispered?

"No, I can manage," she answered sadly, thinking that he was leaving her alone.

"Don't be sad, I'll be back in only a few minutes," he said, just before he softly closed the door

She felt dizziness start to well up over her. What is going on here, she thought. I just need rest, just rest and Edward. She struggled to pull her clothes off. May had left her nightgown on the bed. She slid into it and crawled back under the covers, not caring that her clothes had fallen to the floor.

Edward came back to her, about twenty minutes later. He pulled the easy chair up beside the head of her bed, took her hand in his and sat down. Her hand was cool and shaking slightly. Her eyes were glazed. "What is it Maria?" he whispered.

"Did May tell you anything of what happened today in the garden?"

"She told me that for a time you appeared to be in a daze, that your face looked sad, you uttered something to yourself and then you almost passed out." Edward was amazed that she was still awake and he was greatly relieved that she might wish to confide in him.

"Something happened to me." Maria shook with the remembrance of it as she spoke. "It was like I was looking into another time. I saw people dancing in a grand hall, and they were dressed in old-fashioned clothes. I had strange intense feelings; feelings of longing, sadness and passion. I was overwhelmed and that is when I faltered." Her face looked strained and even paler then before. "Just before it all started I had been enjoying the scent of the roses and the earthy smells of the garden. I remember looking up at the terrace and the windows of the grand hall, when everything started to seem very familiar. Then it seemed to get much darker outside. It was just as if I'd slipped into another time, the music started and a warm light shone from the windows. I saw the dancers, and the feelings started..."

"My poor dear," he said, as he pushed wisps of hair out of her face and caressed her brow, "Has anything like this ever happened to you before?"

"No, never, and I don't feel that this is something to be feared but it is very strange. I didn't want to mention it in front of Dr. Adams, but for some unknown reason I feel secure in telling you about it. This evening when I saw those black shoes for the first time, a similar thing happened. I knew that I had seen the like of them somewhere before. Then I saw them being worn by someone dancing to very old music. I couldn't see the dancers but I could see the shoes going around and around. Then I got dizzy and when the vision and music stopped, I lost my balance and fell sideways onto the bed. Once again, it was as if the sense of familiarity of the shoes triggered the whole thing. The shine of the leather and the glitter of the rhinestones drew my attention inward and then time seemed to slip away again. This was after you left me this afternoon, before I took a nap. This evening when I entered that beautiful room, I just blocked everything out and let the enjoyment and conversation keep my mind off of all of this, but when we were alone and I looked out over the moonlit garden, those intense feelings came flooding back."

"Rest now, Maria, just rest. Deciding to tell me must've been very hard and it's very important that you did," he said, as he caressed her brow once more. "Now that you have confided in me, we can go through this together. This is indeed very strange, but if we don't fear the strange, it won't be able to defeat us. We must learn from it and then grow from it."

She had closed her eyes. He got up, and, leaning down he placed a delicate kiss on her forehead. She squeezed his hand in return as he sat back down.

"You've had a most taxing day, haven't you? I'm going to stay with you, so just try to sleep now. You've told me. Now you can rest and leave your problems with me."

She turned slightly, not letting go of his hand, and pulled the blanket closer around her head. Edward spoke softly now, "Think only happy thoughts. Think about Anna Belle and all of the things that you two are going to be able to do together." He knew that she would go off to sleep now. He hoped that it would be an untroubled sleep.

Behind her closed eyelids, she was hearing his words and thinking that she need only think of his face and his soft kiss on her forehead to make her feel as if she was in heaven. The darkness was coming to cover over her again, but this time the dizziness didn't lurk within its depths. His strong elegant hands had lifted her burdens away. This was a positive healing darkness now, and she slept...

Being a scientist, Edward wasn't blown away by Maria's revelations. He well knew that fear is the route to defeat. One must not let fear creep in. The way to overcome is to learn the facts. If you can't understand them at first, turn them around, looking at the problems from all sides, then study your insights and turn the situation into a positive learning process.

This was indeed a very delicate situation. Edward had heard of Extra Sensory Perception and thought that Maria's phenomena might have something to do with that, so he would start with the study of E.S.P. as well as other paranormal material as soon as it was safe to leave Maria's side. Not tonight, he thought, tonight I must comfort her and protect her from any fear.

Most of Edward's worry was well founded, however, as of yet he had no idea of just how strong Maria's willpower really was. So far, she seemed quite genteel and pleasantly reserved. Their encounters to this point had given little obvious hint as to the shining metal that Maria Stark's will was composed of.

So much had happened today and in this last week. All that had taken place in this short time had changed Edward's life dramatically, and now it would also affect all of the people around him. I must review the factors scientifically, he thought to himself.

a) Albert Green had run the newspaper ad. - Female Recreational Instructress.
b) The appointment was made with Ms. Stark.
c) Maria's accident.
d) The saving of her life.
e) Maria's strong effect on me.
f) Maria's first hallucination (?) in the garden.
g) Teatime, when I found that I am enchanted by Maria.
h) The employment interview - finding out that she'll be perfect for what we need.
i) Maria's second spell.
j) Dinner, I couldn't keep my eyes off of her. It hit me, that I'm jealous of Dr. Adams.
k) Maria asked for my help and comfort. She Confided In Me.
l) She fell asleep holding my hand. I Love Her!
m) Edward Warner loves Maria Stark.
n) I must help her.
   Conclusion - I am madly and hopelessly in love with Maria.
   Edward fell asleep slumped over in the chair holding on to Maria's hand.

May had been waiting for Maria to ring for her and she hadn't, so she decided that it was her job to check on her new mistress and make sure that everything was all right. As she walked towards Maria's room she met one of the guard dogs wandering the hall near her mistress's room.

"What are you doing here big fellow? Your master must have forgotten you," she said, as she patted his head. She slowly opened Maria's bedroom door a crack and first being surprised to find the light still on, she then realized why the dog was in the hall. There sat Mr. Edward fully dressed, asleep in the armchair, holding onto Maria's hand, as she also slept covered up in her bed.

I think this is a good sign, May thought to herself, smiling as she closed the door quietly. She then went into the main room of the suite, through the hall door. After checking to see that the candles had been snuffed and that the fire had burned down properly, she tidied the room, put the lights out, and started back to the servant's quarters.

She was very excited about her job promotion and her big move into the main house. For a general servant to be promoted to a ladies private maid was quite a step up. She admired Maria very much and appreciated her polite, unassuming ways. Mr. Edward had told May about her new assignment just this evening while they had worked to prepare Maria's lavish dining / sitting room. She had been extremely happy to hear about his decision. Tomorrow her belongings would be moved into the maid's quarters next to Maria's room and she wouldn't have to walk these long halls to attend to her new mistress.

Chapter 15

$\mathcal{M}$aria awakened around seven thirty a.m. She was facing Edward so he was the first thing that she saw. He was still asleep and was still holding her hand. She took full advantage of this time to examine his sleeping countenance. He had well defined, strongly, chiseled features. His sandy brown hair had a clean, soft sheen. He was well groomed right down to the points of his fair mustache. Sleeping as he was, there seemed a boyish charm about him. He is very handsome, she thought as her scrutiny shifted to his hands. They were medium sized, with long, elegant fingers. As she continued studying him, he woke.

"Good morning, Milady." He squeezed her fingers gently before letting them go.

"Good morning, my friend. Thank you for staying with me," she said, smiling sweetly.

"I told you that I'd always be here for you," he reminded her.

"Thank you Edward," she said, as she felt tears coming to her eyes, so she looked toward the window, "It looks like a fine sunny day."

"So it is, fair Maria," he concurred, brightly while getting up and going to the window. "I'd like to go to my rooms and shower and change, if you don't mind. On my way I'll order breakfast and have it brought to your dining room, where I'll join you if you don't mind, and we can plan our day. Does that sound alright to you?"

"That sounds like a wonderful start to the day," she agreed.

Edward swept over to where she lay, took her hand and kissed it ceremoniously, then bowed saying, "I'll take my leave, Milady." And he was gone.

Maria got up, put her dressing gown on and went into the next room. She wanted to survey her domain, to see the room in the daylight. She opened all of the drapes and let the morning light pour in. Yes, the room was huge and very lavishly decorated. She walked to where Edward had sat watching her last night. She ran a hand over the back of the couch where he had sat. She had noticed his constant almost wordless attention and had sensed that he had been waiting for Dr. Adams to leave. She walked to the window where they had stood and she had asked him to help her once again. His words echoed clearly in her mind, 'I'll be here always, always for you!'

As long as she remembered his very expressive words, she'd be able to draw strength from them.

After she had showered and dressed, breakfast arrived. A few minutes later there was a knock at the door. She opened it and there was Edward, dressed in casual walking clothes and carrying a large, colorful arrangement of fall flowers, "Good morning again Milady, might I have breakfast with you?"

"By all means Sir, it awaits us," she answered, leading him to the food laden table.

They devoured the meal, both having excellent appetites. Edward suggested that they take a picnic lunch with them and go on a leisurely tour of the estate while the weather was so nice. They should be back by teatime, that way Anna Belle would have time to visit with Maria. Over breakfast they discussed the schooling situation for Anna Belle. It would take a bit of time for Edward to find a suitable tutor for his daughter, so therefore she would be best off staying in school until one could be found. Edward didn't mention to Maria that this would also allow her plenty of time to recuperate, settle in and hopefully deal with this seemingly paranormal phenomena.

As they set out for their tour they took the wheelchair with them, just in case. Outside Maria's room they passed May in the hall. She had asked for permission to oversee the moving of her belongings from the servant's wing to her new room beside Maria's bedchamber. When they emerged from the main entrance of the manor, there was an Explorer - land rover type vehicle waiting for them. Edward informed his driver that he would enjoy driving today, so before stepping aside the driver put the wheelchair in the back of the vehicle for them.

Stepping out away from the building, she asked, "Do you mind if we just step back away from the manor a bit first? I'd like to see the building from the outside."

"By all means, I'd forgotten that you arrived here under a less than fully conscious state," Edward explained, as he led her to a better vantage point. "My ancestors came from Scotland originally and later my family and I moved here from north England, so the manor was designed with heavy British influences."

"I've always been interested in the study of fine architecture, but when I was a student there were no females going into that field. It's still close to my heart. Your parents built a very beautiful and impressive home."

They got into the Explorer and turned immediately south, into the forest along a narrow, paved lane and came out on the south shore of the island at a grand, very tall, gray stone boathouse. The massive structure, like the manor, was adorned with decorative stone work, high peaked roofs and an upper balcony looking out over the water. This elaborate structure housed four large bays for boats inside and two, long docks outside. It was obviously not designed merely for family recreational use.

Here Edward started to describe the history of the estate. "When my parents moved to Canada I was just a boy. They already were very well off through their Scottish, as well as British ancestors. We still have an estate in England and some business interests there as well. But let's get back to the subject of Sinabar. When we came here, the area fruit and vegetable growers had no common market structure. Each farmer was on his own to market his produce, so each farmer often had to travel great distances to sell enough produce to make a living. In order to help the area people as well as building a new business, my father developed a common market. This was well before the building of any of the highways that we have now. He found other buyers for their produce, often a fair distance away, and offered the farmers and their new customers' a system affording each fair market value and also a port for the transportation of the goods. The farmers brought their produce here and independent shippers picked it up, all arranged by my father."

"Your father sounds like a very talented and enterprising man," Maria said.

"Yes his honesty won people's favor and loyalty, but you know, he also had a talent for knowing what would be most beneficial for people in their futures," Edward explained, thoughtfully, as he held open one side of the huge double doors of the boathouse. "Well, that's why the boathouse is so large. As you can see, now we just keep a recreational yacht, a run-about and a fishing boat. Do you fish, Maria?"

"Yes, I do really enjoy fishing," she said, smiling brightly. "Does Anna Belle like fishing?"

"I don't think she's ever gone fishing," Edward said, with a shrug.

"Well we'll find out," she said. "That's one more thing that we can try."

"You girls are going to have a great time together."

After Edward gave her a tour of the accommodations on the yacht, they strolled by the other boats.

"Brian and Gregory use the boats much more then I do. Anytime you'd like to go out on one, just ask Brian, he's in charge of the boats and also in tune with the weather conditions. Being aware of the weather is very important for your safety, out there on the lake."

As they were leaving the boathouse, Edward pointed to a dark hole in the shoreline wall just the other side of the outside boat docks. "See that cave mouth over there? It's a deep cavern that has a tunnel which reaches back to the east wing of the manor and to the pet barn. It has a very interesting historical importance, which I'll explain further when we tour the manor."

"This is very exciting stuff," Maria said, with a grin.

They got back into the Explorer and headed back to the manor and the main driveway. Then they headed east around the island and stopped at a scenic over-look at the end of the island. They walked to a bench that afforded them the full advantage of the view. "Maria, does seeing the water or being near it bring back distressing memories from your accident?" he asked as they sat down and he put his arm around her shoulders.

"I get chills if I let my mind drift back to what did happen, so I haven't yet taken a full appraisal of the accident. Sometime I'll have to deal with my memories. Hopefully you'll be with me."

Edward gave her shoulders a squeeze, "When you're ready, I'll be there." They sat for a short time gazing out over the water, silently pretending to be preoccupied with the view.

When they moved on, the next stop was the charming 'Old McDonald's Barn'; with a gray stone fence around two, small pastures and the rustic, old barn that had been painted gray and white.

"This is Anna Belle's domain, her pet barn and it's full of pets. Brian takes care of it for her, but she's supposed to be responsible for her share of the chores," Edward explained proudly.

"This looks quite charming. It has such a warm and friendly feel. I would have loved being here as a child and I'll love it now," she said.

"Shall we go in and pet the pets?" he said, chuckling.

"Oh Edward I'd love to, but that should be Anna Belle's prerogative. I can imagine that she'd be put out if she didn't get to introduce me to her friends. It'll be very exciting for her," she explained.

"Maria, you're so considerate. I can see now, what a real asset it will be to have a mother here who has actually raised a daughter already," he said, totally in awe of her sensitivity toward others.

"Please tell me the history of the barn?" she asked.

"The barn was built to house the heavy draft horses that they used to transport the produce to the docks, and also three cows, some chickens and other fowl that we used for the house. We also had a small area in the barn for our pets. Now the pets have taken over the whole barn."

"How do you get here on foot from the house?"

"It's quite close to the house actually. See? You can just see it over those trees," he pointed out. "From the corner of the garden closest to Brian's wing, the east wing, there's a well-marked path. The path has lights all along from the manor to the barn. If you can't sleep at night and the weather is good, it's a nice walk out through the garden. Actually it's the only place to walk at night without a flashlight and someone to accompany you."

They got back into the Explorer and drove out the causeway to the larger stable. It was lunchtime so Edward suggested that they take the lunch in with them.

"Where can we sit and eat here?" Maria asked.

"There's quite a nice lounge, for entertaining visiting horse people. It's well equipped and we'll be very comfortable. I think that you'd agree that it's a bit too cool to sit outside for our picnic." As they entered the stable through the office and went into the lounge, they were met by a short, blonde man of twenty some.

"Maria, this is Brian's right hand man, David Cook. David this is Maria. You'll probably be seeing a fair bit of one another. David takes expert care of the horses. And David, Maria will be spending time with Anna Belle, teaching her riding and many other things. Oh, and Maria has a horse that we'll be bringing here to stay."

"That'll be very nice Maria," David said, making a quick, little, bowing gesture.

"Thank you David, it's so nice to meet another horse person." Maria extended her hand and smiled warmly.

David took her hand and gave her a toothy smile, "It'll be a pleasure to care for your horse for you."

Edward interrupted, "We've brought a lunch on our tour of the grounds, and we'll be having it in the lounge, seeing that it's so cool outside. If you're around later on you could show us around the stable."

"Very well Sir. When you want me just knock on my apartment door," the young man replied.

He left them and they made themselves comfortable in the lounge. Emma had out done herself preparing their lunch. There was thickly sliced, roasted ham with a honey mustard spread, potato salad, pickles and rolls; complimented by spicy, pumpkin pie, fresh fruit and steaming, hot coffee. She had put together a meal that held a fond remembrance of summer and a spicy reminder that fall was here.

Maria and Edward were enjoying getting to know one another. He was telling her about the building of the stable when he and Brian had been in their teens, and very much interested in the horse world. They had been quite competitive with each other, but in a positive way. They had traveled to horse shows all over North America and made quite a name for themselves, as top competitors. As Edward had gotten more and more into scientific studies his interests had become split between science and his previous interests; while Brian stayed in the horse world with his only distraction being the overseeing of the grounds and stock. Brian also took great pride in taking care of the roses, this becoming his main hobby.

"Edward, you've been holding out on me," she said, with a sly smile creased the corners of her lips. "You are undoubtedly a very fine horseman. You've just been away from it for a while."

"Not too far away from it," he said with a boyish grin.

"Then between Brian and yourself, why hire someone else to teach Anna Belle horsemanship?"

"Brian is Anna Belle's best friend, thankfully, seeing that I haven't had much time for her, but neither one of us could deal with a child in a full time, positive learning situation. That's why I had Albert run an advertisement for someone who had teaching experience as well as a successful horse career. As you now know, I needed to find a female who could teach her, as well as be her companion and role model," Edward explained, while standing up and stepping next to where she was sitting. Then after resting his hands on her shoulders and bending toward her to land a little kiss on her forehead, he continued, "Then you came along and showed us what we've been missing. I can see now that Anna Belle has been missing a caring woman's attention; someone who can be a friend to her, as well as a motivator, and a guide, and God knows that I've missed having a positive woman's caring and companionship for most of my life, except for that of my mother and Emma to a small extent."

"Edward, you haven't said very much about your ex-wife," she said, dreading the subject even as the statement left her mouth.

He walked to a window and stood staring out, his hands clasped tightly behind his back. He was silent for a few minutes, as if measuring how much to say on the subject.

Maria feared that she had been too intrusive, too soon in their relationship.

"Reanna is an oversexed, promiscuous viper!" he blurted out, not turning from the window. His voice had become quite cold, now. He twisted his hands methodically, his arms still tight behind his back as he continued, "I'm very lucky to have dear, little Anna Belle; because before she was even born I was tempted to kill her mother, the black-hearted bitch. She never wanted to get pregnant.

She made a mistake with her pills, and then, as she realized too late, she made the further mistake of telling me that she was pregnant. She wanted an abortion, as soon as she found out. I wouldn't let her kill my child, so I was forced to take action." He never once turned or acknowledged that he was speaking to anyone; he just stood there staring off into the distance. After a few moments pause as he made a crucial decision, he went on, "For now, let's say that besides having Dr. Bill Adams' help, I still had to go to unusual lengths to save my daughter. The rest of the household, including the ones that were fired for their collusion with Reanna, must have thought the whole matter an awful scandal, but no one said anything for the baby's sake. A great deal of money iced things over with Reanna, so the divorce wasn't quite the scandal that it could have been. Part of the agreement in order for her to receive the payoff was that she had to insure that she would leave the continent and never return. The viper signed over full custody of Anna Belle to me. As far as she was concerned she couldn't sign the papers fast enough. If she hadn't fully complied with my wishes, I would have filled the international gossip rags with a colorful expose of her twisted sexual appetites and life style, as well as her black heartiness. Many times I've wished that I would have done that anyway as that would have shown her to the world clearly as the evil creature that she is."

Maria was dumbfounded. So many fearsome questions crowded into her head that she couldn't put simple words together. He held so much rage toward the mother of his daughter. She just sat back in her chair, her eyes as big as saucers.

"I should've listened to my mother," he went on, "I know that's an old cliché, but it is... oh, so true. My parents warned me about the bitch, from the first day of our short, whirlwind courtship, and afterwards. I thought that they were just being overly protective, and I didn't listen!" He had turned from the window and was now walking quickly, back and forth. "She drove my parents away. She went out of her way to make them so uncomfortable, that within a few months they decided to totally uproot their lives and flee to our estate in England, just to be away from us. It may have been a good thing because they wouldn't have approved of the tactics that I was forced to use. They both died about a year later."

Maria had to stop this tirade that she had unwittingly released, for both of their sakes. What can I do to get him out of this train of thought? Quickly, she stood up and stepped in front of him. He was so surprised that he halted there and stood staring down at her.

She raised her arms and with her hands over his head making small circular motions, and a stern serious look on her face she commanded, "Demon! - Be gone!" with great emphasis.

Still looking deep into his eyes, she gave him her sweetest smile, dropped her arms around his neck and stepped into his arms. He picked her up, walked to the couch and sat down with her across his lap. He looked into her eyes again, questioning, as if looking for any sign of doubt or disapproval. He raised a hand and traced her lips with his finger, still not detecting any negativity, he leaned down and parted her lips with his own, lightly at first, as if in askance, and then, upon sensing her answer, they melted together. Time stood still for them both. Neither one had realized how much fervent longing had been stored away in their hearts.

Maria perceived multicolored, sparkling fireworks flashing against the black velvet background of her mind's eye. She was floating luxuriously, willing herself to be part of this new being that was partly she and completely he.

Edward was falling deeper and deeper into red velvet ecstasy. His hand was at the back of her head. At first he was caressing her hair, but that soon changed to holding her head so that she couldn't pull her head away from his, if she had wanted to. She didn't mind this assertiveness. She was lost in their mutual heat.

They both felt it - the longing, the passion, the complete knowing of each other, the remembrance of being torn apart after not being together for long, not together long enough.

Stop, stop, and STOP, sounded louder and louder from the depths of his soul. It nagged him and nagged him, till he forced himself to pull away from her. In amazement he stared down into those smoldering eyes. His thoughts swirled; I've known this soul before, loved and lost this soul before. I've merely just existed in this lifetime for the purpose of finding this soul again.

Maria hadn't initiated the halting of their kiss, but she knew that it was best - before their fire could flare out of control. When she finally forced her eyes open, the look that she encountered in Edward's eyes was one of pure shock. "What is it Edward?" she asked in great surprise.

"I have the strangest feeling. I've just now recognized you," he voiced his amazement, "I've just recognized my soul mate," he stated confidently.

"Yes Edward," came out of her mouth without her knowing from where, "Let's take some time with this. We have a whole lifetime to be together, this time."

"Yes, by all means my dear, we must come to know one another again," he said warmly, "You bring light and joy into this, till now, barren life. I'm willing to slow down and enjoy this. Please, let's not be self-conscious and uneasy with each other. Let's just enjoy each other's company and learn from each other."

Chapter 16

*H*aving come back to reality once again, Edward and Maria went out into the stable to see each of the horses. They didn't call on David to guide them because they didn't want to break the spell of being alone together.

"Now you've seen the horses that are here at this stable. A few years ago Brian talked me into investing in racehorses. We bought two thoroughbreds that are away at the track right now."

"That sounds very exciting," she said brimming with enthusiasm.

"The next time one of them is racing we'll have to go, so you can be excited about the horses and we can show you off," he finished with an endearing chuckle.

She just grinned back at him.

"There are also Anna Belle's two miniature horses and her pony at the pet barn, I almost forgot about them." He put his arm around her shoulders and squeezed playfully, "I'm just a bit distracted, and with good reason, wouldn't you agree."

She slipped her arm around his waist and hugged him. He tipped her chin up with his fingers and kissed her warmly. They started walking back through the barn. To break the pregnant pause, Maria asked, "What's Anna Belle's pony like?"

"He's as cute as a button. It took Brian a full year to find a well-trained riding pony for her. He's a crossbred, taffy colored gelding, who knows the show ring well. Brian thought he'd be ideal for Anna Belle to learn on and then maybe even show if she's that interested. We gave him to her for Christmas last year. We almost had him under the tree but he was a bit too big, so we hid him behind the tree. It was a good thing that Brian had rubber shoes put on him."

"What did Emma think of having the pony in the house?" she asked with a mixture of awed surprise and mischievousness.

"Brian had to promise to pick up any of his droppings, as soon as dropped," Edward replied, grinning.

"I can see that you boys are still as spoiled as you probably were as children," she said, laughing.

They ended their visit to the stables and headed back toward the Sinabar causeway. When they came to the place where Maria had stopped the first time that she had seen Sinabar, she asked Edward to stop. She just sat and gazed out at the island, it would always be an enchanting sight. When she spoke it was with a shaky voice, "If you hadn't seen me on the cliff top that evening, I would have drowned, without a doubt. If you hadn't been so strong and determined, I would have died."

She looked at him with tears in her eyes, "I have no other way of thanking you."

He reached over and wiped the tears from her cheeks, "Your life is my reward, and as they say, I'm responsible for you now, so please let me take care of you so you might learn to enjoy life here." Edward smiled meekly. He was still a bit insecure about being with a beautiful, intelligent woman like Maria. He knew that he loved her desperately but he felt that she hadn't had enough time to come to love him to that extent, or so he thought.

They just needed to have time to spend together.

"I believe that it was fate that we met as we did and that things will now have a chance to unfold properly," she said, as she reached over and squeezed his hand.

She knows how I'm feeling. She knows my thoughts, Edward was thinking as they headed back. "Let's get back to the manor and take up our tour again," he said, smiling down at her.

As they passed the boathouse on the causeway, for the first time Maria had a fleeting memory of coming to and seeing the Doctor and Edward inside somewhere. "Is that where I came to life, after you carried me from the water?"

"Yes, that's where we four men first met you," Edward answered as he drove slowly through the woods that surrounded the manor. "I love these trees, I feel that I personally know each and every one," Edward said, while grinning like a child.

As they pulled up in front of the manor, Maria was once again awed by its grandeur. As Edward got the wheelchair out of the back of the vehicle she realized how relieved she was that she hadn't needed it.

"Maria, we have an hour and a half before teatime. If we're still going to continue our tour, I'd like you to sit in the chair and have a bit of a rest while I wheel you around this old house so you can see it, or most of it."

She was tired, so she didn't give him any argument. As he wheeled her in the doorway, a huge black and white harlequin Great Dane met them.

"Oh, this is Duke, or should I say 'The Duke'. We named him after John Wayne, no not after an old British relative," he said, chuckling merrily. "He's one of the puppies that Anna Belle has raised."

Emma came rushing up to them, "Oh, I hope you don't mind, Ms. Maria. Mr. Edward told me earlier that I could let the dogs wander as usual today," she explained, as she tried to pull Duke off of Maria. He was expertly licking Maria's face, seeing that she was sitting lower then his normal head carriage. Emma went on, "I hope that you don't mind the brutes, they can be a bit over zealous after they've been kenneled in the daytime, which they have been since your arrival."

As Maria managed to clear her face, of the dog, she replied, "I love dogs Emma. Please don't feel that you need to confine them because of me."

Edward had been standing back, laughing heartily over this scene. When he could manage to speak, he warned Emma that they'd be famished at teatime. He spoke a stern command to Duke, and the canine, western hero strutted off happily behind Emma.

To start their inside tour they headed to the west wing. They walked past the solarium, the formal dining room, Emma's office, the huge kitchen, and the food pantry. The servants' wing connected to the far west of the manor through a small hallway, where the servants could go directly into the kitchen or down the hall to the east.

They couldn't just walk through the north-west wing because Mallory had long ago insisted that the halls on the first and second floors be closed off, so that she technically had a two story house within the manor. "She said that she must have her privacy. Maybe she just doesn't love dogs as much as the rest of us do," Edward quipped rather snidely and then laughed.

"Do Mallory and Gregory not have any children? How long have they been married?"

"No they don't and I think they've been married about six years. I don't know why they are childless so far. They never talk about it," Edward replied.

Once back at the grand hall they headed east. Immediately off the hall through several, stone arches, was the large, lavishly appointed lounge, so that the grand hall and the lounge made a huge entertaining area.

"This is where our Masquerade Ball will be held," Edward pointed out.

"So the grand hall makes a large dance floor. What will you have for music?" she inquired.

"We'll use a combination; a band for the older traditional music and a D.J. for the more modern. We alternate the two types of music. We'll be erecting a stage over there," he said, pointing to the southeast corner of the hall. Next, they passed the library which had its own entrance into the garden, then a meeting room, and after that, a music parlor. At the far eastern end, there was a hallway south to the garage and north to Brian's wing. They went on through Brian's main floor hall so he could show her Brian's veterinary facilities at the far north end. This facility consisted of three rooms; a dispensary and examining room for small animals, an examining and treatment room for large animals, and, a recuperation stabling room. These rooms were carefully sealed off from the rest of the house by a glass door system.

"I'm amazed that Brian's animal hospital is so meticulous and efficiently equipped," Maria stated.

"Well, he did get his veterinary degree, not for the purpose of hanging out a shingle, but so that he could take care of our own animals," Edward informed her, proudly.

"And what is upstairs in this wing?" Maria asked.

"The upper floor is all guest rooms that are hardly ever used. You'll notice at the end of your hall, where it meets with the hallway to the north, it is closed off by a wrought iron gate. These days, that gate functions to keep the dogs out of the unused guest room area. To the south, at the end of your hall, over the garage is a full gymnasium, which you are welcomed to use. Well, I've been very stupid. You could've been using the hot tub all of this time for your recuperation. Have May accompany you to the gym, whenever you feel like it, and have a comforting soak. It'll help you sleep if you use it in the late evening before you go to bed," he said, grinned down at her, "Maybe I could join you there some evening?"

"And will you invite Bill Adams to come along as our chaperone?" Maria asked, laughing as she gazed up at him sweetly.

"You are a little minx! Not this time. We'll be on our own, and besides, I'm not going to give Bill any more chances to win your affections," Edward teased.

She just cocked one eyebrow and smiled a conspiratorial, little smile. This made Edward laugh all the more.

"And on the third floor...?" she asked.

"Yes, there's a third floor, just over the main, central part of the manor. That's my living area and my laboratory. Would you like to see that now?"

"By all means," she said merrily, "You must have a terrific view from up there."

"Yes I do. From up above the trees I can see the whole island. I have a bird's eye view you might say." As the elevator door opened on the third floor, there stood a Doberman. "It's alright Jake, she's a friend."

"Is this another of Anna Belle's pups?" Maria teased, as she patted Jake on the head.

"Yes, I'm afraid so," he said, with a smile, "although when he started to grow up, I took Jake on, as my own dog. He was a bit of a handful for Anna Belle. He stays on the third floor unless I'm walking about, then I take him with me. Twice a day, one of the kitchen boys, collects all of the dogs and takes them out to a long kennel run that's on the far side of the garage. There they get to have a run and do their business."

This floor had a short hall running opposite to the one on the other floors, north / south, with large windows at each end. On one side of the hall was the door to Edward's rooms and the on the other was the large, steel door of the laboratory.

"I see that you've made some decorating changes on this floor," Maria observed.

"Yes this door to my lab is a security door."

"I understand from Dr. Adams that you are a nutritional scientist. While being very important, I'm sure; I would have thought that to be a rather tame or safe occupation."

He smiled at this assumption, "Yes, among other things, I do work in the fields of biology, microbiology, botany and other studies such as metabolism, all interacting with the study of optimal nutrition. Yes, these subjects may sound 'tame', but unfortunately there are many food companies that would pay fantastic amounts of money just to get a look at my findings, before the other guy. For them, it's of the utmost importance to get a head start in the world market. This is called industrial espionage. The food industry, unfortunately just like many others, is highly competitive. And that's not even considering the media. Those people can be diabolically resourceful."

Maria was frowning while contemplating this need for security. Noticing this, he continued lightly, "Well that's enough about that. I don't want to bore you. Come and see my abode."

"I'm not bored. I'm fascinated, but we'll have plenty of time for me to learn about your work," she explained, wanting to see his rooms. She was curious about his tastes and his interests.

This manly, living area was more austere than the rest of the house. It had been decorated using the elegant attitude of 'less is more'. There was more than a hint of the Orient here; touches of black, lacquered furnishings, bits of inlaid mother of pearl, dark wood furniture with creamy white brocade complimented with just a hint of gold treading, gleaming black, slate floors with thick, creamy white, fur scatter rugs here and there. Unlike the suites on the second floor, Edward's apartment was fully self-contained. It was comprised of; a small kitchen, a beautiful dining room overlooking the lake, a laundry utility room, a sitting room complete with a piano, a movie projection room, and two spacious bedrooms complete with two large balconies. One of these balconies faced out toward the boathouse and lake to the south and the other faced north overlooking the garden and the causeway to the mainland. His elegant bedchamber was large and airy, and following the theme of the rest of this regal apartment, the furnishings here were of dark wood upholstered with creamy white brocade and gold. The curtains and bedspread were also white and gold.

Maria walked around his room slowly, taking in every cherished article. Showcased on the wall facing his large bed was a wonderful portrait of Anna Belle at about the age of five. In this oval portrait with heavy golden frame, Anna Belle was wearing a red velvet dress with a white lace collar. The little darling was standing, holding a fluffy, little, white dog. This portrait of his daughter dominated the large room. There were several small photos of Anna Belle and one of an older couple that could only be his parents. They were standing, arms around each other, in the garden in front of the Fairy Fountain. Maria picked up the photo of Anna and Sinclair Warner and taking it with her, she sat on the brocade love seat that faced the fireplace.

Edward had stood in the doorway, casually leaning against the door jam, quietly watching her survey the sum and total of his life. He wasn't surprised that her gaze simply scanned over the framed certificate of his knighthood that had been presented to him by the Queen Of England, and, in passing it by she picked up the photo of his parents and sat down to examine it. He moved languidly to the love seat and sat beside her.

When she spoke finally, she said softly, "There's a strong magical quality about these two people and their fairy."

Taken aback by this, he stated, "Your power of insight is very strong Maria, for you've just summed up the intrinsic essence of their love, and their life together."

"Tell me what they were like?" she asked, wistfully.

"They were both very strong-willed, creative people, but they didn't fight, they didn't even argue. In situations when others might have argued, a knowing look would pass between them and then a decision would be made. It was like they had been together always." His expression changed from one of wonderment to one of profound sadness as he went on, "They died together, quickly and without any warning, and then they were gone."

Maria felt the hot sting of tears coming and that familiar constriction of her throat, "What happened?"

"They were boating in a small run-about on Bassenthwaite Loc, near our estate in England, when the boat mysteriously blew up, killing them instantly. However, the local constabulary didn't find anything amiss, so there must have been a problem with the engine," Edward finished sadly.

Maria took his hand and gave it a squeeze to comfort him. "Where is your estate?"

"It's in Cumberland County, northern England. It has its own small loc and is in what is referred to as the Lake District. It's a mountainous area near Keswick. When we're next in the library, I'll show you pictures and the location on the map."

He raised her hand that held his and kissed it. "Thank you for diverting me from my parent's accident. Now lets go out onto the balconies, while there's still good light." He took the photo and placed it on an end table and led Maria to the north balcony. They passed through large, glass doors, out onto a covered, parapet style area with a bench seat running all around the wall. Maria knelt on this padded bench and leaning on the parapet, gazed to the north and down to the garden, to the barn and causeway that lead to the mainland. It was a breath taking view, now that the deciduous trees were changing color. Their eyes were treated to a fabulous array of fall colors.

Edward noticed that Maria had started to shiver, so he put his arm around her and held her close. They knelt there together as he pointed out places of interest. As he spoke, she rested her head against his chest and breathed in the scent of him, along with the freshness of the world. This was their world and their time, again. They were together again in this magical, new time.

Chapter 17

*O*n returning to the second floor, Edward pointed out Anna Belle's suite and four guestrooms. "Do you want to go back to your suite to freshen up before we meet the others for tea?"

"Yes, that would be a good idea," she replied, as they started back to her rooms.

"I think that we've covered most of the building," Edward said.

"Is there a basement?" Maria asked, teasingly, wondering what else could there be?

Edward's brows shot up, "Why yes there is. Seeing that we have been discussing my family's history, there's another story that I should divulge."

"By all means," she replied, with her head cocked towards him in great interest.

"When my parents were having the foundation dug for this manor, they found a tunnel under where the library is now located. It ran from beside the south shore boathouse - that cave that I showed you, under the manor, and to a very old foundation that was later built into what we now refer to as the pet barn. They decided to take advantage of this oddity, so they built the house over the tunnel and at the south end, the docks and boathouse were built beside it. At the tunnel's north end, where the pet barn is now, there was a stone foundation where a building had been burnt down. So now you know our basement secret. A tunnel joins all of the original estate buildings: the main boathouse, the manor house and the pet barn. When my parents discovered the tunnel, they also found hidden evidence that showed that it had been used back during the Civil War times, as part of the Underground Railway. That may explain why the building at the end of the tunnel had been burnt down. The tunnel has probably harbored a few pirates over the years as well. You saw the large mouth of the tunnel when we were at the boathouse."

"What a colorful past this island has had," Maria mused, as they entered her suite.

Edward, gave her shoulders a squeeze, and replied, "And we'll hope for an exclusively rosy future."

She smiled up at him, but at the same time she wondered why she felt some doubts. All of this seemed entirely too good to be true.

"I'll be back to escort you down to tea in about half an hour. Is that alright?" he asked, grinning boyishly.

Maria's smile was answer enough.

Mallory arrived at the solarium early, hoping to have her curiosity quelled. Emma was busy overseeing the tea setting.

"Emma, has Edward said anything to you about Maria?" Mallory questioned.

"Now, Mrs. Warner, you know that I'd never repeat anything that any member of the family has said to me."

You mean anything that 'your' dear Edward might say, you old bat, Mallory thought to herself. She resented Emma's smug loyalty to 'The Family'. She never once thought that Emma would hold such loyalty to her.

Brian strolled into the now artificially lit room, and picked up the newspaper, seeming not to take notice of the women.

"Brian, has your dear brother Edward had anything to say about Maria Stark?" Mallory tried again.

"No, as a matter of fact he hasn't, Mallory."

"Why does everyone enjoy keeping me in the dark?" Mallory shrilled, slamming a magazine onto the table.

"Before you get yourself any further bent out of shape, I might remind you Mallory that perhaps Edward hasn't had the time or the inclination to talk to any of us about Maria. I did see them driving about the grounds today. I imagine he was giving her a tour, which would seem to indicate that she'll be staying among us, at least for now."

Emma heard Edward approaching and went to meet him in the hall to inform him that Anna Belle wouldn't be joining them for tea, as she wasn't feeling well. She'd be having some soup and going to bed early.

Edward and Maria were talking quietly and walking arm in arm with one another as they entered the solarium. Mallory looked up in surprise.

"Maria, this will give you an opportunity to talk to Brian about your horse," Edward was saying. "Brian, Maria has a horse that we need to have moved here," he further stated to his brother.

"How very nice, Maria," Brian said, with genuine warmth and interest. "Please tell me about your horse, my dear."

"Shavano is an Appaloosa gelding. At this time he's at a friend's stable, just north of Toronto. He's very quiet and he hauls well. I'll be quite happy to have him close by. He'll be quite helpful for Anna Belle's riding lessons," she explained.

"Would you prefer to have him at the pet barn and close at hand for you and Anna Belle or would you like to have him at the big stable?" Brian asked.

"The pet barn would be wonderful Brian, thank you very much." She felt that she was going to like him, immensely.

"Good afternoon everyone," Gregory said, as he entered and sat down next to Mallory, "Maria, I'm particularly glad that you're able to have tea with us today."

"Thank you Gregory, I'm feeling much better today."

Edward stood up, "Now that we are all here I'd like to take this opportunity to let you know that Maria came here in the first place to work with Anna Belle, and because she is more than qualified for that position, she will be doing so. However, there are other reasons for her to be staying here. One of those reasons is that she has graciously consented to be my Lady for the Masquerade Ball."

"Very good, Edward!" Brian heartily interrupted, and before he could continue, Gregory who was smiling, added teasingly, "It sounds as if what you're not saying, may be very important Edward. Are congratulations in order?"

"That may very well be the case Gregory, but first we had better give the lady time to see if she can tolerate us," Edward answered, laughing heartily.

We'll see about that, Mallory was thinking. "Well Edward, I'm glad of the fact that for once you'll have a date for the ball," she said, a bit sarcastically and then continued having remembered something of consequence, "Oh, I have a bit of information for you. You will recall that I was friends with poor Reanna, when she was here."

"Poor Reanna!" Edward exclaimed loudly, as he interrupted her. "I certainly wouldn't refer to her in those terms after the sizable settlement that I was obliged to give her," with a vexed look he continued, "and what information regarding that person, could we possibly be interested in?"

"Well, I've continued to correspond with her, and, well... I..." she stuttered nervously, "I've invited her to the ball."

"You what!" Edward exploded, "Where is your head, woman? That black-hearted viper will not darken the halls of this house, ever again. Part of the settlement agreement was that she could never return to this continent, let alone this house."

"Only - for Anna Belle," Mallory started falsely and froze, seeing the rage in Edward's eyes.

"I'll not have that poor child's life disrupted by that, that 'thing', not even for a moment," Edward flared at her. "Do I make myself clear?!"

Mallory had been totally unnerved at this point. "Well, she has accepted my invitation. She will be coming," she stated blankly.

Edward was obviously struggling to control an even greater rage, "The door men will have orders to not allow her to enter, and, if she tries to slither in any other way, we'll be watching for her." His glance around the room seemed to be gathering up the support of his two brothers, and having succeeded at that, he then leveled an icy glare at his sister-in-law. "You have stepped over the bounds this time, Madame. Please do not, under any circumstances, consider yourself as speaking or acting on behalf of this family or this household, ever again." He turned away from her to signify her dismissal.

"But the ball," Mallory wined, then stopped abruptly.

Edward's voice was calm and cold but lashed like a whip, "You'll be welcomed to attend of course, but Emma will take over with its production." He had not looked her way again.

Mallory looked as if the last breath had been knocked out of her, and, in fact, her status in this family had been. Her face was like florid pink stone, vibrating tensely, about to crumble and fall apart. She rose abruptly, shoving her chair back loudly, and ran from the room.

As soon as she was gone, Edward, whose icy appearance had begun to melt, turned to Gregory. "Did you have any idea of this plan, Gregory?" Edward asked in a spent and haggard manner.

"No I didn't. I knew that she had been in some contact with Reanna over the years, even though I'd tried to quell it. Believe me I had no idea that the woman would ever consider coming back here," his younger brother said, shaking his head. "Don't be too hard on Mallory, Edward. She just has poor judgment sometimes."

"Poor judgment is quite an understatement, this time, brother," Edward stated, slumping into the chair beside Maria. He slowly turned to her, "I'm so sorry that you had to witness this fiasco, Maria." The ice had totally melted from his eyes. "I hope that I can persuade you to believe that life with the Warner's is not often this confrontational," he said, giving a mock, sheepish smile.

"I'm just thankful that Anna Belle wasn't able to join us for tea and entertainment." Maria made an attempt at a warm smile as she rose to her feet. "I think I'd best retire to my suite for a rest before dinner," she said placing a supportive hand on Edward's shoulder.

He rose, asking, "Would you like me to walk you to your rooms?"

"No, that won't be necessary Edward. You have things to attend to. I'll be fine."

She looked over to Brian, who was conspicuously studying the newspaper.

"I'll look forward to chatting with you later, Brian."

"Oh, yes, that would be pleasant," he said dropping one corner of the paper to peer over at her, "I look forward to it also." Brian beamed at her with surprised relief. She nodded to Gregory and left the solarium.

⸺◦◦⸺

Maria walked slowly towards her rooms pondering what she had just witnessed. She felt a bit sorry for Mallory, however foolish the woman may have been. She wondered at the Edward, that she had come to know, reacting so severely. And what about this business that he had alluded to this afternoon; about being tempted to kill Reanna, about having to us unusual methods to save his daughter, to keep Reanna from having an abortion? Oh well. He had probably been over stating the facts.

She walked on past her suite and May's room, down towards the end of the hall. There was still a dim light streaming in through the large windows that faced southward to the open lake. A shiver ran up her spine. There was no sound in this part of the manor except the echoing sound of her foot falls on the slate tile floor. Edward had said that the second floor of Brian's wing was made up of guestrooms that were seldom used. And he had said that at the end of her hall there was a wrought iron gate blocking the entrance to Brian's wing. Yes, he had made a passing remark that it served to keep the dogs out of that unused area.

The end of the hall was growing dark, now. She didn't know where a light switch might be for this area. Slowly her eyes started to become accustomed to the poor light. Thanks to the farthest reaching rays of evening light coming from the south window behind her to her right, she could just make out her shadow falling across the silvery gray, elaborate bars of a large, iron gate; the entrance to the east wing hallway that ran to the north. She took a few more steps and bent down to feel how low the gate was. She discovered that it was scarcely two inches from the floor. Yes that would be low enough to keep the smallest of Anna Belle's dogs from entering. She reached up and found, to her surprise, that she couldn't reach the top of it. That's odd that anyone should have such a foreboding enclosing structure within the house, she thought. She leaned on the gate and tried to see down the hall, and sure enough, further down the hall where the large windows overlooking the garden started, she could just make out the dim evening light shining in, casting eerie shadows across a long unused hallway. As she held onto the gate, leaning on it trying to see down the hall, she heard a sound. It started low, a moaning intake of air that soon escalated to an exhaling, sobbing wail. While she stood as if riveted to the gate, the ragged sobbing sound went on for several minutes, then slowly died down again. Maria stood in silence, doubting her ears. Had that sorrowful sound that she'd just experienced, resulted from one of her spells, an eerie imagination of another time or was someone indeed crying, now? She shook her head. She wasn't dizzy. This didn't seem like her earlier spells. Then she remembered the turbulent meeting of wills that she'd just observed. It must've been Mallory that she'd just heard, through an echo somehow, but an echo from all the way across from the other side of the manor seemed hardly plausible.

She tried to open the gate but it didn't budge, and after reaching into the darkness at the end of the gate, she found a heavy lock, similar to one you might expect in an ancient dungeon.

She turned to face the other side of the hall, where now she could make out the outline of another large door, which must be the door to the gymnasium. She reached it and found that it wasn't locked. Not knowing where she might find a light switch, she closed the door again, not wishing to fall over a piece of exercise equipment. She noticed again how quiet this part of the manor was. Her thoughts went to Edward once again as she started back toward her suite.

I care for this man deeply; more deeply than I could have ever imagined possible, she pondered as she walked. What if he wasn't over stating the situation with his ex-wife? What if he had imprisoned Reanna behind that gate until she bore his child? She had probably had the best of care. He had said that Dr. Bill Adams had helped him. Maybe it really was the only way that he could save the life of his child. What kind of woman could she be, to try and deprive her husband of having a child, to threaten to kill his child? If I was he, and that was the case, could I refrain from resorting to drastic actions? No, I think not!

She shook her head once more. "What have I gotten myself into?" She looked around quickly. She had startled herself, for she hadn't meant to speak out loud. There was no one around to hear her. She had no idea of the history that these people had built; Mallory, Reanna and Edward, so she was not equipped to make any judgments one way or another. Surely she couldn't let any of this affect how she felt. She could only wait and learn, while she risked falling more and more in love every day. Deeply entwined in these perplexing thoughts, Maria went to her bedroom and decided to lie down for a while. In a few minutes she'd call May to help her get ready for dinner.

Chapter 18

$\mathcal{E}$dward stormed into Emma's office, which was between the grand hall and the kitchen. He was quite beside himself. All of this was just too much to sanely contain: Mallory having the audacity to invite Reanna here; his possibly having to keep himself from killing Reanna with his own bare hands; having Anna Belle's life disrupted by Reanna; submitting Maria to all of this, and, possibly shattering any hope that he now fostered for a new life with Maria. This already translated into a dreadful situation.

Finding Emma working at bringing some accounts up to date, he told her everything that had happened. Emma turned quite pale. She well understood what this would mean to Edward, not only how it might affect current matters but also the renewed heartache that opening this old wound would cause him.

"That Black Hearted Bitch will be stopped at the door. We'll have extra guards on duty. She'll not be allowed to disrupt our lives again," Edward ranted.

"Mallory did this?" Emma questioned, as she got to her feet and came from behind the desk. "Why would she do such a thing, Edward?"

"Why, indeed? Reanna must be using her, to some end. She must have a plan of some sort, but what could she want, here?" he replied, as he sat down and was holding his head in his hands, elbows on the desk. "Emma, are you up to speed with the arrangements that Mallory has made for the ball?"

"Yes, she has gone over every step with me," she assured him.

"Good, I've removed her from the project. It's all in your capable hands, once more. I'm sure that she had you doing most of the work anyway. Make sure that you keep an eye out for any irregularities that might possibly have anything to do with Reanna. Make sure you check the credentials of anyone extra that Mallory may have hired. I'll take care of hiring more security people."

"Yes Sir, I understand. Mallory must be quite upset," Emma added.

"I don't care. After the jeopardy that she's put this family in, she's lucky if she's allowed to attend."

"She must not have realized," Emma said, with a baffled expression. "Reanna has undoubtedly pulled one over on her."

"Emma, you are in charge of the ball and the household entirely," Edward declared, "I know that I can trust your capability and your judgment. If you notice anything odd or have any problems, bring them to my attention immediately."

Emma gave him her usual assured nod, as he left her and headed for the third floor.

<hr />

Mallory and Gregory didn't appear at dinner that evening, so Maria and Brian had an opportunity to talk about horses over their meal. Once again Edward sat back and appeared to be observing her quietly, compiling information. He was in a strange, darkly preoccupied mood. It was decided that Brian and Maria would go the next day to pick up Shavano and get her horse settled into the pet barn where Shavano and Anna Belle's pony would be close at hand for Maria.

As Brian left them after enjoying dinner, and was on his way to tend to the animals, Maria again felt exhilaration at the thought of being alone with Edward. She felt a need to comfort him; yet she found his quiet contemplation, quite daunting. When Brian had said good evening and left them alone together, the delight of spending time alone with Maria jogged Edward out of his funk. "How are you feeling now, my dear?" His eyes were no longer dark and forbidding. The excitement of having her to himself and his concern for her welfare had quickly changed his demeanor.

"I feel better, Edward, thank you," her replied, her voice lingered on his name. "I had only one short dizzy spell today when I stepped out of the Explorer too quickly, and I felt a bit weak at teatime. I don't think that any of that is anything to worry about, though."

"No wonder, with the ruckus that you were witness to. I'm very sorry!" he said, rising from his chair and coming over to hers, where he extended a hand to her and helped her to her feet. Still holding her hand he asked, "It's quite balmy outside this evening, would you be up for a stroll in the garden?"

"Yes, that would be wonderful," she smiled up at him eagerly. "I feel quite fine now that I've had dinner and such good company. Let's enjoy the garden while the weather permits." They walked out into the garden, arm in arm. Edward had picked up her wrap from the back of the chair.

"You look quite delightful this evening in the green and black."

"Thank you Sir, you've quite a talent for color, design and fashion."

"I've never had a particular interest along those lines before, but when I think of you, it seems to be very easy. You make my life much easier. I'm just sorry that Reanna has intruded into our lives. Without even being here, memories of her are intruding on us, through my moods. Reanna is still alive, yet she haunts me like a dreaded ghost. I don't want to let her interfere in our new lives."

They came to stand in front of the fairy fountain. Maria stood gazing at the fairy and just before she looked away, she perceived a gleam in that stony eye. "I think we should take a hint from your parents. This statue represented their love, but it was also placed here for you and I as well as other people with a blossoming love, to remind us to lean on the magic of true everlasting love which can help us travel through life together." Amazed at hearing her own voice uttering this statement, she could do nothing but continue gazing up into Edward's eyes.

Without a word he gathered her up into his strong arms and kissed her tenderly. Before he had the will to take his lips from hers, he felt the moisture of silent tears on her cheeks. He tasted the tiny tears as he kissed them away, only after he had momentarily satisfied his hunger for her lips.

"Tears, my love?" he inquired, whispered gently.

"I shed mixed tears of joy, love and thankfulness for your parents. I feel a very strong bond with them as well as a great influence from them."

"Well if that's the case then, from now on we should think of them with joy and use their role model to be a reminder to us of everlasting love. Wouldn't you agree?" he asked.

"Yes, that would work for us both, I'm sure." They walked on until they came to a bench and Edward put the wrap down for them to sit on. Sitting down Edward asked, "Would you tell me some things about your life?"

"Well, luckily I haven't had the extreme problems that you've had. I married right after finishing high school. I guess you could say that peer pressure was the largest factor in my getting married so early. You know the scenario… your friends are all getting married, it's hard to get along at home, you're looking for security, you're foolish enough to think that you can change one another, and therefore you think that you can make it work. You're damned right from the start. Romance and desire may have almost played out before the wedding. I guess you might not have felt the same pressures, being a bit insulated from the normal struggles of society here on your parent's estate. Unfortunately, so many people fall into this relentless pattern; never having a chance to experience real love, lasting passion and love of the soul."

"The picture that you paint is extremely jaded." Edward stated, having been taken aback by her astute overview.

"Jaded yes, made that way by the type of struggling relationship which after you've dragged yourself through it, you realize that except for having a child and experiencing the love of and for that child, you feel like you've wasted twenty years of your life. The marriage was a waste; my daughter Sylvia was not. I love her dearly."

"Well, that leaves us both in about the same situation. A wasted marriage, but we both have wonderful daughters to show for it. The main differences being that I had wealth and work to fall back on and you didn't. Well we can solve that without too much trouble. I'll be very pleased to meet your daughter. Do you think that she might come here for Christmas, if things are smoothed out by then?" he asked.

"Let's not look too far ahead. When things are right, there'll be time for that."

"Neither of us has had a very happy life so far, surely there are happier days ahead for us. Let's start working on that right now," he said, taking her hand in his and smiling down at her.

It was very dark now. Rays of light beaming from inside the manor attempted to illuminate patches of the garden around them. The night air was conflicted with the remaining barest hint of rose scent; the musky smell of the rich, pampered soil and the astringent, aromatic scent of the evergreens wafting from the north edge of the garden.

Looking up into his eyes she could see the golden sparkle in those very changeable blue eyes. She could feel their warmth sweeping over her. "Do you really think that we have a chance at happiness?" Maria whispered.

"Yes my love, just think back to the fairy fountain." This brought a little smile to her lips, and he continued, "Yes we just have to take the steps. Chances aren't just given to you; you have to make them, just like you deciding to come here. You took an important step." He stared down into her eyes, looking for a reaction. And he got it when that sweet little smile widened and the corners of those big beautiful brown eyes crinkled to complete that unforgettable smile. He put his arms around her and drew her to him, tilting her chin up with his fingers and covered those full, rich lips with his own. He kissed her deeply, holding her tightly to him, feeling his body melting into hers, and dwelt there for a long while in the warmth of the night.

Maria knew now, as she felt her senses heighten, that she was lost in this man; lost in those blue eyes and those strong arms, lost in him forever. Forever with this man felt very familiar.

Coming back to a more physical level, she realized that she was quickly passing the boiling point. She pulled herself free in order to survive the rising heat. "Let's walk for a while," she murmured as she looked into those smoldering eyes.

"If you wish," he said, trying to regain his breath, "but please give me a few minutes to compose myself."

"Have you noticed the stars? They're dazzling tonight," Maria said, attempting to make light conversation, for she was blushing, and with good cause. She had just realized that after being so aroused, jumping up and going for a brisk walk might not be so easy or comfortable for a man.

"I'm afraid that I haven't noticed them at all, for I've been totally dazzled by this lovely woman by my side."

"Where's the path to the pet barn?" Maria stammered.

He slowly got to his feet and extended a hand to her. She was quick to jump to her feet and pull the wrap around her shoulders. Putting his arm around her waist he said, "Come, we'll go for a walk to the barn, if you'll promise to take it easy on me."

They started towards the wooded end of the garden, and then turned toward the corner of the east wing. There was a light at the corner shining down on a white stone path, which lead into the woods. Along this path, ground lights shone up into the trees giving them a tall, eerie appearance. They walked into the woods, arms around each other's waists.

Brian had been at the pet barn feeding the animals. He had just turned the barn lights off and was starting back towards the manor, when he heard footsteps on the stones and subsequently recognizing Edward's and Maria's voices, he stepped off of the path and into the woods, not wishing to intrude on their privacy. The two walked by slowly, talking quietly. Brian thought as he watched them; I hope my brother has a better chance at happiness this time, with our Lady of the lake. Anna Belle needs Maria so badly. Brian's heart sometimes ached for his little niece who often exhibited obvious maternal needs. If Maria is the right woman to finish this puzzle, she could draw us all closer together. Reanna must be kept away at all cost!

Maria found the walk enchanting; the warm, fall breezes, the white stone pathway with artfully groomed bushes and trees; the old, stone barn with its stone fenced barnyard, and, of course, Edward's company. They walked as far as the barn.

"It's so peaceful tonight and this scene creates such a tranquil storybook picture," Maria whispered.

"Yes it is wonderful tonight," he agreed.

"I take such great joy from observing nature. Whenever I feel so inspired by the world around us, I have to take time to thank the Lord Almighty for his creations and for his allowing me to experience it so," Maria confided.

Edward took her gently into his arms and they both gazed up into the stars, "I'm very glad that you feel that way Maria, I'm inspired by your spirituality. I remember feeling that way long ago, but that feeling has been lacking in my life for some time."

They turned and walked back to the garden. Edward was warmed by the possibility of sharing a spiritual life with the woman that he knew he would be falling more and more in love with every day. "Maria, have you thought about the prospect of getting married again, or is it too soon after your divorce to think about it?"

Stopping and looking up at him, she said very seriously; "I think, when considering the proposition of marrying once again, one should be thinking more in terms of recognizing if that person is the right mate for you, and whether you can feel comfortable being yourself with that person, rather then worrying about the timing."

"You speak with wisdom beyond your years, Maria. I'm quite astounded by your intellect."

She laughed, "I don't know where my words come from sometimes."

As they walked along laughing, Edward thought about her answer to his marriage question. How remarkable her views are. That had better be enough pushing for right now, though, he mused.

"Are you warm enough, Maria?" he asked.

"Yes, I'm very comfortable," she said, meaning more then just how warm she was.

He noted that possibility and decided to play at that same game, "We were talking about nature earlier, sometimes the weather can get very wild out here."

"Really, I hadn't noticed," she said, laughing heartily, "I think I can hold my own in so called 'heavy weather'."

They both laughed, now, realizing that they had both been speaking with tongue in cheek.

Edward straightened up first and continued, "Really, sometimes we've been cut off from the main land for as long as a week, but we're always well prepared. Emma keeps the house well stocked with supplies, at all times."

"Emma seems well prepared for most anything."

"Yes she is, she's been nanny to all three of us boys, you know. But getting back to weather problems, if we have wind problems, we have the underground tunnel. When you're in the pet barn you'll see a large door that looks like it goes into the stone wall. It really is the end of the tunnel. If we were to have a strong gale that would threaten the integrity of the barn, we can take the animals underground and keep them comfortable. There's also a large animal door at the north end of Brian's wing, which is where the tunnel enters into the stable room of his veterinary clinic. That makes it very handy for Brian to get to the animals if the weather's bad. Also in the tunnel under the library area, there is a modest living quarters, set up and stocked for a month, just in case of emergencies."

"What about the possibility of rising water from the lake?" Maria asked, in amazement.

"The tunnel goes uphill quite a bit from the tunnel mouth, to the large area under the house. If the lake was to rise, the cave mouth could be flooded but the rest of the tunnel would be dry. It's quite a bit above water level."

"I'm glad that your family's been so safety conscious. You never can tell what may happen in the future."

They were back in the garden again and as they came to the bench where they had sat earlier and shared their second kiss, they stopped, stood holding hands and looked longingly into one another's eyes. Edward reached up and moved a fallen tendril of her hair, back into place. Maria squeezed his other hand.

Edward was thinking I must distract myself, "Would you mind looking in on Anna Belle with me? I want to see how she's feeling."

"I'd love to Edward, I'm so glad that you asked me," Maria purred.

She felt a pang of inner pain, at the loss of this very private moment, but she knew that for now it was for the best. They went into the manor and headed for Anna Belle's room.

"Edward I'm very interested to hear about your work and your travels."

Edward hesitated, then spoke, "Really, well perhaps sometime when we need some dull, dinner chatter."

Maria scoffed, "You must have a very interesting career. I'm truly interested."

"Thank you Maria, you're being extremely kind," he said, with a small sideways smile.

Chapter 19

The plan the next morning had been for Maria and Brian to meet at breakfast and go together to bring Shavano to his new home. It was a dull, damp morning and Maria awoke with an agonizing headache. Finding this out, May ordered Maria a breakfast tray instead and quickly went down to the solarium to inform Edward and Brian of the situation. The two brothers went up to Maria's rooms to see what they might be able to do for her. They found her in bed with an ice pack on her forehead.

"I'm so sorry, Brian, that this had to happen. I was so looking forward to seeing Shavano today," Maria said, venting her frustration.

"Maria," Edward butted in, "how are you? Can I get Dr. Adams for you?"

"I've a dreadful headache Edward, but other than that, I'm fine."

From the look on his face she knew that he was wondering if anything odd had happened. "No really, it's just a headache, Bill is due to see me tomorrow and I think that'll be soon enough."

"Very well, if you're sure," he said, not the least bit convinced.

"Yes, I'll stay in bed for now, with this ice pack."

Edward walked to the chair beside her bed and taking her outstretched hand, he sat down. Brian took this opportunity to interject his possible solution, "Maria, you said that your horse trailers well."

"Yes, he has traveled quite a bit and he's very quiet."

"Well in that case, why don't you just call ahead to the stable owner and inform them that I'll be there to pick the horse up, say, shortly after noon. I'll take David with me and there'll be no need for you to make the trip," Brian suggested from were he stood, leaning his tall body against the door jam.

"Oh Brian, that would be wonderful! I'll call Sarah at the stable and let her know that you're coming." Maria said, smiling with great excitement.

"And I'll send a check with you Brian, to take care of any money that's owing," Edward stated. "Just stop at Emma's office and pick one up."

"Edward, I don't want you to do that!" Maria objected.

Edward grinned, "Don't worry; it'll be coming out of your first pay check."

Maria tried to look stern but ended up smiling. She had already explained to Brian where the stable was, when they discussed the situation at dinner the day before.

Brian had noticed that Edward had settled in as if he was going to stay and nurse her. He's going to make a dutiful husband, he thought to himself. Brian was happy for his brother.

"I'm off then," he said giving them a salute. "I'll have May let you know when we're back and Shavano is tucked in at the pet barn." He saluted again happily and was gone.

The room was quiet now. A furrowed brow marred Edward's handsome countenance.

"I really am alright Edward. It's just an awful headache. Maybe the weather brought it on."

"Can I have May bring you anything?"

"No, Emma sent me some of her herbal tea that she prescribes for headaches, and I've had it," she said, while tightening her face into a grimace.

He chuckled. "Oh yes, I've had many occasions to enjoy that particular herbal blend of Emma's," he stopped to make a similar face, and then continued, "yes many times. I used to have quite a time with headaches, and in the last ten years or so I've had a severe problem with migraines, so I must know of every type of remedy by now. Emma's tea has helped me many times though when I've had an ordinary headache." He took a small, green bottle out of his pocket, "I've brought some essential oil that I've used successfully for aromatherapy treatment of my own headaches. The scent is very pleasant. You gently rub it into your temples and jaw joints. Would you allow me to do this for you?" He moved from the chair to sit on the bed beside her.

"That would be very nice Edward."

He took the ice pack from her brow, "We might start by putting this at the back of your head." He raised her head gently and put the ice pack at the back of her head, where her skull joined with her spine. After opening the bottle, he then lifted her hair away from her face. "Are you comfortable now? Put your arms down at your side and just try to totally relax." Maria smiled and did so. He put some of the oil on his fingertips and began to massage her temples. His touch was ever so delicate and the aroma was wonderful. It brought roses to mind, and sandalwood... and something else. With closed eyes, she was enjoying the relaxing scent and savoring each touch of his fingers. Edward took his time and continued on much longer then was necessary. Emma had done well to remind him to bring the oil. He had used it many times on himself and had felt much better for its soothing effects. Now he hoped that he would double the oil's positive affect with his loving massage.

Maria was breathing softly and regularly, now. He had no idea whether she had fallen asleep and was dreaming of some far off land or if she was here with him. He was happy to continue, for it gave him a way of having physical contact with her and also giving her comfort.

She had been intoxicated by the divine fragrance of the oil, its heat combined with the relaxing rhythm of Edward's fingers. She concentrated on that glorious touch, until it penetrated every part of her being. She let herself drift, let everything worldly fall away. As she drifted farther and farther away, she started to become aware of an almost tangible presence floating through the forest of her soul, joyously drinking of her, while nurturing and refreshing her at the same time. Her essence floated as if in glorious dance, being caressed, supported and sublimely comforted. She felt a small glowing fire building at the core of her being. Her senses were all, keenly aware of this extreme pleasure. That wondrous, beloved presence was with her. Its figure began to take form in her mind's eye. It was a male figure, resembling Edward. She thought it must be Edward, but it wasn't. She could see him clearly now. He had long hair tied back and he was much younger than Edward. His large, imploring eyes were filled with sadness.

From the outer world she could hear herself moaning, his name came to her lips, Edwin. Edwin had provided her with all of this comfort, sense of well being, and more...

She felt her worldly muscles stretching, as if she had been still for a very long time...

She was coming back now. She moaned luxuriously and stretched again. His beloved face stayed in front of her. Her eyelids were trying to part. She began to form his name again. Her lips parted. "Ed..."

She was back to real time, and Edward was staring down into her fluttering eyes. He was sitting on the side of her bed with one hand resting lightly on her shoulder, a concerned look on his face. "I'm here Maria. I'll always be here for you."

"Ed - ward," Maria stammered. She felt hot blood rushing to her cheeks.

"Maria, you're blushing. I was massaging your temples and you must have drifted away into a dream. I must surmise that it was a very interesting one, from the sounds that you uttered and the color of your cheeks," he said, with a wide grin.

"It wasn't a dream Edward. It was nothing like a dream. I was meditating on the rhythm of your touch and something else took over. I floated far away and I saw a face. At first it was you, but then it changed subtly. He didn't have a mustache and he had long hair tied back. He looked so much like a younger you, but his eyes were very sad. Do you have an ancestor by the name of Edwin?" she asked, as she sat up and was gripping both of his hands as if she was worried about floating away again.

"Yes, several actually," Edward answered her skeptically.

"He was so much like you, and he was vitally important to me," she said, feeling that familiar stinging across the bridge of her nose, so she started to fight back the tears. She didn't want to say anything further about the passion and the longing that Edwin's face had represented to her.

Never the less he had sensed the impact that she felt. "It would seem that we have some family ties, I just hope that they're not too close," he said, jokingly, trying to lift her spirits.

"Long ago, some part of me loved this Edwin very much, and now, in the real here and now, I love you!" This fell out of her mouth so naturally that she shocked herself. She had not thought about admitting to it. It just came out. And there it was, hanging in the air between them.

Edward was totally blown away. He had been contemplating on the paranormal possibilities that he'd been reading about last night. Time stopped. Yes, she had said that she loved him. This was more than he could've dared to hope for. A self-conscious smile creased his face and a tiny tear seeped from one eye as he asked, "Could you repeat that last and most important phrase for my feeble recollection? I'm afraid that I may be in shock."

"I Love You Edward!" she repeated, smiling through her tears as she reached her arms up around his neck.

Moving closer, he gathered her up into his arms and embraced her as if he would never let her go; and their tears ran freely.

"Maria I've loved you ever since I pulled you from the icy lake, but for some reason it feels as if I've loved you always."

"Maybe you have Edward. Maybe this is our second time around." They each pulled back, apart ever so slightly, and stared into the other's eyes.

"That might in some way explain the spells of recollection that you've been having."

"Wouldn't that be wonderful? That would mean that we are fated to be together; that there's something stronger than life and death, between us!" Maria said, excitedly.

"The fact that you feel the way you do, here and now, is wonderful enough for me, but we'll have to put some research into this past-life premise."

"My headache has cleared now. It's almost as if the headache and the dizzy spells that I've been having are like warnings or wake up calls, telling me that more information is trying to leak through to me. That's what it's like. Each spell heralds a small glimpse of another time," she explained, while looking at him, wide eyes filled with wonderment.

"The oil and TLC must have worked," he said, with his warmest smile, but as the facts hit him his expression changed to one of seriousness, "The oil. One of the components of the oil is rose petal essence. Was it not the walk in the rose garden that preceded your first spell? You said that you felt that these recollections might be triggered by senses."

"Yes, familiar sights, smells and emotions seem to be the key," Maria said, pondering over this.

"We may have a major breakthrough here and we'll have to look into it, but that's enough from this scientist, on the matter. Right here and now, I want to celebrate the fact that we're in love," he said, pulling her to him once again and kissing her passionately. Maria melted into his embrace and returned his fervor, with great, inner joy… and so they sat for sometime… just holding one another.

After having lunch together in Maria's dining room, Edward talked her into having a nap until Brian called from the barn. "Let's meet Anna Belle and take her to see Shavano and her pets, after she gets home from school this afternoon and you've had time for a nap."

"That sounds like a wonderful idea," Maria agreed.

"Sleep well my love. Think of this as your castle, with me as your shining knight and Anna Belle as our princess. You should have no worries now, so sleep well. I'll come and meet you later," he said, before he kissed her forehead softly and was gone.

Maria was tired and overwhelmed by this morning's revelations, as well as the implications of it all. For now, in real time and from another lifetime long ago, for them to come together and their two souls to meet again; to be madly in love again, it was incredible. Edwin - Edward, I'll have to ask Edward if he will allow me to simplify matters and just call him Ed, she thought as she laughed softly to herself. She was very tired. She went to sleep thinking of the golden life that she could have with Edward, Anna Belle and Sylvia.

Still there was something. Its identity was eluding her, but it was there. Something dark was there lingering in the background, within her existence.

Chapter 20

*S*havano came out of the trailer looking for new friends. He whinnied pleasantly and hopefully, to which he was promptly answered by a chorus of the pony, the two, miniature horses and sundry other amiable creatures. The men and Maria's horse had had a good trip. Shavano had bonded with Brian right away, responding to his kind and confident ways.

Edward had gone to speak to Emma after he left Maria and told her of their plan to go to the barn with Anna Belle. They would forgo teatime, but they would take a thermos and some cookies with them. Maria was now resting and wasn't to be disturbed. He and Maria would be having dinner with the family tonight.

When he met Anna Belle in the grand hall after school, she was very excited to hear about this plan. He had a small picnic basket with him and he asked her to change into suitable clothing for going to the barn.

"Meet us at Maria's suite when you're ready, Anna Belle," her father said, with a big grin before he headed off in that direction.

Maria was dressed and busy straightening up her room. She just couldn't get out of that habit. She had donned jeans and a warm, wooly sweater. In greeting, Edward took both of her hands, stood back and looking at her proudly, he said, "I can't yet fully take in, my great, good fortune."

"Our great, good fortune, you mean," Maria said, happily.

"Thank you Maria!" he exclaimed, smiling and pulling her to him. "Anna Belle is on her way here to meet us," he continued, "Would you mind having dinner with the family tonight? I'd like to show you off, even though they've no idea of the future that lies ahead."

Maria laughed skeptically and said, "Yes, that would be fine."

"Maria, after dinner tonight, might we discuss our future?" He hadn't wanted to push her, but now that they'd declared their mutual love maybe they had something further to discuss.

She smiled sweetly, "Yes Edward."

One more step was accomplished, he thought to himself. He was quite elated. Just then Anna Belle tapped on the door. In greeting, Maria gave her a big hug and then they were off to the barn, gibbering merrily.

Emma saw them come through the grand hall and out across the garden. She smiled knowingly and crossed her fingers. This fairytale might just work out, she thought.

Earlier, Edward had instructed her to order flowers for Maria's suite, three large bouquets for the main room, colorful mixtures picked to go with the gold and cream decor and also a large, flowering plant for the bedroom. "Hibiscus would be nice," he had said, "just no roses this time." She had wondered at him not wanting roses for his lady. Never the less, the flowers would be delivered while they were out and she'd have them displayed in Maria's rooms before they returned.

Maria was so happy to see Shavano comfortably settled in a large stall beside the pony and the miniatures, that she forgot herself and impulsively hugged Brian and gave him a kiss on the cheek. Brian was taken aback by this at first but after looking to Edward over her shoulder and seeing his broad smile, he realized that this was alright so he relaxed and ever so gingerly hugged her back. "I'm glad Maria that you're so pleased with our humble accommodations here at this barn," Brian reflected, "Your horse is a fine animal and he's been a pleasant companion."

"Oh Brian, I just love the atmosphere here. It's so clean and cozy. It makes me think of a barn straight out of a children's storybook. I'm sure that Shavano's also going to love it and his new companions." Maria was beaming as Anna Belle tugged at her sweater, impatiently waiting to introduce Maria to all of her friends, so the two of them went about petting and cuddling each of the individual animals.

Edward and Brian where left standing and admiring the scene. Brian was a quiet, introspective man and he hadn't seen such a broad smile on Edward's face since they'd been teenagers. "I'm very happy for you brother, and doubly happy for little Anna Belle. It seems that you've been given a second chance."

"Thank you Brian, I hadn't realized that the situation was that transparent," Edward said, quietly and confidently, "Yes, God has truly given me a second chance."

"The positive energy between the two of you and Anna Belle is so strong that any intuitive, caring person couldn't help but feel it," Brian said, reverently.

Brian and Edward had been very close when they were young, but they hadn't had the chance to be as close since Edward had married Reanna. Brian was a very sensitive person and the negativity caused by Reanna had pushed him away. He had tried to comfort Edward after the breakup but Edward's bitter turmoil had kept him at bay, so in order to help where he could Brian had focused his loving attention on Anna Belle. He had gladly taken on the task of watching over her. He understood that Edward had needed to bury himself in his work in an attempt to cope with what had happened, so, besides caring for his niece, all he had been able to do was pray for them all.

After meeting and fussing over all of the occupants of the pet barn, the four of them sat down on bales of hay and had tea and cookies. Anna Belle had been happily babbling on about all of her little friends, talking so fast that they repeatedly had to ask her to slow down so they could understand her. "This is just great. The only ones missing are Emma and the dogs," she chirped.

"I don't think that the dogs would let us have our tea in peace, do you?" Edward asked.

"Well maybe not, especially not YOUR dogs, Father." The little girl giggled and they all laughed heartily. "Do you think that we could do this again sometime?" Anna Belle asked, pleadingly.

Edward looked questioningly to Maria.

"Yes Anna Belle, I think that we will," Maria answered.

"Maria, are you going to be my riding teacher?"

"Yes, I am Anna Belle and we're going to do many other fun things together, also with your uncle Brian's and your father's help."

Seeing that this seemed like the opportune time, with all of them there together, they sat and discussed their plans for Anna Belle and Maria. Brian was thrilled to be included in these plans. Between their exciting discussion and grooming the horses, they just barely had enough time to get to the manor and get washed and changed for dinner. Anna Belle was allowed to have dinner with the adults this night.

During dinner, Edward reached over and lovingly patting Maria's hand, he whispered, "I know of one little girl who's going to sleep extremely well tonight."

Maria whispered back, "I think you can make that two." They laughed together comfortably and Anna Belle smiled widely to see her father enjoying himself. She also, already loved Maria.

Mallory was being very sullen tonight, as she watched this scene from under veiled lashes. She thought that Gregory hadn't even noticed 'the couple', and that the smiling Brian looked like the cat that had swallowed the canary. This can't be good.

Emma, as usual, had outdone herself with dinner. She had adorned the dining room's grand, oval table with a beautiful arrangement of pink, violet and white flowers, intertwined with two different colored, leafy vines trailing out over the crisp, white tablecloth. Dinner consisted of: steaming, wild mushroom soup, a cold, Italian vegetable medley, dressed roast duckling complimented with cranberry sauce, and a large, crown roast of pork, mashed potatoes, green beans, cauliflower, and of course, freshly baked bread, as well at least six different types of dessert. Maria made note that eating like this regularly meant that she was going to have to watch her weight, but hopefully Anna Belle would keep her busy enough to solve that problem.

Chapter 21

$\mathcal{A}$fter dinner Edward and Maria accompanied Anna Belle to her bedroom. They took turns reading her a story, and after tucking her in, they bid her good night. Her eyes were closing even before they got to the door.

"Madame, would you like to retire to the library or your sitting room?" Edward asked, with mocked formality.

"Well Sir, speaking frankly, I find your library a bit too formal. Would you mind spending more time in my sitting room?" Maria answered, equally as formally.

Edward laughed, "By all means my dear, I revel at the chance to be with you once more in your suite." She threw him a coquettish smile.

"However," he continued, "I'd like you to stop with me at the library first. I've something interesting to show you."

She hooked her arm in his, "By all means Sir," she replied, as they started down the hall toward the stairway. "If Emma is still in her office, could we stop in there for a minute? I'd like to compliment her on tonight's feast."

"As you wish," Edward replied, smiled warmly.

Catching Emma at her office, Maria thanked and complimented the family's long time employee and almost family member, on the fine repast. Edward asked Emma to have one of the boys go up to Maria's suite right away to lay a fire for them in the sitting room.

"I've already taken the liberty of having that done, Sir."

"Thank you Emma, for being so thoughtful." On the way to the library, Edward speculated, "It seems that the people around us are beginning to anticipate our actions."

As they entered the library, Maria took a seat in the chair that she had used during their interview, and thought how that meeting seemed to have taken place such a long time ago. Edward walked to a large stack of framed paintings that were leaning against one of the bookshelves. "I've found something that I'm sure you'd like to see." He motioned to the pile and started to look through them. "These are old family portraits that have been brought here from the estate in England. They were hanging here, in the manor, until I had them taken down." He pulled out the third painting and brought it over to rest on the floor in front of her. "Is the light here all right?" he asked, as he tilted it toward better light for her.

Maria drew her breath sharply, and held it, for there before her, stood a wonderful likeness of Edwin Alexander O'Donnell. "That's him!" she gasped.

"I thought this must be who you meant when you called him Edwin and said that he looked so much like me. Maria, please meet my great Grandfather on my mother's side, Sir Edwin Alexander O'Donnell," Edward spouted, with great pomp and ceremony.

"Thank you very much Edward, but as you can attest, I'm quite sure that we've already met." There was absolutely no doubt in Maria's mind. "I know him! I saw him in my head, this very morning." She reached out to the portrait and her hand began to shake. She looked up at Edward. "That face, it's your face!"

Edward was struck by her appearance. In it he saw total confusion and sadness. She was starting to sob. "It's alright Maria," he said, as he leaned the portrait back against his desk and quickly knelt down beside her. Embracing her, he whispered into her hair, "Maybe I shouldn't have shown you the damned painting, yet. After we talked yesterday, I started a very interesting research path on reincarnation and past-life remembrance. Then this morning after your vivid recollection of Edwin, I knew whom you meant. Do you have any knowledge of the term reincarnation?"

"Only that it's a belief that souls live over and over again," she replied, as she took a tissue from her pocket to dry her face. Edward got up and pulled another chair over next to hers, "Exactly! It's a well documented belief that the soul is reborn in another new body, as in the Hindu religious belief. It has a very widely accepted history."

"What frightens and confuses me are my half remembrances of Edwin - the strong feelings that I don't understand, versus the new feelings that I have for you. It has all happened so fast." Tears were welling up in her eyes again, and starting to fall. Edward leaned over and kissed away the first tear and then the next. His lips felt like butterflies caressing her cheeks. She tried to smile bravely. "I guess I just need some time and lots of TLC. Let's go up to my sitting room."

As they stood he hugged her close for a few minutes and then led her from the room. They walked to the elevator and most of the way down the hall, in silence. Just before they got to her suite she asked, "Where were the portraits hung before you had them taken down?"

"They were spaced out along this hallway. I had them taken down when we were trying to modernize this old house," he said, gesturing to the long hallway.

"I think you should have them put back up. It's very important to preserve family history, especially for Anna Belle's sake."

"Whatever you command milady, after all you are to be the next Mistress of the Manor," he said, with a wink, as he opened her door.

"I am? Is that a form of a proposal Mr. Warner?" she asked, as she went through the door and into her luxurious suite.

"It is Ms. Stark, but please, you must understand that I want you to take as much time as you like before you give me your answer," he stated as he escorted her to the large sofa and bade her to sit.

Folding his long legs, he got down on one knee, took her hand in his and slowly began kissing it. He started at each fingertip and worked his way to the back of her surrendered hand. After he had meticulously covered every bit of her hand with sensual kisses, he lifted his gaze and let his smoldering eyes look up into hers. Then he slowly turned her hand over and giving it his full attentions he sensuously kissed her warm palm, letting his lips linger there before he looked up again. Maria's eyes betrayed her emotional reaction. There was no doubt as to the love that they held for one another.

"Please Edward, come and sit beside me, we have a lot of getting to know one another, to do. I - I mean we have a lot to talk about."

He moved up to sit beside her, still holding her hand, his jaws tightened in earnest. "My love, I have a declaration to make to you," he said, rushing on nervously, "It's a serious subject that I feel compelled to discuss with you, now."

This tone of frankness subdued her as she sat back on the couch, "By all means, Edward." She couldn't yet keep from lingering over his name.

"I don't mean to push the matter unduly, but I would like to possibly announce our joyous event at the Masquerade Ball. It's less than two weeks away and I'd like you to give me an answer by then." He paused and took a ragged breath, "It's getting more and more difficult for me to maintain a socially acceptable decorum while in such close contact with you, my love. You are very alluring."

"Edward, I must say that I'm learning to appreciate your candor and as far as your first request goes, I'm fairly sure that my answer to your proposal is going to be yes. The only reason that I've asked for some time, is to clear up this confusion in my mind about this possible past-life situation, and, it's far reaching effects on us. You must admit that it's a bit bizarre."

Edward's eyes gleamed over an equally brilliant show of teeth, "Thank you Maria. You've given me a new life and made me a very happy man. As for this other situation, I'm not worried at all about how it will affect us. In fact, I'm intrigued by it. I've found that there's a doctor who practices in dealing with these occurrences of past-life remembrances."

"There is such a doctor?" Maria was so excited that she almost jumped up.

"Yes. A physician in this field can sometimes access these past-life existences and even treat problems by hypnotizing the subject and regressing them through their past-lives."

"I'd like to see this doctor, Edward. I'm very excited about learning more about this and more importantly, about us!" Maria said, barely contain herself as she sat on the edge of the sofa. After re-establishing her composure she asked, "Could you please tell me more about this doctor?"

Edward had gotten to his feet and was strolling around the room as if in deep thought.

She could tell that his mind had jumped far ahead, possibly to another topic all together. "Oh, yes, of course! His name is Dr. Simmons and his office is near the University of Toronto. I'll call him tomorrow and convince him to see us."

"We're very lucky that he's so close. I can hardly wait. I guess that I should make some notes of what I can remember of the different spells, so that I don't get all tongue tied when we see him."

"That might be a good idea. It should definitely make you feel more at ease to have it written down." he said, coming over behind the sofa where he began to massage her shoulders. "I agree with you Maria that this is very exciting, indeed. We're in love and now we are about to venture into a whole new realm of science, together. I'm very proud of you my dear. I had hoped that you, to, would also have the soul of an adventurer. We are well matched." He smiled covetously down at her, and then, reminded of something more serious, he began pacing the room again.

"What is it?" she asked, realizing that she was beginning to be able to sense his moods more acutely now.

"Maria, as far as our amorous activities go, I just want you to understand where I'm coming from. As you must know, I feel very passionate towards you, but I want you to know that I don't think of sex as a recreational sport. It's not a subject that I take lightly. I guess that stems from my staunch up bringing, combined with my disastrous relationship with my first wife."

Noticing that he was clasping and re-clasping his hands as he walked, Maria knew that he had something that was troubling him and that he needed to get it off his chest so she sat listening, quietly.

When he found the words, he continued, "Well, in not wanting to make any further mistakes in that area, I've not been with a woman, ah . . . sexually, since Anna Belle's conception came to light. That was almost eight years ago. You see, Reanna, my 'dear' ex-wife did such a number on me, that I've not even been mildly attracted to anyone, until the night in the boathouse when I first saw your lovely face." He sat down close beside her and clasped one of her hands in his. "So you see Maria, love and passion are such new feelings for me that I stupidly tried to ignore these feelings for that first week that you were here. I thought I was physically ill or something, and then I slowly began to understand that my strange symptoms were not from an illness, nor a mere interest in you, but from something much more compelling that was overpowering my will." He turned his face away from her and laughed a short, sardonic laugh. "Those nights for that first week, before I introduced myself to you, I'd have been mortified if anyone had caught me standing outside your door. But there I stood each night in the dark, with the door open just far enough, leaning against the doorframe watching the moonbeams playing across your alluring body. I was furtively admiring your glorious hair and the form of your body under the light bedclothes that covered you. I listened for your breathing, yet never daring to enter your room. I didn't need Emma's or Bill's very considerate reports to know how you were doing. I couldn't keep myself away from you, even then. Yet I didn't know why.

Unfortunately, the short time that Reanna and I were together, it wasn't because of real, lasting love. I don't know if she is capable of really loving anyone. She certainly didn't love me. We were together because of her greed, lust, and her talent for manipulation. For my part, I was dazzled by her beauty and false charms. Then, after the battles and the wounds that we inflicted on one another, soon there was nothing left but hatred and loathing."

Maria sat, wide eyed, for if she'd been astonished before, by his frankness, she was completely shocked now. Seeing her expression, Edward forged on, "So you see, I have reason to feel most inadequate, but never-the-less I am quite aroused by you. I know that by telling you all of this now, I may have totally blown the whole situation, however, it is very important to me to have you know exactly how I feel."

"On the contrary, my dear man, you've only made yourself more endearing to me. It's refreshing to know that under your suave, very handsome exterior, there's a person of honesty, modesty and integrity."

He lifted her hand and kissed it gently, "Thank you Maria, I'm touched by your kindness and sincere understanding." He noticed that the fire had died down low, and once again he was conscious of her need for rest, so he must now force himself to leave her side. Groaning audibly, he leaned over to kiss her forehead and got up to leave. Of course, she sensed his meaning.

"Oh, I almost forgot that Dr. Adams will be coming to see you tomorrow morning. I'll ask him to stay for lunch with us."

"That's not necessary, Bill doesn't need to see me again right now," she said, frowning.

"Oh, 'Bill' is it now?" Edward said, from behind a teasing smile. "I doubt that 'Bill' would miss any chance to see the very lovely Maria. I can tell that you're by far his favorite   patient."

"Well, I guess that I shouldn't cancel then and spoil his day," she said, feigning vanity.

"Touché, my love. Tomorrow afternoon I'd like to have a lady come to see you. She'll be bringing your masquerade costume for your first fitting. Will that be convenient for you milady?"

"Oh definitely, I can't wait to see it! Who am I going to be? Please tell me?" she begged him.

"No, no, you're not getting it out of me now. You'll see tomorrow, when you have the costume on and you look into the mirror," he answered, with a grin.

"Who are you going to be? Will it be your true 'alter ego' as Mallory puts it?"

"Well, I can tell you this much. I had my costume made before I met you and I don't know if I would call it my 'alter ego'. I'm going be a masked buccaneer, a pirate. So we'll see what unfolds that night," he said, with a boyish grin.

"How very interesting," Maria purred, as they walked toward the door.

"You see Maria, for as much as I down play the masquerade idea for Mallory's benefit, I really do enjoy dressing up and acting a bit out of character for the evening," he said, with a wink.

At the door he took both of her hands again, "Tomorrow is going to be a very busy day for you, my dear." He raised her hands, carefully turned them both, palms up and tenderly kissed each of her wrists, "This will have to do me for the night," he said, as he kissed them both, once more and then added, "And last me all night."

Then he was gone.

Maria went into her bedroom and sat on the edge of the bed. She was reeling. She slowly raised the wrists that he had kissed so tenderly, and touched them to her lips.

Chapter 22

"*M*ilady, Milady," softly; knock, knock.

Her eyes flew open.

"Milady," he called, a bit louder. It was coming from the inner door of her suite.

"I've slept in," she said incredulously, to herself. "Yes Edward, come in please."

The door swung open and there stood Edward with an immense bouquet of yellow, purple and white flowers, and flashing that handsome, boyish grin of his. "I'm very glad that you were sleeping so well, my pet. Your breakfast is here."

"Thank you Edward, I had a wonderful rest," she said, while swinging her legs out of bed and putting on her dressing gown.

Edward whisked her over to a beautifully set table that had been placed in front of the window overlooked the rose garden. A refreshing breeze from the narrowly open window fluttered the table linen as the brilliant sunshine lit up the dishes, the crystal and the cutlery with a marvelous gleam. The aroma of the rich, Columbian coffee was scrumptious and invigorating. They lingered over a breakfast of fresh fruit, cereal, warm croissants, juice and that aromatic coffee. It was one of those glorious mornings that you would want to savor for as long as possible.

Maria sat with her back to the sun, enjoying the feeling of it on her shoulders. One couldn't have lived the life of a horse trainer without the body suffering a tad from wear and tear.

"I had forgotten that you where joining me here for breakfast this morning," she said, smiled conspiratorially, "But believe me that was the only thing that I could've forgotten about what was said last night."

"Was it that much of a harrowing evening?" he asked, with a sheepish look.

"No, not at all. We confirmed our love for one another and agreed that we would tell the rest of the world on the eve of the Masquerade Ball." Before she could say anything further, he had launched himself out of his chair and was picking her up out of hers. He held her to him so tightly that she could feel her vertebrae popping. "Apparently," she managed to squeeze a chuckle out, "that was what you wanted to hear."

He was still quiet. She couldn't see his face; it was buried in her hair. Her feet were still off the floor. She could feel that he was fighting for control of his feelings. As he gently lowered her back down to the floor, she managed to pull her head back so that she could look up into his eyes. She was touched to see that those large, handsome eyes were brimming with tears.

"Are you sure Maria? You will become my wife?" he asked, breathlessly.

"Yes, I'm sure my love. I will be Mrs. Edward Warner," she answered, without any hesitation or doubt.

"I was so afraid that I'd messed things up terribly last night. I didn't sleep. I walked the floors above here most of the night. I'm surprised that you didn't hear me."

"My poor dear, I'm sorry that you felt that way, you left so quickly . . ."

"I thought that I'd better go before I made more of a fool of myself," he confided.

"I could never have that impression of you," she said, as she stood on tiptoes and kissed the tears away from his cheeks, licking the salty droplets from her lips.

He smiled the most strikingly, radiant smile that she had ever seen. "We're engaged then; you will be my Lady of the Manor." He spoke from a place of profound wonderment.   Once again, she stretched up onto her toes and this time she kissed him soundly . . . His arms came tighter around her, to support her. . . She lived on his breath and he on hers. She was cleaved to him and neither had the will to pull away. Eventually a greater need for oxygen forced its way between them. Their lips parted hesitantly, but their arms persisted to hold them together, tightly.

"Maria . . . Maria," he panted, "I can't move away from your heart, nor your arms. How are we going to survive, apart, until we're wed?"

"It won't be long, Edward, it can't be!" she said, with such a low voice that he just barely heard her. She released her arms and gesturing towards the sofa, and she moved to sit down. He supported her weight until she was sitting, then he sat several feet away from her still breathing laboriously.

This time he spoke first, "We'll see, after we've talked to this physician about past-life regression, we'll know better. We don't need his observations to confirm how we feel about one another, but I know that further knowledge and understanding about your spells will ease your mind about the future, and then we'll be able to set a date." He was back in control once more.

"Thank you for being so considerate." Her face was very serious now. He noted that even when she wasn't smiling, she was strikingly beautiful in a strong, confident way. She went on, "I want you to understand that I also feel compelled to marry you as soon as possible." After telling him this, she relaxed back into the corner on the cream and gold brocade sofa.

"I have a call in to Dr. Simmons office and I hope to have some good news for you, later today," Edward assured her. "What type of a wedding would you like my dear?"

"I hadn't even thought about that," she said, with an astonished look. "I don't feel that I'd want to have a big wedding. What do you think?"

"I don't care one way or another, but I'd like to give you whatever you desire, so think about it and don't be afraid to be elaborate if you wish." He looked thoughtful for a few seconds, and then said in a pleading manner, "Maria, the doctor will be here shortly, and that means that I must leave you. Before I go, will you promise me something?"

"Yes Edward, what is it," she said, out of concern.

"It pains me greatly, to have you out of my sight. Will you promise to spend as much time with me as possible, while we wait to be wed?" He knew that he loved her with all of his being, but he had no idea yet, why, he couldn't bear to be away from her.

"Yes Edward, I crave your company as well. I definitely would enjoy spending as much time with you as possible." She rose from where she was sitting, leaned down and kissed his forehead. He took her hand and kissed it gently, hesitating to give it up.

She said, most regretfully, "I had better go and dress before Bill gets here."

"Could you and he meet me in the library when he's finished with your checkup, then we can all go to lunch together?" he asked, speaking more brightly now. "Mrs. Doyle the dressmaker will be here at two o'clock. I'm also waiting for a courier to arrive from New York City today. He'll be delivering your engagement present."

"What, already... A present already, isn't that a bit fast?" she quizzed, with one cocked eyebrow and a mocked scowl.

"Madame, you forget how organized we scientists can be. I ordered it last week," he confided with considerable satisfaction.

"That was a bit presumptuous of you, was it not?"

"No, I somehow found faith and I prayed almost continually," he said, rising and taking her in his arms, he kissed her before she had a chance to say anything further about it. When she did break free she was laughing softly, "You're going to have to let me go, if I'm going to be presentable when Dr. Bill gets here," she said, pulling away, but he still held her hand.

"Don't you flirt with him? Be kind. He's already in love with you," he leveled a concerned look at her. "We're going to have to let him down easily," he said, relinquishing her hand reluctantly.

"No-ooo. . ." Maria reacted, with a surprised expression, "What makes you think that?"

"The looks that he affords you, tell all, my dear. There's no doubt, he's smitten."

"Then I guess that I'll have to make sure that I'm the model patient, and nothing more," she replied, still having a hard time seeing what Edward had understood from that first faithful night on the causeway.

"That's a sensible 'engaged' lady!" he chided, as he left the room, shaking his head. She really has no idea of the commotion that she causes us poor defenseless men, he thought, as he made his way to the library to call Dr. Simmons again.

Maria scurried into her bathroom to shower before Dr. Adams arrived.

Chapter 23

$\mathcal{T}$he dear doctor arrived right on time. He was wearing his best, gray tweed suit with a white rose in the lapel. He had thought of bringing her flowers or something, but then thought better of that idea. After all, this is a medical appointment; not a date, even though he wished it was. Hopefully there still was time for that.

"How are you feeling today, Maria?" he asked, after taking the seat that had been offered.

"I'm feeling just fine, thank you Bill." She noticed that he had taken great care in his appearance today. Surely Edward was exaggerating in Bill's case.

"Well, for my follow-up injury report, I'm going to have to give you a thorough examination. May we go into your bedroom where you can disrobe and lie down comfortably?" He noted a quick flash of insecurity and something that he took to be indecision following it, across her surprised, facial expression; so before she could object, he added, "Please feel free to call May to assist you by being present."

Without hesitation she went and pushed the buzzer to summon May. "I had no idea that a further examination would be in order, but I do recall Edward instructing you to be thorough. If this will satisfy you, ah..., I mean for your report, then by all means," she finished, with a weak little smile.

May arrived and Maria motioned her to join her in the bedroom. As they were about to go through to the bedroom, leaving the doctor sitting waiting, he said, "Just disrobe and lay down with a sheet over you, then have May call me."

The doctor was very professional. After depositing his opened black bag conveniently on the chair beside the bed, he went right to work, checking all of her vital signs. He was careful to always guard her dignity by using the sheet effectively and considerately. Asking all of the pertinent questions that a physician asks, he palpated her abdomen for any enlargements or painful areas and next checked her lymph glands. He then asked her to roll over so that he could check the areas where she had been bruised.

"The bruising is still visible, but just barely," he said, as he moved on and examined her spine and neck. "You seem to be in very good shape Maria, almost perfectly healed," he said, while closing his black bag. "I'm all done now. I'll wait for you in your sitting room while you dress."

When he had left the room, Maria thanked May for being there with her. "I'm so glad to get that over with. I'm not one for going to a doctor for every little thing, so now that I've got a clean bill of health regarding my injuries, I shouldn't have to worry about seeing one again for some time," she said to May, as she put on her dressing gown. "Could you get those tight fitting, black jeans out for me? Yes, and the lilac, silk blouse, and that cute little, black, crochet vest with the black beading. I'll also need the narrow belt with the western buckle and the little, black, dress boots." Maria gave these instructions as she sat at the dressing table brushing her hair and putting on some makeup. "I haven't seen much of you, May, in the last day or so. Have you gotten nicely settled in next door?"

"Yes Ms., I hope I haven't been neglecting you too much?" May asked. "I've been busy, and when I've come to see to you, Mr. Edward has been here."

"No, don't worry at all May; I'd have buzzed for you if I'd needed you. And yes, Edward has been here quite a bit." She stopped there, without giving anything further away and just smiled as she went on, "How is your room, is it comfortable?"

"Oh yes, Ms. You'll have to come to see it when I get it all set up. I've never had living quarters like this before," May answered, and continued to chatter as she got Maria's clothes ready for her, "There's a large bedroom with a fire place, a big bathroom with my own tub and shower, a walk-in closet and storage area, and a big, glorious window looking out over the garden. I feel like a proper lady, Ms. I'm very lucky to be in your service, and I'm very thankful. You'll never want for better service while I'm around, Ms. Maria." May's eyes were gleaming with pride and excitement.

"I'm very happy for you May," Maria said, as she got into her clothes and was running the brush through her hair one last time.

"Ms. Maria, I don't know quite how to say this properly, but I feel that I should reassure you. Now that Emma is my only staff supervisor, under yourself and Mr. Edward of course, I've no reason to be discussing anything with any others of the staff, or with anyone, even including Emma. That being said, I hope that you'll feel at ease, in the knowledge that I'll be perfectly discrete and loyal to you. You're my care, solely, and taking care of your wishes and needs is my duty. I consider this a privilege and I'm happy to be loyal to you, Ms." May concluded, with a little curtsy.

"Thank you May, I'm quite sure that you and I will get along just fine and that we'll be together for some time to come." Maria was pleased. She knew that it had cost May quite an effort to declare herself so, and she appreciated the assurance that she could depend on May. She would have liked to let May in on the plans for the future, but no, she'd better wait until the date was set.

Maria was dressed and confident now; this was her style of daywear and she hoped that Edward would approve. She'd try it out on Bill Adams first.

As she entered her sitting room, she found him standing at the window surveying the garden. "Maria, I'm so delighted that you are doing so well. You are absolutely radiant," he said as he went to sit down, but she stopped him.

"Thank you Bill. If you don't mind we should go down to the library to meet Edward before lunch," she said, as she took him by the arm and headed him toward the door.

He was suspect, as to the reason for her radiance. Surely a person couldn't glow like that all of the time. She was quite beautiful in her own right, but this is beyond that. "Have you gotten comfortably settled in now?" he quizzed.

"Very comfortably Bill, and just about fully settled. Brian picked up my horse yesterday so Anna Belle and I are very busy making plans. I still have to pick up my personal belongings in the city. Maybe we'll get around to doing that sometime next week. Edward has taken care of all of my needs, quite effectively," she explained, figuring that that last part was a big enough hint for now.

"I imagine he has," mumbled the doctor.

Maria shot him a surprised and critical look.

He pulled in his horns immediately, "Oh, I don't mean that with any disrespect, maybe I'm just a bit of jealous," he said, tilted his head a bit sideways to give her a long, definitely appraising glance, "but, I could never take any credit away from a man like Edward. After all, he has lived through the 'Reanna - wife from Hell' situation, and has managed as best anyone could, to raise Anna Belle; as well as attaining world renown in the same time span. How could I ever hope to compete?"

Wishing to overlook his derogatory sentiments and his rhetorical question, she stressed a preceding subject that Edward himself had alluded to, "Yes, Edward has told me that you were a great help to him and poor little Anna Belle during the 'Reanna situation'."

He hesitated momentarily, not knowing how explicit Edward might have been in his disclosures about Reanna, to undoubtedly, the new love interest in his life. He then decided that he might play within a little latitude here, but only with great care. For, even though he was enchanted by this gorgeous creature, he did after all need to afford his benefactor some loyal protection. This was definitely a matter of remembering on which side one's bread is buttered.

They were walking down the hall, so Bill pretended to be studying something out through the window, while he decided what might be a safe avenue to take on this matter. "Well all I can say is that Reanna is by far the must devastatingly evil piece of work that I've ever encountered. We, that is Edward and I, were forced to employ extreme measures to protect Anna Belle, before her birth and afterwards, until he was finally able to get rid of Reanna, the she viper. That twisted woman is strikingly beautiful and cunningly able to bend people to her wishes. I'm very thankful for all of our sakes that she's gone. As a reward for my efforts and my discretion, Edward was quite generous then and has continually been quite instrumental in the furthering of my career since those dark days." Bill walked on slowly, looking dourly satisfied and quite pleased with himself.

Maria had listened with great interest, and was now evaluating what he had chosen to say on the matter. He's satisfied that he's told me enough to unsettle me or warn me discreetly, but not enough to disturb his standing with Edward, should I mention any of this to him. I think Bill Adams is trying to impress me, while at the same time, he's being careful to protecting his interest. That's all right. That's fair, she contemplated silently.

"How has Edward been lately? He's had such trouble with those migraine attacks. He's a man who's been very hard on himself, over the years," Bill said, sounding genuinely concerned about his patient.

"He's actually been very well, doctor. We did discuss his past migraine problems and he apparently hasn't had an attack since I arrived," Maria confided.

"I'm glad to hear that, maybe he's easing up on himself. The attacks that he's suffered in the past have been quite extreme."

"Thank you for letting me know, doctor."

"Let me assure you that I tell you these things as a friend to you both, not merely as his physician."

"Then thank you again Bill, thank you very much," she was saying, as they entered the library.

Edward looked up from a book, "There you two are. Hello again Bill, and how is our patient today?"

"She checks out to be absolutely, totally recovered, Edward. I've given her a thorough physical and could find no lasting problems, just a few fading bruises. She shouldn't run any marathons or dive from any cliffs yet, but I think she's just fine, and gorgeous on top of all that."

Bill Adams is completely devastated, Edward was thinking as he rose from behind his desk and took Maria by the arm, "You beautiful women are seldom kind to 'we poor men'," he said, with a wink. "Come Bill, let's take our lady of the lake to the dining room and see if lunch is ready." They all laughed as they walked across the grand hall.

"Bill, do you have your costume for the ball, yet?" Maria asked feeling completely relaxed now that Edward was with them. "Edward has a dressmaker coming to see me today. I'm very excited because I don't as of yet, know who I'm going to be. He's kept it a secret from me."

"Well, I've finally decided, and I have someone working on it," Bill replied, "but we have a complication. I can only give you one hint. The complication has something to do with goats."

"My, my," said Edward, chuckling.

They enjoyed a wonderful meal of lasagna, Caesar salad, cheese bread, lemon sherbet and sliced melon and pears. The conversation was light, entertaining and very witty. Mallory wasn't there to join them. Gregory explained that she was out shopping and that she was on a diet anyway, so that she might hope to get into her costume for the ball. So Maria had the men all to herself, and they were quite overcome with laughter a good deal of the time. There seemed to be no keeping up to her witty exuberance.

As Bill was making his goodbyes, he was thinking that Edward had never looked so good, nor been so friendly, in all of the time that he had known him. And Maria, she definitely had the glow of a woman in love. I guess one and one makes a couple, he said, sadly to himself. Well if they are that good for one another, maybe they were meant to be together.

Chapter 24

*M*aria returned to her suite to wait for Mrs. Doyle. Edward had asked her to have Emma call him, when she had the costume on, if it was wearable yet. I guess he's as anxious to see it as I am, she thought.

The seamstress arrived carrying a very large, leather clothing bag, with May not far behind carrying the ladies sewing basket. May was eager to assisted Maria with her costume. She was almost as excited as Maria who quickly unzipped the clothing bag that Mrs. Doyle had ceremonially placed on the dining table.

What she saw first was brilliant, emerald satin and under that was the same shade of emerald velvet and layers upon layers of emerald crinoline. Mrs. Doyle picked up the dress and held it up in all of its grandeur. The layers of flowing skirts were made of emerald satin, while the sleeveless bodice was emerald velvet. Attached at the high points of the deep V bodice back was a luxuriant, satin wrap that was made to rest in soft folds across her upper arms. The bodice back was tightly fitted and complimented by a large satin bow. The multilayered skirts floated away in a sea of glorious, lustrous, green waves.

Maria stood with her mouth slightly open, in amazement over the lines of the gown and the gorgeous color. "Let me help you into it,"

May said, in encouragement. They took the gown into her dressing area and both women helped her step into it. Maria still hadn't said anything, as the women tucked her in and zipped her up. She then stepped in front of the full-length mirror. "The emerald, it's so rich. I've never worn this color before," she whispered, as the crinoline was put into place and the satin, wrap collar was settled into place on her arms. Maria just stared at the vision in the mirror. Mrs. Doyle was tucking here and putting final stitches there, while May was arranging Maria's hair over the back and on her shoulders.

Mrs. Doyle was fussing about the satin wrap; "Mr. Warner was not quite exact about the length of yer b utiful hair, I'll be droppin' de wrap a wee bit in the back to allow for the full affect of yer b utiful hair."

Maria tried to say something but Mrs. Doyle cut her off saying, "Oh, and it'll just be taken me a wee minute, I'll just be loosenin' dis off here a tad and given a few, wee stitches der. Den every, lil thing will be jus darlin'!" And she was right. In a few minutes everything was complete, right down to the matching, emerald shoes that came out of the bottom of the garment bag.

The velvet bodice had internal ribbing to further slim her from the waist up, to lift and cup her breasts. As Maria looked down, she realized that she had never before seen that much ample breast lifted out in front of her. I've no doubt about where most of the men's eyes will be traveling. She began to giggle merrily. "Mrs. Doyle, the dress is unbelievable! I would've never dreamt that I could look like this!"

"Well apparently, Mr. Warner knew his mind, well. He knew t'would be the dress fer his lady. He ordered dat it be a replica, only in a better color fer his lady, den de one in de movie."

"Who am I to be? From which movie?" Maria had been wracking her brain, but she could not place the design of the dress... not that she had ever paid that much attention to fashion in the movies."

Mrs. Doyle piped up in her broad accent, "Why, yer Scarlett O'Hara of course, from Gone Wit De Wind. Don' ye remember de dress from de original movie? Only, it was sapphire blue. Yer veri b utiful, ye look jus like her," the lovable Mrs. Doyle said, smiling as she was looking into the mirror with Maria, and patted her just below the bow.

"Yer man knew dat de green would suit ye much be'er den de dark blue. I'm feelin' dat he made an excellent choice."

"It fits so well already, Mrs. Doyle, how did you do it?"

Mrs. Doyle's eyes twinkled as she winked at her, "Jus' you ask yer man and yer maid."

Maria felt herself blush a bit this time, at the reference of Edward being her man. The little Irish lady hadn't missed very much during her dealings with Edward.

"It's still in need o' a lil nip an tuck, 'er an der. I'm thinken dat I can finish it now so as ya can keep it."

After they accomplished the minor fitting, Maria remembered that Edward wanted to see it on her. "May, would you please take Mrs. Doyle down to the solarium for a cup of tea, while Edward has a chance to see the gown? I'll clear it with Emma now, as I call to contact Edward. Then you can come back and help me get out of it and Mrs. Doyle can finish the hem." Maria called Emma to arranged to have Edward told that all was ready for him to come and see the gown and for May and the seamstress to take a tea break.

"Ms. Maria, I believe that Mr. Edward is already waiting in your sitting room," Emma replied, "and tell May that the solarium will be fine for their tea, seeing that the family teatime won't be for a while yet."

Emma had sounded very official. Maria hoped that she hadn't stepped over any invisible bounds. Edward was already waiting, how nice, she thought. I'll have to make a special entrance to live up to this gown.

The women left for tea and Maria prepared to make her, 'Gone With The Wind' entrance. Carrying this dress is going to take a whole lot of presence. I just can't believe what a difference a dress can make! She opened the door quietly, just a crack to see where Edward was sitting.

He was sitting in his favorite chair in front of the fireplace, across the wide floor from the bedroom door. There was lilting, waltz music playing in the room. She closed the door again, quietly, to have time to psych herself up. She stretched her spine, lifted her head and everything else high, and opened the door wide. Edward hadn't heard the door, so she cleared her throat softly.

Hearing this he stood up and turned to face her.

He thought that he was prepared, but he wasn't. As she started across the floor, taking the measured steps that the gown would allow, his swift intake of breath was quite audible. Maria seemed to magically float across the floor.

"My God . . . milady you look unbelievably divine!" he uttered, swallowing hard. "I knew, the first time that I saw you standing, and the way that you moved... it was in the solarium, that first time; I knew then that you were as beautiful as Scarlett O'Hara, in Gone With The Wind."

"Oh, Edward you're outrageously complimentary, you must be in love!"

"There's nothing truer then the 'in love' part of that statement, but you are remarkably beautiful my lady."

She reached up and kissed him sweetly, being careful not to crumple the gown.

"I have the final touch for you my dear. This gown may be a recreation and a costume but these are the real thing. I had it designed just for you and therefore it's a one of a kind, just like you." he explained, as he reached inside his tweed jacket and pulled out a large flat jewel case and handed it to her.

"Yes, open it please. It's my engagement present to you. It was inspired by you, my Scarlett O'Hara." His blue eyes were sparkling like stars.

Maria still paused with the case in her hands. She put her fingers on the latch to open it and closed her eyes. When she heard the latch spring open, she opened her eyes and was dazzled by what she saw. It was a large, heart shaped emerald with one, large diamond on each side, clinging to a flattened, gold chain with ten, smaller diamonds embedded in the enlarged, chain links.

"This can't be for me! It's too exquisite." she said, in a hushed tone, her eyes filling with tears.

"It very definitely is for you. It's my heart delivered right to you. The two larger diamonds represent our two daughters." Edward delicately took the necklace out of the case and put it around her neck, "Now my heart is yours forever, and this is a reminder of my love and devotion."

"Edward, you are too good to me, I am just a plain woman," she said, sniffling.

"Don't ever say that again! You are incredibly special, and you are my lady, soon to be Lady Maria Warner, but you surely don't need any title that I could give you, to make you special. You already are!" he exclaimed, while pulling another, smaller, jewel box from his pocket.

"And these finish the ensemble," he said, as he quickly opened the smaller box and showed her matching, heart shaped, emerald earrings with diamonds on each side.

"Edward, darling, this is all amazingly beautiful, but it's way too much!" Hesitating momentarily, she put the earrings on as he handed each of the jewels to her.

"Several days ago, when we were on our Sinabar tour... and I asked you to just relax, get to know me and let me take care of you; do you remember that?" he quizzed.

"Yes, but. . ."

"Well, this is what I meant. I mean to give you whatever you desire and then some," he said, asserting his will as well as his love.

She could find no other come back, other then to say thank you as she melted into his arms, without any worry about the gown.

Chapter 25

Cwo days before the Masquerade Ball, Maria was up early, getting ready for a trip to Toronto. Edward had informed her the day before, that his persistence had finally paid off and that they had an appointment with Dr. Simmons. Edward had been calling, pressuring and cajoling in his attempt to get to see Dr. Ronald Simmons, a psychotherapist who used hypnotic past-life regression to treat his patients.

Maria had been worried, but now she was anxious to get there and find out about the strange spells that she had been having, as well as the nightmares. Edward had mentioned that some of this research was done under hypnosis and this intrigued her.

The building that the doctor's office was in was a newer, three story, white stucco clad building on the outskirts of the university buildings. It was simply marked 'Research Center'. Dr. Simmons's spacious, very modern office was on the first floor. There was no one about, probably because it was before normal office hours. Dr. Simmons met them at the door. "Mr. Warner this is highly irregular for me to squeeze an appointment in like this, but with the fact that you are also a research scientist, I find myself finally giving in."

"Along with the fact of the sizable fee that we agreed on, should we accomplish results," Edward retorted, in a slightly lower tone. He was just letting the good doctor know that he meant business.

They spent the first part of the session explaining the strange spells that Maria had experienced. She had a bit of a hard time disclosing the extent of the emotions that had been uncovered, to a man that she didn't know; but when she realized that if he was successful in hypnotizing her, he was going to hear everything anyway, then she was able to just let everything out. Edward also divulged the strange effect that Maria's appearance had on him.

The doctor started, in a very assuring voice, "Well Maria, with your approval I'll attempt to put you into a deep trance. We'll be recording these sessions and it's up to you if you wish to allow Mr. Warner to attend."

"By all means, I want Edward to stay with me."

Dr. Simmons had her recline on his office couch, with Edward sitting near by. The doctor explained to them that if Maria achieved deep trance, there may be multiple lives that could come up as well as between life stages. However, to get to the lifetime that Maria had been getting glimpses of, he would ask for the lifetime that had included Edwin, then work back into anything else that might affect them as a couple.

Maria turned out to be one of those individuals that are easily hypnotized. When asked to go to her life with Edwin, her voice changed to that of a coquettish young lady, by the name of Elaine. She spoke of Victorian times in southern Scotland, and the handsome young Lord Edwin that she had just met at his cousin's, Celeste O'Donnell's birthday gala. She went on to tell a story of young love and awakening sexuality. They had arranged to meet at several, social occasions and they danced their way into love. Elaine had an overbearing brother, Paul, who after seeing this happening had succeeded in influencing their parents into sending Elaine to live with relatives in England. This spirited young woman rebelled and planned to run away with Edwin. The night before the elopement was to take place, Paul lured Elaine out to the stables where he ruthlessly beat and raped her. Paul had a volatile, dark soul and he had been insanely jealous of Elaine and Edwin's chaste, virtuous love. As he gagged her and pummeled and whipped her with a riding crop, doing his best to scar her, he kept saying that if he couldn't have her, no other man would want her after this. Then he brutally raped her, gloating about how frail she was and how strong and manly he was. Even though he had thought to gag her, his own maniacal raving was overheard, and their father was summoned.

When the entire story came out, the unsuspecting parents were shocked by Paul's evil depravity and Elaine's willful rebelliousness. Fearing that the whole family would be ostracized by society, to save face; the very next day Elaine was sent to a nunnery and Paul to a monastery, where he spent several years before being released. Elaine became a nun, sadly, living under the misguided belief that God was the only one who could possibly love her after her horrid disgrace.

This forlorn young woman lived with the knowledge that Edwin, her virtuous love, would have been left at the agreed upon place, waiting - horses in hand, wondering why Elaine didn't come to him. He had been left in the lurch, left to believe that she was just a shallow, fickle, flirt and that she really didn't love him. She did truly love him. This haunted her for the rest of her life.

After relating her story, Elaine cried piteously.

Dr. Simmons immediately brought her out of the trance. "Maria, your regression was very successful. You took us to a life that brought you together with Edwin O'Donnell. However, your relationship had a very sad outcome. You can listen to the tape at a later time. I feel that as Edwin O'Donnell was an ancestor of Edward's, it may be very important and even crucial, to put Edward into a trance and see if his soul was indeed also Edwin's soul. Assessing that, may be of the utmost importance to your relationship."

Edward hadn't been prepared for this eventuality, but he did see that it might be very beneficial for their relationship. He took

Maria's place on the couch and the doctor was able to put him into a deep trance after several different approaches. "Edward, go back to Victorian times and tell us your name," Dr. Simmons suggested.

Edward in a similar voice but with a Scottish accent said, "Edwin O'Donnell."

"Edwin, can you tell us about Elaine?" the doctor prompted.

Edwin began to tell his story. Elaine had been his first love. With great emotion, he spoke of the way that it felt to hold her as they danced; of how he had to fight the other young men off, to keep her to himself - not only on the dance floor. He had noticed that her brother Paul watched them broodingly and that he hardly ever let them out of his sight. One evening at a dance Edwin had stolen her away, out into the garden. He hoped that they could be away from prying eyes for a time. They had kissed - cautiously, experimentally. Edwin had become heatedly aroused. He'd been self-conscious at first but quickly realized that she might not be able to notice if he didn't press himself against her, as he longed to do. He reminded himself that he was a gentleman and that he must restrain himself. They were young and Elaine was betrothed to a man that she hadn't even met yet, so it was very risky for them to be alone together. Her parents would never let them be together. Paul figured out what was going on and cornered Edwin later on that night, to warned him to stay away from his sister, or he would stop them from ever seeing each other again.

By the time that they met again at the next party Edwin was full of resolve and he had a plan. He once again pulled Elaine out into the garden. He kissed her passionately this time, and felt the ecstasy of her body melting against him and starting to respond to his touch. However, he knew that this was as far as they could go, before they were wed. He told her of his plan for them to elope, two nights hence. Her parents wouldn't be able to do anything if they were legally married and their love had been consummated. He had two horses ready, and they would ride through the night to the home of a relative of his in England where they could be married the next morning. His family, such as it was, wouldn't hold this desperate act against him and his new wife. He was a wealthy man. He didn't need the dowry of a planned marriage and pleased in-laws.

Elaine had agreed, and was very excited about the romantic adventure that they were about to embark upon. Two nights later Edwin was waiting at the predestined rendezvous but Elaine didn't come. He inquired about her the next day and was told by her family that she had decided at the last minute to go away on a trip. Yes, that would have been just what would've been expected to be their answer: if it had been someone else inquiring after her, if it was not he that was asking and if he was with her and married by now. What was this all about? Was he going mad? He kept asking about her, not knowing what else he could do. Finally, two weeks later he heard at the local ale house, that she'd gone away to a nunnery, of her own free will. Edwin was devastated. He was left to think that she'd left him. Had he frightened her away? Had he done something wrong? He had also heard that Paul had gone away at the same time as Elaine had. He felt that all of this was very odd, but he had no way of knowing why or where Elaine had gone, and he was left feeling that somehow it was his fault.

Some five years later his family influenced him into going to England and marrying an English girl. She was of a family that had been friends of the O'Donnell's for some time. Although this arranged marriage hadn't been conceived with the glowing passion and overwhelming love that Edwin had felt for Elaine, the couple lived happily together and successfully raise three children.

Dr. Simmons cut in here, "Soul of Edward Warner and Edwin O'Donnell, have you ever encountered the soul of Maria Stark and Elaine before, in another life.

"Yes I have, several times," drawled, a voice with an even stronger Scottish accent.

"Soul, go to the encounter with Maria's soul that is closest in time before Elaine and Edwin," Dr. Simmons instructed.

"Yes, she is Mary McDonald O'Donnell," Edward answered, in this much heavier Scottish accent.

"And who are you and what is your story?"

"I'm Gavin O'Donnell, Mary and I was betrothed by our dear parents when we were but wee bairn. We met when we were each ten years old. We were lucky to grow up, more or less together, forbye we grew to be soul mates. When we were fifteen we were allowed to marry. Our kin were vera close and times were vera good. Mary and I were blissfully happy and before long, Mary was ta having me wee bairn. There had been other suitors that had come around to try and win me Mary's hand before we were wed, but our parents and Mary had always turned them away. Just after we found that Mary was to have our bairn, one o Mary's cast-off suitors started a clan skirmish. He was mislikin' that the McDonalds had not treated him fairly, and he had it hard for me Mary. So we went to war just cause his feelin's was ruffled. During a fierce foot battle, I knocked the broad sword from his grip. He bolted to a horse that had been held for him, and the treacherous Son of a Witch ran me down with the horse and stabbed me betwixt the helmet and shoulder guard. It did not take me long to die. I did me clan an honor to die well for me wife's family's honor. If only me opponent had fought a fair battle, I'd a lived to see me wee bonnie son - Edwin O'Donnell born. It was very sad that me darlin' Mary was so torn up by me death that she died herself a few days after he was birthed."

"Soul, may I speak to your between time, between Gavin and Edwin?" the doctor asked.

The soul answered with a clear ethereal voice exhibiting no trace of accent, "This is a resting place, with time for judicial assessment, time to replenish the soul and plan for the next session of life. I must be with my soul mate! It will not be as her mate this round. God has given me the opportunity to be with her again but this time it will be as her son, it may not be for long but perhaps it will be the move to set us up to have a full life together, later on in another time. I must make my move now! I can't take the chance of missing her, this time.

Dr. Simmons awakened Edward from his trance. The doctor excused himself and made several calls to cancel other appointments. Coming back to sit down with them, he said, "I think that it's imperative that we listen to the tapes that we've made so far and attempt to analyze the situation." Maria and Edward had been sitting back taking time to think. The Dr. continued, "Maria, you and Edward obviously have had three and possibly more, very intense lives together. I think that we should listen to the first tape now; the one I made of you."

They both agreed, so he rewound the tape and pressed play. Maria was surprised at the change in her voice. She listened while sitting on the edge of her seat. She felt the intense warmth of Edwin's and Elaine's sweet, young love; then the rage and indignation of the violent beating and rape that Elaine's own brother had perpetuated against her. How could a brother do such a heinous thing to his sweet, younger sister, stealing her virginity just to spite the chaste love that she and Edwin had so briefly shared? These two innocent people who had been naturally drawn together had been robbed of the possibility of having a loving relationship and life together, by this evil soul who had been her brother. Then, for Edwin to be left believing that she had left him behind because of something that he had done wrong, once again proved that this life had indeed been very cruel.

Maria's mind flashed ahead to Edward's trance and how he, as Edwin, had felt dejection and guilt. She then thought of Edward, speaking as Gavin O'Donnell, telling of their love, their marriage and early deaths - where they had supposedly been Edwin's parents. This was so very fantastic. "Doctor Simmons, how could this possibly have happened, I mean the close connection between Gavin and Mary, Edwin and Mary, then Edwin and Elaine?" Maria was perplexed, to say the least.

"I'll try to give you an idea of how that might have come about, after Edward has listened to his tape," the doctor said, as he inserted Edward's tape. Edward sat transfixed, first by a voice that sounded similar to his but had a distinct Scottish accent and then that same voice with a much more pronounced, Scottish accent. After they listened to both of the distant lives that he had divulged and then the astounding revelation of his soul in 'the between time', both he and Maria sat speechless, staring at one another.

Dr. Simmons looked from one to the other and then back again. It was as if he could hear the wheels churning, trying to come to some grip as to the extent of this situation. The doctor broke the silence, "They say that one's eyes are the windows to the soul, but in these cases, hypnosis is the method to give the power of speech to the soul. As for a possible explanation of how this could've come about, let me give you further information that we have found about this science, through much study. In further sessions we may find out that your two souls may have come together in other previous lives that we haven't yet discovered. Through meticulous studies of thousands of cases we've been able to prove that there is a 'between lives' existence that is meant to be a period of reflection, choice making, planning and then waiting. Souls which have attained a certain level of evolution may have the opportunity to plan the entrance time and place for their next life. In these cases when souls are sufficiently evolved and have a strong attraction for one another, this is their opportunity to plan a strategy to exist together once more. But keep in mind, there must be a balance. Everything in the universe has a balance. There must be a negative as well as a positive."

Maria interrupted, "What do you mean by a negative and a positive?"

"Well in the first case, of Gavin and Mary; they lived and loved and both died very young. While this may not have been so unusual for that time, there probably was a soul in that lifetime that worked to keep them from living a full life together. This was likely the one who killed Gavin under devious circumstances, therefore playing the negative roll, in that lifetime. Then that same soul may have chosen to meet the two of you in the lifetime of Edwin and Elaine, as Elaine's evil brother, Paul. These negative ones may have been two separate souls, but I'm thinking that there's a good chance that they were the same soul, negatively interfering. And to follow this pattern, that same soul may be stocking you both in this lifetime." The good doctor was relieved that he'd been able to put this puzzle together in a way that he hoped Maria and Edward could begin to comprehend.

"Oh My Heavens! This is so complicated and yet so uncannily obvious from what has come out of our own mouths, and is evidenced by these tapes," Maria said, shaking her head and running a hand through her hair. She looked to Edward for his reaction. He simply stared at her, thinking behind a passive mask.

"Do either of you have any doubts that this is your reality?" the doctor asked, while looking from one to the other.

Maria was shaking her head thoughtfully and returning Edward's stare. He didn't speak immediately, so she did, "I have no doubts, after the spells that I've been having, and after seeing the portrait of Lord Edwin O'Donnell - Edward's great something or other."

"I've no doubts formed either," Edward added resolutely, "and I think I know who the negative soul in this lifetime is." He and Maria looked at one another and said, "Reanna," simultaneously.

"But how could that be, she's a female?" Maria asked.

Dr. Simmons answered with alacrity, "Souls may come back as either sex, which ever suits the grand plan. It's probably only due to good planning that you two have stayed the same sex through each of these lifetimes, at least the ones that we've discovered so far."

Edward's passive mask was now augmented with a crooked grin, as he uttered, "That could explain a multitude of situations," and there he let that subject drop.

Maria asked, "Getting back to Gavin and Mary, Edwin and Mary, then Edwin and Elaine, and then us, why the close time frame between our preceding lifetimes and then the longer span to this lifetime?"

Dr. Simmons took up this task, "There are many scenarios that could be possible here, but two that come to mind are: after the devastating experience and subsequent feelings that Edwin and Elaine must have had, probably, one or both used poor judgment in the 'between life' planning, or the negative soul that may be following your lifeline could've waylaid one of your souls in another lifetime. Actually though, in neither of your hypnosis sessions, did we ask if either of you had lived any lifetimes closer to this one. We just immediately asked to go to the one that included Edwin because that is who you had a point of reference with. Another time, that is if you are interested, we must simply ask to go to closer previous lives."

Dr. Simmons felt haunted by one particular fact here so he reiterated. "Let me digress for a moment here to stress what I feel is the most important fact that we have uncovered. As you have seen, the power which this negative soul has mustered while following you two down through the ages is very real, so by all means be prepared to deal with it this time around," the doctor said, cautioning them.

Edward interjected here, "This evil soul has almost succeeded in reeking havoc in this lifetime, already."

"I think that the both of you had better be very careful, now! Especially if you have an idea of who the negative one is," Dr. Simmons cautioned.

"Doctor, why is it that in this lifetime I've had these spells, these bits of other life recall," Maria asked.

"Well my dear, the theory is that as a soul gets older in terms of the number of lives it has lived, we surmise that as it becomes more and more enlightened, (only if it has chosen the path of greater positive achievement), it may also gain in other-life sensitivity. Your soul may have lived though many lives of positive growth, therefore attaining higher sensitivity and knowledge. Also, it may be possible that your near death, almost drowning experience could have heightened your sensitivity to your past lives.

Edward spoke up, "It is fate, that we be together to overcome the odds."

"That's one way of expressing it," the doctor added, "Fate or good planning, as well as divine intervention. Your souls may have been fighting for many lifetimes to succeed in having a full and satisfying life together. And just maybe His intervention has rewarded you with another chance to overcome evil. So, I would suggest that you both need to be very careful and take good care of one another, but above all, Don't Waste Time!"

Doctor Simmons stood up and extended his hands to Edward and Maria, "I think that we should leave it there for now, you have a lot to digest. If you have any questions, or when you'd like to delve further into your past lives, just give me a call.

Edward shook the doctor's hand and said, "We'll do further research at another time. As for now, we've some planning to do to get caught up in this lifetime." He was smiling devotedly at Maria as they walked to the door.

"Well," said Dr. Simmons, "Good luck to you both and God Bless."

Chapter 26

*T*hey left the doctor's office and asked the driver to take them to Maria's apartment. Earlier May and one of the houseboys had been sent to Maria's previous address with the stable truck and a small trailer. Their mission was to pack Maria's belongings, clean the apartment and return to Sinabar, with Maria's belongings in tow.

When Maria and Edward got into the limousine, they just sat staring into one another's eyes for a long minute, then gravitated to one another's arms and stayed that way, holding tight without saying a word.

As they arrived at the apartment building, May and her helper were putting the last of the boxes into the trailer. Maria had to take one last look at her last home. It wasn't that she had lived here very long or formed any attachments here, but this was the place where she had come to terms with all of the changes that needed to take place in her life. This was where she had decided to go out in pursuit of a new life; and what a life she'd found! Dr. Simmons's phrase 'divine intervention' rang stoically in her mind.

She was very glad to see that May had cleaned the rooms thoroughly. She took a check to the super and told him that she wouldn't need any apartment, ever again in this lifetime. After they got back into the limo and headed home, home to Sinabar, Maria sighed deeply. She was glad to have that chapter over with. It was time for a new one to begin.

She smiled radiantly up at a contemplative Edward, "Where do we go from here, partner?"

"Isn't that brilliantly obvious my love? We set a date, a very important date," he replied, gathering her up in his arms and kissed her with a glowing fervor. When they did release each other's lips, she put her legs up onto the seat and snuggled against him, dreamily involved with thoughts of him and their new life together.

Mallory, as ordered, had turned all of the masquerade arrangements over to Emma. The manor was in turmoil of preparations. The big event was tomorrow night. As the rising clatter erupted from stage builders, extra kitchen staff, and delivery men of every sort, Anna Belle who had been allowed to take a few days off school, was dancing around the grand hall in an imaginary ball gown, to imaginary music.

Immediately after Edward and Maria arrived home from Toronto, he called a local security company and hired a full staff of ten security men, to secure the manor and the surrounding grounds. Two of the guards would occupy the hallway adjacent to Maria's and Anna Belle's suites at all times. Edward wasn't going to take any chances with his two ladies.

The men were told to keep a look out for anything strange, and they were given photos of Reanna. They also received orders, that on seeing her, they were to apprehend and contain her. All guests arriving for the ball would have to show their faces to the gate and door security before entering. Unknown to Anna Belle and Maria, Anna Belle's skipping school had really been for her greater protection. She wouldn't be going back to public school.

The evening of their appointment with Dr. Simmons, Edward ordered their dinner to be served in Maria's suite.

"I'm not going to take a single chance on anything Maria, not one single chance," he said as he wrapped his arms around her. "We're not going to be deprived this time. You and I and our daughters are going to have a wonderful long life together."

That evening they sat together, cuddled up on the sofa, and started to plan their future. They decided to be wed in the small chapel on this very floor, next Saturday, a week after the Masquerade Ball. Maria would send a note to her daughter Sylvia, to break the news to her slowly and she'd call her after the ball to make further arrangements.

"I don't want to get into a lot of explanation right now about why so soon. I'll just tell her that she'll have to wait for details until she gets here. She'll be shocked, to say the least."

"Maria, what would you say to having Sylvia, Anna Belle and Brian standing up with us?"

"That sounds like a very nice idea, Edward, the girls will love it."

"What do you think of Monaco?" he asked, surprising her.

"I've never thought of it. Why?" Maria asked, peering up at him.

"I know of a wonderful resort there and I thought you might like to go there for our honeymoon."

"Oh Edward, that sounds so exotic and romantic," she said, smiled widely and squeezed her eyes shut as she squirmed even closer to him, under his arms, "How exciting, but anywhere with a wonderful bedroom will suit me just fine."

He laughed out loud, "You can be quite a little vixen, I'm finding out," and he hugged her tightly, "Right then! Monaco, here we come! We'll fly out of Toronto on Saturday, after the service. I've longed to have you all to myself since the evening that we had our interview in the library. I had quite a difficult time controlling my thoughts, that evening."

"No wonder! Edward, Edwin, Gavin... no small wonder that "bed" is the most prominent peace of furniture that comes to mind when we're together. No wonder that the temperature just naturally rises when we're together," she said, smiling coyly as she trying to come up with another 'No wonder'.

He laughed out of humorous defense this time, "Now, play fair my pet! Take it easy on me unless you wish to move up our date of consummation."

She half turned and smiled up at him meekly, "No, that's ok, I'll promise to be good... for now."

Regretfully, he calmed his features and pulled his sitting position up straighter, "And after Monaco, I'd love to take you to our estate in England. May and Anna Belle could join us there so that we could have a proper holiday together. If you like it there, we could even stay there over Christmas, and maybe Sylvia would like to join us for her holiday."

She turned so that she could look up at him and put her arms around his neck, "It sounds so delightful, Edward, I can hardly wait!" She reached up and kissed him blissfully, feeling that they were truly part of one another once again. They sat encircled in one another's arms, just holding on tightly to life.

Minutes later he whispered in her ear, "I hope you won't be too upset with me, my love, but I must tell you something. I've already ordered your wedding gown."

She pulled away, so that she could confront him, "You've what!" she exclaimed, doing her best to sound indignant, "Well, I shouldn't be surprised. You've probably made a better choice than I could anyway. What color is it to be, my lord and master?"

"It'll be a glorious creamy, golden honey, very simple in cut, but stunning."

"That sounds like a quite unique color for a wedding gown, but undoubtedly I have perfect faith in your choices, based on experience," she said, with a playful grin.

"You may wish to also take it and the emerald gown to Monaco with us," he said, finishing with a wink.

That brought up a whole new topic. "What'll I do about clothes for our trip, the climates will be different?"

"Don't worry about a little thing like that. Just take a few comfortable things from here and we'll shop for clothes wherever we go."

"What is your estate like?"

"You mean our estate, not my estate. Everything that I own shall be yours also." He bent and kissed the tip of her nose lightly. "Our estate is very grand, by most standards and has been in the family forever. It's a small castle, built into the side of a large hill in the Lake District of Cumberland County, near Keswick. It's very picturesque. The hillsides are heavily wooded and we have our own lake. The place is teaming with wildlife and there's still a fine stable of riding mounts there. I think you'll quite enjoy it."

They sat talking, most of the night and fell asleep in each other's arms while reclining on the sofa. All that they had learned on their trip to see Dr. Simmons, had totally eclipsed all of the getting to know one another that they had accomplished previously. Now, all of the plans that they were making revolved steadfastly around them being together for the rest of their lives, without any doubts, come what may.

Chapter 27

*M*aria, or should we say, Scarlett O'Hara stood in front of the full-length mirror in her room. Her delicately scented body was draped in emerald satin and velvet. Edward's engagement jewels sparkling brilliantly, nestled across the voluptuous expanse of her neckline. May helped her curl her lustrous dark hair into masses of big curls that casually kissed her shoulders and back. She twirled around several times, intoxicated by the feel of the material against her skin, the gentle touch of her curls, and the glitter of her engagement jewels. Mrs. Doyle, the dressmaker, knew her work well and how a woman wants to feel. She had lined the bodice with the same velvet and the structure of it was comfortable yet vampishly supportive and shaping. Her breasts were slightly lifted and cupped in velvety comfort. The bodice hugged her smoothly and super accentuated her small waist. Everything was perfect, right down to the matching shoes and gloves.

Edward had given her the video of the original Gone With The Wind so that she could see Scarlett, her mannerisms, and how she moved in the dress. Not that he thought Maria needed any help in that department. He had known that she was a natural beauty.

"May, what time is it?" she asked.

"It's six-thirty, Ms. Maria. You're ready early."

"That's good," Maria said, almost under her breath. Then remembering May she said, "I want to surprise Edward, by meeting him before he goes downstairs. I just have to touch up my makeup to make it a bit more dramatic. Then I'll go." She finished off her makeup by giving her eyes more definition, adding just a touch of sparkle to the outside corners of her eyes, and darkening her lipstick. She felt slightly breathless. She hadn't realized that she had rushed that much. Earlier in the day she had gotten the idea to meet her lover upstairs in his suite at least half an hour before he planned on coming down. Let her take him off guard for once. Let her throw a wrench into his well-formulated plan, for a change.

May wondered if this was a wise course, but she decided not to say anything. Maria had finished her final touches and was headed out the door. "Have a wonderful evening Ms. Maria. I'm going to go down to the railing that overlooks the grand hall so that I can see you dancing with Mr. Edward. You'll make the most striking couple."

"Thank you May," her mistress said, as she was closing the door. Maria started down the hall towards the elevator. Being so wrapped up in everything else, she hadn't thought about May not going down to the ball. Well, at least she'll have a good spot to see everything from. Her heart was beating as if she'd just run a mile. Was she more excited to be going up to Edward's suite to see him before the ball, than she was about going to the ball? Yes, she was! That's why she'd been so hyper, with palms actually sweating.

Her mind raced ahead as she hurried around the corner toward the elevator... Aah!

She thudded right into a guard who was striding in her direction from around the corner. He had been rushing to investigate after hearing her dress rustling as she walked quickly up the hallway. Luckily he had managed to get his hands out in front of himself and he caught her by the shoulders.

"What's your hurry lady and what are you doing up here?" He was a burly, blonde, young man with a crew cut and a stiffly pressed uniform. He was starting to pull what looked like a photograph out of his pocket. Then Maria realized what he was doing. The photo must be one of Reanna. After taking a closer look at her, he thought better of it and shoved the picture back into his pocket.

"I'm Maria Stark, Mr. Edward Warner's fiancée. I'm on my way up to meet him," she gasped, after managing to catch her breath.

"He didn't say anything to us about anyone going up there, besides him."

"I'm just going to meet him before he has to go down to the ball. It's all right; I just want to surprise him. I'll tell him that you stopped me, but that I talked you into letting me go up." The man was shaking his head as if he was undecided. "It's all right really, I don't have a weapon," she said, laughing.

"Won't the dog stop you?" he questioned.

"I don't think so, he knows me by now."

"Well ok, but if he's mad at me later..."

"I can guarantee that he isn't going to be angry with anyone," she said, giving him a playful grin.

A big smile crossed his face and he gestured with just a quick nod of his head, for her to get on her way. "He's a very lucky man," he called after her.

Deep in thought, she stepped onto the elevator, and the door closed behind her. I haven't seen that guard before. There sure are enough of them around. I thought I saw another one at the end of the hall when I came out of my bedroom. They must be changing shift or something.

He sure was wearing nice cologne, odd for a guard to be scented with something expensive like that. Well, to each, his own.

The elevator stopped and the door slid open. She knew enough to stand still as the dog approached her, to give him time to recognize her. He got up from lying in front of Edward's door and started to growl. His hackle was up. She took one step forward so he could see her better, and she spoke, "It's alright Jake, it's just me." The dog recognized her soft voice and began to wag his tail. She stepped up to him and patted his head.

"Well at least you're glad to see me, let us hope your master is as well. How do I look?" Not really expecting the dog to answer, she took a few seconds to straighten everything, fluff her curls, and tried to compose her breathing. "Ok, this is it!" She knocked on the door. There was no answer. She knocked again, harder this time. There still was no answer and no sound from within. She looked down at Jake, "Is he in there old man?"

Jake made a soft, whining sound, and then to her great shock, he barked loudly, twice. He startled her so badly that she jumped back. It seemed the dog had known what was needed, for just seconds later a grumbling, wet, tall, handsome man with a towel wrapped around his waist and knotted over at the hip, opened the door. He thought that he was simply answering the dog as usual, so he was looking down.

"What is it now, Jake!"

Catching sight of her from the corner of his eye, at knee level, "What..." his eyes were traveling upward, taking their time. "Madame, to what do I owe this very great honor?" His eyes had stopped momentarily at her bust level, and then snapped quickly up to her eyes.

"Lust, I believe," she said a bit sarcastically, noting his appraisal of her appearance.

"Mine or yours?" he quipped.

"Do you really think it matters at this point? May I come in?"

"Yes, by all means, but you must beware of a wet man in a towel. Remember, you've been suitably warned." He closed the door behind her and walked passed her, in the direction of the bathroom. As he passed her he whipped the towel off, from around his waist and began to rub his wet head with it.

Her eyes did a quick appraisal of his well muscled behind before he turned into the bathroom.

"Just give me a minute to comb my hair. Make yourself comfortable," he said, just as he was turning the corner into the bathroom.

She felt a rush of emotion, as her mind swirled with thoughts. How theatrical of him? How vain of him! How sculptured his butt looked! How comical to see his wet footprints on the ceramic tile floor! How am I supposed to move from this spot? How in heaven's name could I possibly 'get comfortable' with him just around the corner, with nothing on, but a smile?

How can he get to me so? I guess I asked for this! He did warn me. This is why I was so excited to get here. He excites me!

She finally managed to move from where he had left her at the door. She walked into the living room and sat on the edge of a large white leather sofa. Before she had any further time to compose herself, he came walking in, wearing only the towel again, with his hair neatly combed. She sensed that, being in his own personal environment, added to his natural assurance level. Further illustrating this, he sat about a foot away from her on the sofa and recklessly put one ankle up on the other knee. "So, you haven't told me yet, why you've come up to meet me?"

She said nothing, as she smiled coolly and slid back into a more comfortable position.

So he started to improvise for her, "You missed me... you wanted to invade what you consider, my inner sanctum... you wanted to catch me, off guard... you wanted a preview of my costume... you wanted to be the initiator..."

She stopped him there, "You're getting very warm." She smiled coyly now and offered no further hint.

"You sometimes would like to be in charge... you just couldn't stay away." He stopped there, knowing that he had hit home on both counts.

This was the first time that she'd seen him without a shirt. She was adoringly surprised at his well-muscled physique, for his age and line of work. He must be in the habit of making good use of his gym, she thought. Can I manage to keep my hands off of him? I need to feel those muscles, run my hands over them, but I must behave myself. We've a ball to attend!

She moved over beside him, putting one hand on the back of the sofa and resting the other wrist on his shoulder with her fingers in his hair, "You're right. I love you and here I am."

"In all of your glory, I might say!" He put his arm around her waist and pulled her to him, "My gorgeous, head-strong woman. I'm totally yours. And I notice anyway, that none of my security measures stopped you from surprising me at my door. I'll have no doubts in the future, as to just how persuasive you can be. Now, what can I do for you, besides assure you that you're undoubtedly going to be the most beautiful woman at the ball and that I'll be the most envied man, because I'm going to monopolize all of your time?"

"Just kiss me and then go and get dressed, I just wanted to be here with you," she said, reached up to simply touch his lips with hers.

But he had other plans.

He slipped an arm under her and being very careful of her gown, he scooped her up, stood up and carried her into his bedchamber, not even noticing whether his towel went with him or not. He then somehow conveyed himself down onto the bed so that he was stretched out with her lying on top of him, his arms still wrapped tightly around her, "Now, let's have that kiss," he whispered into her ear.

What he had said was immaterial, for he had fanned the flames that had been building ever since the evening that they'd met in the icy waters of the lake. Fire and ice; it's always going to be like this for us. All of their joint loneliness, silent suffering, and self-denial came to the fore and was encompassed at that moment. Their mouths met hungrily, relentlessly. Their lips mashing together, thrusting tongues, touching, teasing, sucking in air, sliding lips, shifting bodies, grinding together, holding each others heads tightly together, one tongue caressing the other, licking the flame that was growing hotter and hotter, kindling reaction in their nether regions, blood pumping wildly.

They kissed so intensely that oxygen deprivation was threatening to take its toll. Maria was fighting for air, as was Edward. Slowly she won the battle that her mind was having against every other part of her seething body. She was able to will her already surrendered body to pull her head away. She gasped for air, trembling and fighting to stay strong willed. Must be strong! She managed to take several more ragged breaths.

Edward laid his head back, spent - letting his neck muscles relax, eyes still closed, breathing in short rhythmic breaths. He was trying to regain self-control.

Maria pushed herself up on one shaky elbow, "We're going to be late for our own party."

"What party?" he gasped, and then laughed feebly, "I'm in a world of ecstasy here in my own private, inner sanctum and you have to remind me of the hundred and some other people downstairs, that are going to want me to share you with them. That's as cruel as having to leave this bed without making love to you, Maria, here and now."

She smiled at him apologetically, "Soon my love. As soon as possible, I promise."

She rolled off of him so that he could get up.

She laughed to herself when she noticed that his towel was somehow still in place, although something resembling a tent post under it threatened to force it open. He, awkwardly this time, swung his legs down from the bed and sat up on the edge of it. He looked back over his shoulder and winked at her, "I heard that little giggle of yours, I know, I'm going to have to go and have a cold shower this time, and I'll bring back a cold face cloth for you, Miss red cheeks. Please have a rest while you wait."

She lay out flat on his bed, her heart still racing. Edward truly is a Gentleman!

Chapter 28

$\mathcal{H}$alf an hour later they were ready to face the guests, totally refreshed. She'd rested as he suggested, then got up, straightened everything back into place, fluffed her hair and repaired her makeup as best she could. She went to get a drink of water in his kitchen, also to give him some privacy to dress. After his much-needed cold shower, Edward groomed himself meticulously and started to don his buccaneer garb. He had truly indulged himself in this matter. He'd spared no expense to have the costume designed just the way he had imagined it in his mind's eye. He started with the stockings. They were men's ballet tights, made of heavy, white nylon, similar to ladies panty hose, except the crotch was different. They fit very well. Then the breaches, they were made of rich, black velvet and had bands that tied off just above the knee. The especially handmade boots were next. They were made of very soft pliable black Italian leather, pointed at the toe, with a good inch and a half, walking heel, high uppers that came up above the knee and folded over dramatically. They were gusseted so that they fit snugly. His buccaneer's blouse was impeccably made of a soft, airy, snow white cotton blend. It was tight fitted through the waist and the back, and slashed open in the front from neckline, halfway to navel. It had a high collar that stood up in the back and came to sharp points beside the deep V neckline that showed delicate light brown curls of chest hair. The shirt had large, billowing sleeves, with tight lower arms. Edward stepped in front of the dressing mirror to see how he was doing. The fit was very flattering. He felt a little surge of unexpected, primal excitement. Maybe there was something to this alter ego idea. Well, he would see!

Now it was time for the weapons. He strapped on a wide, black leather belt, which held a decorative scabbard that sheathed an elaborate, antique rapier that had been crafted for one of his ancestors and was cherished by his family. He tightened the large, silver buckle. Next came the chest girth. This black leather belt that he had also had especially made had been designed to holster a dagger and two, jewel handled stilettos that were also from his family's cherished collection. This belt fit from one shoulder, down across his chest, and hugged the bottom of his rib cage on the other side. The dagger was sheathed at the top of his back so that its hilt was just behind his right ear. Both stilettos; finely polished and jewels twinkling were gloved in leather along the front of the belt.

Now the head gear. First he tied on a blood red scarf across the top of his head and knotted it just above the left ear, leaving the tails hanging. This came to just above his eyebrows and succeeded in covering most of his hair, except for his neckline at the back, but his high shirt collar hid most of that. Then he carefully placed the eyeholes of a black sash mask and tied it at the back. Out of a huge box, he lifted a flamboyant, black felt hat, brim pulled down dramatically on one side and sharply up on the other, festooned with a large black, plume feather. He placed it on over the red scarf and tucked the black tails of his mask up under the hat. Most of his face was covered and only the point of his nose and his lower face were visible. No one other than Maria would be able to tell who he was. The final touch was the soft, black kid gloves with exaggerated wrist gauntlets. He pulled them on slowly, stretching each finger, enjoying the sensuous feel of the tight softness as he flexed his fingers and made taught fists.

Fully clad now and looking ready for mayhem or gallantry, he stepped in front of the mirror again. After adjusting his mask for optimal vision, he surveyed his adornments. "Wow, I love it!" he said, to himself as he affected a gallant bow. He managed this by: keeping one leg straight, stepping out the other leg and cocking the heel of his boot, bending at the waist and making a spiraling gesture with the arm and hand on that side while keeping his other hand on his hip. Looking up, he then bowed further over that leg inclining his head forward. "Oh my, that feels good and my hat didn't even fall off!"

He felt youthful, taller and magically lighter, and he couldn't wait to get onto the dance floor with his gorgeous lady. He would unmask later in the evening and shock everyone with the joyous announcement that he and his eternal love, his lady, would be wed in one week. His skin tingled with excitement. He felt strongly virile, as never before. He gazed into the mirror once more before he went to join Scarlet O'Hara.

"Which one of my gallant ancestors am I tonight? It's time to go and join my love and find out." he whispered.

His lady was standing in the dining room in front of a large window overlooking the garden. She had been watching as their guests had been arriving steadily, some of which had even wandered out into the romantic setting of the candle lit garden. A window was open somewhere, emitting faint, lilting music. Maria swayed slightly to the rhythm.

Edward walked up behind her quietly. Not wishing to startle her, he whispered, "I'm here my love, but please don't turn around yet. He stepped up close behind her, sliding one arm around her waist and leaned her back against him. He passed his other hand in front of her and gently cupped her chin between his thumb and forefinger. As she relaxed against him the hypnotic music enwrapped them both and they swayed together.

Maria hadn't realized that these simple contacts could be so provocative, so sensual...

She had seen the glove on his left hand, as he reached around to take possession of her face. She reveled in the sensation of the kid-clad fingers holding her chin and delicately touching her throat. Her eyes were almost completely closed now as they swayed, totally relaxed. "I love the scent of leather. This is so dreamy," she murmured, "I could do without all of that metal poking me though, I take it that it must be part of your costume?" The hilt of his rapier was rubbing against her rib cage and the handles of the stilettos were digging into her back.

"I'm sorry my love. Hopefully when we're dancing face to face, it won't be such a problem. As to the term 'costume', I don't feel that it is. I feel much too comfortable and normal in these clothes, maybe without the weapons.

"Weapons! For heaven's sake let me turn around and see you!" she wiggled a bit as she begged.

"Let me warn you first that I've purposefully dressed so that no one will be able to tell for sure, who I am. That way, part of the evening will be just for us alone. Then later I'll take my mask off and we can make our announcement. Are you ready for the world to know that we're to be wed?"

"Yes, very. Now, may I turn around and find out who you really are, at heart?" she asked, while trying to contain herself.

He let his left hand roam slowly down over her breasts and down her rib cage to her waist, then firmly grasping that thin waist he pushed her out away from his body and turned her around.

"Oh, my! She stepped back even further to have a better view. "I've thought of you as being elegant before, but this is rakishly debonair!" A hot, searing thrill ran down her spine as he gallantly bowed.

"One thing that's for sure," she said, in a low, throaty, voice after she recovered herself. "I'm very glad that you'll be making that announcement tonight, for then all of woman-kind will know that you are mine, and I won't have to worry about fighting them all off." Stepping forward she took both of his hands, still not able to take her eyes off of him. "I'm thrilled that you feel so at home in these clothes because I'm going to want you to keep them for a long time, and wear them just for me! I agree that this look totally suits you. We're going to have to do some more research and see which lifetime this influence comes from."

His reserved smile didn't quite hide a look of intense passion and hunger, "I'm so gratified that this," he gestured to his outfit and his body, "pleases you and entices you so, because this is me and I am completely yours." The field of electricity around them was like a sparkling cloud that they might not be able to find their way out of, unless one of them made a determined attempt, right away.

He snapped out of it first. He turned on one heel and presented her with his right arm. "My lady, I think we must face our guests now," he said, with great authority, then smiling down at her as they left the room he continued, "before this goes any further and we are forced to bolt the door and retire for the night."

"Yes, I agree totally, yet reluctantly."

They left Jake on guard and took the elevator to the second floor. Edward thought that if they entered the grand hall via the staircase, instead of the elevator, they might not be so conspicuous. The plan didn't work. It was as if the orchestra had been waiting for their entrance. In fact, Brian had been waiting and he tipped them off. The minute he saw Maria, he motioned to the band and they stopped what they where playing and switched to a wonderfully lilting waltz. Although he'd been out-witted, Edward didn't miss a beat.

There was a hush in the crowd as they reached the bottom of the stairs, and the middle of the dance floor cleared.

"It would appear, milady, that the dance floor is ours," he whispered to her, as he held her arm out and gallantly led her to the middle of the floor. He made a flourishing bow to her, then taking her in his arms he literally swept her off her feet, his strong arms guiding and slightly lifting her as they glided around the dance floor. She was amazed at how little effort it took to stay with him. She left the driving to him as she floated almost effortlessly.

"I'd no idea that a man could move this well," she murmured.

He chuckled softly, "It was my mother. She and father were wonderful dancers and she insisted on teaching all of us boys. The other two dance adequately, but Mother always said that I was a natural. Dancing must be like riding a bike, for I haven't danced in a very long time, and besides, you have me walking on air. You're like a jewel in my crown - beautifully brilliant and wondrously light and portable. I can do anything while you're in my arms."

"You flatter me so milord, I think your natural finesse for dancing may be an influence from our dear Edwin. Oh, by the way, I meant to ask you if you'd mind if I simplified matters and shortened your name to Ed."

He drew back a bit in their embrace and looked at her for a second, his mask hiding his expression. Then it dawned on him, Edward - Edwin. "Well, now I get your drift. I have been so enjoying the way you say my name, let's see if that feeling wears off after a while, then maybe I'll let you shorten it up. Will you grant me that?"

"Yes Edward, my dear. I'd grant you just about anything!"

The waltz finished, and the crowd applauded. Couples started to join them on the dance floor, as the second piece started. This was a slower, more modern waltz. Edward gathered her up much closer now. She settled herself so that she was slightly sideways to him, with her right leg ever so seductively between his legs and she resting her hip against his middle, here she was able to meld to his movement. This closeness, while dancing, was new to her but it quickly became instinctual for both of them. They looked like shear poetry as they moved together. The fingers of his hand at her back started high on her spine and slowly moved down her spine, from one vertebra to the next, causing a sensual thrill that impelled her even closer.

"I love you," he whispered, into her hair emphasizing each word carefully.

Maria thought that she would melt. She clung to him, eyes closed, reveling in the feeling of his body in movement. Bliss filled her mind and she forgot that there was anyone in the room. Every part of her body felt that glorious ache that just being close to him made her feel. They stayed on the floor for one more dance, smoldering in each other's eyes. At the end of this tribute to their love, they pulled apart slowly, as if from a long, breathless kiss, and walked casually through the other dancers, to the lounge at the side of the hall.

Edward got them drinks and they stopped at one of the many hors d'oeuvres tables. Maria chose several hot and cold canapés and put them on a small plate, the idea being that they'd make their way out to the garden for a few minutes of glorious anonymity. That was one of the perks of being in costume. Some people might guess who Edward was but none of the guests would know for sure, so he didn't have to be the host of the evening, yet.

The orchestra was taking a break and soft, medieval, flute music was playing in their stead. Odd-looking creatures and notable, social figures alike were milling together visiting with one another. Before, neither of them had noticed anything about the room or the people that had surrounded them, they'd only had eyes for each other. They'd been oblivious to the beauty, the comedy, and the commotion that was all around them, while missing what a fantastic, visual portrait was being enacted. Now they could see it all. The lounge, as well as the garden, was ablaze with soft candlelight. In the grand hall itself, the chandeliers had been turned down a notch, to extend a warm romantic glow. Edward had said that one porter would have the sole job of attending to the more than one hundred candles.

Edward motioned to her to start heading towards the door to the garden. However, before getting to the door, they were accosted by a large, hairy beast with curled horns and large, brown, glassy eyes. The stag had his horns lowered and was in a mocked charge, as he slid to a stop in front of Maria, a hairy arm reached out and taking her hand, bowed over it and attempted to kiss her hand.

"Your physician, at your service, my beauty! However, I dearly wish that it was the Beauty And The Beast that was the 'love duo of the ball' instead of the Beauty And The Buccaneer." Dr. Adams said, as he raised the beasts head and winked at them both.

"Well Bill, your costume is quite appropriate," Edward said, with a chuckle. He was thinking about how thankful he was that now, he need no longer worry about Bill Adams as competition for Maria's affections.

The doctor did his best to put forth a fake sneer in answer to Edward's jibe, "Maria, please save me a dance later on. Please have pity on a poor stag."

Maria laughed and promised to spend some time with him later on in the evening. She and Edward finally broke away from Bill and the rest of the crowd. They leisurely walked arm in arm through the candle lit garden. The air was calm and thankfully a bit cool, with just a hint of floral sweetness. Most of the roses were finished now and some of the vivid annuals were in final bloom. Alexander and Cleopatra walked by them, whispering happily. Their costumes were meticulously appointed.

"Maria when we have to go in, shall we make our announcement?" Edward asked, sounding very serious and distressed.

"Yes we should, but have you told Anna Belle yet?"

"No, I hadn't even thought of that. She'll be extremely happy and excited. She loves you already, and this'll mean the world to her," he said, smiling proudly.

"I think that we should tell her privately before you tell everyone else. But why did you sound so forlorn, just a few minutes ago?

"I was remembering that our wedding is a full week away. May I ask you your opinion about something crucial?"

"Yes, of course Edward, what is it that's bothering you?"

"Is it important to you that we wait till after we take our vows before we make love?"

"No, at this point that isn't my concern. We know that we love one another and that we're going to spend the rest of our lives together. It's not as if either one of us is a virgin, to cherish deflowering in the wedding bed. We've each been married before. No I feel that I'd rather let nature take its course, in the light of our histories."

"Oh Maria, I think that your decisiveness and thoughtfulness may be saving my life. It's funny how actuality throws a different light on situations. Before, I never would've thought of being in this situation and being willing to forgo social convention, let alone talking so openly about sexuality. I sounded distressed because I knew that I would die if I had to wait to have you."

Chapter 29

"Then, lets find Anna Belle and you can tell her our news before you tell everyone else," Maria suggested, trying to bring Edward back to reality.

"The little dear is at the ball with Emma. I gave her permission to stay up until after the fireworks as long as she stays with Emma. They shouldn't be hard to find. Emma's dressed as the Queen Mother and Anna Belle as young Elizabeth. They make quite a pair."

"We'll have to look for them," she said, smiling.

"Yes, and with you at my side I'll tell them our news." Edward was positively glowing.

Tweety Bird ran by them, being chased by Sylvester. They were laughing loudly and Sylvester almost tripped up the patio steps. Tweety reached the door first, but waited as Sylvester got there to open the door, after bowing extravagantly for the big yellow chick. The Buccaneer led Scarlett O'Hara back to the grand hall and they started their search for the Queen Mother and Elizabeth.

As they started across the hall, they were approached by the very same security guard who had nearly collided with Maria earlier, on the second floor.

"Sir, begging your pardon," he said, making a stiff bow to Maria. "Ms.," he looked back to Edward again, "Mr. Warner, we may have a glitch in the laboratory security system. Could you come with me right away?"

Edward was startled, "A problem...?" He turned to Maria. "I'll have to go for a few minutes, my love. I'll be back as quickly as I can. Why don't you continue looking for Anna Belle?"

Before she could agree, Edward and the guard were headed for the elevator.

Maria decided to watch for Anna Belle as she took advantage of this opportunity to take in the sights and the sounds of this wonderful event. She saw Mallory and Gregory; she was dressed as Marilyn Monroe and he was Dick Tracy. Maria had heard ahead of time, about their costumes so she had no trouble identifying them. The other personage that Edward had tipped her off about was Count Dracula - Brian. The vampire was leaning against the wall at the edge of the lounge, watching the strange figures on the dance floor as he talked to a short person dressed as Napoleon. Maybe that's David Cook from the stable, he looks about the right height, she was thinking.

There was Anna Belle and Emma, happily dancing not far away from Dracula. Emma's dress was pale aqua lace, layers on top of layers of lace, with considerable added padding, and a matching wide brimmed hat and gloves. Anna Belle wore a white Princess style gown with a pale aqua sash to match Emma's dress. She had a gold colored, jeweled crown on her little, light brown head. She appeared as quite the regal little Princess.

The band was now playing light modern, contemporary music. A very elegant witch and her huge black cat danced close to Maria. She started to walk around the hall toward Dracula and the two Royal Ladies, when she stopped to watch the Pink Panther dancing with Inspector Clusoe. The Panther's tail kept tripping the Inspector, causing him to laugh loudly. She was about to move on, when a gloved hand took her by the elbow, and the Buccaneer was at her side again.

"That didn't take very long," she queried.

"Not a big problem," he mumbled.

A lilting waltz was just started and he steered her out onto the dance floor once more. For some reason he didn't pull her quite so close this time. She noticed that for some reason he wasn't wearing his weapons now. He must have decided that they were too cumbersome for dancing. Like before his fingers started to work their way down her spine. Maria was moving to the music and letting her mind travel. The prolonged anticipation of joining together and taking part in certain love maneuvers could be nearly as erotic as the actual acts. She stretched and experienced a seductively, electrical convulsion as his fingertips skillfully located each vertebra. Her body uncontrollably arched achingly toward his body, momentarily surrendering to the seductive power of those fingertips.

A low guttural chuckle welled up from within the throat of her dance partner. Maria instantly snapped back to reality. She leaned back and gazed into the Buccaneers face, wondering about this uncharacteristic behavior.

"I knew that his old habit of 'fingers moving on the spine' would both relax and entice you, my dear," her partner sneered, revealing the lack of light brown mustache over rounder, fuller lips. "Hush now, my sweet," this unknown Buccaneer purred.

"Who are you?" Maria hissed, as a bolt of recognition hit her that this was not her Edward. She stopped still, and stared defiantly up into those unknown eyes. A chill ran down her spine as the answer hit her. Reanna! It must be!

The imposter read her body language and taking her by the waist, forced her to resume the dance, "Dear Edward must have filled you in very well regarding his ex-wife," she whispered into Maria's ear.

"Now don't blow this Maria, you don't want to endanger everyone here as well as yourself. We're going to finish this waltz and then we're going to retire to the library. Don't worry; we just need to have a little chat, just you and I."

"Where is Edward?" Maria asked, through her teeth, low under her breath.

"I imagine that he's busy taking care of business Maria. Why else would he leave you unattended, my pet?" She pulled Maria closer to her as they danced on.

Reanna whispered in her ear, the way that Edward had, earlier in the evening, "I'd like to taste your beautiful lips, right here Maria, but something tells me that you might react rather badly, so let's just quietly walk to the library."

Maria impulsively recoiled after hearing this woman's sexual suggestion.

Edward was deep in thought about the lab security as the elevator reached the third floor and the door slid open. Jake, the Doberman was lying in front of the laboratory door. He didn't offer to get up. Noticing this right away, Edward not thinking of anything else, ran and knelt down to attend to the dog.

The guard, coming behind him, had stealthily slipped a small sealed plastic bag out of his pocket. Following close behind Edward from the elevator, he took a dampened cloth out of the bag and bending even closer, he reached around and clasped it over Edward's nose and mouth. With his other hand on the back of Edward's neck, his fingers were pressing in just the right location to keep his victim from putting up any fight.

Edward was loosing consciousness quickly, that scent... halothane! The sweet taste at his soft palate, his vision became confined to a graying tunnel; the tunnel was closing in... And he was out like the proverbial light. Such was the result of a civilized knock out drug that an espionage agent might use. The counterfeit guard wrapped on the lab door three times. It opened and his partner emerged to help him drag the unconscious scientist and his dog into the lab where they dropped them in front of the computer area.

"Have you had any problems locating the Agri - Boost project files?" the guard imposter asked his partner.

"No, I didn't have a single problem. There's a cover description file that is linked to batch document files, so I got the list of the batch files and copied all of them," Fred, fake guard number two said, smiling self-assuredly.

John, the agent that had brought Edward up to the lab, nodded to the unconscious body and exclaimed, "That's these scientist types for you. He must've been relying on this doggie here and some high tech locking devices to protect his project secrets. I guess he never expected to be hiring agents from the other side to guard the hen house." He chuckled, "I guess you could call this a real, inside job."

Fred rose from in front of the computer and deposited five discs into an inside jacket pocket, "Well I guess that it's payback time for dear Edward here. Reanna wants him finished off and we owe her, big time. Can you figure her? Have you ever heard of one woman taking on three men like that? That was some orgy! That slave of hers, Sebastian, he put on some show, didn't he? I thought that woman was going to do us all in, for good."

"Not even in my wildest dreams, Fred, not even in my dreams. Remember, she promised us a second go, if we pulled this off the way she wanted. Do you think we'll be up to it, if we can catch up with her again, I mean?"

"I hope you remembered to take your vitamins John," his partner said, laughing loudly.

"What are we going to do with this guy and his pooch?"

"Well she wants him finished off for good and we have this charge set for eleven - fifteen, so it'll go off during the fireworks, just as Reanna wanted. That'll be an hour from now, so we'd better throw him in this closet just across from the computer and the bomb. He won't be able to get out of there and this bomb will decimate everything in this area."

They took Edward's arms and wrapped his wrists together with duct tape. Then they put a piece across his mouth, and, without even turning the closet light on, they hauled him and then the drugged dog, into the dark storage closet. Fred slammed the door and blocked it by propping a chair under the doorknob. Not having any further cares about Edward, they left the lab and got into the elevator.

"Do you think we have any chance of getting together with Reanna - the sex-crazed, for another orgy as she promised?"

"I think that if we were ever to have that opportunity again, there's a good chance that we both might not live through it. Remember that she needed us alive to do her dirty work for her, this time. We might be better off just to consider ourselves extraordinarily lucky, and leave it at that." John wasn't laughing now. He had sensed something evil about that woman.

After disabling the elevator so that no one else would be able to go to the third floor seeking the missing Edward, they left the elevator on the second floor as to not draw any unwanted attention. They walked calmly to the gymnasium and once inside, they escaped through a window. Not wanting anyone to notice them leaving the grounds, they got into their hidden delivery van, changed into delivery uniforms and simply drove off of the island.

"Well that's two less guards that Edward's estate will have to pay," Fred said, chuckling. He was driving and once on the mainland he pulled over at an inconspicuous spot and parked the van, facing the island.

"What do you think you're doing?" John asked.

"What do you think," he said, as he made himself comfortable, "I wouldn't miss this fireworks show for anything!"

Chapter 30

$\mathcal{E}$dward woke up with that sweet taste still in his mouth, his head resting against the dog's side. It was very dark. He had no idea of where he was. The feeling of the dog's hair against his face was startling. He took in a long nasal breath, trying to allow his head to clear so that he could think more effectively. His hands were stuck together in front of him. Who ever had done this hadn't even thought it necessary to fasten them behind him. He was glad for their overconfidence. They must've thought that he'd be unconscious long enough for whatever it was that they'd planned. They hadn't even taken his weapons. He took in a more careful breath, through his nose, utilizing this as an investigating tool. Realizing that his mouth was covered, he reached up and tried to remove the tape. This wasn't going to be an easy task, considering his mustache. It turned out to be a very painful ordeal. Recognizing the scent of the dog brought new fear to his mind. Had they killed him? No he could feel the dog's side faintly rising and falling. He could just barely hear a faint heart beat. Jake must still be unconscious. At least he's still alive. He remembered now, he'd been coming up to the lab with one of the new guards, and seeing Jake lying in front of the lab door, he'd knelt down to help him, then the guard must've covered his nose and mouth with something. That smell and the sweet taste must be halothane, an inhalant anesthetic. "What is going on!" he exclaimed, trying to shake the cobwebs from his brain.

"Here I am in the dark with a drugged dog and feeling still a bit high myself. Well, at least whoever did this wasn't a killer, at least as far as I can tell." He brought his hands to his mouth and discovered that they'd also used tape on his wrists. With his fingers he eased one of the stilettos out of its sheath. Putting its handle between his teeth he carefully started to cut the tape. It was very tough so this took some time. The dog started to stir a bit.

"It's ok Jake," he mumbled, to the dog as he worked away at the restraining tape. Eventually he cut through it after inflicting a few minor cuts. He then rolled over and sat up, rubbing his mustache and lips. Now that he was turned around, he could see a crack of light under the door. He reached out to his right and felt the leg of a shelving unit. He then crawled to the crack of light and felt his way up the door. Using the doorknob he was able to get to his feet. He felt for a light switch and finding it, turned it on.

The light was far too bright at first, between having a dreadfully painful head and being in the dark so long. He scrunched his eyelids together tightly then slowly tried to open them again. "It's the lab closet!" he exclaimed. His next move was to check the dog to see if he had any other apparent injuries. Finding none he patted him on the head, "You'll be alright Jake after the drug wears off. Take your time old man." He got up to check the door. He couldn't budge it. "What is going on out there?" He put his ear to the door to see if he could hear anyone, but couldn't hear anything except some loud ticking.

"There's no clock out there." He froze in that position as the truth hit him like a well aimed axe. "A BOMB!"

"They do mean business," he muttered to himself, "How can I get out of here and warn the others?" Then it dawned on him, "The dumb waiter. It wasn't meant to carry people or even dogs, but it'll do. The villain must not have turned the light on in here or he'd have seen it. Chalk one up for the good guys."

The small elevator was a four-foot cube. Edward put the dog in and shoved him to the back, and then sat in beside him. He reached around to press the last button down and got his arm back in just in time before the door slid shut.

The little elevator had just started its decent, when there was an earth shattering blast. Edward's hands flew up to cover his ears. The cube tilted a bit sideways, its cables screeched as it continued a now laboring trip to the main floor. Debris began raining down, loudly pelting on its top. Because of its awkward tilt, it was scrubbing against the wall and sparks were flying. The cube lurched sharply, again, as the cables shredded further. Edward had no way of knowing how far they were from the bottom of the shaft, at the main floor supply entrance next to the kitchen. He held his breath. There was a final PING as the last cable broke and they dropped. The small elevator hit the bottom of the shaft with a bone jarring crash. Edward's head rebounded off of the door casing. Jake let out a startled yelp. Luckily, they'd been just ten feet from the bottom. Debris was still raining down the shaft. Edward recovered quickly from the jolt of the crash. Thank God it hadn't fallen from any higher.

The door only offered to open about a foot and a half, and then jammed. It was open far enough; Edward managed to get to his knees and laboriously crawled through the hole, dragging Jake with him. They had just cleared the hole when a huge chunk of stone crashed down on the dumb waiter and totally annihilated it.

Jake was fully awake now, and as Edward bounded toward the door to the hall; the dog was right on his heels. Stone and glass was still falling as they ran down the service hall jumping over rubble, and ducking falling debris, passing the kitchen and the dinning room and skidding out into the grand hall.

People were screaming and crying, not knowing which way to move to escape the falling debris. The building had stopped shaking now and the lights were flickering, threatening to go out. Running headlong, Edward tripped over someone who was lying on the floor in shock. He slid to a stop as he came across the grand hall. He saw that one of the chandeliers had fallen, knocking down two unsuspecting guests. Sylvester was lifting it and helping them up. Everything was beginning to settle down. Edward's eyes fearfully searched the hall. Something was obscuring his vision. He brushed his sleeve across his forehead and eyes, discovering that his forehead was bleeding and that his blood was dripping down over one eye.

Most of the glass of the wall facing the garden was shattered and some was still falling. The man in the devil costume, and a guard were trying to keep people back away from that area.

Dr. Adams, with the head of the Stag costume now discarded, had formed a triage area in a more stable part of the lounge and was attending to first aid. Emma was helping and May was sitting on a nearby couch trying to calm Anna Belle. Neither of them was hurt. Emma saw Edward coming and she pointed toward him to show his anxious daughter. She jumped up and ran to him, "Daddy, you're here, but you're bleeding," she said, reaching to hug him around the waist.

"Yes dear, I'll be fine," and looking to Emma he asked, "Where are Maria and Brian?"

Emma had been in the process of exclaiming, "Thank the Lord Edward, you're alive!" Having heard his question she stopped to think, "I don't know Edward, the last time I saw Brian, he was going out the door with someone; and Maria, the last time I saw her, she was going down the hall towards the library with you."

"What? I went to the lab. I didn't take Maria to the library," Edward stammered wildly, wiping the blood away from his eyes again. He stopped, trying to pull himself together, "Has anyone called out for ambulances and the fire department?"

"Yes, thankfully the telephone line is still intact," Bill Adams said, coming over to where Edward was. He then reached out and swabbed his patient's forehead with alcohol and slapped a bandage over the laceration.

The searing burn of the spirits helped Edward to clear his mind; "You're doing a great job Bill."

"What happened, does anyone know," Emma asked.

"Someone set off a bomb in the laboratory, trying to kill me," Edward answered, looking around searching every group of people that he could see. "Where can Maria be? Anna Belle, stay with Emma and May," he said over his shoulder, as he headed toward the library.

Just then David Cook came running in and caught Edward's attention as he was about to leave the lounge. David was so breathless that he was bent over at the waist and holding onto his knees trying to get enough oxygen to speak coherently.

David had run all of the way from the boathouse, spurred on by the earth shaking blast that had decapitated the manor house right in front of his eyes. He finally reached the manor and as he had vaulted over the front door that stood half fallen across the opening, he was thankful to see that there seemed to be fewer injuries then one would have expected. Just as his legs were about to give out, he saw Edward who was about to leave the hall so he ran to Edwards side.

"Mr. Edward," he said, stopping to try and breathe. He struggled to speak again, for he carried a most important message. "They took Maria!" he puffed, "They have her on a yacht," he struggled again, "Brian's on the boat too, he's stowed away in the dingy."

Edward took hold of his shoulder, "Who took her, who was it?" he said, franticly.

"I don't know!" David gasped, "A big guy and a tall, slim, dark haired woman who was wearing a costume just like yours."

"Reanna!" Edward blurted, his face had gone white. "It must be her." Edward turned, and bolted across the hall. As he reached the door, he turned long enough to say, "David, please help here and then stay with Anna Belle and Emma." Then he was gone into the dark, with the house still creaking and groaning, some people crying and others helping their friends.

Chapter 31

$\mathcal{E}$arlier in the evening, Brian and David Cook had created and enjoyed an intriguing game of guessing the identities of the vastly incongruous costumed guests. This observational pastime had entertained them for most of the evening, for seeing that neither of them was accompanied by a personage of the opposite sex, it would seem that taking advantage of the music and the dance floor was out of the question. Brian, who had a love for boating, made a suggestion that the best vantage point for enjoying the fireworks would undoubtedly be from out on a boat. David, not having anything better to do, agreed with this and they decided to walk to the boathouse.

It was a glorious, moonlit night and the walk along the narrow, paved, ribbon of road, under the pines, was both invigorating and placid. As they reached the boat yard, before they went inside, Brian was surprised to see a large yacht tied up to the outside dock closest to the cave. He asked David to sit on the bench just outside the boathouse and keep an eye on things, while he went to check this yacht out.

"I don't know of anyone who was invited to the ball that might have come by boat or why anyone would've parked it way over there," Brian said, "I'll check it out and see if I can find out whom it belongs to." As an after thought he added, "If you see anything unusual go back to the manor and get Edward. Something just doesn't seem right."

"Sure Brian," David answered, as he sat down. From the bench he had a clear moonlit view of the yacht.

Brian boarded the yacht and first examined the pilot tower. Finding nothing to indicate the ownership of the vessel, he descended below deck to investigate further. Before he got very far he heard voices. Someone was coming. He peered out a porthole just in time to see two figures trudging through the sand, coming from the direction of the cave. The bigger figure was carrying something that looked like a body, slung over his shoulder.

Brian had just enough time to run back to the aft deck. He frantically looked for somewhere to hide. The voices were getting louder now and he could hear their footsteps on the dock. There was a dinghy hanging from the back, with one corner of the cover not snapped down. He made a run for it, flung the cover up and dove inside, hitting his head on a seat and his knee on the side. "Oow, I hope they didn't hear that bang," he thought, "It's ringing pretty loud on the inside of my head."

Just as he pulled the dinghy cover back down, he heard the voice of a woman, from just beside the boat, as she stepped on board.

"I never dreamt that this would be so easy," she said, gloating as he heard her boot heals clicking on the yacht deck. "I have his precious kitten in my clutches and in a few minutes he'll be toast."

Brian thought that the female voice sounded familiar and he turned around soundlessly to peak out through the hole, which he had come in through. A figure stepped into his line of view. It was the Buccaneer. His heart jumped, he was about to call out happily to his brother when in one movement this Buccaneer reached up and pulled the scarf and hat off. Black hair cascaded down her back as she turned and looked right past him, toward the manor.

Reanna! He had almost blurted that name out, and as he reached to cover his mouth with his hand, a freezing chill ran down his spine.

There was a thud on the deck, as a large male trudged onto the deck carrying a body. He unceremoniously swung the burden down and let it bump onto the deck, "You could've helped me a bit, unless you don't mind if she has a few more bruises," the man grumbled. Brian strained his eyes to see who the captive was but it wasn't necessary, for as the ruffian turned her over toward Brian, the moonlight caught the full glory of the jewels around her neck. There was no doubt. It was Maria, either unconscious or dead.

"Take our pet below to the special cabin," Reanna ordered.

The fireworks had begun and Reanna stayed on deck to watch the cascading colors. Brian couldn't budge from his hiding place; he had seen a gun in her hand. Something had really tickled her fancy, for she was laughing hysterically. What was that she'd said after she'd come aboard? Something about having his kitten and he soon being toast? Did she mean Edward? What could she have done? His only hope was that David had seen them and had gone to get Edward. The banging of the fireworks and her unsettling laughter rang loudly in his ears.

The man came back on deck and readied the yacht for launching.

"Take your time Sebastian, I want to see the grand finale," Reanna said, through that wicked laughter.

David had seen the two figures emerge from the cave, with the man carrying a woman's body in a flowing gown. The moonlight danced on the jewels hanging tangled in her hair. He also saw Brian dive into the dinghy, just in time. David knew that it was time to go for help. He started to run towards the house, hoping that he'd be able to quickly find Edward. Before he was half way there, a devastating explosion literally rocked the ground so fiercely that he had a difficult fight to stay on his feet. He looked up thinking of the fireworks, when to his horror the whole top floor of the manor blew upwards into the black sky that had only moments ago been lit with the pulsing color of the pyrotechnics. His mind was stunned but his legs kept on running. Bits of stone and glass rained down on him through the pine trees overhead. He hadn't thought it possible, but he ran even faster.

As he got closer, his eyes scanned the manor. Although most of the upper floor near the center of the house had been blown away, luckily because the main structure was stone and steel, it looked as if there was little or no fire. It was a good thing that it hadn't been the older part of the house.

He must find Edward!

Chapter 32

After removing Maria's gown, Reanna took her own Buccaneer costume off. While she was still naked, and Maria was under deep sedation, she lay down behind Maria who had been dropped onto the bed on her side.

The two women lay naked on the large bed; the upper satin sheet lay rumpled at their feet. As her unconscious captive breathed deeply, Reanna traced over her sleeping form with gliding fingertips, stroking, and petting. Kindling her own smoldering fire, Reanna wondered if through her drugged, state Maria might sense this tactile stimulation.

She whispered next to Maria's ear, "And if you do, I hope that you'll mistake my touch for Edward's, only to make your future realization of his death all the more poignant." Reanna rose up on one arm from behind her peacefully slumbering captive. She kissed her own fingertips and traced Maria's full lips.

"What a beautiful kitten you are, 'Edward's Maria'." Her finger tips stroked down under Maria's chin and down her neck, until they reached the delicate point of one of Maria's softly rounded breasts. Reanna delicately pressed a kiss on the curve of Maria's neck. She had no intentions of halting her own mounting urges. She cupped her captive's full breast roughly in her hand; her own body reacting involuntarily in a stiffening, sexual spasm.

She lay back behind Maria now, enjoying the thrill of the spasm and the scent of the body beside her, she relaxed into the movement of the boat rocking on the waves. There was no stemming the sexual tide that had begun to wash over her. Her pleasure glands were swelling and her juices gathering to overflowing. She imagined a drop falling onto her inner thigh and she was stiffened by another hot spasm. Reanna reached one hand down, stroking between Maria's buttocks, but before she could reach Maria's cool, inner thighs, Reanna's sexual hunger rocketed toward ecstasy, and withdrawing that hand from Maria, she slipped it between her own thighs. Her other hand cupping her own taught breast, she rocked back and forth with the motion of the boat, moaning deeply as she attained full, intoxicating release.

As Reanna recovered, her first thoughts were of Edward being blown up, amidst the festive fireworks. How fitting! And now she had his little sex kitten as her captive. The triumphant captor rose slowly from the bed, pressed a kiss on her fingertips, and touched it to Maria's buttocks, before she pulled the satin sheet over her prisoner.

"I believe the game will be quite different when you're awake," Reanna said, as she pulled on a black, skintight, body suit with a zipper down the front and a wide belt, which partially concealing her gun. She removed Maria's engagement jewels from her unconscious body.

"Thanks for the gift Edward, sweetheart. It's very fitting that I should have them, now that you're no longer with us." She laughed as she collected up her costume and Maria's gown, making sure there was nothing left in the cabin. She left the barren room and Maria, her captive, never knowing of the liberties that had been taken. Reanna quietly locked the door and went up on deck.

Sebastian was expertly piloting the yacht through the night. He smirked as he noted the rosy glow still adorning his partner's face.

As a survivor of frequent encounters, he was very familiar with that glow. He'd guessed that the quiet comfort of their captive wasn't the only reason why Reanna had instructed him to take his time. He'd learned over time that jealousy concerning Reanna's sexual prey was wasteful and indeed even dangerous, should she sense it. He was more than willing to accept her veracious appetites as he reveled in being allowed to take part on some occasions, in being a small part of her life and her misadventures.

Sebastian was a tall, broad shouldered, pretty faced bull. Reanna had found him in his native country of Greece. He'd been drawn to her enigmatic energy like a moth to a flame. Her accelerated sex drive and her money kept him inevitably enslaved. He would follow her anywhere just as if he truly did have a ring through his nose.

Brian could see them both clearly now, but he also saw that they were both armed. He'd have to bide his time and wait for just the right break. In his resourcefulness he had quietly lifted the dingy oar out of the ore lock and had it ready. It'd be his only weapon, so he needed just the right chance to use it.

Reanna spoke to Sebastian quietly, smiling and rubbing her hand up and down over the contour of his backside.

Earlier, after Maria's captors had abducted her from the library, Reanna, Sebastian and the hiding Brian had heard the catastrophic explosion at the manor, just as their yacht had pulled away from the dock. Maria on the other hand, had been dead to the world as Sebastian had carried her from the library, through the tunnel and cavern, across the beach, onto the yacht and had deposited her onto the bed that she was on, so she had no idea of the mayhem back at Sinabar.

Chapter 33

$\mathcal{M}$aria now floated only half conscious, languidly confused, under the last throws of a drug induced sleep. She was in a large bed that seemed to be levitating up and down, slowly, methodically undulating.

There was a constant, low droning sound, relentlessly intruding on the rosy, warm glow that still enveloped her senses, as she was rocked rhythmically.

As a few more senses fought their way toward alertness, she began to realize that there was another sound, a steady, swishing noise coming from somewhere near her head. The luscious warmth, the rocking motion and that constant sound, whispered to her that she didn't want to wake up.

A fantasy stirred within her mind, suggesting that maybe she was a tiny infant, back in the comforting confines of her mother's womb. This soothing, mental image flitted through her brain; however a more powerful entity from deep within, knew that it must struggle to awaken her. It must fight through the plush comfort, the sensual movement, and this overwhelmingly seductive feeling of extreme well being.

She stretched luxuriously, feeling the strong, elastic power of her muscles and the cool gliding of her taught flesh between the lustrous, satin sheets that caressed and engulfed her naked body. This felt heavenly!

NO! NO… reverberated on the inside of her skull, FIGHT IT! FIGHT IT! FIGHT IT… Fight this seduction of your senses.

Her inner strength was winning out. Seconds later she stretched again, her eyes sluggishly pushing open. Her numb mind still couldn't fully react to the imminent peril, which was her situation. Her senses slowly kicked into gear one by one, laboriously putting together the clues of her nefarious surroundings.

Naked? I'm naked! No wonder these satin sheets make me feel so erotically comfortable, she thought.

"Edward," she whispered, starting to feel a flood of inner warmth, but no, this warmth quickly abated and completely vanished as she realized that he couldn't have set this scene. Her groggy mind slowly pulled the facts together; the rocking, the swishing, the droning of an engine, and the tiny yet luxurious room. "It's a boat. I'm on a boat!" she exclaimed.

Maria struggled once again to clear the residual drug affect from her mind. "What happened, how did I get here? Why?"

⚜

She began to roll back time, to recall her last memories.

I was dancing in the grand hall at Sinabar, when that woman, Reanna, Edward's ex-wife, made sexual advances toward me on the dance floor and forced me to go with her to the library. Reanna had been dressed in Edward's costume, which had made it possible for her to trick me into this compromising situation. Then after threatening violence to get me into the library, Reanna tried to continue her lured advances. I succeeded in pulling out of her grasp and managed to move around the room to stay out of her reach.

Reanna appeared to become quite relaxed then and even more confident. She tried to lead me into a discussion about Edward's sexual prowess. I tried to change the subject by mentioning the work that I was going to be doing with Anna Belle, as I continued to maneuver to keep the desk between Reanna and myself.

Apparently, Reanna wasn't to be dissuaded, "Edward hates me!" she spat out as she strolled around the room, hands clasped behind her back.

I remember thinking that somehow this woman knew about the strong connection between Edward and I, and she now wanted to try to further intimidate me. Reanna's speech became light and coy as she continued ranting, "He hated my lust for the fairer sex, as well as men. How ludicrous he was. He could never tolerate the fact that while I enjoyed our own steamy sex play; I was also 'playing' with a few of the young women of the household staff, how selectively sectarian of him. I hadn't let any of my 'fem. play' interfere with his time with me. I simply recruited the girls to fill in for the times that he chose to immerse himself in playing with his test tubes." Reanna had chuckled lowly, letting her upper lip turn up distastefully into a sneer. She advanced toward me, forcing me further back toward the bookcase, behind the desk, as she continued, "After I seduced the girls into my way of... doing... things, they enjoyed me and kept very quiet about our little rendezvous', but then Edward had to walk in on three of us one afternoon; and that spoiled everything."

I said nothing, as I backed away quickly to stay out of this depraved woman's reach.

I was almost pressed back against the bookcase.

"I'm afraid that Edward's great pride was sorrowfully bruised," Reanna gloated, and laughed quite loudly.

Maria remembered that her gaze had been riveted on the other woman's hideously contorted face. She had heard a sliding sound somewhere behind her but before she had been able to act, a large hairy arm had clamped across her chest from behind and simultaneously she had felt a needle jab into her gluteus maximus. All she had remembered after that was Reanna saying, "Now I'm going to doubly enjoy my revenge on Edward for imprisoning me and then exiling me, by taking my time ravishing his little lady and by seeing to it that they are never together again," followed by that villainous laughter that haunted her, even now, through her memory.

Chapter 34

*M*aria pushed herself up on her elbows. She couldn't believe all that had happened.

She shook her head and reached for her necklace. It was gone and so were the earrings.

Reanna must have taken them from her. The remembrance of that woman's contorted face and the images conjured up by her last statement, made Maria's flesh goose bump. What could she expect next?

"I've got to do my best to avoid further drugging, I must stay alert. Edward will come. Someone will come," she said, out loud in order to make these statements more convincing. Now her mind was able to start dealing with the physical realities of her situation. The luxurious comfort and warmth of her drugged state was completely worn off now. Shivers ran down her spine. There were no clothes here that she could see.

She stood up and leaning on the bed, ripped the sheet off of the bed and wrapped it around her torso like a cocoon. When trying her sea legs, she found that it took a few minutes to get used to the motion. She reached for what looked like a closet. It was completely empty. She walked over to the larger, main door and of course it was locked.

Maria shook her head to clear the cob webs away. Reanna was her captor and there was at least one accomplice. She remembered nothing after the drug had taken effect and she had collapsed into the burly arms of the person behind her. What could Reanna possibly want with her? She remembered the woman's distorted sexual appetite, which Edward had alluded to, and that Reanna herself had reveled in telling her about while they had been together in the library. A new chill ran over her flesh.

But why take her on a boat? Surely Edward and the others would realize that she was gone, but how would they know about the boat?

Who would come through that cabin door next? Would it be Reanna or a man? Years ago when Maria had mentally confronted the monumental controversy of how to react in a possible rape situation, she had weighed carefully, the information which she'd gleaned from actual reports and her own personal reaction and physical ability. She felt that having a strategy in mind, just in case, would be half of the battle to decide whether the victim managed to survive or not. The personal stand that she had come to; if the perpetrator had the upper hand, was to seem to comply with the attacker's wishes and wait to get him in a vulnerable position and then while he is off guard strike out with everything you have. Unfortunately, she'd never figured on having to use this strategy to protect herself from a woman. It wasn't hard to know where you could do the most damage to a man, but a woman? Maybe in this case the best target would be the solar plexus, just under the rib cage or the head. Having come to terms with this, she decided that the only thing that she could do for now was to make herself feel as secure as possible. She had no intention of letting her attackers have things their way without a battle.

She took the sheet that she was wearing loosely wrapped around herself and tore a strip from around the bottom. She then wrapped the sheet tightly around her this time, tucking in the top corner, securely between her breasts and wrapped the torn strip around her waist, several times, tying it tightly at the side, being careful to tuck the ends in. This action alone helped to build her confidence. She felt better, having her body snugly girded and her arms and legs free of encumbrances. Now she needed to do some deep breathing, to relax and re-energize. She sat on the edge of the bed, facing the door, praying to God that He might give her calm and much needed resourcefulness, but mainly that He would send help. This made her think of Edward. Was he all right? Could he possibly know that Reanna had abducted her, by boat? How could he suspect that? She remembered the sound of the sliding bookcase and Edward telling her about the tunnel from the house to the cave by the boathouse. Everyone's attention would've been on the other side of the island, because of the fireworks show. He'd have no way of knowing. He might even think that for some reason she had just left on her own.

Surely, he wouldn't believe that she had just left him.

⁂

Some time later the door opened quietly and there stood her nemesis, Reanna. Maria automatically stood.

"Why Maria, your fashion sense is simply stunning, even now," Reanna purred, "How resourceful of you!"

"Why have you taken me from Sinabar, and where are we going?"

"Away from destruction and into chaos," Reanna quite matter-of-factly stated, as she walked over in front of a long mirror on the wall and stood admiring her figure, sliding her hand from just above her waist, down over her hip, as if stroking a cat. She also watched Maria, in the reflection of the mirror.

"What do you mean...What destruction?" Maria asked, uneasily, as she stood not moving from the bedside.

"Oh! Forgive me, Maria, I'd forgotten that you were in la-la land when the really big boom sounded." A surreptitious smile crossed Reanna's face.

"The really big boom, you mean the fireworks?"

"No, no Maria," Reanna said, turning to face her prisoner in order to catch the other woman's full reaction, "The really, really big boom, when I blew the grand manor up, up and away." Reanna gestured upwards with her arms and an explosive smile.

This verbal blow was far greater then any physical blows that her captor could've dealt her. Maria's knees buckled and she sank down onto the side of the bed. Reanna moistened her lips, slowly, with her tongue. She was enjoying this, savoring it.

Maria blinked several times and tried to push a word out of her mouth, "W... why?"

"Oh, let's just say greed, hate, passion, and ego. Roll that all together. Yes, that would answer why," Reanna appeared very much like a serpent, her tongue flicking out occasionally, as she spoke.

This woman truly is a demon. Of this Maria had no doubt. "What about Edward and Anna Belle, your own little daughter?"

"That little... 'Edward's creation', simply leapt from my loins!" Reanna spat. "She was never mine, she was Edward's little prize. I never wanted her! And as far as your new love, Edward, he'll be dead for sure, blown to pieces. I left explicit orders that he was to be tied close to the bomb. Just what he deserves for trying to rule my life. So now - one, two, three, I've gotten rid of them all. First his parents in England, then Edward himself, the little brat, that naïve, blonde Mallory and maybe even the brothers, all gone in one big finale to their wonderful, fireworks show. What a blast!" Reanna chuckled merrily. "Edward's finished, I've got you, and the fewer the family survivors, (and I don't expect any), the less court battle for the money," she paused theatrically, "Ah ha! Now, can you see why I'm so ecstatic? You and I are here, the deed is done, and there'll be no one left to say that I was even on the island. Sinabar is now history, and I've got my revenge on a plate and served up with all of the money too."

Maria's mind wasn't yet registering much of Reanna's sadistically gleeful tirade. She sat stone-faced with only her eyes showing any reaction. Her spirit was searching, calling, Edward, Edward!

Reanna once again turned to the mirror, laughing quietly now, seemingly self absorbed in her glowing victory. She smiled at herself, as she craftily checked Maria's reflection to observe her numbness; looking for any sign of her victims pain and possible weakness. Seeing none of this, she wheeled around and left the room, slamming the door loudly this time before she relocked it.

Chapter 35

*R*eanna joined Sebastian once again at the helm. "You did disable all of the boats at the docks, didn't you, Sebastian?"

"Yes, they've no way of following us, even if there are any survivors. I cut all of the ignition wires," her handsome partner said, smiling smugly.

"Good fellow." Reanna purred, as she leaned against her comrade and kissed him heatedly. When he was willing to pull himself from her grip, he asked, "Why are we headed in this direction? It would've been so much shorter to just cross the lake and have the car waiting."

Reanna was annoyed at his simplicity. "This is yet another safety measure, my dear fool. If there was anyone who might have noticed us on the island and suspected that we'd left by boat, they'd check for us along the immediate Canadian coast and also straight across the lake. No one would be apt to check the farthest, tourist ports."

"Very well El Capitan!" Sebastian smiled, and snapped to a salute.

"It should take us about an hour to get there and Franco will be waiting with the limo. We'll have to sedate her again," Reanna said as she stretched, "Do you still have the Demerol?"

The tall, bronzed, muscle man nodded. Reanna smiled and started down the stairs again, "Join us in the cabin in fifteen minutes. Have yourself and the injection ready."

<hr>

Reanna had left Maria sitting on the bed, after deflating her with the news of the bombing of Sinabar. With this report of the subsequent death of Edward and probably many others, still ringing in her ears, Maria maintained her existence by deliberately breathing deeply and slowly, fighting to center herself. Every part of her mind and spirit was reaching out to Edward, "I must rely on my instincts now," she whispered, to herself, "Edward, you are not dead! He is not dead!"

Maria lay back on the bed, gathering her energy. "This woman... This monster doesn't know who she's dealing with." Deep from within her, a new strength began to well up. She had never before had to fight for her own life or for that of a loved one, but it looked as if this time she might be forced to do just that.

She heard someone coming down the hall. She positioned herself on the far side of the bed, on her side, facing away from the door, eyes closed. The door key turned and Reanna stepped into the small room. As before, she wore the skintight, black spandex, body suit with zipper front and a wide belt around her thin waist, over accentuating her ample bust line. Maria could see her image in the mirror, through partially closed eyes. This time Reanna had dramatically added to her attire. She was wearing the emerald and diamond jewelry that Edward had so lovingly given Maria. Maria held on to her anger, tightly, quietly, waiting for the right opportunity to unleash it.

"Hello again my pet, are you well rested now?" Reanna asked, with faked concern, "We had a rather heavy petting session, after your arrival, while you were but partially conscious. I suppose, you can't tell me if it was good for you, but I can tell you that it was great for me."

Maria's blood ran cold, but she didn't move. She realized that her taunting jailer hadn't locked the door behind her.

"Come, my pet. It's time to play," Reanna teased.

Maria still feigned sleep.

Reanna, feeling very self-assured, came around the bed to Maria's side and sat on the edge of the bed in front of her captive's thighs. She reached out to touch the presumably sleeping Maria. Maria was prepared. She scissor kicked her top leg over Reanna's head and caught her shocked captor, between her legs, just below Reanna's bust line. Maria snapped back over onto her back, flipping Reanna back onto the bed and Maria up into a sitting position with Reanna still wreathing between her legs. Reanna's arms were momentarily trapped with her upper body as she tried to twist her way free.

Maria took her one clear chance at a good shot. She clenched a fist, aimed and punched with all of her might at Reanna's nose. Reanna had been flopping like a beached barracuda, but she managed to turn her head at just that moment so that Maria's blow caught her across the cheekbone.

Maria's other hand had gone for Reanna's hair. Reanna's head lolled back momentarily, but she had wiggled loose enough to reach around her side and toward her gun that had been concealed in the back of her belt. In Maria's assault with her hands, she had unfortunately loosened the grip of her legs. Reanna had used this chance to jerk the gun out of her belt, bringing it up between Maria's thighs and right into her face.

"You play rough, little one," Reanna gasped, breathing raggedly as she moved her other, now free hand, up to her cheek, "I think I'm going to need some ice."

Now staring into the barrel of the gun, Maria heaved an exasperated sigh, unsnarled her fingers from Reanna's hair and threw herself back onto the bed.

"I'd prefer not to have to use this gun just yet, so don't try my patience again," Reanna said as she got up from the bed and was now leaning on the wall, "If I had to shoot you now, we'd be missing out on a lot more fun. You've surprised me, Maria! I had you pegged for more of a kitten than an alley cat."

Suddenly, there was a loud, crashing noise from the other side of the boat. Reanna made a dash for the doorway and out into the hall, not bothering to even close the door.

Chapter 36

*I*n reaction to David Cook's reported sighting at the dock, Edward ran like he had never run before. He headed for the boathouse. As he ran under the pines, he heard the fire trucks arriving. He couldn't think about that now. He knew that the situation at the house would be taken care of. All he could think about now was Maria, and the fact that she could be in Reanna's hands. David's description of the abductors was vague, but Reanna had jumped into his mind as if she had willed herself there.

He tore into the boathouse, pushed the door behind the speedboat up and jumped into the speedboat, turned the key and nothing happened. He reached under the dash and came up with the severed wires, "Damn," he swore. He leaned over the back of the boat and scanned the watery horizon. He squinted hard and could just make out the lights of a boat, heading southeast. He scanned again. There were no other lights anywhere to be seen on the horizon.

"That's got to be her, at least I know what direction they are headed." He quickly checked the ignitions of all of the boats, but as he had suspected they had all been disabled. He ran to the tool room, got wire strippers and electrical tape, and started to work on the speedboat's wiring. It seemed like it took forever but soon he was roaring out of the boathouse in the direction that he'd seen the yacht's lights fading away earlier. If they haven't changed course I should be able to catch them, he was thinking. What then? I should've stopped to get a weapon, but then I would've lost too much time. Which of these options would be of more importance? Maria in Reanna's hands for any amount of time is too much to risk. What I find when I catch up to them will tilt the scales.

He stood above the windshield, hoping to see more clearly but the wind beating against his face making his eyes water soon drove him down behind the glass. He must clear his eyes for the search. Thank the Lord that it isn't a bit foggy tonight, and, for that full moon. It'll make any light surface shine. They'll also have a fair chance of seeing me coming, so there's no point in my trying to come along side quietly. I'll have to run up along side of her and take a leap.

He was running the boat at full throttle, and with the aid of clear visibility, it wasn't long before he caught sight of a light and the glimmering outline of the yacht. That's got to be her. Please God! Who else would be out here running this late at night, and at this time of year?

Sebastian had been so intent on where he was going and thinking about what was going on down below, that he hadn't noticed Edward's boat gaining on the yacht. He heard its engine only moments before the speedboat hit up against the side of the stern of the yacht.

"What the Hell ..." Sebastian exclaimed as he jammed the controls into automatic pilot. He then nimbly climbed down onto the main deck, shouting, "Reanna get up here!"

The moon was so bright that it was almost like daylight, except for an eerie silvery glow that touched everything. Things happened very quickly, but to the participants of this deadly dance, their movements seemed as if happening in slow motion. This scene would've appeared as a glowing, two-dimensional movement in real time.

When Brian heard the speedboat engine and the crash against the yacht, he ripped the snaps of the dingy cover open and with an oar in hand he landed on the stern deck.

With the momentum of the crash Edward had been catapulted, instead of successfully jumping, up against the stern deck railing.

As Sebastian jumped the last two steps from the pilot deck to the stern deck, his attention was on Edward. As he landed, his gun was already being aimed at Edward who was clambering to get over the railing. Sebastian then caught sight of Brian's movement out of the corner of his eye, but before he could swing his gun around to bear on Brian, he felt as if a bomb had gone off in his head as Brian's oar met the back of his skull.

Edward had managed to get over the railing, but before he could advance, Reanna startled both brothers by rushing onto the deck from below with a gun in her hand. She took two steps out onto the main deck and shouted, "Stop, you fools!" and took a deep breath. Sebastian had collapsed unconscious, onto the deck. The two brothers froze not knowing whom Reanna would take her first aim at. They had a second to look from one to the other and back at Reanna's gun.

Brian made a move to throw the oar at her like a javelin, but Reanna got one shot off which deeply grazed his shoulder. The oar clattered to the deck beside her feet. Brian had seen where Sebastian's gun had hit the deck and he managed to take a dive in that direction.

Maria charged up from below, tackling Reanna around the waist, stopping her from having time to train her gun on Edward. The force of Maria's tackle took both women careening into the railing at the back corner of the deck.

Brian retrieved Sebastian's gun and rolled into a firing position.

Edward ran to get between the two women. Reanna struggled to gain her footing and bring her gun around to bear on Edward or Maria, whoever was in front of her. She stabilized herself preparing to fire from where she now leaned on the railing. Edward grabbed Maria and pulled her away from Reanna.

Just as Reanna was ready to squeeze the trigger, Brian fired. Reanna was hit and the force toppled her over the low railing of the yacht's stern.

Maria had fallen to the deck quite heavily, so Edward knelt down beside her to make sure that she wasn't injured. He cradled her to him. "Are you alright?" he gasped.

"I've just got a few bumps and bruises, Edward. Where is that woman?" she asked, glancing toward the railing where Reanna had gone over.

Brian took a look overboard and then realized that the yacht was still moving. He climbed up to the pilot deck and after pushing the throttle into neutral, he turned to shout to Edward, "Where did she go overboard?"

Edward straightened up so that he could see over the railing, "Must be about a third of the way back, between where we are now and where the speedboat is floating."

Sebastian, who had been knocked out cold, was now starting to come to. He lay on the deck moaning. Edward jumped up and getting a rope out of the dinghy, he tied the henchman's hands and feet together.

Brian put the yacht into motion and turned it around, stopping part way back to where the speedboat was. They all scanned the surface for any sign of Reanna. Edward was straining his eyes in vane. "We'd better put down the anchor and radio for help. I hope we can reach the O.P.P. from here." Brian went to do this as Edward and Maria stood on each side of the bow, studying the surface without seeing any sign of the body.

"I can't see any sense in diving now, when we don't know exactly where she went in," Edward spoke, with great concern.

Maria agreed and added, "It must be very hard to see under water when it's dark, even with the aid of the moonlight, although the jewels may still sparkle. She would have to still have them on."

Brian came down to join them, "I got hold of the O.P.P. It'll take them at least three-quarters of an hour to get here. Any sign of her?"

Bitterness had seeped into Edward's voice, "No, thank the Lord! I hope that she's gone for good!"

"I've never shot a person before, but to tell you the truth, I had no trouble shooting Reanna." Brian spoke, meekly, "She's given us so much pain in the past and she was trying to make sure that none of us had a future." He turned to Maria, "Are you really all right my dear, I know that she must have been shamelessly taunting and abusing you?"

Edward had torn off both of his sleeves and was making a bandage and a wrap for Brian's shoulder. Luckily, it was only a flesh wound and he was able to stop the bleeding.

Maria moved closer to Brian, "Well, let's put it this way; I've had better dates." She tried to chuckle as she carefully put an arm around him and hugged him warmly, "I think it'll take us all a little while to get over this experience." As she smiled up at Edward, she added, "But we won't let it put off our wedding, will we Edward?"

"What, you've got it planned already?" Brian asked. "I'm so happy for you both." He gave them both a gleaming smile, "But I'm even happier for Anna Belle. She'll finally be getting the mother that she needs." He gave Maria a big hug. "When will it be?" he asked.

Edward spoke up now, coming out of some serious contemplation, "Next Saturday, if this problem causes no further complications. Yes, it'll be as soon as possible," he shot Maria a conspiratorial glance. "We've already wasted too much time, haven't we Maria?"

"Oh, really? What do you mean?" Brian asked, from under furrowed brows.

"That's an answer that we'll gladly give you, at another time when we can sit down and give you a full explanation," Edward said, closing the subject for now. "Maria wouldn't you like to go below and have a rest until the authorities get here?" he asked, and as he led her to the stairway and below he continued, "I'm sure that they'll need to question us when they arrive."

"As long as I don't have to lie down in that seduction pit again," she answered, shakily.

Edward looked at her with great concern, thinking to himself that the authorities weren't the only ones that would want to know just what had happened to her, but he would leave that for another time. "I'm sure that we can find you another cabin. You'll need some rest."

Brian knew that his brother needed to talk with him before the police arrived, so he sat and waited for him to return. The sky was already starting to get brighter and the water even calmer, as his brother joined him once again on the main deck.

"Edward, what happened at the house?" was Brian's first concern.

"Anna Belle and Emma are fine. They're just a bit shaken up, but there were many people injured. I don't know about Gregory and Mallory. Bill Adams had already started to gather up the injured and was administering first aid when I left. At least one of the men from the security agency that I hired to keep Reanna out was actually an espionage agent who must've been in collaboration with her. I think they might've been trying to steal the files on my latest nutritional science research, but that black hearted bitch must've also given him extra inducement to murder me and others by blowing up the manor," Edward quickly explained.

"Oh my God, Edward! We had no idea of the extent of her wickedness," Brian exclaimed.

"Well you know, Brian, I've a feeling that we still don't have a full picture of Reanna's evil excesses."

"What are the conditions at Sinabar?"

"As far as I know, the bombers misjudged the integrity of the manor's structure. From what I could tell as I was making my hasty departure, a good part of the third floor (being the lab, and my suite) is now missing and there may be internal and ceiling damage on the central, second floor. I heard the fire trucks arriving as I was running to the boathouse. I'm hoping that there wasn't much of a fire problem," Edward explained.

"I just can't comprehend the extent of this whole situation, Edward, and the violence that has taken place this evening. It started out as a celebration and ended up almost killing us all." Brian was shaking his head slowly, and then as exhaustion welled up over him he rested back against the deck chair and let his eyes fall shut.

"Reanna has obviously been planning this for some time. She had to have shopped around until she found a powerful ally, with enough clout and resources to pull this off. There are mega-corporations that would benefit greatly from having a preview of my research files before my work is made known to their competition and the general public. You might say that they'd be able to make huge profits by being able to beat the others to the market place."

Brian was shocked, "Did they get to the files?"

Edward started to laugh sardonically, "You know, I don't think so. He took me to the lab and if they did succeed in hacking their way into that computer, then they'd only have found false files under the headings that they would have looked up. They were simple enough to think that I'd have the culmination of my work stored on that computer. If they copied those files, their employers are going to be in for a rude surprise. I dressed those files up to look like the files that they'd have benefited from, but when they call the actual work up, all they're going to find are computer games. Someone is going to get a shock. The bulk of my research wasn't on that computer at all." Edward and Brian laughed together, more out of release of tension and relief, then actual merriment.

"Edward, how do you think the investigation of this incident will go?" Brian asked, with a worried look.

"Brother, please don't have any doubts. You did what had to be done. If you hadn't taken control of the situation and fired on her when you did, one and probably all of us, would have been dead before this was over," Edward said, reassuring him.

"I know that now. It's just that I never would've thought that I would be able to kill anyone, even in self-defense," Brian admitted.

Edward got up and clapped a hand on his brother's good shoulder, "Try not to think of it that way, Brian. You saved my wife-to-be and me from sure death, and we'll be in your debt forever."

"Thank you brother, I'm just delighted for you and Anna Belle. Now you'll have a chance at some normalcy. Maria seems to be a wonderful person. Congratulations!"

"The thanks go to you Brian. Do you think that you'll be able to oversee the rebuilding of Sinabar, while we're away on our wedding trip?"

"After we make some plans, I'm sure that I'll have no problem. Will you be away long?"

"We haven't finalized our plans yet, but I'd like to take Maria to Monaco for several weeks, alone, and then take her to our estate in England. I think we'll have Anna Belle with May and possibly Maria's daughter Sylvia join us there, for an extended holiday. Particularly to get away from the chaos here, but also, neither of my ladies has been to England yet."

They had noticed a cruiser approaching for the last few minutes, and now it was pulling along side. The brothers welcomed the officers aboard and sat down to tell them the whole, incredible story.

Chapter 37

"*W*ell, Mr. Warner, we won't need to question Ms. Stark right now, you'll want to get back to your house to see how things are there. I'll speak to her later, which will be soon enough. If your ex-wife has been under water or out of your sight all of this time, I think we can assume that she's dead, especially if she was wounded. We'll be sending divers down as soon as it's fully light. We'll be confiscating the yacht and we'll be taking Mr. Sebastian into custody pending charges. We have his gun and from what you say, the gun that the woman had must have gone overboard with her. So the three of you are free to take the speedboat and head home, if the boat hasn't been disabled."

"Thank you, Constable Harmer, for being so considerate of my fiancée. We'll be waiting at Sinabar to see you later on in the day."

Brian had gone with another officer in the cruiser, to get their boat. Edward went to Maria, woke her up gently and lifting her up, carried her from the yacht to their waiting boat. She was exhausted. She just partially wakened and leaned comfortably against Edward's chest. They said goodbye to the officers and he cradled her back to sleep as Brian piloted the boat home. Luckily, it was almost fully daylight now and the water was calm.

The damage to Sinabar manor house was quite evident from the water, even before they docked. Maria was stunned by it, not having heard the full story as to what had happened. Edward tried to fill her in as they got into the Explorer that had been left at the boathouse for them and they traveled the stone littered road back to the manor. He explained once again, about the state that things had been in when he had run to the boathouse, but most importantly he assured her that Anna Belle, Emma, and May were alright.

When they got out of the truck in front of the manor, the three of them stood looking up at the ruined part of the house. Maria then stepped between the two men and taking them each by the hand, said, "Structures can be easily rebuilt, it's our loved ones that are important. God has seen fit to protect them and us, so let's join them and give thanks."

Anna Belle was with Emma in her office. Hearing them coming, she along with four dogs ran to meet them with Emma following close behind, scolding the Great Dane for knocking over furniture in his exuberance to see them.

"Daddy, Maria, and Uncle Brian, you're alright! We didn't know where you were. It's been so exciting here. Mallory and Uncle Gregory had to go to the hospital. The guards have been stalking around checking everything. People have been calling to see how we are," all of this was a steady stream, pouring out of Anna Belle's little mouth.

Maria and Edward had bent down to her level and her arms hung around their necks, hugging them tightly. "Slow down Anna Belle, we can't keep up with you," her father chided. Standing up again he reached his other arm out to Emma and pulling her to him he hugged her.

"How are Gregory and Mallory?" he asked her quietly, while Maria distracted Anna Belle by playing with the dogs.

"Mallory was cut quite badly by falling glass and Gregory broke his leg while trying to rescue her. He had picked her up and was attempting to get her to Mr. Adams to stop the bleeding when he tripped over several, large pieces of stone that had fallen from the second floor. They were both taken to the hospital in Toronto.

Anna Belle dodged away from Maria and ran to Brian, who momentarily forgetting about his shoulder leaned down for her to throw her arms around his neck. He picked her up and being quickly reminded about his wound, grimaced for a second but didn't make any move to put her down.

"Brian, you need to have one of the drivers take you in to the emergency to have that shoulder taken care of," Edward was saying, "I'm going to call Bill Adams to see if he can see you there."

"Daddy, can I go to, for the ride?"

Brian looked from Edward to Maria for their reaction. They both nodded in affirmation, so Brian answered, "Sure she can come along to hold my hand, then later we may stop for a treat." He took the little girl by the hand and started towards his wing. "Let's go to my room first, so you can help me change my shirt," he was saying to her, as they left.

Edward took Emma by the arm and led her to one of the comfortable sofas in the lounge, so that the three of them could sit in comfort together. "What damage do we have to deal with?" he asked Emma.

"Well Edward, it's quite a mess, but it could've been a lot worse if there had been more fire involved. The elevator is out of course. The central part of the third floor has been obliterated, though I imagine you noticed that from outside. The ceiling over Anna Belle's suite is gone, but surprisingly there is only minimal damage to the contents, and the same is true of the bedroom part of Ms. Maria's suite." She stopped here and looked to Maria, "May is moving your personal things, Ms. Maria, to the gold room in Brian's wing."

"Thank you Emma."

Emma resumed her report to Edward, "Pretty well all of the glass in the second floor central hallway has shattered, as well as you can see here in the grand hall and the solarium. Flying stone from the third floor smashed many of the windows facing the garden side.

I've sent for tarpaulins to cover the exposed, second floor rooms and much of the furniture up there is being moved into the gymnasium, which hasn't been seriously damaged by the blast."

"No, I hadn't noticed much of the interior damage, as we came in. I only had eyes for Anna Belle and yourself," he said as he leaned over and hugged her again.

Emma's eyes filled with tears, "Thank you Edward, we were so worried about the three of you, not knowing what had happened to you or what had caused all of this destruction."

Edward grimaced now, "We can sum it up in one word Emma, and that is 'Reanna'. It's quite a story and you'll hear it all later on. There'll be some police officers coming to talk to us later today, but I can happily tell you that the villainess is gone for good."

Maria asked, "Emma, what about the guests, were there many injuries?"

"Oh yes! I had totally forgotten the other people," Edward exclaimed.

"Other than Mallory and Gregory, there were fifteen other people injured, that I know of. Most of the injuries were from the glass or falling stone, because the people were near the glass or out in the garden watching the fireworks. Elderly Mr. Costa, from the vineyard, had a mild heart attack just from the shock and commotion. Mr. White, the cabinet minister, has a fractured shoulder. While in the middle of the garden, he was struck by a falling, stone block as he attempted to shield his wife. She has a sprained ankle and some bruises. When the stone started raining down, what hit the patio, bounced back into the wall of glass, sending the shattered glass everywhere; flying glass shards caused so many of the injuries. Mallory has a large cut down the side of her face and other cuts to her shoulders, chest and arms. Dr. Adams was luckily able to stop the bleeding in time. She'll probably need corrective surgery. Along with Mallory and Gregory, Mr. Costa and Mr. White were taken to the Toronto hospital. Many of the others, less seriously hurt were taken to the hospital here in town. We are very lucky that

Dr. Adams was here. He was wonderful!" By this time tears were running down Emma's face.

"I'm sure that you've been wonderful, as well Emma," Maria purred, as she patted Emma's hand, "You need to take time to rest now."

"I've kept Anna Belle right with me and busy doing things, so that she wouldn't have time to remember too much and worry. I didn't know quite what to do about the manor, so I just put all of the staff to work cleaning and covering things in the exposed areas. Falling stone also smashed down on many of the cars that were in the parking yard."

"Emma, don't worry any more. I'm here now and I'll take over. Was your apartment damaged?" Edward asked.

"No, just minor, some cracked windows."

"Are the kitchen staff able to function?" Edward asked.

"Yes, the firemen turned the gas and the power back on after everything had been checked and the lines to the lab and your suite were capped off. The kitchen had only minor damage."

"Fine, then. I would like you to leave orders for your meals and other needs with the kitchen staff, and I want you to spend the day in your apartment resting. Maria and I can take over from here and May and Brian can take care of Anna Belle," Edward said, in an almost ordering tone.

"But Sir, there is so much to do, people to contact and deal with..." Emma objected.

"Emma, if I know you, there's already a list sitting on your desk of everyone to be contacted. We'll tend to that. I must call Bill Adams and have him meet Brian at the emergency, and also call Gregory. Oh, by the way Emma, this'll be a quick way to break in the new Mrs. Edward Warner to be. Yes, life with the Warner's. Are we having fun yet?" he said, with a mischievous grin as he gently pocked Maria's side.

Emma's jaw dropped.

"Yes Emma, you heard me right. Now, I didn't think that I could shock you any further. We will be wed on Saturday."

"B...but, but the arrangements..." Emma sputtered, through a big smile and more tears, tears... of joy this time.

"Whoa, right there. Most of the arrangements are already made. Now scat. Go languish in your rooms or take a walk in the woods, but get some rest. It's going to be a hectic week and we need you well rested. I don't want to see you until lunchtime tomorrow, and yes, please join us for lunch so that we can talk further. We'll manage just fine for now." He helped her up and feigned pushing her in the direction of her room. "Do me one last duty though. Please call May from wherever she is and ask her to meet us in your office."

Emma knew that there was no more use in trying to protest, so she left to find May. What wonderful news, she was thinking. Her cherished Edward was going to marry the love of his life. She sensed that Edward and Maria where made to be together and that they and everyone around them would experience new joys in life. It was hard for her to leave her post, with all of the pressing duties, but she knew that Edward was thinking of her well being, so she did comply, with new warmth shining in her heart.

May met Maria and Edward in Emma's office. Emma had spilled the glorious, good news. There had been such a shortage of good news lately, that she just couldn't help herself. The only part that had surprised May was how soon the wedding would be, under the present circumstances.

They had ordered a big breakfast, to be served in the office.

"May, I'd like you to help Maria this morning while Anna Belle is with Brian, but this afternoon I'd like Maria to have a rest, so could you take Anna Belle shopping or do something in town just to keep her mind off of the problems here? And also, May, I'd like you to keep her with you tonight. Emma is on leave until noon tomorrow," Edward requested.

"Yes Sir, I'd be delighted to spend time with the dear girl!"

Maria and May discussed what needed to be done first while Edward made his phone calls to Bill Adams and Gregory. His brother assured him that he was well, except for the broken leg and that he'd be home tomorrow. However, Mallory would be staying in the hospital for at least two weeks. She was having some specialized surgery.

"Gregory, I don't want to get into details about this crime, on the phone. We'll have a talk when you get here. But I'll tell you that it was Reanna and that she tried to murder us all, with considerable help from others, so you see it's a good thing that Mallory isn't going to be here for a while. I'll see you as soon as you get back. Oh, and also Maria and I are to be married on Saturday. Thank you. Goodbye."

"Well my dear, we won't have to worry about having Mallory at our wedding. Because of her need for surgery, she'll be in the hospital for at least two weeks," Edward related with a tone of near satisfaction. "Can you two ladies call the florist and send an arrangement to each of our unfortunate guests with a copy of this note?" He read the note aloud, as he sat and wrote it: "We are gravely sorry that you were subjected to the violent explosion during our masquerade ball. We hope that you are as well as can be, and that if you have any problems due to the crime that was perpetrated against us, please contact us. There will undoubtedly be further information about the bombing in the news media. Sincerely, Edward Warner and family."

"Yes, we have the guest list and we can attend to this," Maria said.

The doorbell rang and May went to answer it. Maria and Edward were looking over a brochure of floral arrangements and making a decision, as to which arrangement would be suitable.

May interrupted them momentarily, "Sir, four men have arrived together. I've shown them to the library to wait for you and Ms. Maria. One of the men is O.P.P. Constable Harmer. What would you like me to do in the meantime, Sir?"

"Well, we'll just turn our plans around a bit. The investigators will probably need to speak with Brian when he gets back, which should be soon. When he arrives please ask him to wait for us in the lounge. Then you could take Anna Belle to town and also stop at the florist. This is the arrangement that we've chosen. Take the guest list and this note with you and see that the florist takes care of sending them all out. That would be very much appreciated, May. Oh, and also find something else to occupy Anna Belle and yourself for the rest of the day."

Chapter 38

$\mathcal{E}$dward and Maria walked arm in arm to the library. Maria was thankful that they'd taken time earlier, to change and freshen up. Edward introduced Maria to the officer in uniform, Constable Harmer, whom had taken Edward's and Brian's statements on Reanna's yacht in the wee hours of the morning. Constable Harmer, then introduced them both to Constable Bill Campbell of the R.C.M.P., as well as agents Edwards and Morris from the F.B.I.

Edward was anxious for a fresh update, "Constable Harmer, was there any sign of Reanna as a result of your search this morning?"

"No Mr. Warner, there has been no sign of her, the jewels, or her gun. The search is still going on."

"Mr. Warner," Constable Campbell started, "later in our discussion it will become apparent as to why we are all here. We've all read the statements that you and Brian Warner gave Constable Harmer earlier this morning. Now, we're all starting on the same page. Could you please start us off by telling us what you know about Reanna Barton?"

Edward gave them what information that he knew of her background, which wasn't a lot, also he told them what she had done to his family and where he had been sending her settlement checks. He also told them that his sister-in-law had foolishly carried on correspondence with her behind his back, and that she was likely Reanna's source of information to plan this whole crime, as well as her method of gaining entry and having an exact copy of his costume. Then he went over everything step by step, from the time he left Maria's side at the party, to when he met Constable Harmer on the yacht.

Maria sat through this, silently taking in all of the details. It all seemed to her like a nightmare that must have taken place long ago.

Constable Campbell woke her from the nightmare, "Ms. Stark, may we call you Maria?"

She nodded. "Yes, please do."

He went on, "We know that this has been quite an ordeal, especially for you. It seems that this woman went after you singularly. It appears that she arranged for the espionage agents to do her dirty work for her, by killing Edward after they retrieved the files that they wanted, and then she personally went after you. Can you tell us what happened from the time that Edward first left you on the dance floor?"

Maria was prepared for this. She hadn't told Edward anything about the details, before hand, but she was prepared now. It was like she was in a trance. She began reliving each step and each fact in great detail. She even included her feelings and mental insights. The men sat back and watched her relive the entire event. When she finished explaining the fight on the deck and Reanna toppling overboard, one of the F.B.I. agents said quietly, "I wish every person abducted or every witness could explain the whole event with such clarity and insight." The others murmured in agreement.

Edward discreetly dabbed at moisture under his eyes. He rose and went to comfort Maria, reassuring her that it was all over now and that this should never have happened to her.

Constable Campbell spoke up once more, "Mr. Warner, did the spies get what they came for?"

"No, gentlemen they did not. All they got were a collection of computer games, disguised to appear to be my project files. Luckily neither Mallory nor Reanna knew that I had a new computer room added on to this library last summer. My files are on a computer that is concealed quite well," Edward explained, now sporting a sly smile. "My fiancée is safe. My project is safe. Now, if Reanna is out of our lives for good, we'll be able to count ourselves blessed."

Constable Harmer said in answer, "I doubt that there is any possibility that your ex-wife could still be alive, in that depth of water and so far from land."

Agent Edwards of the F.B.I. spoke up next, "Mr. Warner, does your brother Gregory know about your computer in this room?"

"No, as a matter of fact, I think it was installed while he was away. My brother manages our family's original business of agricultural produce marketing and shipping, from an office in his wing and the main office in Toronto. He has a management staff there but he still travels quite a bit.

"Does he ever have business reasons to travel to say, Iran or Iraq?" the agent asked.

"Yes he does. We've been promoting our exports to those countries for the last two years." Edward answered, with a quizzical look. "Why do you ask?"

"That brings us to why the F.B.I. is being represented here," the agent continued, "Well before this bombing took place, we were getting to the point in a very crucial investigation where we were going to have to come and interview you. The bombing worried us and compromised our investigation. It has also given us an opportunity to talk to you about this other matter, without tipping our hand and scarring anyone off. Although, it could somehow turn out that these two situations are parts of the same matter. You see, we, being agents of the F.B.I., may be here under false pretences.

"What is this other matter? Why is there the need for these slippery tactics?" Edward was more than a little annoyed.

"Please calm down Mr. Warner," F.B.I. agent Morris spoke up, "I'm afraid we have further bad news for you. We've had your family under surveillance for four months now, and when Ms. Stark turned up here, we checked her out also. The good news is that Ms. Stark checks out to be exactly who she says she is, with no criminal ties and squeaky clean."

"The nerve...!" Edward started...

"Hold on Sir. You'll see why we have had the nerve, and the right," agent Edwards put in.

Agent Morris continued, "Your brother, Gregory Warner has been implicated, and evidence proves this out, as an arms trader and smuggler."

Edward jumped to his feet. "You've got to be totally out of your minds! Why would my brother need to be involved in anything illegal, especially something so vile?"

"Please, Mr. Warner, sit down and we'll tell you of the evidence that we have," pleaded agent Morris.

Maria went to Edward and taking his hand, she led him to sit beside her on the sofa.

The agent continued, "We have video tapes showing Gregory in New York City, making deals with a known arms trafficker, and we also have tracked illegal shipments from various ports in the U.S. to your family's warehouse in Toronto. We also have shipment, flight records from Toronto to these various, unfriendly, countries. We didn't want to make any bust until we knew who in your family, was involved. We have been investigating you, Brian, and then Ms. Stark. We found that none of you seem to be involved with Gregory and his actions, so we were ready to take action tomorrow. Then the bombing took place and shook everything up, possibly revealing a new angle to this whole thing. Although, after hearing your story about Reanna, I can see no obvious connection between these two crimes. We understand that Gregory will be getting out of the hospital tomorrow."

Edward sat in silence, staring straight ahead.

The other federal agent asked, "Mr. Warner is there any possibility in these situations... that Gregory and Reanna may have anything to do with one another?"

Edward still stared straight ahead, "Apparently, anything seems to be possible, judging from everything that has come to light in our lives in less then twenty four hours. I seem to have no idea of what is going on. Why... why would he do something like this, he certainly doesn't need more money?"

Maria spoke up softly, "Sometimes there are other reasons, beyond money."

"Mr. Warner, we have a proposal to put in front of you," agent Morris suggested, "We need you both to be very quiet about this right now. Don't tell Brian yet. If Gregory comes home tomorrow, would you please ask him to come into the library to talk about the bombing? Then just to see what he has to say, lead him into the subject of irregularities at the Toronto warehouse and then mention that you've heard whispers about possible illegal activity. We'll be behind the false wall and we'll also have the room bugged."

"Would you like me to give you my brother on a silver platter? Is that what you're saying?" Edward stormed.

"We know that this is a terrible shock for you, on top of what happened yesterday and this morning, Mr. Warner. However, this way we can assure you that it'll be much safer for your brother, than if we have to bust in on him at the warehouse. We're prepared to give you the choices here; which option do you think would be the best course of action?" agent Morris asked.

"We'll see, we'll see... bug the room and come tomorrow, and hide in the tunnel. We will see." Edward looked twenty years older and he sounded hollow.

Constable Harmer spoke up next. "In regard to the other matter, the abduction of Ms. Stark and the suspected death of your ex-wife, Reanna, we find that your stories all substantiate one another's. Also, what you've had to say, jives with what we've found out so I'll be writing this case up and classifying Reanna's shooting, as self-defense. Due to Brian's involvement in the shooting and as a formality, I'll have to speak to him again and have him sign a statement. Reanna's accomplice, Sebastian, will be charged with conspiracy in Ms. Stark's abduction and confinement, and possibly other conspiracy charges."

R.C.M.P. Constable Campbell spoke up and explained that as far as the bombing and industrial espionage went, there would be a full investigation and that he'd also be working in co-operation with the F.B.I., on their case. He then stated, "We'll all be working on these cases and I assure you that we'll strive to protect you and the rest of your family from any further problems."

Edward asked, "Will there be any problem with Maria and I leaving the country on Saturday? We're to be wed and are planning to leave for Monaco, Saturday afternoon."

Officer Harmer spoke first, "Oh my! Congratulations! As far as the O.P.P. investigation goes, I can't see any problem as long as you let us know how to reach you if there should be any other developments."

Agent Edwards chimed in, "Congratulations! If everything goes well tomorrow with Gregory, and we have a confession out of this, then it shouldn't be a problem."

Constable Campbell came over to shake their hands, "It appears that you are a lucky couple after all. I dearly hope that you'll have some peace after this blows over. Why don't you go and rest while Constable Harmer gets Brian's final statement, if he's here, and then we'll all be gone out of your hair for now? We'll come back tomorrow morning to set up in here and hopefully that'll be over quickly."

Edward rose and holding Maria's hand, they started to leave the room. "I guess that I'll have to see you tomorrow. I don't expect Gregory much before noon, so you'll have ample time to set up. I'll send Brian in, he's probably back from the hospital by now."

They left the library, and, walking hand in hand, they met Brian in the lounge. "Well old boy, they say the abduction and Reanna's death is a cut and dried case. The different agencies are here to investigate the subsequent bombing and industrial espionage. They just need your final statement," Edward said, and then on second thought he asked, "Are the adjoining gold and green rooms in your wing open for us to use?"

"Yes, we thought you might have need of them. Emma had already arranged to have them prepared," Brian answered, with a small smile.

"Thank you brother, I think we need to have a rest," Edward explained, "May will take care of Anna Belle and I've also sent Emma to have a rest. She's worn to a frazzle. Can you meet me here around three thirty so that we can survey the damages and make some plans?"

"That sounds good. You two need some time alone together."

Maria was dangerously near to tears as she said, "Thank you Brian, for everything."

Brian went to the library and the tired couple walked along arm in arm, slowly, not saying a word until they reached the first guestroom in Brian's east wing.

They entered a richly appointed room that appeared to be right out of a Victorian movie. The heavy furnishings were of dark, waxed wood, standing on a dark green, wine and beige, Indian rug. The large window was dressed with luxurious, heavy, green velvet curtains and the walls of the spacious room were hung with beautiful, pictorial, British hunt tapestries. The focal point of the room was a huge bed and on the opposite wall was a massive fireplace with an ornately carved mantle. Two sumptuous, wine colored leather armchairs awaited them, facing the already glowing fire.

Edward noticed Maria's look of wonderment. "Brian loves the rich, Old World style. His rooms have been left quite, completely original, except for a few, modern comforts that have been added."

"It's a manly room and very lush. I like it. It has a strong, comfortable feel about it," Maria observed.

Edward checked to see if the door of the adjoining room was unlocked. It was, so they also peered into it. This second bedroom was a similar style, only the decor was done in gold accents instead of green. He slipped his arm around her waist and was holding her loosely. "Which room would you like my dear?" he asked in a heavy, English accent.

"Either one, my love, as long as you are in it. I need to lie in your arms and just talk and sleep. I feel numb and just a bit lost."

"Come, I'll comfort you and keep you safe. We both need a rest and we can sit and talk later on." He led her into the gold room.

The first thing she wanted to do was to change into something more comfortable, so she investigated the closet. "Someone was very thoughtful. My things are already here." She chose a comfortable, velour dressing gown, went into the bathroom, stripped down, freshened up, and put the dressing gown on. When she came out, he had already stripped down to his shorts and gotten into the bed. She looked at him quizzically and he said, with a mock frown, "I said I'd comfort you and that we'd rest, that's all, ok?"

"Ok." she said, and climbed in beside him. "I'm too numb to think any more," she declared, with tears starting to sting her eyes again.

"I know my love, I feel the same way," he kissed the tears from her cheeks, and pulled her into his arms. "Just sleep, my love." And they did.

Chapter 39

*M*aria woke first to find that she had turned in her sleep. She was now lying on her back with Edward facing her, on his side, with his arm draped comfortably across her waist. By just turning her head slightly, she was able to lay still and watch him sleeping. She was thinking, what an incredibly attractive man he was. His finely trimmed mustache aided his already debonair appearance. Her eyes wandered over his exposed arm; just enough muscle to have good definition and plenty of strength, without being bulky. Her appraising glance traveled back and rested lovingly on his face.

He's so gentlemanly and considerate, each time that we've been together and now in this bed, he's been content to kiss me and hold me, never pushing for further gratification. Never have his lips been demanding, she continued to ponder. She well knew that a lesser man wouldn't be capable of exercising such restraint. Yes, she knew that he craved more of her, as she did of him, and if he hadn't shown such restraint she would've crumbled and given in to that shared, physical need. No wonder she had loved him from one lifetime to another, over and over again. Comforted by her thoughts and his radiant warmth, she let her mind wander through that deeply embedded knowledge that true everlasting love had won out this time and that they were going to get to enjoy that love for the rest of this lifetime. They would continue to love and protect each other and watch each other's backs. This time their relationship had the added benefit of the knowledge that they were meant to be together, that there was this time, as before, a higher reasoning for their being together, nurturing one another. They also knew about the evil that could engulf them if they weren't vigilant and prepared for it. A shiver ran down her spine and brought her back to reality.

Scanning for a sense of the time of day, she spotted a beautiful clock on the mantle. One thirty, Edward was to meet Brian at three thirty and they needed to have something to eat. She turned on her side to face him and slid her fingers through his luxurious hair. Softly she kissed his cheek.

"That is precisely how I'd love to be awakened every morning," his voice was rich and husky from sleep, "at least when you're awake first."

"I will love to oblige you, my lord," Maria answered, seductively. Her eyes widened and she pushed herself up on one elbow, having realized what she had just said and how it sounded.

"Need I ask where that phrase came from?" he asked, with a swarthy smile on his lips.

Maria rolled her eyes as if looking inwardly, "I don't know Edward. It just slid out and then seemed so appropriate."

"Is this a flash back from another time, perhaps?" Edward mused, as he sat up, pulling the sheet up with him.

"You know, I haven't had any more dizzy spells and visual or emotional spells since we were regressed. It's as if the spells were a force that was trying to bring our past lives into today's focus. Like the Lord on high was trying to make sure that we came together and He was also warning us of the evil around us, to kind of stack the deck this time around. I feel sure that was what was happening to me, so, thank you Edward and you to Lord," she said, looking up, "for knowing how to help bring us together and our past-lifetimes together into focus."

"I'm very glad that you're so strong about this my dear," he said, reaching out to stroke her hair.

"Now, I seem to sense little things that I hope will enhance our relationship." Something stopped her before she went on, "Does this 'other lives, bits and pieces' bother you, Edward? Do you feel that it'll take the freshness of our 'getting to know one another' away?"

He grinned, "Not at all. I am, however, a bit jealous that you are so sensitive to these remembrances and I'm not... as least not yet. I think it will add many extra dimensions to our relationship. Maybe you can teach me to be more open to this sensitivity to our past, or maybe it'll just rub off, literally," he said, as he reached out and pulling her to him, he squeezed her tightly.

She giggled, "I woke you now, because you're to meet Brian at three thirty and we need to eat."

"Yes your ladyship," he snapped his hand up as if in salute, "we shall eat. You get some clothes on and I'll order a late lunch and have it served in the lounge."

As she was changing behind a very elaborate, Victorian dressing screen, he went into the adjoining room and picked up the house phone to order lunch. "Which soup would you prefer - turkey vegetable or beef barley?" he queried.

"Beef barley," she replied.

When she was dressed, she went into his room to find him lying on his bed, day dreaming. He was dressed in jeans and a teal T-shirt. She'd never seen him clad so casually. "I like this look," she said, smiling as she sat on the bed beside him.

"All the better to climb through household debris, but if you approve, I'll dress this way more often, at least here at home."

"What'll you do regarding the F.B.I. proposal about Gregory?" she asked, not being able to steer away from the subject any longer.

"I was trying to avoid thinking about it just now but I suppose I must," he said, scowling, as he stared out the window. "The options that they've put forth don't leave much room for consideration. If it must come down to me letting him talk his way into a confession in the safety of my library versus a 'shoot - m - up' bust to catch him at the warehouse, surrounded by weaponry, I must choose the deception in the library. Is that how you see it?" he asked.

Yes, I must agree with you. Have you ever seen any evidence of his being capable of doing what they've accused him of?"

"No, I mean not something illegal like this. He's always been very business minded and very capable of running our businesses, so I guess I'd have to say that he definitely can be shrewd in his dealings." He laughed sarcastically, "I suppose he's gotten very good at marketing and transporting, so he might have found it challenging to move into more dangerous, but above all, illegal goods. I had no idea that he might aspire to such levels. No wonder he and Mallory haven't had any children, he's been too preoccupied with making deals, living on the edge and trying to stay ahead of the various agencies involved. Our business has been showing a profit all along. I wonder how entangled it and we are with his illegal business," he stated.

They got up and left the seclusion of their temporary rooms.

"Maybe you've answered your own question about why. Maybe it's the danger and the excitement of this other life that has seduced him into crime. That might be your answer," Maria speculated.

Edward looked at her with yet even more admiration and gratification, "You'll always amaze me, I'm sure. You're an exceedingly intuitive person," he said, hugging her to him as they walked toward the main part of the house.

"I'd never have dreamt of Gregory doing such a thing. This makes him a pirate. I'll let the agents set the stage and I'll try to get him to talk about his other life. We'll see what happens. If this works, he may hate me for the rest of his life but at least he'll be safe, I hope."

They came to a window seat, and stopping in front of it, Edward motioned to her to have a seat, "Please sit with me for a few minutes Maria, there's something that I must ask you." They sat in the golden rays of sunlight and he took her hand, "Do you remember the very frank conversation that we had in the garden just before the disguised spy came and took me away from you on the dance floor? Was it only last night... it seems like at least a week ago? Sorry, I got lost there for a minute. Do you remember that important conversation about letting nature taking its course?" he asked frankly.

Maria smiled sweetly, "Yes, I remember your question and my answer."

He pushed on like an apprehensive teenager, "Do you think that we might be able to check with nature this evening and see what part of the course we find ourselves on?"

"Yes, I think that might be a very good idea."

"I love you completely Maria, and even through all of the discourse around us, I feel blessed and honored," he stated, as he pulled her to him and kissed her as if there was no tomorrow. In this kiss they took strength from each other and flooded it back again, striving to be one with each other. "I do need you so, Maria!" he murmured into her hair, after he had managed to drag his lips away from the delicacy of her mouth for a second, only to search it out again, immediately, not being able to quench his thirst for her. She twined her arms up his back, fingers slipping through his hair, melding her body to his, moaning softly as she gave herself completely to his kiss and his embrace. There was no tomorrow anymore, only the promise of tonight.

They eventually pulled apart, both panting and flushed. Maria couldn't get a word in here anywhere, for as soon as he was able to, Edward was saying, "I didn't dare mention this subject while we were in either of the bedrooms, for fear that I'd not be able to contain myself any longer. I love you Maria and I want you to be my wife and my best friend, always." He raised her hand, palm up, and kissed it ravenously.

Maria was struggling to calm herself, trying to stem the tidal wave that had washed over her. She longed to go with it, to ride it till it blew itself out and once again tranquilly lapped the warm contented shore, preparing for the chance to rise again. She formed her words carefully, breathing deeply, "Thank you Edward, without a doubt, I feel the same way."

He leaned toward her as if to kiss her again. She shot her hand up and pushed on his chest to keep him away, "No, don't. If you kiss me again right now, we're going to have to get back to one of those very inviting beds." She looked around to distract herself, "I'm glad this part of the house is so private. Please Edward, just relax for a few minutes and try to think of something else. My legs feel like noodles." She leaned back against the corner of the window seat and closed her eyes, her breathing more relaxed now.

Edward's laughter tinkled like crystal, wind chimes. "It seems that nature can be a bit tumultuous."

They both laughed and then sat back smiling at one another. After a few minutes they were able to get up and resume their walk to the lounge. Maria laughed again, "I think we'd better get to our lunch, we need to replenish our energy!" They walked, arm in arm, to the lounge where a cold buffet had been set out with a cauldron of steaming hot soup. They both ate ravenously, smiling and laughing over the smallest things. Brian came along and joined them, and was a bit surprised by their merriment. Edward noticed Brian's seriousness and made himself come back to earth. "Well Brian, how did your meeting with the authorities go?"

"As well as could be expected, they seemed quite satisfied with what they had heard from the two of you. So after I signed my statement, they assured me that the matter of the abduction and Reanna's death would be closed. That is, except for Sebastian being charged and their needing us to testify when they are able to set a trial date, which seems to probably not be in the near future. I'm still not quite clear on why the F.B.I. agents were involved."

Edward turned away to pick up a piece of dessert, "Maybe they've been investigating Reanna and Sebastian regarding some other crime." Edward turned to Maria, "Well my love, do you wish to walk with Brian and I as we have a look at the damage and decide what should be done? I'm sure we could value from your opinions."

She'd been sitting watching Edward and wondering how she had ever lived without him. "Thank you, I think I'll follow along behind you two and just count my blessings." She got up and putting one hand on Brian's shoulder, she stretched up and placed a small kiss on his cheek and said, "Brian, I just want to give you my thanks and appreciation for being there for Edward and I. I count myself very lucky to have you as my brother-in-law."

Brian blushing lightly gave Maria a warm hug, "Thank you Maria, I look forward to having you in our family, even more then you could know. I feel that you're very special and that you're just what we need to hold us all together."

In that moment it came to Maria that she had known Brian before, that they had been close, maybe as parent and child or as siblings. On impulse she hugged him again and standing on tiptoes she whispered in his ear, "If you ever need me for anything, I'll be there for you."

He smiled down at her rather sheepishly and said, "I have no doubt."

Chapter 40

"Anna Belle, my dear, Maria and I are going to get married this Saturday. What do you think of that?" Edward asked, while assisting her with her chair at the table as they assembled for dinner that night.

"You are?" she squealed, with a mixture of surprise and glee. "Am I going to have Maria as my mother?" she asked, as she got off her chair again and ran to where Maria was already sitting.

"Yes, you are my dear," Maria answered, as Anna Belle was jumping up and down beside her.

"I'm so happy!" the little girl exclaimed, as she reached up to hug Maria.

Edward came and stood behind them and while giving them a joint hug he stated, "And we'd like you to be in our wedding party."

"Does that mean that I get to have my picture taken with you?" she asked.

"Yes, you sure will Anna Belle." Maria helped her up and settled her on her lap, "We'd also like to have you as our flower girl and my daughter Sylvia will be my bridesmaid."

Anna Belle looked up sweetly and asked, "Is she a little girl like me?"

"No she's a big girl and she's away at college right now. That's why you haven't met her yet."

"You mean that I'll get to carry flowers at the wedding?"

"Yes, my dear," her father answered, "Now if you sit down and have your dinner, we'll try to answer all of your questions."

Brian had come in and was seating himself at the other end of the table. "Brian, seeing that we're talking about the wedding party, we'd like to ask you to be the best man. Would you do that for us?" Edward asked.

"By all means Edward, I'd be honored," he said, beaming at his brother and Maria.

"We're going to keep it simple. It'll be at eleven o'clock, with a luncheon to follow. If the weather is nice, we could have the ceremony in the garden. But if it's too cool, we can have it in the chapel, if the glass could be put back in time," Edward continued, "We'll make sure that the cleaning crew concentrates on the garden and the chapel, just in case."

"And I'll make sure that the flowers are beautiful for your special occasion," Brian assured them.

"We'll be gone for an extended wedding trip, Brian, so we need to come to agreement as to the repairs and then we'll leave all of that in your capable hands," Edward said.

"Have you any ideas about the third floor?" Brian asked.

"Well, Maria and I were discussing that just before we came in. How about taking off what remains of the third floor, completely except for the elevator? Then, utilizing the elevator, have a domed, combination solarium and observatory built."

"Well, that's quite an idea. It'd be great to have an observatory totally glassed in. That would afford us all, the enjoyment of that wonderful view from up there. I could grow a whole new range of plants with that amount of light," Brian stated, and then fell silent as he began to contemplate the possibilities. Of course he found this proposal very exciting.

Edward was thinking aloud as he went on, "I won't need that third floor suite any more; there's plenty of room on the second floor for Anna Belle, Maria and I. Oh, and also May of course. When the repairs are finished, we'll have May move into the suite next to Anna Belle's to allow us more privacy and to keep Anna Belle company while we're away."

Maria smiled at this arrangement.

Edward continued on, "And as for any future work that I'm going to need a lab for, it'd probably be more practical to have a separate building across the parking area, beside the road to the boathouse. Actually, maybe it could be tied in with the old footman's building in front of the entrance. It need only be a small, single floor building for my lab and office, but I'll take care of that when we get back. Brian, if you could oversee the house repairs and the building of the observatory that would be wonderful.

Brian sat looking very pleased indeed, as he replied, "I'm thrilled at the opportunity and I very much like your choice of site for your new lab. We won't have to take out hardly any trees and if some mad scientist or spy decides to blow anything else up, it might not affect the manor so much." Everyone laughed with great relief now that they felt that they truly could put that nightmare behind them.

"I guess the new lab building will need its own security system, won't it?" Edward asked, with a chuckle.

This new feeling of freedom and progress set the tone for a very pleasant, family meal time.

After dinner was finished Edward said to Brian, "We'll draw up some preliminary sketches tomorrow, say mid-afternoon. Maria and Anna Belle will be having a busy day at the pet barn tomorrow." Turning to his daughter he said, "Maybe you might be able to have a pony ride tomorrow, little girl." As they rose, he took his daughter by one hand and Maria by the other. "Lets go and build a fire in the lounge and you two can chatter my ears off. Please come along Brian, if you think you can handle the girl talk."

Begging off, Brian wanted some peace to think about the flowers for the wedding and the new plants that he'd be able to grow in the new observatory. "I'll join you later to have something before going to bed," he said, backed away pretending fear.

Edward called after him, "Don't make that too late, we're going to have an early bedtime tonight." Maria gave Edward a veiled smile and Brian smiled to himself as he walked away.

Maria had written Sylvia a letter last week, breaking the news about their up coming wedding. So now she called her to arrange the final details. "Hello dear, how are you?"

"Mother I just got your letter on Friday. You're getting married! Who, where and most importantly, why? Your letter didn't say much other than when... this coming Saturday. Mother, I don't believe this?" Sylvia said, finishing this tirade of exasperation.

"Well, if you'd let me get a word in edgewise, I'd be able to give you more information. Can you leave there on Friday morning?"

"I can leave here on Thursday morning. I don't have any important classes till Monday. Where and how am I to go?"

"We'll send a car for you. It'll be a dove gray limousine. Hold on for a minute." She took the receiver away from her ear to speak to her fiancée, "Edward, could we send the car for her on Thursday morning?"

"Yes, that'd be fine. Why don't you, go too and that way you could take Sylvia shopping in Toronto, for a dress for her and whatever else you may need," he suggested.

"That's a wonderful idea, thank you." She put the receiver back to her ear to resume her conversation with her daughter, "Sylvia, Edward has suggested that I go as well, so that we can stop in Toronto to shop for a while. I'd like you to be my bridesmaid, so we need to go shopping for a nice dress for you."

"You do, thanks Mom. Edward sounds like a great guy, but why so fast?" Sylvia demanded.

"Just wait, you'll understand once we've had a chance to talk... after you get here and meet Edward and his daughter. I'll be there

Thursday morning at nine o'clock. Just pack a few things for the weekend. Bye for now. I love you."

"Well, I guess I'm going to have to stay in suspense for now then. Thanks Mom. Bye."

Edward spoke, looking concerned, "That was short."

"Well, I didn't want to get into too much of an explanation over the phone. Actually I don't know just what to say, yet. I thought I'd just let her get here and see and feel," she said, as she sat down beside Edward and Anna Belle, in front of the glowing fire. "This is going to look like a fairy tale to her, and I want her to understand that this whole situation, especially our love, is very real." They sat and answered as many of Anna Belle's questions as they could. At nine o'clock they called May to come and take the little girl to her temporary bedroom next to May's room.

Edward and Maria curled up in front of the fireplace and stared into the flames. Edward murmured to her, "We're going to help create the very best of lives for our two daughters. If we're going to our estate in north England after our holiday in Monte Carlo and Anna Belle is meeting us there, we'll be spending Christmas in England, so maybe Sylvia would like to also join us for her holidays. Do you think that would be nice?"

"Oh Edward, do you think she could? That would be so wonderful! She's never been away from Canada other than a few short trips into the U.S. It'd be so educational for her. I'm so excited for the girls that I haven't even thought of how excited I am for us." She smiled up at him and he kissed her warmly. Stretching out luxuriously she said, "You know, my love, this is just too much for me to take in. I've always been so financially stressed, paying the bills and managing the business. Just buying Sylvia a suitable winter coat and boots when she needed them, was always a daunting task. I feel a bit off balance now that the stress has been lifted and with all of this talk about travel. I feel just a bit lost."

"Now, now Maria, have no worries. I'll take care of things for now, so you can just relax. However, when you wish to do things on your own, you'll have all of my resources to back you. By Thursday I'll give you your own credit cards, but if you need anything before then, you can take the household card with you. I already have your passport and we'll apply for one for Sylvia. Oh! Did I tell you that we also have a fishing lodge in Scotland? It used to belong to my mother's family. When my grandparents left it directly to me, I was still very young but I remember being quite astounded. I wonder if maybe they somehow knew something that I didn't have any knowledge about, until just recently," he mused with a little, mischievous smile. "Well, anyway, we'd better also visit it while we're over there." They talked for a bit longer, till Brian came in pushing a teacart. On the cart, as well as tea, there was a selection of dainty sandwiches, biscuits and fruit.

"Thank you Brian, this is very thoughtful of you," Maria said, smiling up at him as he offered to pour.

"Well dear sister to be, I've an ulterior motive besides wanting to serve you this repast," Brian said, as he turned and smiled at her, sheepishly.

"Oh?" Edward said, a bit stiffly as he untangled himself from Maria and got to his feet.

"Yes, Maria, I have something that I must divulge to you. I normally wouldn't wish to discuss this with anyone, but as I've come to know you, I believe that I may be frank with you, and, that you might be able, I hope, to be more understanding than most."

Edward, she noted, had clasped his hands behind his back and had started to pace back and forth in front of the fire. In taking her attention away from Brian, just for an instant, he had caused her to noticed that he was wearing his, 'Oh, here it comes' look. So she quickly, shifted her full attention back to Brian who was now pouring the tea. He was carefully, placing Maria's tea cup on the coffee table near her knee. During this delicate process, Brian also hadn't missed this body language exchange, "Yes, Edward is one of the very few people who knows my secret, and I can understand his apprehension in my breaking the news to you, but as I have said before, I can feel that you are a very special person so I am almost comfortable in telling you this now, before you have time to wonder about it."

Maria spoke slowly and with great empathy for Brian, "Yes Brian, please go ahead."

"I'm afraid that I must refer back to the chaos of last night, so please bear with me. Maria, do you remember seeing me talking to someone at the ball, who was wearing a Napoleon costume? Well, that was David Cook. He and I were going to go out in one of the boats to watch the fireworks. That's how we came to see Reanna's yacht. I went aboard it to see if I could find out whom it belonged to. Then Reanna and Sebastian came out of the tunnel carrying your drugged body. I jumped into the dinghy to hide, and seeing this, David ran back to the house to get Edward. Well, the reason that we were there to begin with, was because we didn't have partners for the dance. In short, David and I were on what you could call a date. We are both gay. We don't have a serious thing going on, but both feeling a bit ostracized at the party, we just wanted to get out of here and spend some time together." He let the subject drop there, and waited for her reaction.

Maria slowly got up from the sofa and walked over to Brian, and smiling at him with great affection she said, "I'm deeply moved and impressed that you chose to confide in me." Then she kissed him lightly on the cheek, saying, "Please extend my thanks to David for his part in saving our lives. There are no two men, besides your brother here, that I'd rather have looking out for me and our two girls." Having said this she picked up the tray of dainties and offered them to the two men, "Now, let's enjoy these refreshments."

The two men had both been holding their breath, first in worry about her reaction and secondly, in awe of her grace and wisdom. They now broke into stress relieving laughter, and she joined them.

"Well Maria, I think I can speak for both of us in saying that we are both truly impressed with you and your acceptance," Edward said, as Brian nodded in agreement, having lowered his eyes as he stroked his chin. The men were very relieved that they were all going to be comfortable with one another and very glad that the nightmare of the previous evening could now finally be put behind them.

They talked together for a while, about further arrangements for the wedding. Brian asked, "Will that be two bouquets and a flower basket for Anna Belle? What types of flowers would you like and in which colors?"

Edward spoke up describing Maria's gown to Brian.

"I think I'd like antique white roses with just a touch of fuchsia and light blue, and also green ivy trailing from mine," Maria stated.

"That sounds as if it'll go quite nicely with your gown," Brian agreed.

Chapter 41

*S*hortly afterwards, Maria and Edward were walking to their rooms, "You know my love, your reaction and especially what you said to Brian, was the best gift you could ever have given him," Edward was saying, as he squeezed her shoulders. "I'm very proud of you, and thankful."

"Brian is very dear to me," she said. "His sexual preference makes not a bit of difference to me."

Maria couldn't have possibly seen because of the dimly lit hall, but Edward's eyes had misted over as he became even more serious. As they continued walking, he stared straight ahead and voiced his fears in the form of a question, "Are you truly sure that you still want to marry into such a nest of oddities: a workaholic scientist, a homosexual and a gun running pirate?"

"I've never been more sure, Edward. I'm marrying you because you're the only one for me and we've finally found one another again." She reached up and ran her fingers through his hair as she continued, "About that workaholic part, you're not going to continue on that way are you, now that you're going to have a brand new life with me and the girls?"

"No. I don't imagine that you're going to allow me the time or the energy, my dear, although I do plan on studying this reincarnation and past-life regression science, just a little bit."

They had reached the door to the green room, his room. They went in through it and Maria headed for the door between the two rooms. She turned and looked at him, beseechingly. He answered her unspoken question with a command, "Meet me back here as soon as possible, I'll start a fire for us."

She smiled at his attitude and his inference. After quickly showering, she put on just her dressing gown, and brushed her hair out until it shone and cascaded loosely over her shoulders. May had already turned down the bed and left a carafe of milk beside it. Maria laughed as she ruffled up the bed a bit, and picking up the milk, she knocked on the adjoining door.

"Come in my love," Edward answered. He was sitting in a large chair in front of the fire, wearing nothing other than a handsome, dark green robe edged with fine, gold brocade. "What's that you have there?" he asked.

"Its milk that May has left. She takes excellent care of me."

"May is a dear isn't she? I must remember to give her a raise."

"Yes, especially now that you won't have to pay a coach / companion for your daughter."

"Somehow, I think that having a beautiful wife and two daughters are going to be a whole lot more expensive, but I'll enjoy spending every penny." He motioned to her to come and sit on his lap. "Maria, there's one thing that we've overlooked in our many discussions, and it's come to the time when some decisions need to be made. Are you presently using birth control or have you considered the need for birth control, and if so, what is your preference?"

She was getting used to his straightforward approach and as a matter of fact, she liked it. So as she sat on his lap in the big fireside chair, the fire crackling as if in conversation, she took a moment to breathe in the manly scent of him, which had been further enhanced by a lightly spiced cologne.

Her hesitation before answering heightened the intrigue.

"Well, due to the manner in which you've put your questions, I will reply in order. No I haven't needed it for some time. As to taking precautions, yes, I believe that we should wait till life has settled down a bit before we consider having a child, and yes I have internal birth control available and I've already taken care of it."

Edward appeared dumbfounded. He was stunned at the second part of her response.

She grinned, having beaten him with his own tactic.

He swallowed hard and managed to spit out his response, "Do I correctly understand you to mean that you might, in the future consider having my child?"

"By all means Edward, I'm very excited about having a child with you."

"Please excuse my shock; I hadn't let myself dare to even consider the possibility." He reached out, and taking her hand in his, he pressed it to his lips, still staring into her eyes.

She reiterated, "I'd love to have your child, but for now, I'm prepared to use internal birth control until such time as we've made this important decision together."

"You are an angel!" he exclaimed, burying his face in her hair and hugged her tightly.

The lights had been turned down very low so that the firelight flickered throughout the room. The bed had been turned down. Maria pulled loose the sash at the waist of her dressing gown, so as she stood up and stepped back, between him and the crackling fire, the silky gown slipped silently to the floor.

Edward sat for several long moments, lovingly drinking in every curve of her perfect form, which was silhouetted by the firelight, a vision glowingly framed. He felt the kindled stirring of his loins. He reached out with one hand and tenderly traced those glorious curves with his tingling fingertips. He caressed her thin waist and let his fingertips slowly slip down over the gentle swell of her hip. It had been a very long time since he'd touched a woman, so. He took in a deep, ragged breath, forcing himself to take his time, savoring every slight feeling, sense and emotion, before he would be compelled to let his stronger need take him over.

Maria stood unmoving, her eyes imploring, letting him find his way.

His eyes fastened on hers now and as he was about to stand, she said, "Let your robe fall away."

He pulled the sash and left the robe, like an empty imprint on the chair, as he stepped in front of her. Her hands went out and catching him by his hips, she made him stand away from her. Letting moments pass, she surveyed his elegant body, freeze framing it in her memory.

This was a new and honest introduction to one another, with no shyness and no shame, just loving awareness and sweet appreciation.

"I love you Edward Warner!"

"I love you Maria!"

An enveloping, undulating imagery had been created by the mingling of their forms with the torrid light and energy of the flames behind them, which toiled to devour the darkness. This ravishing new entity reflected, flickering and licking ravenously across their dark shadows on the rich expanse of colorful tapestries which lavishly depicted ancient British lore.

She stepped to him as if drawn by the most powerful of magnets. His arms came around her waist and they melted together. Their mouths met and their own fire took over. He reached down and scooped her up in his strong arms. They were almost breathless now. Her fingers were clenched in his thick, tawny hair, holding his head to hers, caressing his tongue with hers. He turned and carried her to the bed. She pulled away long enough to get into the bed and move over to the middle; the fresh, jasmine scented sheets feeling surprisingly cool against her simmering skin.

After he turned the last remaining light off, the firelight took over completely, sumptuously illuminating their sight of one another, adding even more voluptuous motion to their bodies. Edward slid in beside her so that he lay on his side facing her, his upper arm over her body, "My darling, you have the luscious body of a goddess! I'm overwhelmed by your perfection and your beauty!"

She sighed and stretched, "You aren't so bad yourself," she said, with her best Mae West impression, as she ran her eager fingertips through the light brown curls on his chest, reveling in their tawny, softness. She was transfused with eager tenderness.

He slowly swept his hand down over her side enjoying her ample curves. Then, as he reached back, further behind, he cupping one cheek in his hand, and slid her closer to him. She eased her shoulder over closer and wrapped her arm around his neck. His mouth sought hers once again and this time he marshaled no control over his ravenous desire. He took full purchase of her body and soul, searing her lips, her neck and one of her breasts with his burning lust, as if to consume her.

This further ignited her primal passion and they were recklessly lost in turmoil of movement matching movement, need-quenching need, climax seeking climax.

After they each attained the heights of total oblivion and captured that elusive ecstatic release, they lay spent. They then rolled apart slightly, but not out of each other's arms. That hold was too precious. With each new breath they replenished what had been eagerly spent on the momentary quenching of their shared desire. They now lay beside one another, searching each other's face. In response, a totally blissful smile eased across her beautiful face, and she began to relax. He sighed in relief and smiled in refection. She rolled onto her back to get even more comfortable, so he slid up beside her and put his arm across her waist, nestling his face in her flowing hair.

"Rest well my love," he whispered.

Edward went to sleep thanking God for all of the blessings that He had bestowed on him; the second chance at marriage, the second chance of having children and the biggest blessing of all was the everlasting love that Maria's soul brought to him, yet once again.

Maria was thanking God for His love and His wisdom which had brought her and her beloved together again, for the children that they already had and the possibility of creating new life with Edward.

Their lives had been very hectic and exhausting for the past few days, so they both slept soundly, comforted by each other's presence.

Chapter 42

$\mathcal{M}$aria awakened first, again, in the very early morning. She was well rested. She slid quietly out of the bed, as not to wake him. After going into her bathroom she checked her diaphragm, and after brushing her teeth and hair, she snuck back into his bed. She watched him sleeping for several moments, but her exited anticipation was too much for her. As before, she reached out and ran her fingers through his hair. She leaned forward and was just about to plant a kiss on his cheek when he moved his head so that her lips brushed his.

"Hello, my little angel with the flowing glorious locks," he almost sang.

Before he had time to ask, she said, "I'm well rested, are you?" She was smiling broadly as she stretched seductively.

"What an eager little darling you are, but first I must excuse myself for a moment," he said, as he got out of the spacious, love warmed bed.

While he was in the bathroom, Maria got out of bed and went to the window. She pulled open the heavy, velvet drapes and tied them back. It was a brilliantly sunny morning, one of those wonderfully joyful mornings, which made it difficult to fathom the devastating commotion that had taken place in the past forty-eight hours.

This day is as bright and new, as our new life together promises to be, she thought as she smiled to herself. She opened the window and found that there was a fresh, crisp breeze, which was kissed with a heavenly pine scent, as it blew in from the lake and through the forest. Everything was so fresh. She hugged her naked body, in response to the wonderful, new exhilaration that poured through her veins. Smiling still, she anxiously climbed back into her lover's warm bed.

Coming out of the bathroom, Edward eagerly bounced back into bed, refreshed and smelling very enticing. However, Maria gave him no chance to say anything or even kiss her. She took immediate control of any impending opportunity. She slid her hand down his front, intent on fanning his already obvious desire; she caressed him lovingly, teasingly, as she offered her pretty mouth to his.

After inciting him to hot, moaning delight, she kicked back the sheets and threw one leg over his prone, pulsating hips. He looked up at her in delighted surprise as she expertly mounted him. He momentarily closed his eyes and let her take full command of his movements, his hands kneading her voluptuous breasts, tenderly yet equally demanding, sporadically catching her pert nipples between his sensitive fingers.

Carrying most of her weight on her knees, she created a wonderful posting rhythm, driving him almost to the brink of supreme stimulation, she then slowed her rhythm ever so slightly; roughly tweaking one of his nipples between her fingers, distracting him from the edge, momentarily enjoying the slow motion, only to shift her position ever so slightly and by increasing her rhythm once again heightening the stimulus. This time she pushed her steed beyond any threshold of control. As their mutual explosion neared culmination, she leaned down and lusciously devoured his waiting mouth.

In a crescendo of mutual sound expression, rhythmic movement, tingling nerves, dizzying breathlessness and exploding resolution, together they reached the ultimate peak of supreme existence. Holding it as long as possible; then giving in to their grand gratification, they floated back down to earth like two bronze colored oak leaves loosely curled together, floating as one, luxuriously on a soft comforting breeze.

When his breath came less labored, and he still held her tightly to his chest where she had collapsed in exhaustion, he cleared his throat and said resoundingly, "My Love, You Ride Divinely!"

Chapter 43

Some hours had passed and the breeze blowing in through the window and across their rumpled bed, whispered warmly that the fall sun was now much higher. Edward rose from their serene love nest, donned his robe, and, while running his long fingers through his tussled hair, he called the kitchen and ordered a sumptuous breakfast to be served in his room.

Maria was physically tired but she radiated vitality like never before. She made a sweet picture of satisfaction and contentment.

When the knock on the door came to herald the arrival of breakfast, she discreetly picked up her robe and retired to the bathroom to freshen up. After she was gone, Edward jumped up and anxiously hurried the servant in. The young woman arranged a beautiful breakfast setting quickly, while Edward riffled through some drawers looking for something; all the while keeping a watchful eye on the bathroom door. He sighed with relief as his hand closed over a small, velvet covered, jewel box. He then asked the serving woman to place the jewel box on one of the plates and cover it with a silver dish cover. Having this accomplished, he shooed the woman out just as May was bringing in fresh cut flowers. He whispered to May that Maria was in the bathroom and that everything was set up perfectly. May took the hint and with a big smile she centered the flowers on the foldout table and left quietly.

"Maria, my love, breakfast is served."

When she reentered the bedchamber, Edward formally seated her in front of a glittering array of covered dishes and fragrant, fresh white and red roses with baby's breath. She smiled up at him lovingly, as she lifted the cover from the plate in front of her.

"I guess that I'd better not be too hungry," she said, for on the plate was the small jewel box. She smiled at him teasingly, "What is this Edward? As you can imagine I really am quite hungry."

"Well my love, everything has been so hectic lately. Oh, just open it."

After seeing the earnestness of his expression, she did so, and gasped! It was a ring with one very large perfect emerald, surrounded by diamonds. She looked up from the ring in silent awe, only to find him wearing a sad, somehow guilty frown on his handsome countenance. She had never seen him look so forlorn.

"I'd planned to give this to you at the ball right after we were to announce our engagement, but unhappily, I didn't have that opportunity. It was meant to be your engagement ring, but now remembrances of Reanna still reach out to mar its beauty and the purity of love that all of the emeralds were meant to bestow and remind us of, forever."

"Oh, my dear man, you give Reanna too much credit. I'm a very practical woman," she said, smiling kindly. "I love this ring and from now on, it'll represent the clarity of our love and of our relationship."

He gathered her up in his arms and held her to his heart, "You are perfection my love. God has granted me a wonderful opportunity!"

She put the ring on and was delighted to find that it fit perfectly. It was very difficult to keep from admiring it as he served her with her real breakfast. They both ate heartily.

He suggested that she take some time to luxuriate in bed while he went to the library to meet with the law enforcement agents. She agreed with him and after giving him a warm generous kiss, she curled up in bed again.

After dressing, he forced himself to leave her as he headed to the library. He found that the constables and FBI agents were already there waiting. He showed them the hidden passageway and they set about arranging their surveillance gear. Just as the men were satisfied that everything was ready, the phone rang.

It was Gregory. He was calling from an airplane.

"Edward, dear brother, I hope that you and the others are all well and that things have settled down since the bombing."

"Yes, everything is fine here Gregory, where are you?"

"I'm out over the ocean now, and it'll be better if you don't know where I'm destined. You may or may not have found out about my armament import / export endeavors, but you'll undoubtedly hear about it soon. Don't worry. I've been very careful not to involve the family business in my private enterprises. My secretary, Marion, at the Toronto office has really been running the Warner businesses for the last two years. She is very capable and has been completely devoted to the family. Thankfully, she knows nothing about my private enterprises or where I'm relocating to. Marion will continue to be an asset to you and the family businesses. I have my own financial situation well in hand now and it's time for me to move on."

"But Gregory, what's going on?" Edward asked, with a note of exasperation.

"I've left a detailed letter for you at the office, which should explain things well enough. I'm giving Mallory a divorce, so when she's well enough to leave the hospital, she'll be going to stay with her family. Please have a great life, Edward. Don't screw up and miss your chance with Maria, our lady of the lake. Ha, ha! Take a leap of faith and get on with your life, and understand that I've gone to a great extent to make sure that there's no reason for the family to suffer because of my choices."

"But Gregory..."

"Goodbye for now, brother. Say goodbye to the others for me." And the line went dead.

Edward turned to look at the impatiently waiting faces of the law, "Well gentlemen, you've been out-finessed. Gregory is now out of the country and I've no way of knowing where he's going. He tells me that he's left full disclosure in the form of a letter, at our Toronto office. He has also assured me that his unlawful business isn't in anyway tied up with the Warner family businesses."

"Damn, he must've gotten wind that we were on to him!" exclaimed Constable Campbell of the R.C.M.P., as he sat back into one of the leather chairs.

Agent Morris of the FBI said, "We're going to have to search his residence here, Mr. Warner and then we're going to have to search this Toronto office and speak to the staff there. Mr. Warner, are you sure that you've no idea where he's going?"

"Absolutely none, he wouldn't say."

After Edward called a porter to show the officers to Gregory's wing, he went to find Brian. It was time to let his other brother in on what was going on. He found Brian in the garden, devotedly tending the delicate flowers in their mother's fairy fountain. They sat on the nearest bench and Edward filled his brother in on everything that he'd recently learned about their brother Gregory.

"This is absurd, why would he have anything to do with something like this?" Brian asked, in utter amazement.

"I felt the same way when I first heard about all of this from the F.B.I. agents."

"That's why they were here on Sunday," Brian stated.

"They almost got him today, but he outsmarted them." Edward went on, "A large part of me is outraged and having a hard time dealing with the inevitability that Gregory can only come to a bad end, following the road that he's chosen; but a small part of me was also elated when I knew that he was out of the law's reach, for now."

"I think I know what you're saying, even though I still can't comprehend his motivation."

Noticing that Edward was a bit distracted, Brian asked, "How is the wedding plan progressing?"

"Fine, I think. Things will fall into place. You're taking care of the flowers and the location, while Emma is taking care of the luncheon. Maria and I are taking care of making a few invitations and she'll go to pick up her daughter, Sylvia, on Thursday."

Edward seemed to have all of his ducks in a row, but Brian felt that he still came across just a bit nervous. While staring at the flowers Edward continued, "I'm going to have another, full grown daughter. I do hope that she likes us!"

"I can't wait to meet her, and as you say, things will fall into place Edward. If she's anything like her mother, things will be fine."

Edward had been fondly gazing towards the east wing. He got up from the bench and headed for the door, "See you at dinner, old man."

Brian smiled to himself, "Lovers in love!"

Chapter 44

Chursday morning started off bright and cool as Maria hopped out of bed very early, stretching and smiling, eager to begin the day. She was in a hurry to have breakfast and leave to pick Sylvia up at the college.

Edward squinted at her as he yawned and watched her rush around the room. Noticing that he was awake, she came to his side of the bed and sitting down beside him, she reached down and kissed him eagerly.

"I'm as taut as a violin string this morning," she said, "I just couldn't stay in bed any longer."

"May I hazard a guess that this has a lot to do with you having to face your daughter today?"

"No it couldn't be that!" she complained sarcastically, with a sheepish little smile. She shrugged her shoulders and hung her head.

"My sweet darling! Don't make this worse then it has to be by letting your imagination run away with you. Try to relax and keep a rein on things. If she sees that you're relaxed and happy, as you have been for the last three glorious days, then she'll be less apprehensive about all of this."

"Thank you, I know the scenario but I just needed you to lend me some of your calm confidence."

She curled up on the bed beside him and they started the morning off, just right.

———

Maria arrived at the college at the agreed upon time and Sylvia was waiting at the dormitory door, suitcase in hand. The driver rushed to relieve her of it and opened the car door for her.

After the door was closed for her, she said, "Mother, I don't believe this yacht of a car, and that driver! If he hadn't had his hands full, he might have picked me up and sat me in on the car seat. What's with all of this luxury?"

"Get used to it sweetheart, this is common everyday fare for my fiancée's family," Maria answered as she leaned over and embraced her daughter. "How are you? You look great!"

"I'm doing very well mother. My classes are going well and I like dormitory life, but we haven't got time to talk about me when so much is happening in your life. What is Edward like and how did you meet him? This has happened so fast! Are you sure you want to do this, on the spur, so to speak? You haven't been abducted by aliens have you?" Sylvia finished her questions with big eyes and an equally big smile.

"No, there are no extraterrestrials involved in this decision, and before we get too involved in our conversation, have you heard of any posh places to shop for a bridesmaid dress? Edward has suggested a couple of places in downtown Toronto but if you have any other ideas we can check them out as well."

They decided to go with the shops that Edward had suggested, so Maria lowered the communication window between them and the driver and gave him the instructions. She had decided to fill her daughter in on how this whirlwind courtship had come about, but thought it best to leave out their past-life revelations, for now. Sylvia was so enthralled by the scope of her mother's story, that they were still deep in conversation when the chauffeur pulled up in front of the first dress shop.

Both women were stunned by the array of finery that was presented for their perusal.

Little did Maria know that Edward had called the two shops that he'd suggested and after talking to their owners, he was satisfied that Maria and her daughter would receive the finest welcome and the most devoted service. Sylvia tried on many gowns at both locations and finally decided on a lusciously layered green chiffon dress at the second location, where they were also able to purchase the accessories to complete her bridesmaid ensemble. Maria also had her pick out two slightly more casual outfits for dinners at Sinabar. Sylvia was aglow with all of the pampering and special attention.

When back in the car and speeding towards Maria's new home, Sylvia confided, "I'm so happy for you Mom. Maybe this Edward Warner is the right man for you. God knows that you certainly deserve the best that life has to give. I harbor no animosity toward you having a new life with a man who will treat you well. I've known for some time that you and father didn't have a satisfying life together, I just never dreamt that you'd be able to find Mr. Right so quickly."

Maria was moved to tears, "Thank you my dear for having such a mature outlook."

She hugged her daughter as they discussed the plans for the wedding service.

It was still daylight as they approached the gates of Sinabar, so Maria instructed the driver to proceed slowly so that Sylvia would have a chance to take in the glorious views. She asked the driver to stop at the overlook from which she had taken her near fatal plunge. As she and Sylvia walked toward the area that she had fallen from, she felt a strange deja vu, and worried that the area might not be safe. However, she soon saw that Edward had ordered a stone retaining wall built back a safe distance from the edge. They stood at the wall, gazing out at the island and Sinabar manor house, much the same way that Maria had on that faithful evening not that long ago.

"It's like an enchanted scene in a fairy tale book," Sylvia said softly, eyes wide trying to take it all in. Her mother was silently staring down into the dark blue, roiling waters, her thoughts engulfed by the horror of what it felt like to be nearly consumed by those waves, but then her spirits were magically lifted by the wonderful memory of that strong arm coming around her nearly frozen body, just before she had lost consciousness for what would've been the last time had Edward not found her. She quietly took her daughter's hand and walked back to the limousine.

As they pulled up in front of the manor and stepped out of the car, Sylvia was just recovering some form of dignity and was managing to pull up the hinge of her jaw to close her mouth, when Edward came through the door of the grand hall. As he approached, her jaw threatened to drop open again. The phrase 'Prince Charming' didn't quite cover her first impression of him. Before he got too close, she pulled on her mother's arm, "Mom, he's gorgeous!"

Maria smiled to her approaching lover and whispered to her daughter, "Stop drooling my dear and get ready to meet your future stepfather," she paused, still smiling at Edward and then addressed him. "Edward, please meet my daughter, Sylvia. And Sylvia, this is Sir Edward Warner, my fiancé."

"Hello Sylvia," Edward said, taking Sylvia's outstretched hand, and with his left hand he touched her lightly on the shoulder, while bending down to kiss her gently on the cheek.   Sylvia stared up at him for several moments until she regained her composure. "I'm... I'm very pleased to meet you, Sir Edward."

"My Dear, you're certainly very welcomed here, and please feel free to call me Edward."

He led them into the grand hall and up the staircase. Rooms had been prepared for Sylvia, beside Anna Belle's suite. Sylvia's eyes were busy trying to take everything in. Maria smiled to herself, remembering how she'd felt when she'd first been escorted around the manor.

Edward stood in the doorway admiring the two ladies. Sylvia wasn't quite the shadow of her beautiful mother. She was a bit shorter and rounder then Maria. Her hair wasn't as dark as her mother's and their faces were only slightly similar; still she was in her own right, an attractive young lady.

"I'll leave you ladies to your catching up and we'll meet again in the dining room at seven thirty. I'll then enjoy introducing you, Sylvia, to my daughter Anna Belle and my brother Brian." Taking Maria's hand he kissed it gently and made a slight bow, "Till later my love," and he was gone.

As the door closed, Sylvia laughed softly and threw herself on to the white poster bed, "Mother, wow! You're in Heaven here! I can feel it! You're absolutely glowing, and so is he when he's beside you."

"I'm very relieved and glad that you understand my dear. Now, let's go for a walk so that I can give you the grand tour."

<hr />

At dinner, Sylvia and Anna Belle delighted their elders with their immediate friendship and their bubbling chatter about the upcoming wedding arrangements. After they had exhausted that topic, Anna Belle stated, "Father has hired a tutor for me, Mr. Jones. He smells like a hospital... you know that chemically, clean smell. He's dreadfully afraid of the dogs. I have to have one of the staff take them all out of my rooms when he's coming. He does seem kind of quiet and nice though. Father says that I don't have to have lessons tomorrow, because you're here and we'll be frightfully busy getting ready for the wedding on Saturday."

"Anna Belle, please take a breath. You do have to breathe once and a while, you now. Sylvia might like to get a word in edgewise," her father taunted her. He took this opportunity to continue, "Sylvia, as to our further plans, your mother may have told you that we'll be flying to Monte Carlo, Monaco after the wedding luncheon, for our wedding trip. One of our drivers will take you back to school Sunday, whenever you're ready to leave." He rose and taking an envelope out of his breast pocket, he walked to where she was sitting, "When we leave Monaco, we'll be flying to London for a short stay, and then we'll be going on to our family estate near Keswick. Anna Belle will be joining us there and we'd like to invite you to also join us there for your Christmas holiday. I've contacted your school about the dates," he said, as he held the envelope out to her. "This is your airline ticket, your passport application, and, some expense money. I do hope that you'll consider joining us. Christmas at our ancestral home will be quite charming."

Sylvia had tears in her eyes as she looked from Edward to Maria. She had a lump in her throat and couldn't speak right away.

Maria sensed this problem and said, "As you'll soon learn, Sylvia, Edward is a man intent on taking care of all of the details and I'm finding out that he also has a very big heart where his women are concerned."

Sylvia's gaze shifted upward to meet Edward's smile, "Of course I'll come. I'm just shocked to be considered part of your family and to be offered such a wonderful opportunity to travel." Tears ran down her cheeks. Edward put a gentle hand on her shoulder and replied, "Of course we're going to love having you as part of our family."

Sylvia stood up and hugged him, smiling through her tears at her mother. Anna Belle got up and ran over to hug them both. After sitting down again, Anna Belle used this lull in the conversation to ask, "Uncle Brian, can you take us to the barn with you tonight when you go to check on the animals?"

Brian was quite enjoying this family atmosphere, and he was clearing his throat to answer when Edward interrupted to answer the question for him. "I'm afraid that it's too late my dear and much too cold out there tonight. Why don't you help Sylvia get settled in tonight and maybe Brian will have time to take you both to the barn in the morning, if you can manage to get up early enough?"

Anna Belle was about to start to pout, but Brian acted quickly to concur with Edward,

"If you girls can meet me in the solarium at eight o'clock for a quick breakfast, then afterwards we'll go to the barn to feed everyone else."

"That sounds like a good plan," Sylvia interjected, "I'm a bit tired this evening after all that's happened today. I've gained a whole new family today," she said, smiling. "Thank you everyone."

"You're quite welcomed, Sylvia," Edward spoke softly, showing the full extent of his sincerity, "Now Anna Belle, take Sylvia up and show her around your suite and hers. And don't keep her up all night chattering. Remember you have a date with Brian in the morning."

The two girls left the room giggling; one little one and one very happy, young woman.

Edward gazed after them as if mesmerized, "God has blessed us both Maria. Wouldn't you agree Brian?"

"Yes brother, they are two wonderful girls and they appear to fit together like two natural sisters." He cleared his throat and laughed, "Maybe, even better!"

Edward picked up on the joke and laughed, also remembering what this house had been like with three young brothers tearing around, tormenting each other.

Maria fondly looked from one brother to the other, surmising what their little joke was about, she said, "Surely you boys must've been proper little angels and you must've all gotten along just fine."

Both men broke into merry laughter. Brian spoke up first, "We drove our dear parents' right around the bend some days."

Edward chuckled and shook his head, "Even this house didn't seem to be big enough in those days."

Chapter 45

Jt was Friday morning, the last full day before the wedding day. Everyone was up early and met in the solarium for the beginning of their day.

The construction and cleaning crews had been working overtime and had succeeded in completing the glass walls of the grand hall and the solarium. The chapel on the second floor, just above the grand hall, had been made suitable for the service. The manor was bustling with extra staff, cleaning and working in the kitchen. The garden had also been cleared of debris and was in the process of being freshened up with some new planting.

Maria helped herself to some fresh fruit and asked, "Ok, Edward and Brian, what needs to be done today to have everything ready?"

The men looked at one another and replied in unison, "Not much."

Edward forged ahead with a more exact answer, "Brian assures me that though the chapel is not perfect by any means yet, it will, however, be suitable for our small service, and that all of the flowers are resting in anticipation. Emma reports that everything for the luncheon is being prepared today or tomorrow morning. Your dress is here for your approval today, but I know that it'll be wondrously perfect. The one thing that you and I have to do is have a chat with

Reverend Paul Thompson at one o'clock today. May is packing your traveling bags, as we speak. The details all check out my love."

She had, of course, been confident that her intended would have everything systematically under control. "Then what shall we do this morning?"

"The weather is wonderful today. Why don't we go for a quiet walk and just relax together?" Edward suggested.

Maria laughed at how delicately he had put his suggestion. She now, thankfully knew that she wasn't the only nervous one.

The girls pried Brian away from the morning paper and headed him towards the barn. Sylvia waved absentmindedly as she left, "I'll talk to you later Mom."

The newly-weds-to-be took their coffee and walked out onto the terrace to survey the repairs. "Let's sit by your mother's fountain," Maria suggested, "It's such a special place."

"Since the circumstances that we find ourselves in dictate the proof of reincarnation, I now harbor hopes of meeting the souls of my parents once again. We could only benefit from such a wonderful opportunity," Edward said, divulging a heart felt sentiment as he gazed at the delightful, dancing fairy.

"That's a very comforting thought," she replied.

"There has to be a positive balance somewhere, sometime. Just think, my brother in this life, could have been my father or even sister in a prior life, or even simply a neighbor. I'm going to enjoy this study immensely. England and Scotland will be fertile ground to start this learning adventure.

They went back to their rooms after a quiet stroll around the garden. Edward presented her with a large, white box, and also a shoebox. "Here's your gown and your shoes, my lady. I think I'd better leave and send May to assist you."

Maria laughed excitedly, "Good idea."

So he headed for the door, "Meet you at lunch."

Maria couldn't even wait until the door was closed. She tore the ribbon off of the box and ripped the top off, "Ohhh!" The gown was light honey froth, gold lame'; with a loose, folding neckline that was designed to swoop from one shoulder to the other. The scooped bodice was quite fitted and came to a point just below the waist, front. The trim skirt was long and flowing. She had slipped into it before May knocked and came in.

"Oh Ms. Maria, how does he do it? I mean, he always knows just what will make you look like a Goddess. It must be a gift!"

"Yes, a gift from the past," Maria uttered, without thinking, as she gazed at herself in the mirror.

"What was that Ms.?" May asked, not having heard clearly.

"Oh, nothing. It does look glorious doesn't it, and it fits just right?"

"It's perfect Ms. Maria, you look wonderful. Here are the shoes," May said, taking them from the box and handed them to Maria. They had been crafted from ultra soft, kid leather that had been tinted to match the dress. "They sure do look like dancing shoes to me."

Maria put them on and danced around the room to see how they fit and how the gown would flow when she moved. The beautiful gown draped from her hips snuggly and trailed just slightly. She felt divine.

"Mr. Edward has instructed me to carefully pack this gown, so you can take it with you on your trip. I can see why he'd want to squire you around the dance floors of Europe in this glorious gown."

"I know that you'll take good care of it May, just as you'll take excellent care of us in England when we meet you and Anna Belle at the estate."

"Me, in England Ms.?" May gasped.

"Yes May, who do you think is going to bring Anna Belle to us and continue to take care of us while we live there?"

"I get to go to England?" May was still stunned.

"Yes May, Edward agreed that I could be the one to have the delight of asking you."

"Ask me, there could be no question, if you want me, of course I'll be there Ms. Maria, and I'll love it! I love to travel! I'm so excited! Listen to me, you can just tell me to 'shut up May'."

"Shut Up May!"

The girls met Maria in the dinning room, before the men arrived.

"Mom, the pet barn is just great. The animals are all so comfortable and friendly. The atmosphere is so warm there," Sylvia said, as she came to sit by her mother. Anna Belle was busy chasing one of her small dogs out of the room.

"I knew that you'd enjoy being there," Maria said.

"Mom, when I saw Edward for the first time yesterday, I was amazed at his appearance, not just because he's so handsome but because I thought that I'd seen him somewhere before. This morning I realized why. This summer I met a British actor at Stratford who could be Edward's twin. His sir name is Alexander and he seemed to be quite a ladies man. Rumor had it that he'd been involved with most of the younger actresses who had walked the stage there, at one time or another. That's part of the reason why I was so taken aback. But there's no doubt, your Edward is a foxy man."

Edward and Brian just happened to be walking into the room.

"Speaking of that foxy man, himself," Maria got up, and, putting her arms around his neck, kissed him heartily, "The gown is divine, my love, and it fits like a glove."

"I'm so pleased that you like it," he said, giving her another kiss.

Anna Belle had taken a seat next to Sylvia and they were grinning at one another as lunch was served. Brian was obliged to loudly clear his throat twice before getting the attention of the two lovebirds, so that lunch could begin.

At one o'clock, the Minister arrived and was brought to the library to meet Maria and Edward. The latter got up to welcome him and introduced him to Maria, "Paul this is my wife-to-be, Maria. My dear, this is Reverend Paul Thompson."

The Reverend was cordial to Maria, but rather quickly turned back to his host, "Edward, I was shocked to hear less then a week ago, after that horrible bombing, that you were planning to marry so soon."

"It would be abnormal Paul, for you not to be surprised, and even dismayed at the timing that we've chosen. However, let me assure you that this is a very special situation. I can't go into details at this time but believe us when we tell you that this is meant to be. Neither Maria nor I have any doubts that this is the right timing and the right move for us. Someday I hope that we'll be able to explain our motives further." Before the Reverend could give any further objections, Edward went on, "The wedding will be at eleven o'clock tomorrow morning, here in our newly repaired chapel, with just a few close friends as guests. We want to keep the service very simple."

The Reverend knew that there'd be no chance of persuading Edward to put this wedding off, so he asked a few questions about the service and the vows; then left without saying anything further.

When they were alone Maria took Edward's hand and asked, "After we finish the service in the chapel, could we go out to your mother's fountain with just the wedding party for our own, more private vows?"

"Of course, I'd be honored," he said, pulling her into his arms, "are you going to give me any hint as to what you intend?"

She ran her fingers through his lustrous hair and looked deep into his eyes, "No, let's just open up our sensitivity and let our hearts speak."

"As you wish." he leaned down, their lips met gently, yet sensuously as they held each other for some time.

They spent the rest of the afternoon with their daughters, approving their dresses, talking about flowers, and having a bit of a rehearsal in the chapel. Emma had planned a sumptuous dinner of roast duckling and pheasant, with all of the trimmings. She knew that they probably wouldn't have much in the way of appetites tomorrow.

Everyone agreed that it'd be a good idea to turn in early that night. Although Anna Belle and Sylvia were doing a lot of giggling and secret conspiring, so their elders didn't imagine that they'd actually be settling down very early. Maria was thankful that they were in a separate wing of the house, away from the girls, but at the same time she felt a tinge of sadness that after the ceremony, they wouldn't be seeing the girls for some time. She and her beloved Edward would be starting off on a wonderful, new adventure. Yes, the rest of this life and others would definitely be adventurous.

Brian had gone to check on the animals at the barn and the girls had run out giggling, after kissing them good night. They were alone again at last. Edward had sensed her feelings about the girls, "It'll be wonderful to have the two girls together with us for the Christmas holidays."

"Yes, thank you for being so generous with Sylvia. She was so touched that you'd do all of that for her, especially when you don't even know her yet."

"She's almost as special as her mother is and I'm very happy to invite her into our family."

"Thank you dear," she said and as she got up from her chair she suggested, "Let's go to the library, I'd like to see those portraits of your ancestors again." Edward just smiled and taking her hand in his, they walked to the library. He now had one of the larger portraits hung behind his desk. It was an early painting of his parents that'd been done shortly after their wedding. His mother had been a shorter, quite refined lady with light brown almost blond hair - nearly the same shade as Edward's. She possessed a pretty face, with a very sensitive mouth, and she had undoubtedly the bright light of love in her eyes. Sinclair was a tall, stately, handsome man with his arms proudly encircling Anna's shoulders.

"The artist has captured their essence very well. They always remained very much in love. As I've said before, my marriage to Reanna was very much against their wishes. I was young and enchanted, and I guess you could say that I was stubborn to a fault. After a very short time, my parents found it uncomfortable to live under the same roof with her. I was still wearing rose colored glasses, which kept me from recognizing the cause of the friction and the conflict. My parents had often talked about taking an extended holiday at home in England, so they went. Four months later they were killed when their boat exploded on the lake." Maria shivered at the thought. Edward noticed this and came to her side to rub her shoulders.

"I have no doubt at all that they'd have loved you completely and would've been very happy for us," he whispered, as he leaned down and kissed her neck.

"Can I see the portrait of Edwin again," she asked?

"By all means, my love," he replied as he went to the stack of portraits leaning against a bookcase and brought out the second one.

"It's so uncanny that this man looked so much like you," she whispered, staring into the eyes of Edward's long passed, family member. "If your hair was long like that and you didn't have a mustache, you could pass as twins. I wonder what poor Elaine looked like?"

"She was the whole world to Edwin, so I imagine that she must have been very special," Edward assured her, as he put the portrait back in the front of the pile so that it could be readily seen.

"Shall we think about retiring now, Maria?"

"Yes. Tomorrow is going to be a very full day, and then some," she replied as she rose to meet him at the door, where she slipped her arm around his waist.

As they walked to their rooms in the east wing, they talked about the plans for the trip that they would be starting on, tomorrow.

Chapter 46

$\mathcal{A}$t two a.m. Maria was awakened by something. At first she thought that it was something internal that had forced her awake, but as she lay there taking stock, she ruled that out. Maybe Edward had moved. They hadn't closed the heavy window drapes, so bright silvery moonlight cascaded across their bed. This enabled her to see that her loved one was lying on his back beside her, sleeping peacefully. She smiled as she thought how boyish he looked when he was in his world of dreams.

A loud, mournful sound echoed out of the darkness.

Maria lay frozen in shock, holding her breath and listening. The sound went on and on. She reached over and shook his shoulder, "Edward, did you hear that?"

He mumbled something and pushed himself up on one elbow, "What?" he said, shaking his head.

"Don't you hear that sound? Where is it coming from?" Maria demanded, hardly breathing. She took one deep breath and held it, waiting for the sound again.

It started again, only at a higher pitched now and even more mournful then before.

"I hear it now," he whispered incredulously after a quick intake of air. "What or who could that possible be?" Quickly, he was out of bed and donning his robe. He started fumbling at the side of the bed for his slippers. In answer to this frustration, he thought to reach back and switch the light on. It was quite cool in the room, as their fire had gone out earlier.

Maria sat, nearly paralyzed by the eerie sobbing.

"It seems to be coming from above us; from the second floor," Edward said, as he stood up. He reached into his bedside drawer and put something into his robe pocket.

"If you're going to hunt it down, then I'm coming with you. I'm not staying here alone. Wait a second." Maria vaulted out of bed and grabbed her robe.

He stood at the doorway to the hall, listening to the sound, trying to envision where it could be coming from. Maria found a pair of shoes and met him there. Once they were out in the hall, the sound was more muffled.

"Do you notice the difference from out here?" Edward asked. "That must mean that the origin of the sound is the room above this one, it's coming from just above us. There's a stairwell between here and Brian's suite. Let's take it," he said, producing a candle from his pocket.

As they mounted the steps, Maria confided, "Once before, I heard sobbing from the second floor hall near my old rooms. It was on the evening that you and Mallory had that terrible fight in the solarium."

"You did? Why didn't you tell me?" Edward exclaimed.

"Well, it happened at the time when I'd been having those odd spells and I couldn't tell whether I'd imagined the sounds; or if they might have been an echo from Mallory's rooms, somehow. You must remember how upset she was. So I figured that it was probably inconsequential."

They had arrived at the landing of the second floor hall. All seemed quiet. Edward took her by the hand and indicated for her to stop, and listen. A breeze drifting down the hall played havoc with the flame of the candle, causing it to flutter precariously. The electricity to this floor of the east wing had been turned off, for fire safety reasons and also because of the fact that it went for long periods of time without being used. As Edward thought back he realized that indeed, this floor hadn't been used since he had imprisoned Reanna here - seven and a half years ago.

The low moaning, sounding definitely like a distraught woman; filled the stale, cool air of the long, unused hallway. The thought of Reanna was still rattling around in his brain so he tried to push it to the back of his consciousness. They advanced farther along the hall to precisely above the room that they had been sleeping in. Sure enough, the sobbing was louder here. Edward paused outside the door and looked down at Maria. She clung to his side. He reached out to turn the doorknob. The knob turned but the door didn't open at first. It was stuck. The sound that emanated from the room subsided to a low whimpering. Edward put his shoulder to the door to give it a hefty shove. There must've been debris on the floor on the other side because the door scraped over something. The door was less then half way open as he stuck his arm in through with the candle. As he did so, with Maria peeking from under his outstretched arm, they peered into the dimly lit room. They were just in time to witness a translucent white filmy cloud moving from over the bed toward the fireplace and disappearing, that woeful sound echoing after it. It was now gone.

"Did you see that?" Edward barked as he put more shoulder against the door and shoved it all the way open this time.

Maria stood staring and listening. The room was silent now.

Edward moved to the fireplace mantle and lit another large candle that he found there. This added a stronger, yet eerie glow to the room. Maria hurried to the bedside and as she expected, she felt a cold indent on the bed covering. Her hand smoothed the area and then automatically came to her face as if she was trying to sense something else.

Edward stood with his back to the fireplace and stared at the indent in the bed and then looked to Maria. She'd said not a thing, but her eyes were as wide as those of an owl on the hunt. Her gaze followed the direction that the apparition had taken from the bed to the fireplace. The chimney cover must have blown off some time ago because the otherwise perfectly preserved room was littered with fall leaves and other wind born debris. That was what had encumbered the door.

They stood transfixed as they looked from one another back to the fireplace.

"Oh my God!" Maria exclaimed. The glow of the candle flame was close beside a nameplate on the bottom of the huge portrait that adorned the wall above the fireplace. Maria read the inscription reverently, out loud "My Darling Elaine." She walked to the mantle and lifted the large candle up and backed away so that they could see the subject of the painting. A pretty, young girl of seventeen or eighteen peered down at them with soft, lustrous, brown eyes. Her hair was raven black, pulled back from her heart shaped face and pinned at the back with ringlet curls hanging down just past her shoulders. Her very maidenly dress was light green. She cradled a small white and brown spaniel in her arms.

"Well, I guess that answers your question about Elaine's appearance. She was quite a young beauty," Edward said, as he moved his small candle toward where the portrait would have been signed. "And here's another shocker. It's signed Edwin A. O'Donnell. It would seem that our Edwin was quite an accomplished artist. I'm sure that I must've been in this room at one time or another, but I can't say that I've ever noticed this painting... not that I would've had any reason then to take note of it."

"Edward, what did we just see? That must've been a spirit!"

"I must agree, I've never had the pleasure before, but I've no doubt after seeing it myself." He backed up and sat down on the foot of the bed and continued, "But why all of the sobbing and wailing?"

Maria came and sat down beside him. "I think it was just trying to get our attention. It obviously was in a disturbed state and I feel that it was drawing us here to find Elaine's portrait. When I touched the depression on the bed it was cold, but I sensed a positive feeling of energy."

"Yes, one normally would associate cold with the spirit world. And yes this spirit may be here with a positive motive or maybe not." He paused and scuffed his foot over some leaves on the floor. Thoughtfully, he continued by saying, "I just don't know at this point, but I do know that which ever was intended, this may well be a warning from our past; a warning to be ever vigilant, to watch over one another and be prepared. Oh, maybe I'm just over tired, so much has happened to us lately."

"I know Edward; we do have good reason to both be overtired but please remember that we do have a head start in knowing the danger and how to take care of one another. We love one another and we will always be there for one another. We can't have anything better then that."

He brushed his foot through more ruble on the floor, "Look at this room. All of these leaves and things must've come in through the chimney, the windows look secure." He got up to check the windows. The bars were still in place and the windows were locked. Once again, the bars reminded him of Reanna's imprisonment. He really didn't want to go into that subject with his wife-to-be, right now. "The windows are fine. The cover must be off of the chimney. We'll have the repair men take care of it while they're here."

Maria sat staring at Elaine, "Edwin must have painted her from memory, and maybe that was enough to make him lose interest in his artistry. They had a very sad existence, Elaine and Edwin. For some reason that spirit wanted us to take note of this part of our past-life relationship. This is very timely - just before our wedding."

"Speaking of our wedding, my dear, we'd better get back to bed with hope of getting some sleep." He took her by the hand and after blowing the large mantle candle out he led her carefully back down the dark stairs to their room.

Maria didn't fall asleep for some time. She couldn't get that sobbing sound out of her head.

When they awakened in the morning, they discussed what'd happened during the night, as a way of acknowledging to one another, that it really had happened. They both agreed that they'd better set this subject aside for now, so they could go about the matter of getting married this morning. Therefore, they wouldn't be discussing it with anyone else right away.

On their way to breakfast in the solarium, Maria heard a harp singing. "That's very pretty, where's it coming from?"

"From the chapel, my dear," Edward replied, "they're practicing for the wedding. I thought it'd be a nice touch to have Celtic music for our celebration." Edward winked as he smiled down at her and squeezed her hand.

"How appropriate! It sounds divine. Are there any other surprises coming my way?"

In answer, he just grinned down at her as he seated her at the table. Brian and the girls were there ahead of them this morning. Emma and May were there as well. Everyone was chattering about how things were going and what still needed to be done. Apparently, everything was running according to schedule. After breakfast everyone was going to their rooms to prepare themselves. Two hairdressers were coming in at nine o'clock, one to do the girls' hair and one to do Maria's hair.

"Father, do you not have anyone coming to do your hair for you?" Anna Belle said, laughing as she teased her father.

"No, I believe my hands are just steady enough to do it myself, unless you'd like to come and do it for me?" He winked at her and they all laughed. "Emma, I almost forgot about our guests. They'll probably be arriving anytime after ten o'clock. Please ask the doorman to escort them to the lounge for refreshments and then to the chapel at say, ten forty-five. The musicians should be done practicing by ten thirty and they'll then begin their repertoire," he explained.

"The music is very pretty, Father. What is it?" Anna Belle asked.

"It's traditional Celtic music, the music of our ancestry. The quartet is from Toronto. They play the lute, the flute, the harp and the bagpipes. Apparently they're quite well known, but I've never heard them before, so I hope they're as good as their reputation indicates."

Sylvia spoke up, "Mother, we'd better go and start to get ready. If Anna Belle and I are ready in time, can we come down to your room to see you?"

"If you're ready by ten forty-five, but if you're not, I'll see you in the chapel at eleven."

The two girls winked at each other and left to meet their hairdresser. Maria was trying to quietly finish her second cup of tea. After hearing the doorbell, Emma and May disappeared to meet with the hairdressers. Edward came over behind Maria's chair and gave her a hug, "I must leave you now, my love. I have a few little things left to attend to. Brian, would you walk your sister-in-law back to her room? May will be waiting to attend you, my dear."

Maria was swallowing the last of her tea and shaking her head, to the negative, wishing to state that this wouldn't be necessary, but before she could speak, Brian said, "That would be my great pleasure, Edward."

Knowing that she would only be outmaneuvered, she simply smiled and took Brian's outstretched hand as he offered to assist her from her chair.

As she and Brian approached her door, he said, "When you're ready, I'll accompany you to the chapel. I'll be sitting out here in the hall awaiting you. Knowing Edward, I'm sure that my dear brother won't need me for anything else. Besides, he's already given me the most important job – escorting his bride-to-be."

"That's very nice of you Brian. I'll see you shortly." She realized that because she had no one to 'give her away', Brian was taking on the role of her escort.

Chapter 47

$\mathcal{A}$t ten-fifty, May assured Maria that everything was perfect. Maria took one more, long glance at the regal woman in the mirror, hardly recognizing herself. She walked to the door, opened it and stepped out to meet Brian.

He'd been sitting in a window seat, admiring the bride's bouquet, which he was proudly delivering to his sister-in-law to be. He looked up as he heard the door opening. Maria stopped in front of him. There was silence.

The initial smile that he had been wearing faded to a very serious, yet pleasant, contemplation. He shyly dropped his gaze back down to the flowers in his hand. "There are no flowers that could rival you, this day, Maria." He looked back up at her, deep into her eyes this time, with an almost sad smile, "This day, Edward Warner will be the most blessed man on this earth." He rose and gently handed her the flowers.

She was so touched that she had to raise a finger to dab away a tiny tear that was forming already. "How dare you Brian; making me tearful already. At this rate my makeup will never last through this," she said, as she stood on tiptoes to plant a delicate kiss on his cheek. "Thank you for such high praise."

As they walked toward the chapel, Sylvia and Anna Belle, who couldn't wait there, came hurrying down the hall to meet them.

"Oh Mother!"

"Oh Mother!"

Maria had distinctly heard two different voices, and she smiled with great delight.

The girls stopped some distance ahead of them. Sylvia spoke up this time, "Mother you are simply radiant!"

"Yeah, there's a bright glow around you," Anna Belle stated, in total amazement.

Maria just laughed and replied, "Well, if you say so. I guess I can take that as a good omen."

They walked the rest of the way, with the girls chattering excitedly about the flowers, the music and the guests. As they reached the chapel door, Brian realized that the bride-to-be needed some time to compose herself, so he took the girls with him, to wait just inside the door while Maria stood at a window overlooking the garden. She and Edward had both agreed that anytime they needed strength and assurance, they'd think of Anna Warner's fairy fountain standing silently in the garden. Maria was looking down on it now. "By all God's magic we've come this far, may He watch over us all, forever. Please say a prayer for us Anna and Sinclair, for I go now to join with your son."

She felt a rush of assurance as she approached the chapel and entered. Brian and Edward had both been watching the door from in front of the altar. Edward smiled confidently and Brian signaled the musicians. The girls knew what to do; they'd been practicing before the guests had come in. Anna Belle started down the isle with a large basket of flowers and a beaming smile. Sylvia started down just as the younger, little lady reached the altar and stepped to the side. Maria waited until the two young ladies were settled, and then she stepped forward from the shadows of the doorway into the brilliant light that was emanating through the large windows.

As she started down the isle with the natural sunlight gracing her form, Edward felt as if a strong fist clenched around his heart. A lump formed in his throat and his confident smile changed to a humble smile of adoration. The ancient music filled his head, as she seemed to float toward him. He was thinking, she's so perfect, so dream like. This feeling must be what people refer to as being 'spell bound'. I know this feeling will last forever. After all, we've already carried it between us from the beginning of time.

She reached out and laying her cool, soft hand in his, she brought him back to reality. She was grinning as she leaned toward him and whispered, "I love yer bonnie knees." To her great surprise, he was wearing a kilt. Actually he wore full, Scottish, formal attire.

Still smiling, he paused for a moment and then he laughed out loud, having momentarily forgotten about wearing the kilt.

Reverend Thompson cleared his throat to gain their attention and then proceeded with the ceremony. It was short and sweet, just as Edward had suggested. Neither of them could wait until he got to the kiss. So when he did say, "Now you may kiss the Bride," they were well primed.

Edward kissed her as if they'd never touched lips before; as if they'd waited all of this time and he just couldn't contain his passion any longer. She melted against him and to her great surprise he reached down and picked her up as if she was a tiny kitten. He started towards the door and curtly said over his shoulder, "If you would please remain here everyone, we'll be back shortly." The wedding party briskly followed after them, while everyone else including the Reverend, started whispering and looking from one to another. Brian, who went through the door last behind the wedding couple and the two girls, decided on second thought, to stick his head back through the door and clarified matters for the guests, "They want to make special, private vows to each other, in the garden. So if you'd please wait here, they'll be back to sign the register and we'll then have pictures taken." He ducked back out and ran to catch up with them.

Bill Adams spoke to the tall, blonde lady sitting beside him, who'd introduced herself as Sara Cummings, one of Maria's friends, "Leave it to Edward to be the dashing dramatic." He grinned and continued as the woman bobbed her head in agreement, "But I guess I can't fault him for it. Maria is one of the most beautiful and delightful women that I've ever had the pleasure of meeting."

"Yes, she always has been a very nice person and a wonderful friend, especially when anyone needed her," the woman sat back down again, "although, I'd no idea that she could look so beautiful and happy. I guess that she's been hiding her light under a basket. I don't think that her first husband ever gave her much of a reason to be happy."

Edward carried his new wife all the way down to the fountain. The romantic, Celtic music could still be heard from the chapel, thanks to Brian's ingenuity. Still holding her, Edward kissed Maria again, then setting her on her feet in front of the dancing fairy, he said, "Maria, my bride, from what we've learned about our history, our past-lives; we know that we'll always have to be vigilant and prepared. We may possibly even have to resort to unusual methods to protect this very precious life that we are going to have together; this new chance that we've been gifted with. Therefore, I give you my solemn vow that I'll do everything humanly possible and then some to protect you, this blessed union between us and our family."

For a few seconds, shades of the sorrow from their multiple pasts played across Maria's sweet face. She swallowed hard and bit back the tears that threatened. "My beloved Edward, I echo that vow. This time we are forewarned as well as being stronger, and we also have God, as well as Anna and Sinclair backing us up."

They took each others hands and turned to the fairy with the gleaming eyes. Maria said softly, "I Love You Edward Warner."

"I Love You Mrs. Warner and you are welcomed to call me Ed if you like."

Maria laughed and threw her arms up around his neck, hugging him close as they both laughed heartily.

Their family just looked at one another, not understanding the reasoning behind anything that had been said, other than the 'loving each other' part. Reading this from their inquisitive expressions Edward simply said, "When the time is right we'll translate these vows for your greater understanding. I promise."

The newly-weds smiled at one another and Maria said, "Let's get back to our guests now."

Edward looked back at the fountain, "Thanks Mom and Dad."

Back at the chapel, with all of the guests looking on, they completed the necessary signing and then everyone enjoyed the wonderful music and a delectable luncheon that was served in the lounge.

By three o'clock the photos had been taken, the bouquet had been thrown; friends had visited and given their congratulations; the couple had gone and changed into their traveling clothes; their formal clothes had been packed and put into the waiting limousine; and the newly-weds were at the door, ready to leave.

Now came the hardest part, the goodbyes. Edward had handed May an envelope that held the airline tickets and passports for her and Anna Belle. His daughter was now in tears. Maria hugged her and whispered, "We'll see you soon and then we'll have a great adventure." Edward picked Anna Belle up and made her promise to be a good girl for Emma and May.

Sylvia smiled sadly and hugged them both, saying, "I'll see you at Christmas, for sure. Call me when you have a chance. Edward, I know that you'll take good care of her so just have a great time."

Brian hugged Maria and when she looked up at him, he kissed her full on the lips, however quickly and discretely. "I'll get the repairs done and I'll be looking for you to come home safe and sound. I'll be missing you both every day." He started to shake Edward's hand but then pulled his brother to him for a hug.

Both Edward and Maria felt that if they didn't get into the car quickly, they wouldn't be going at all, so they let the chauffeur help them into the car without looking back again. Edward moved over to the side and after putting several cushions behind his back in the corner, he leaned back and pulling her to him he said, "I'm so glad that the wedding service was so short. I hope that you didn't mind. I just couldn't wait to get my arms around you again and taste that voluptuous mouth of yours. Even there in the chapel I had trouble controlling myself. Am I turning into a wicked, depraved and possessed man, Maria?"

"No, you're just madly in love," she replied as she turned so that she could give him a long, pleasurable kiss. When she came up for air she added through her smile, "With maybe a touch of influence from much older times. Carrying me out of the chapel the way you did, surely gave our guests quite a start, even though the women thought it very romantic."

"The women, what about that ladies man, Bill Adams? What were you two whispering about at the bar?"

"We weren't whispering." She reached back to feign a swat to his shoulder. "If you must know, he was giving us his congratulations, saying that he wished that I'd fallen in love with him, but that you and I appeared to make the perfect couple and that you deserve a chance at a perfect life. But he did finish his statements by saying that if I ever had second thoughts or just decided that I didn't really love you, that I should let him know." She finished with a sidelong glance at him and a hearty laugh.

"Well that scoundrel!" Edward scoffed, "Remind me when we come back home, to keep an eye on that man whenever he's anywhere near my wife," and he gave her an affectionate squeeze.

"Maybe if he's very lucky, by that time, you won't have him to worry about. Do you remember my friend Janet that I introduced you to while we were in the lounge?"

"Yes, the small attractive lady with the warm, mouse brown hair."

"Well, she's unattached right now and is a dear friend of mine. If you were keeping such a good eye on Bill and I, did you not see us laughing together, and then me taking him over and introduced him to Janet? Well they spent the rest of the afternoon together, and then rather then her riding home with Sara Cummings as planned, she consented to leave with our ladies man and dear friend, Doctor Bill."

"Why, my dear you're quite talented aren't you?" he said, kissing her forehead. She gave a low, guttural chuckle, "Yes, as you should well know," she replied, as she turned a bit so that she could snuggle in closer.

"Well, my pet, just rest now. It won't be long before we're in the air."

"We'll probably have a lot of rigmarole to go through at the airlines." This murmur came from her face pressed into his sweater at his chest.

"As a matter of fact, we won't have anything to go through. The car will pull out onto the tarmac. I'll carry my then very tired wife, onto the jet that I've hired. The chauffeur will put our bags on board. Our dear friends from the R.C.M.P. will have cleared us for take off and then we'll be in the air. Once on the plane we'll get very comfortable, have dinner and when you wake up we'll be over Europe."

"Oh Edward, I should've known that you'd have organized only the best. What did you mean about the R.C.M.P.?"

"Our former acquaintance, Constable Campbell contacted me about our travel arrangements. It seems that because my brother Gregory hasn't been apprehended, it remains their duty to keep an eye on our comings and goings. So I arranged another trade-off agreement with him. I agreed to keep him informed of any traveling that we do and to let them search our jet, in return for him having his specialists check out our pilots, giving the jet a thorough going over, and securing all safety factors. So, thanks to the R.C.M.P. we'll be flying under the safest conditions possible."

"You are wonderful, Ed..." She was falling asleep.

Edward grinned to himself. He couldn't see her lips from this angle, so he didn't know if she'd meant to call him Ed or if she'd simply dozed off in the middle of saying his name. He didn't mind a bit, he just was very glad that she was so relaxed. He wasn't. He hadn't mentioned that part of his reasoning for using the R.C.M.P. resources, was because the idea of terrorist intervention had occurred to both he and the constable, whether it be resulting from his scientific work or his brother's illegal weapons dealings. He wasn't going to take any chances. Realizing though, that the law enforcement officers and anti-terrorist specialists should know their work, he finally closed his eyes and tried to get some rest.

Half an hour later they arrived at the airport. His driver knew the routine. He drove straight to the security station. Edward woke Maria up so that he could get out of the car to take care of the security clearance, which would allow them to drive out onto the runway area. Constable Campbell had been waiting for him inside, "We've given the jet a thorough search and mechanical going over. It checks out okay and the two pilots seem to be the best men available. Their records are impeccable."

"So you're sure about what or who is not aboard the plane, and we are assured of having a safe trip. I think that this has been a worthwhile compromise. Thanks Constable," Edward said, as he turned to go back to the car.

"If you don't mind, I'll get a ride with you out to the jet to pull my men off," the Constable said, getting in beside the chauffeur.

As Edward helped Maria from the car to the jet, she was surprised at the level of security. After she was settled comfortably aboard, Constable Campbell came in to give his wedding congratulations and to say goodbye. She was more then a little tired, "How nice of you to take such good care of us Constable Campbell, thank you."

Campbell just winked at Edward and replied, "Just taking optimal care of our favorite people. Goodbye Mr. and Mrs. Warner," and with this, he disembarked from the plane confident that nothing had been overlooked.

Edward's driver was making the trip with them. After they were settled in their seats, he came in to inform then that dinner would be served as soon as they were in the air.

"I didn't realize that Richard, your chauffeur would be traveling with us." Maria said, as she stretched and yawned.

"He's much more then our driver. Richard is our 'Jack of all trades'. He always travels with me as my secretary, manservant and bodyguard should the need arise. Please feel confident in relying on him for any need. He has had specialized training and is reliable as well as undoubtedly loyal."

Chapter 48

*T*he transatlantic flight was totally uneventful but the dinner was very notable. The Champagne was delectable and the chateaubriand was perfection. So much so, that the satiated bride fell fast asleep shortly after dinner and slept all of the way to Monaco. After they were very quickly cleared through the Nice - Cote d'Azur International Airport, a Rolls Royce pulled up in front of the main entrance. Richard put all of their bags into the back and changed places with the driver. It was raining ever so lightly as Edward ushered Maria to the waiting vehicle and held the door for her.

As they drove close along the shore of the Mediterranean Sea, what she managed to see of the countryside was rugged and very steep. Monte Carlo was a very short drive from the airport, so before she knew it they were easing to a stop. Having arrived at their destination, they stopped in front of a huge ornate building which had been designed to replicate an ancient French palace. It was the Hotel De Paris, on Casino Square. Fancy masonry work and gilded woodcarving rose in lofty arches, with brilliant colored flowers everywhere. It truly looked as if it was a palace. Maria felt like Alice in Wonderland as she stepped from the Rolls. Doormen scurried to collect up their bags as Edward took her proudly by the arm and escorted her in through the enormous, elaborately decorated lobby.

They were taken immediately to a huge suite of rooms that overlooked the sea. Maria went out onto the spacious, flower laden balcony. The rain had subsided and the sun was beginning to peer out from behind a gray cloud. The scene was exquisite; the sparkling brilliant blue water of the sea crowned by a translucent rainbow reaching out from an expanse of white billowy clouds to the south. Colorful, sailboat sails dotted the calm, blue expanse. Edward had come out behind her, without her noticing, mesmerized as she was. He stepped up tight behind her and she felt his strong arms encircling her waist. He leaned down and whispered in her ear, "It is Heavenly isn't it? I just knew that this was one place that you couldn't help but love."

"I have very few words. I just can't seem to take it all in."

"Well my dear, having experienced the effects of jet travel many times before, I'd suggest that we enjoy some of the wonderful local fruit that room service has provided along with some tea while we rest and just enjoy this gorgeous view. Does that sound good to you?"

"Yes, it certainly does, but I'm also looking forward to lying down on that sumptuous looking bed before too long," she said, as she reached back and ran her persistent hand down over one of his cheeks and further down his outer thigh.

"That sounds like a date, Mrs. Warner, as soon as we've had some refreshments, then…" He turned her around and pulled her to him, landing many small kisses on various parts of her face, teasing her until she determinedly pushed herself up on her tiptoes and planted her lips over his. They swayed like this for several long moments, bodies pushing together, firmly attached at the lips, forgetting the posh world that surrounded them.

She pulled away abruptly and ran back through the sitting room to the bedchamber, echoing behind her, "Okay, let's have a snack."

He laughed, holding out his empty arms to the sea, then turned and followed her. After a prolonged session of torrid lovemaking, they languished around for the rest of the day. Late in the afternoon, he rolled over to her and kissed her neck, nibbling just a bit. "My love, I'd like to take you out dancing this evening after a late dinner. Do you think we're up to it?"

She chuckled and then crooned, "Well, if we could stay out of this bed for awhile we might have a faint chance."

"I like the sounds of that. What a wonderful problem to have. Do you think that perhaps we should order up another bed, just to use for sleeping?"

She laughed again as she cuddled up beside him, "To tell you the truth, I don't think it would make any difference." They slept for a couple of hours, then got up and sat on the balcony. Edward took this chance to tell her about some of the history of the area. That evening they dressed in their finery and went out to dine and dance the night away. Edward was an accomplished dancer, which made even the more complicated ballroom dancing, effortless and fun.

So went many of their days. Between lovemaking and eating and dancing; they strolled through the beautiful public gardens of Monaco and visited the vast aquarium and oceanographic center, which was of great interest to them both. They also spent considerable time wandering through endless, unique shops. Edward lavished her with haute couture clothing and finery, as well as buying many unique things for the two girls.

He wasn't very interested in the casino nightlife, which is so integral to Monte Carlo, but he thought that Maria might like to at least see it while they were here, so he arranged for them to tour several of the larger casinos. They'd be leaving for England tomorrow, so it'd be their last chance, on this trip. The casinos were even more lavish then some of the ballrooms that they'd swirled their way through, so he thought she should have this experience, besides, there was someone that she just had to meet.

Occasionally, patrons would recognize Edward, as he had traveled in these social groups years ago. Maria enjoyed being introduced to a wide array of celebrities, members of royal families and other high rollers. She was impressed with the caliber of people that were her husband's acquaintances, but even more so, they were impressed with Edward for his good taste and luck in finding such a vivacious beauty.

As they entered the Casino Royal, Edward steered her towards a raised dais off to one side of the crowded, main floor.

"There's someone very special that I'd like you to meet. She's been a good friend of our family ever since I can remember," Edward whispered in her ear as he propelled her toward the dais.

Getting closer, Maria noticed a group of women involved in a conversation with a wizened, yet regal, older lady. She was wrapped warmly in a wine, velvet shawl, which could not hope to conceal the glittering gown that hung over her frame. Their approach had attracted the attention of the lady's entourage and they moved aside so that the woman could have full view of who was stepping up onto the dais.

"Edward Warner, you handsome rake, I thought that you and yours had abandoned us forever. I truly had just about given up all hope!" Eyes black and cool as onyx flashed amiably across Edward and slowly came to rest on Maria's countenance, "Pray, who is this fresh, exquisitely beautiful flower?"

"Princess Francesca Joseph, I'm delighted to introduce you to my new bride, Lady Maria Warner," Edward proudly stated, bowing low to the dowager Princess and then turning to Maria, who was bobbing a polite curtsey, he said, "Maria, this is Princess Francesca Joseph of Liechtenstein, who has long graced my family with the dear favor of her friendship." He bowed once more over the Princess's hand, and raising it to his lips, kissed it graciously.

The grand lady raised her other hand to the women that had surrounded her previously and motioned for them to leave her while she visited with her new guests.

"My dear young man congratulations on your blessed union and to you also Lady Warner; regardless of how unhappy you've made the rest of us unattached and most envious females." The gaze of those vibrant black eyes reluctantly moved from the proud groom's face and warmed considerably as it toured from Maria's ankles, slowly, without apology, up to her now blushing face.

Recognizing the bride's flushed complexion, the Princess interjected, "Oh, come now Lady Maria, don't be put off by an old woman with the ways of the Old World. I didn't mean to offend you. On the contrary, I applaud you."

Maria took the small bony hand that had been outstretched to her. "Thank you Princess Joseph, I'm overwhelmed by the pleasure of meeting you, Madame."

"You're too kind my dear one. In your lifetime you'll meet many a prominent personage who will not hold a candle to your own brilliant flame." The older woman pulled her gaze away from Maria long enough to give her condolences to Edward. The aged Princess took his hand and holding it between her own, she said, "I must tell you how shocked I was to hear about the passing of your illustrious parents. When I heard, it was too late to attend the service. This world will greatly miss your beloved parents as I'm sure that you must."

"Thank you Princess. My parents thought very highly of you and your philanthropic activities."

"Thank you Edward. Now, would you consider letting me visit with your dear wife, while you go and play baccarat or some other manly game?" she said, dismissed him. "There's a good man, let the women chatter for a while."

Knowing what an eccentric Francesca was, he just laughed and rested a reassuring hand on Maria's shoulder as she sat down beside the aged monarch. "I can take a hint. I'll see you in a little while," he said to Maria, before he walked off through to crowd to find a gaming table.

After admiring his form as he walked away, the Princess turned her full attention toward Maria, who now felt a bit like a doe in someone's headlights, "You must forgive an old lady, Maria. I might come across as being very bold and short with people, but that's just a side effect of my age, as well as my background. I sense that this is the only opportunity that I'm going to have to communicate personally with you before you leave to start another very important stage in your life. Is that true?"

"Well, yes... we're leaving for England tomorrow morning," Maria said, still not know where this conversation might be going.

"That's why I was so abrupt with Edward. I wish that I hadn't had to cut him off at the quick like that, but it's of the utmost importance to you both that I should have this chance to speak with you, alone. My manners, or lack of, are not the only trait that has progressed with me from the 'Old World'. I have the Sight, and I've seen some of your future as well as having knowledge of Edward's and his families past. There are things that I must pass along to you if you and he are going to survive, and a great wrong is to be righted."

Maria really was transfixed now, blinking occasionally, under the strong power of this woman's presence.

The Princess went on in great earnest, "You have the power! You possess the positive power that has now joined with Edward's and will continue to grow, nurtured by your everlasting love through age after age. You'll finally have a strong fighting chance to destroy a great evil, a demon that has plagued you both since the beginning of time."

"You know... you know about our past-lives together?" Maria stuttered, exhibiting her shock.

"Yes my poor dear, I've seen it in your souls. I saw it in Edward when he was just a young boy. I saw that he was only half of a whole, only part of what was to be a great, strong, positive entity. I could only wait. I saw the pain and the despair that has haunted him into this life. Now I see that you're the other half; the half that will complete this power force and focus it; the other part of that positive energy that we in this life have been waiting to witness." The Princess stopped but did not withdraw her gaze from Maria's eyes, this gaze which extended deep into Maria's soul.

"Yes, I feel your questions. Yes, you are finally living the life that you were always meant to live. No, danger has not left your future. You've only succeeded in staving it off for a short time. The demon has only receded, waiting to regain its fierce, evil power once more."

"What! What..." Maria attempted to marshal her thoughts.

"Listen to me girl! Just listen. You'll meet a guide, near a lake, close to where the evil grows."

"A guide, what do you mean, a guide?" Maria asked, in great earnest.

Francesca gave her a dark look and Maria subsided into silence. After regaining Maria's attention she simply said, "One of two will be waiting, as I have, for you to take up the staff of power." The Princess withdrew her hypnotic grasp from Maria's soul as if it had been a surgical probe. Francesca blinked tiredly, and sitting back she pulled her velvet shawl tighter around her diminished body. It was like someone had flipped a switch. The powerful presence who had easily probed and scanned Maria's mind and soul had disengaged by simply withdrawing her glance.

Maria's sense of wonderment and her newly, regained balance was short lived as the unbelievable weight of this foretold challenge settled in on her. The Princess knew all about what she and Edward had just come to understand as their continuing reality. She'd known of their devastating pasts. Maria's memory turned back to the conversation that she and Edward had gone through with Dr. Simmons after their regression therapy. She recalled the doctor explaining that it wasn't uncommon for independent souls to seek out the same time frame and locations in the continuum, so that they could live out lives in contact with other souls that they had interacted with in past-lives.

The Princess had let her attention wander over the crowded room around them.

"Princess Francesca Joseph, we've known you in other past-lives haven't we?"

Her gaze came slowly back to Maria and enveloped her with a warm, healing glow. "You've come to the correct summation, my dear. But I've nothing further that I can give you at this time. I've summoned your husband. When he rejoins us, collect him up in your capable hands, love him dearly every minute and be on your way tomorrow, hopefully as prepared as I can help you to be."

The Princess looked away and only seconds later Edward stepped up onto the dais.

They sat for a while, speaking of old times and Edward's family, reminiscing as any old friends might do. Then the Princess stood up and let them know that she was very tired and needed her bed. As she stood, Maria was amazed at her height and her regal posture.

A tall, attractive, young man seemed to appear out of nowhere, as soon as she made a move to stand. He stepped up to this gracious lady and gave her his arm for support.

The Princess turned to Maria and said, "Never fear, your future will be a bright one, together at last. And as you may have already realized, this everlasting love is worth the battles that will inevitably come. You'll always be able to overcome, my dears," she pronounced and she walked away.

Edward was smiling at the lady as she left. Maria stood on tiptoes and kissed his cheek saying, "She must've been quite a stir and quite a force to be reckoned with, in her day."

"She still is!" he said, with a sly look as he took her arm and they started to make their way to the door.

"What did you mean earlier when you mentioned her philanthropic efforts?"

"You see all of the activity here? Well, Francesca built Casino Royal many years ago when she first came to the French Riviera. Since the day that it opened, eighty percent of the profit that this casino makes has gone to nurture a hand full of various humanitarian charities. I think she manages to educate and feed a large populace of the third world's poor. I guess you could say that she takes from the rich and gives to the poor, while making sure that the rich have a very good time giving. She's always kept in touch with my research toward better nutritional assistance for the less privileged. That's why I wanted you to meet her."

"You were right, it was very important. Let's get back to our rooms and I'll tell you all about the revealing conversation that she and I had, or I guess I should say, that she had. By the way, how did you know when to come back to our table?" she asked.

"Oh! She called me. She's always been able to do that. She telepathically summoned me. It's one of her many talents. I knew that I was bringing you to her tonight for some special reason, and after giving you two a chance to talk, I can't wait to hear why."

When they got into the car, Maria wrapped her arms around his neck and rested her head against his chest. She was trying to recall the Princess's words of warning; trying not to dwell on the content, as much as trying to put everything in order before she spoke to her husband about this strange encounter. Later, that sumptuous bed in their suite, held them safe and warm as she revealed the extent of Francesca's knowledge of their situation as well as her ominous foretelling of what their futures would hold.

Maria said, as she pushed herself up onto one elbow, "She used sparse, simple phrases, almost as if she was speaking in some code. Her exact words were, 'You will meet a guide, near a lake, close to where the evil grows,' and then she said, 'One of two will be waiting, as I have, for you to take up the staff of power!' Then as we were parting, you heard her say that our 'everlasting love' was worth the battles that would come and that we'd always be able to overcome."

Edward stretched and clasped his hands behind his head, "Well I guess that the best part of what she sees in our future is that we overcome any battles and survive to have a bright future together. As to her actual wording, she was undoubtedly repeating the cryptic words that had come to her, as to not mislead you. If there were anything further, that might be of help to us, she would've told you. I completely trust Princess Francesca and her paranormal powers."

"This is all so bewildering!" Maria said with exasperation, as she cuddled up to his side under his protective arm. She murmured, "Well, as you say, at least she sees us loving one another and overcoming all."

They held each other close throughout the night, occasionally whispering endearments and encouragement, both deep in thought about their dubious future. After only a few hours of actual sleep, Richard came to wake them in time to prepare for their flight.

It was still early when they left their suite. Richard led the way, pushing a huge baggage cart loaded down with the few bags that they'd arrived with plus the copious new suitcases and boxes that they had accumulated. Maria looked over her shoulder, fondly, as they passed through the lobby, and she thought of the sweet memories that they were carrying away from this exquisite love haven.

It was no time at all before they were pulling up at the airport, and were comfortably seated in the jet. Edward leaned over to her and with his fingers he gently pushed back a stray curl that brushed her face, "Maria, I don't want you to worry about the prophecy that the Princess made." He kissed her forehead softly.

She smiled sweetly as he looked down into her eyes. "Edward, there's no sense in either of us worrying. That'd only be a waste of precious time and energy. Worry only defeats causes and promotes negativity. There's no way of changing the future; there's only the opportunity to live it well, loving each other, one day at a time."

He took her hand in both of his, saying, "We've made it this far and we know that the future will be bright for us."

The jet had been taxiing down the runway and now it hurled itself upward with a great energetic thrust, making a large arcing turn through the dull, morning sky. As their aircraft broke through the dense, smoke like clouds, brilliant sunlight flashed radiantly through the window and across their bodies. Edward squeezed her hand reassuringly, "See, we've come thrusting through the clouds and into a bright new day, the first day in the rest of our long lives together. Now as we hurl into our future, our next stop will be London, England."

"I love you, Ed," she purred.

"I love you, Lady Maria," he said, with a smile.

"The power of this love will overcome all odds. That's what Princess Francesca was telling us, to have faith in Love," she said, thinking aloud, "Have Faith and Thank God for His Favor."

Next Segment Of This Story

Nocturnal, mysterious occurrences are rumored to be taking place at and near the Warner ancestral estate in the ruggedly beautiful Lake District of northern England.

Although it is the festive season, Maria and Edward who do arrive amid gaiety and invitations to fabulous social events, also experience undercurrents of secrecy, nervous whispers and dark apprehensions. Even though they are welcomed cordially by the estate staff as well as the local gentry, something is very wrong here.

The couple begins to reanalyze the prophecies made by their good friend Princess Francesca Joseph.

Fate leads them to a resplendent social occasion at one of the royal residences, where they are both sublimely shocked to come face to face with a woman wearing Maria's emerald and diamond jewels which Reanna, Edward's presumed deceased ex-wife, had undoubtedly been wearing when she was shot and fell overboard into Lake Ontario.

Maria and Edward try to prepare, but prepare for what?

Look for this next book by Deborah May Marshall in the future.

About The Author

Deb, as she stringently prefers to be referred to, was inspired as a teenager to write television plots, but was too involved at that early age, with learning about life to devote serious time to her writing. While life is still very hectic, now in her early fifties, she is now indulging her desire to be a story teller.

Until recently, Deb has strenuously maintained a successful career as a horse breeder, trainer and riding coach. This career has often existed as a backdrop to the other twenty two jobs and careers that her life experience has afforded her. While finishing high school she also traveled to Toronto to study and work as a model, only to find that city life was not for her. This experience accomplished, she continued to college to study secretarial sciences and then on to become a cosmetician and a lecturer in personal / professional development.

Being an avid self educator, her study interests range widely from psychology, theology, parapsychology, natural sciences, nutrition, use of medicinal herbs, gardening, alternative medicines and treatments, business marketing, many crafts – including fashion design, universal energies, communication with God and counseling.

Deb adores and actively stewards her small horse heaven located in the picturesque Thousand Island resort area of Ontario. Proudly, a confirmed nature inspired eccentric, she revels in every opportunity to offer up gratitude for her family and friends, her home amongst the rocks and trees, her many animal friends, as well as her creative abilities – both natural and paranormal.

This enigma, humbly makes herself available to many people as a God mandated spiritual counselor – calling on her experiences and abilities to relax, stabilize and empower people in the natural ways of God and the universe.

Made in the USA
Las Vegas, NV
06 May 2022

48536930R00215